Thirty-Day Affair
MAUREEN CHILD

The Prince's Mistress
DAY LECLAIRE

MILLS & BOON
Pure reading pleasure

All the characters in this book have no existence outside the imagination of the author, and have no relation whatsoever to anyone bearing the same name or names. They are not even distantly inspired by any individual known or unknown to the author, and all the incidents are pure invention.

First published in Great Britain 2008
by Harlequin Mills & Boon Limited,
Eton House, 18-24 Paradise Road, Richmond, Surrey TW9 1SR

ISBN: 978 0 263 85894 5

51-0308

Printed and bound in Spain
by Litografia Rosés S.A., Barcelona

100 Reasons to Celebrate

We invite you to join us in celebrating Mills & Boon's centenary. Gerald Mills and Charles Boon founded Mills & Boon Limited in 1908 and opened offices in London's Covent Garden. Since then, Mills & Boon has become a hallmark for romantic fiction, recognised around the world.

We're proud of our 100 years of publishing excellence, which wouldn't have been achieved without the loyalty and enthusiasm of our authors and readers.

Thank you!

Each month throughout the year there will be something new and exciting to mark the centenary, so watch for your favourite authors, captivating new stories, special limited edition collections...and more!

Thirty-Day Affair
by Maureen Child

Is Nathan Barrister your *Millionaire of the Month?*

1. It's your job to keep a millionaire content for his month-long stay in town. You:
   (a) Fill his house with fresh flowers
   (b) Fill his refrigerator with gourmet goodies
   (c) Fill his mind with thoughts of…you!
2. How to argue with a millionaire:
   (a) You don't
   (b) Gently suggest he might consider someone else's opinion
   (c) Tell him exactly what's on your mind: money doesn't mean a person's always right!
3. You've found yourself stranded with your millionaire in a snowstorm. You:
   (a) Throw a log on the fire
   (b) Bundle up in a woolly sweater
   (c) Have two words: body heat
4. Your millionaire has just offered you the trip of a lifetime. You:
   (a) Accept gleefully
   (b) Wait ten seconds pretending to consider his offer…and then accept gleefully
   (c) Turn him down. You're holding out for a honeymoon!

The Prince's Mistress
by Day Leclaire

"I guess this is good-bye."

"It is." Lander paused. "If that's what you really want."

"We settled this already."

"You can leave." He shifted closer and covered Juliana's hand with his, preventing her escape. His breath stirred the curls at her temple while his voice murmured seductively in her ear. "You can get out and we'll never see each other again. Or you can stay. Think about it. We can have one evening together before we go our separate ways. No one has to know. I can arrange that. No media attention. No spotlight. Just a man and a woman doing what men and women have done throughout the ages. One night, Juliana."

Available in March 2008 from Mills & Boon® Desire™

Thirty-Day Affair
by Maureen Child
&
The Prince's Mistress
by Day Leclaire

❧

Expecting a Fortune
by Jan Colley
&
Fortune's Forbidden Woman
by Heidi Betts

❧

The Millionaire's Seductive Revenge
by Maxine Sullivan
&
The Tycoon's Hidden Heir
by Yvonne Lindsay

THIRTY-DAY AFFAIR

by
Maureen Child

MAUREEN CHILD

is a California native who loves to travel. Every chance they get, she and her husband are taking off on another research trip. The author of more than sixty books, Maureen loves a happy ending and still swears that she has the best job in the world. She lives in Southern California with her husband, two children, and a golden retriever with delusions of grandeur.

You can contact Maureen via her website: www.maureenchild.com

Dear Reader,

It was very exciting to write the first book in this new series. MILLIONAIRE OF THE MONTH is a continuity that my friends and I came up with, and we had such a great time planning it all out and creating these stories.

The series is set near Lake Tahoe and takes place in and around a mansion built on the shores of the lake. Six men, all once friends in college, are forced to deal with the memories of who they once were when the terms of a seventh friend's will dictate that one of them a month must stay in this lodge to honour a long-ago promise.

My hero, Nathan Barrister, is a man who makes his own rules. He believes in living his life on his terms and never looks back. Keira Sanders, though, is a woman who won't be ignored. She slips into Nathan's life and has no intention of slipping back out again.

I really hope you enjoy the books in this series as much as we did writing them!

Love,

Maureen

To Christie Ridgway, Susan Crosby,
Liz Bevarly, Anna DePalo and Susan Mallery.

Great writers all,
they made being a part of this series so much fun!

One

"Hunter," Nathan Barrister muttered as he stared at the mammoth wood-and-stone mansion on the shores of Lake Tahoe, "if you were here right now, I'd kill you for this."

Of course, Hunter Palmer wasn't there and Nathan couldn't kill the man who had once been his first—and best—friend, because he was already dead.

The ice around Nathan's heart thickened a little at the thought, but he used his long years of practice to ignore that tightening twinge. Regrets were a waste of time.

"As big a waste as the next month is going to be." He climbed out of his rental car and stepped into a mound of slush he hadn't even noticed.

With a disgusted sigh, he kicked the dirty snow off the polished toe of his shoe and told himself he should have listened to the clerk at the rental agency. She had tried to tell him that renting a four-wheel-drive car would make more sense than the sports car he preferred.

But who the hell expected snow in March for God's sake?

A wry grin curved his mouth briefly. *He* should have expected it. He'd grown up back east and should have remembered that snow could hit anytime, anywhere. Especially this high up in the mountains. But he'd spent so much time trying to forget his past, was it really surprising that even the *weather* had the ability to sneak up on him?

The air was cold and clean, and the sky was so blue it made his eyes ache. A sharp wind whipped through the surrounding pine trees, rustling the needles and sending patches of snow falling to the ground with muffled *plops.*

Nathan shivered and shrugged deeper into his brown leather jacket. He didn't want to be here at all, let alone for a solid month. He never stayed *anywhere* for more than a few days at a stretch. And being here made him think about things he hadn't allowed himself to remember in years.

Reluctantly, he headed for the front of the house, leaving his bags in the car for the moment. The crunch of his shoes on the ground was the only sound, as if the world were holding its breath. Great. Fifteen minutes here and his brain was already going off on tangents.

He shouldn't be here. He should still be in Tahiti at his family's hotel, going over the books, settling disputes, looking into expansion. And next month, he'd be in Barbados for a week and then Jamaica. Nathan moved fast, never giving himself a chance to settle. Never risking more than a few days in any one place.

Until now.

And if there had been any way at all of getting out of this, Nathan would have taken it. God knows, he'd tried to find a loophole in his friend's will. Something that would have allowed him to keep both his own sense of duty in place and his sanity intact. But even the Barrister family lawyers had assured him that the will was sealed nice and tight. Hunter Palmer had made sure that his friends would have no choice but to honor his wishes.

"You're enjoying this, aren't you?" Nathan whispered to his long-dead friend. And when the wind rattled the pine trees, damned if it didn't sound like laughter.

"Fine. I'm here. And I'll try to make the whole month," he muttered. Once he'd completed Hunter's last request, he hoped to hell his old friend would stop haunting his nightmares.

A long white envelope with his name scrawled across it was stuck to the heavy wood front door. Nathan took the short flight of snow-dusted wooden steps, stopped on the porch and tore the taped envelope free. Opening it, he found a key dangling from an ornate keychain and a single sheet of paper.

Hi, I'm your housekeeper, Meri. I'm very busy, so I'm not here at the moment, and chances are you won't be seeing me during your stay. But here's the key to the house. The kitchen is stocked and the town of Hunter's Landing is only twenty minutes away if you need anything else. I hope you and the others to follow enjoy your time here.

Without thinking, he crumpled the short note in his right hand and squeezed it hard.

The others.

In a flash of memory, Nathan went back ten years. Back to a time when he and his friends had called themselves the Seven Samurai. Foolish. But then, they'd been seniors at Harvard. They'd done four hard years together and come out the other side closer than brothers. They'd had their lives laying out in front of them like golden roads to success. He remembered the raucous evening with just a few too many beers when they'd vowed to build a house together and reunite in ten years. They'd each spend a month there and then gather in the seventh month to toast their inevitable achievements.

Yes, it was all supposed to work out that way. And then…

Nathan shook his head and let the past slide away. Jamming the key into the lock, he opened the door, stepped inside and stopped just inside the foyer. From there, he could see into a great room, with gleaming wood walls, a huge stone fireplace with a fire already ablaze in the hearth and lots of plush, comfortable-looking furniture.

As jail cells went, it was better than most, he supposed. He thought of the housekeeper and the nearby town and hoped to hell he wouldn't be bothered by a lot of people. Bad enough he was stuck here. He didn't need company on top of it.

He wasn't here to make friends. He was here to honor a friend he'd lost long ago.

An hour later, Keira Sanders grabbed the oversized basket off the passenger seat, leaped down from the driver's seat of her truck and slammed the door. Her boots slid around on the slushy ground but she dug in her heels and steadied herself. All she needed was to meet the first of Hunter Palmer's houseguests with dirty snow on her butt.

"Great first impression that would make," she murmured as she looked the house over.

It shone like a jewel in the gathering night. Light spilled from the tall windows to fall on the ground in golden spears. Smoke lifted from the stone chimney and twisted in the icy wind coming off the lake. Snow hugged the slanted roof and clung to the pines and aspens crowding the front yard. Winter tended to stick around this high up on the mountain, and she wouldn't have had it any other way.

There was something about the cold and the quiet hush of snow that had always felt…magical to Keira. In fact, at the moment, she'd like to be back in her cozy place in Hunter's Landing, sitting beside her own fire, with a glass of white wine and a good book.

Instead, she was here to greet the first of six men who would be spending thirty days each in the lakeside mansion. Nerves jumped in the pit of her stomach but Keira fought them down. This was too important—to the town of Hunter's Landing and to her, personally.

Just two weeks ago, she'd received a very legal letter from the estate of a man named Hunter Palmer. In the letter, the late Mr. Palmer's attorney had explained the unusual bequest.

Over the next six months, six different men would be arriving in the town of Hunter's Landing, to spend thirty days in this gorgeous mansion. If each of the men stayed for the entire month, at the end of the six-month period twenty million dollars would be donated to charity—a large chunk of which would belong to Hunter's Landing—and the house itself would be donated to the town as a vacation home for recovering cancer patients.

Keira took another deep breath to settle the last of her nerves. As the mayor of Hunter's Landing, it was her job to make sure each of the six men held to the stipulations of Hunter Palmer's will. She couldn't afford for her small town to miss out on a windfall that would allow them to have a spanking-new clinic and a new jail and courthouse and…

Her head was spinning as she smiled to herself. She tightened her grip on the basket and checked to make sure the lid was latched down. Tugging at the lapels of her black jacket, she straightened her shoulders, plastered a smile on her face and prepared to meet the first of the men who could mean so much to Hunter's Landing.

She was good with people. Always had been. And now, with so much riding on the next six months, she was more determined than ever that everything go right. Not only would she ensure that each of the six men would stay his entire thirty days at the lakeside lodge, she was going to make sure they knew how much this all meant to her hometown.

With that thought firmly in mind, she gulped a deep breath of frosty air and headed for the front door. Her boots crunched in the snow but, when she hit a patch of ice, her feet slid wildly. "Oh, no."

Eyes wide, she held tightly to the basket and swung her arms in a desperate attempt to regain her balance. But her feet couldn't find purchase and as she tipped and swayed, she knew she was going to lose both her balance and her dignity.

"Ow!" she shouted when she hit the ground, landing so hard on her butt that her teeth rattled. The basket tipped to one side and she groaned, hoping that the contents were tightly sealed. "Well, isn't this perfect."

The front door flew open and light spilled over her. She blinked up at the man silhouetted in the doorway. Oh, man. This so wasn't how she'd planned to meet Nathan Barrister.

"Who're you?" he demanded, making no move to come down the steps to help her up.

"I'm fine, thanks for your concern," she said, wincing as icy, wet cold seeped through the seat of her jeans. So much for first impressions. Maybe she should crawl back to her truck and start all over.

"If you're thinking of suing, you should know I don't own this property," he said.

"Wow." For a moment, Keira forgot all about getting up—forgot all about the fact that this man and five others just like him could mean a windfall for Hunter's Landing—and just sat there, staring at him in amazement. "You're really a jerk, aren't you?"

"I beg your pardon?"

"Did I say that out loud?"

"Yes."

"Sorry." And she was. Sort of. For heaven's sake, none of this was going as planned.

"Are you injured?"

"Only my pride," she admitted, though her behind hurt like hell and the melting ice beneath her wasn't helping the situation any. Still, might as well make the best of the situation. She raised one hand and waved it. "A little help here?"

He muttered something she didn't catch and, considering his attitude so far, she considered that a good thing. But he came down the steps carefully, grabbed her hand and pulled her to her feet in one quick motion.

His fingers on hers felt warm and strong and…good. Okay, she hadn't expected that. He dropped her hand as if he'd been burned, and she wondered if he'd felt that small zap of something hot and interesting when they touched.

She brushed off the seat of her pants while she looked up at him. For some reason she'd expected him to be an older man. But he wasn't. Tall and lean, he had broad shoulders, a narrow waist and long legs. Considering how easily he'd plucked her off the ice, he was strong, too. Not that she was heavy or anything, but she certainly wasn't one of those stick-figure types of women that were so popular these days.

Ordinarily, a man like him was more than enough to make her heart go pitty-pat. However, the scowl on his truly gorgeous face was enough to make even Keira rethink her attraction. His black hair was stylishly cut to just above his collar. His blue eyes were narrowed on her suspiciously, and his hard jaw was clenched. And his full mouth was tightened into a grim slash across his face, letting her know without a doubt just how welcome she wasn't.

"Wow. Are you really in a bad mood or is it just me?"

He blew out a breath. "Whoever you are," he said, his voice a low rumble that seemed to dip all the way inside her to start up a slow fire, "I didn't invite you here. And I'm not interested in meeting my neighbors."

"Good," Keira said, grinning at his obvious irritation, "because you don't have any. The nearest house on the lake is a couple miles north."

He frowned at her. "Then who are you?"

"Keira Sanders," she said, holding out one hand and leaving it there until rudimentary good manners forced him to take it in his.

Again, there was the nice little buzz of connection when his skin met hers. Did he feel it? If so, he wasn't real pleased about it. Keira, on the other hand, was enjoying the sensation. It had been a really long time since she'd felt the slightest attraction for anyone. Purposely. "Been there, done that" sort of summed up her feelings about romance.

But she had to admit, it was really nice to feel that sizzle.

Still shaking his hand, she smiled up into his scowl. Gorgeous, but crabby. Well, she'd dealt with irritable people before, and there was just no way she was going to let his bad attitude affect Hunter's Landing's chances at getting money that would be a godsend to the small town. "I'm the mayor of Hunter's Landing and I'm here to welcome you."

"That's not necessary," he said and dropped her hand.

"It's our pleasure," she said, hanging on to her good cheer by her fingernails as she turned to pluck the basket out of the snow. "And," she continued as she walked past him, headed toward the front door, "I've brought you a welcome basket, courtesy of the Hunter's Landing Chamber of Commerce."

"If you don't mind," he countered, following after her quickly.

"Not at all," Keira said, walking into the house and stopping just inside the foyer. "I confess, I've been dying to see the inside of this place ever since they started building it last year."

It took a moment or two, but she heard him come in behind her and close the door with an exasperated sigh. He was not just crabby, but very crabby, apparently.

But that was okay. She'd win him over. She had to. She had to make sure that he and the five others who would come after him here would complete the terms of the will that would so benefit her hometown.

"Ms. Sanders…"

"Call me Keira," she said and turned to give him a quick glance and smile.

"Fine. Keira." He shoved both hands into the pockets of his slacks and rocked back on his heels.

He *really* didn't want her there.

"Don't worry," she said, stepping through the arched doorway into the great room, "I won't stay long. I only wanted to welcome you, let you know that you're not alone here."

"I prefer alone," he said flatly and she stopped halfway across the room and turned to look at him, still standing in the foyer.

"Now, why is that?" she wondered aloud.

His features tightened even further, until he looked as though he'd been carved from stone. Not really a people person, Keira decided, then shrugged.

"Anyway," she said loudly, setting the basket down atop a hand-carved coffee table that probably cost more than her monthly house payment. "I've got a few goodies here to make your stay more comfortable."

"I'm sure I'll be fine."

She ignored him and started rooting through the basket, pulling items out, one after the other, with a brief description of each. "Here's a certificate good for free coffee and freshly made doughnuts every morning at the diner. And a jar of homemade jam—Margie Fontenot, the late mayor's widow, makes the best jam in the state. A bottle of wine from Stan's Liquor Stop, fresh bread from the bakery, a bag of ground Jamaican coffee beans—" she stopped to sniff the bag and sighed at the aroma, then continued "—there's a jar filled with the best marinara you've ever tasted, from Clearwater's restaurant—you really should get over there for dinner while you're here. The outside dining area overlooks the lake and there's no better place to catch a gorgeous sunset—"

"Ms. Sanders…"

"Keira," she reminded him.

"Keira, then. If you don't mind—"

"And," she went on as if he hadn't spoken, "there are a few more goodies in here, but I'll let you discover them on your own."

"Thank you."

"Now," she said, turning to face him from across the room, "is there anything else I can do to help make your stay more interesting?"

"Leave?" he asked.

Keira shook her head at him, as if she were sorely disappointed. Wandering the great room, she ran her fingers along the deeply carved mantel over the fireplace and, just for a second or two, enjoyed the heat pouring from the hearth. Her gaze swept the rest of the room and lingered on the view of the lake out of the floor-to-ceiling windows. The moon was just beginning its climb across the sky, and the water shimmered with a breath of light as if waiting for the show to start.

She gave herself a moment or two to calm the flash of irritation inside her. Wouldn't do to insult the man whose very presence could mean so much to her town. But at the same time, she wondered why he was being so nasty. By the time she'd centered herself and turned her gaze back to him, *still* standing in the foyer as if he could force her to leave by simply not welcoming her in, she was wondering something else.

Why did he intrigue her so much when his rudeness should have put her off immediately?

And how was she going to make this man connect with Hunter's Landing and make a commitment to see this through when he so obviously wanted nothing to do with her or the town?

Two

Nathan had had enough.

He'd been at the lakeside mansion for a little over an hour and already he had an uninvited guest.

Plus, Keira Sanders seemed to be oblivious to insults and clearly didn't care that she was very obviously not wanted.

His gaze swept her up and down more thoroughly than he had when he'd first found her sitting in the snow. Her jeans were faded and hugged her long legs like a second skin. Her long-sleeved black sweater came down to her thighs and, ridiculously enough, made her figure look more exposed than hidden. Maybe it was the way the soft-looking fabric clung to her curves, but whatever the reason, Nathan could appreciate the view even while wishing she were anywhere but there.

Her shoulder-length, reddish-blond hair hung loose in waves that seemed to dance around her animated face whenever she moved—which was often. He'd never seen a more mobile woman. It was as if she couldn't bear standing still. She was wandering the great room, her fingers touching, stroking, everything as she passed and he couldn't help wondering what those fingers would feel like touching *him.*

Yet as soon as that thought hit his clearly fevered brain, he knew he had to get her the hell out of the house. He wasn't interested in a monthlong fling. That was more commitment than he'd given to any woman he'd known in the last ten years.

Best to just get her out of the house now. And if that meant being even ruder than he had been already, fine.

"Thank you for coming," he said, waiting until she gave up examining the bookshelves to look at him again, "but if you don't mind, I'd like you to leave."

There. A man couldn't be any more plainspoken than that.

"Wow," she said softly, her green eyes sparkling in reflected light from the fire, "nobody ever taught you how to treat your guests?"

He swallowed hard and pushed away the thought of just how horrified his grandmother would have been at his blatant rudeness. "You're not a guest," he said tightly, reminding her as well as himself. "You're an intruder."

She actually laughed at him. "But I'm an intruder who brought you gifts!"

Nathan finally left the foyer, since it seemed clear that standing beside the door wasn't going to be enough to convince her to step through it. He'd never met anyone else quite like her. She seemed impervious to rudeness, just rolling right along with a cheerful attitude that must, he thought, really annoy the hell out of people who knew her well.

"Look," Nathan said, walking across the polished floor toward her. "I've tried to be polite."

She blinked at him and her smile widened. "Really? *That* was trying?"

Frowning, he ignored the jab and said, "I appreciate the gifts. Thank you for taking the time to come out here. But I would really prefer to be *alone.*"

"Oh, I'm sure you want to settle in," she said, waving one hand at him, blithely ignoring his attempt to get rid of her. "And I won't stay much longer, I swear."

Hope to cling to.

"I only wanted to let you know that Hunter's Landing is ready to help you and the other men who will be staying here in any way we can." She wandered to the big-screen TV, picked up the remote and studied it for a second or two.

If she turned the damn thing on, she might never leave. Nathan walked to her side, took the remote and set it down on a nearby table. She shrugged, walked to the windows overlooking the lake and stood staring through the glass as if mesmerized.

He watched her and couldn't help feeling a little mesmerized himself. The fall of her hair on her shoulders. The curve of her behind. The defiant tilt to her chin. She turned to look at him and her wide, shining eyes fixed on him with a slam of power he didn't want to think about.

"You'll only be here a month," she said quietly, "and

maybe you don't realize just how important your stay and the others' are to Hunter's Landing."

Nathan sighed and resigned himself to at least a few more minutes of conversation. It seemed plain that Keira Sanders wasn't going to leave until she was good and ready. "I know about what your town stands to inherit from the estate."

"But you can't know what it means to us," she insisted, half turning to lean one shoulder against the cold glass. "With that influx of cash, we can build a new courthouse, expand our clinic…" Her voice trailed off and she smiled as if already seeing the changes that would happen to her town.

"And speaking of the clinic," she said quickly, straightening up and walking toward him. "I want to invite you to the town potluck dinner tomorrow night. We're raising money to get the expansion started and—"

"But you'll have the inheritance—"

"Can't count on that until it's reality, can we?" she pointed out, neatly cutting him off before he could finish his sentence. "Anyway, our clinic is good, but it's not nearly big enough. Of course, there's a terrific hospital in Lake Tahoe, but that's a long drive, especially in the winter snow. We need to be able to take care of our own citizens right here and, with the potluck dinner, all the money collected will go directly into the fund for…"

She was talking so fast Nathan's ears were buzzing. He had no interest in going to her community fundraiser and he suspected that she didn't really want him there, either. What she wanted was a donation. Wasn't that what everyone wanted from him in the end?

With the Barrister family fortune behind him, Nathan

had long ago accepted that he was seen first as a bankbook and second as a man. Which suited him fine. He didn't want friends. Didn't want a lover or a wife. What he wanted was to be left alone.

And he suddenly knew just the way to hurry Keira Sanders out the door: Give her what she wanted. What she'd really come for. While she continued to talk in nearly a stream of consciousness while hardly pausing for breath, he stalked across the room to where he'd dropped his briefcase on one of the overstuffed, burgundy leather chairs. Quickly, he opened it, grabbed his black leather checkbook and flicked his ballpoint pen.

Shaking his head, he wrote a check made out to Hunter's Landing, and then tore it from the pad and walked back to where Keira was still smiling and outlining the plans she had for her little town.

"So you see, it would be a great chance for you to meet everyone in town. Nice for you to see the place you'll be living for the next month and maybe it will help you see how important it is to us that you and your friends complete the stipulations of Mr. Palmer's will." She finally took a breath. "If it's okay with you, I'll pick you up tomorrow about six and drive you to the potluck myself. I can take you on a tour of the lake if you'd like too and—"

"Please," Nathan said, interrupting her when it became obvious it would be the only way to keep her quiet. He held out the check and waited until she'd taken it, a question in her beautiful eyes. "Accept this contribution to your clinic fund."

"Oh," she said, "that's very generous of you but—" She stopped, glanced down at the check and Nathan actually *saw* all the blood drain from her face. She went absolutely white and her hand holding the check trembled. "I…I…you…"

Her mouth opened and closed, she gulped noisily and wheezed in a breath. "Oh. My. God."

"Are you all right?" Nathan reached for her, grabbed her upper arm and felt the tremors that were racing through her body.

She raised her gaze to his, waved the check in a tight fist and swallowed hard a time or two before trying to speak. Apparently, he'd finally found the way to make her speechless.

"Are you *serious* about this?"

"The check?"

"The *amount,*" she said harshly, then added, "I've got to sit down."

And she did.

Right there on the floor.

She pulled her arm free of his grasp and folded up on herself. Leaning her head back against the closest chair, she looked up at him in stunned amazement. "I can't believe you—"

"It's just a donation," he said.

"Of *five hundred thousand dollars,*" she pointed out.

"If you don't want it…"

"Oh, no!" She folded the check and stretched out her right leg so she could stuff it into her jeans pocket. Then she patted it carefully and gave him a grin. "We want it. And we thank you. I mean, the whole *town* is going to want to thank you. This is just wonderful. Completely generous. I don't know what to say, really—"

"And yet you keep trying," Nathan said, feeling

oddly embarrassed the longer she went on about a simple donation.

"Wow. My head's still spinning. In a good way," she insisted, then raised one hand toward him. "A little help here?"

Nathan sighed, reached for her hand and, in one quick move, pulled her to her feet. She flew off the floor and slammed into his chest with a *whoosh* of air pushed from her lungs. His hands dropped to her waist to steady her and, for a quick moment, he considered kissing her.

Which surprised the hell out of him.

Keira Sanders wasn't the kind of woman who usually attracted him. For one, she was too damn talkative. He liked a woman who appreciated a good silence. And she was short. He liked tall women. And he preferred brunettes. And blue eyes.

Yet, as she looked at him, her green eyes seemed to pull at him, drawing him in, tugging him closer than he wanted to be.

With her breasts smashed up against his broad chest, Keira felt a rush of something hot and needy and completely unexpected. The man was as closed-off as a dead-end road, and yet there was something about him that made her want to reach up, wrap her arms around his neck and pull his head down for a long, lingering kiss.

And it *wasn't* the huge check that was sitting in her pocket like a red-hot coal.

"You're a very surprising man," she finally said when she was pretty sure she could speak without her voice breaking.

His hands dropped from her waist and he stepped back so quickly that her shaky balance made her wobble unsteadily before she found stability again.

"It's just a check."

"It's more than that," she assured him. God, she couldn't wait to show his donation to the town council. Eva Callahan would probably keel over in a dead faint. "You have no idea what this means to our town."

"You're welcome," he said tightly. "Now, if you don't mind, I have some work I have to get to."

"No you don't," she said, smiling.

"I'm sorry?"

"You don't have any work," Keira said, tipping her head to one side to study him, as if getting a different perspective might help understand why such a deliberately solitary man could give away so much money without even pausing to think about it. "You just want me to go."

"Yes." His frown deepened. "I believe I already mentioned that."

"So you did." She patted the check in her pocket, swung her hair back from her face and gave him a smile. "And I'm going to oblige you."

A flicker of something like acceptance shot across his eyes, and Keira wondered about that for a second or two. But then his features evened out into a mask of granite that no amount of staring at would ever decipher.

"Okay then," she said, starting for the front door, only half surprised when he made no move to follow her. He'd seemed so anxious to get rid of her, she'd just assumed that he'd show her out once he had the chance. But when she turned to glance back at him, he was standing where she'd left him.

Alone, in front of the vast windows overlooking the lake. Behind him, the water silvered under the rising moon and the star-swept sky seemed to stretch on forever. Something inside her wanted to go back to him. To somehow make him less *solitary.*

But she knew he wouldn't welcome it.

For whatever reason, Nathan Barrister had become a man so used to solitude he didn't want or expect anything to change.

Well, Keira wasn't going to allow him to get away with an anonymous donation. She was going to make sure the town got the chance to thank him properly for what he had done for them with a click of a pen.

Whether he liked it or not, Keira was going to drag Nathan into the heart of Hunter's Landing.

By the next evening, Keira was running on adrenaline. She'd hardly been able to sleep the night before; memories of Nathan Barrister and the feel of his hands on her had kept her tossing and turning through some pretty detailed fantasies that kept playing through her mind.

Ridiculous, really. She knew the man would be here for only a month. She knew he wasn't interested—he'd made *that* plain enough every time he looked at her. But, for some reason, her body hadn't gotten the message.

She felt hot and itchy and…way more needy than she'd like to admit.

Apparently it had been way too long since she'd had a man in her life. But then, the last man she'd been interested in had made such a mess of her world that she'd pretty much sworn off the Y chromosome.

Then grumpy, rich and gorgeous Nathan Barrister,

rolled into her life and made her start rethinking a few things. Not a good idea.

She spun her straw through her glass of iced tea and watched idly as ice cubes rattled against the sides of the glass. It felt good to sit down. She'd been running all day, first calling an emergency meeting of the town council so she could tell them about Nathan's donation. And, she smiled as she remembered, Eva Callahan had behaved as expected, slumping into a chair and waving a stack of papers at her face to stave off a faint.

Once the meeting was over she'd had to take care of a few other things, like depositing that check, talking to the contractor about the renovations to the clinic, settling a parking dispute between Harry's Hardware and Frannie's Fabrics and finally, coming here to the Lakeside Diner.

Being mayor of a small town was exhausting, and it was really hardly more than an honorary office. Her duties consisted mainly of presiding over town council meetings once a month, playing referee to adults old enough to solve their own problems and trying to raise money for civic projects. And yet, she seemed to always be busy. She didn't have a clue how the mayors of big cities managed to have a life at all.

But then, Keira thought, isn't that the way she wanted it? Keeping busy gave her too little time to think about how her life had turned out so differently from what she'd expected. She picked a French fry off her plate and popped it into her mouth. Chewing, she glanced around the crowded diner and took a deep breath. Here, no matter what else was going on in her life, Keira could find comfort.

The Lakeside Diner was a tiny coffee shop and more or less a touchstone in Keira's life, the one constant she'd always been able to count on. Her parents had owned and operated the diner before her and she herself had started working here, clearing tables, when she was twelve.

Then, when her parents died, Keira had taken over, because there was her younger sister, Kelly, to provide for. Now, she had a manager to take care of the day-to-day running of the diner, but when she needed a place to sit and recharge, she always came here.

The red Naugahyde booths were familiar, as was the gleaming wood counter and the glass covered cake and pie dishes, the records in the jukebox her father had loved hadn't been changed in twenty years. Memories crowded thick in this diner. She closed her eyes and could almost see her dad behind the stove, grinning out at her mom running the cash register.

This diner—like Hunter's Landing—was *home.*

"Hey, Keira. Can I see it?"

She opened her eyes, startled as an older woman slid onto the bench seat opposite her. Sallye Carberry grinned, and held out one hand dotted with silver rings.

"See what?" Keira asked.

"The check, of course," Sallye prompted. "Everyone in town is talking about it. Margie Fontenot told me that she'd never seen anything quite so pretty as all those zeros. I just wanted an up close peek at it."

"Sorry, Sallye," Keira said, taking a sip of her tea. "Already deposited it."

"Well, darn." The older woman slumped back against the seat and huffed out a disappointed breath that waved the curl of bangs on her forehead. "That's a bummer."

Keira laughed.

Sallye waved one beringed hand. "That's okay, I'll settle for meeting the man himself. I hear he's a real looker. He *is* coming to the potluck so we can all get a look at him—I mean thank him—isn't he?"

There was the question.

She knew damn well Nathan wouldn't want anything to do with the town or their potluck dinner. She knew he didn't want their thanks and was pretty sure he wouldn't want to see her again any time soon. So anyone with a grain of sense would keep her distance, right?

The last thing she should do was go back to the lakeside mansion to see a man who wanted nothing to do with her.

And yet…

Keira checked her silver wristwatch, saw she had a couple of hours until six and took one last sip of her tea. Sliding from the booth, she looked down at her late mother's best friend and nodded. "He'll be there," she said firmly.

Three

Nathan felt like a prisoner.

And damn it, he shouldn't.

He *preferred* being alone.

But this kind of alone was too damned quiet.

He stepped out onto the deck overlooking Lake Tahoe and let the cold wind buffet him. His hair lifted in the icy breeze, and he narrowed his eyes as he stared out over a snowy landscape. Silence pounded at him. Even the soft sigh of the lake water slapping against the deck pilings seemed overly loud in the eerie stillness.

The problem was, Nathan thought, he wasn't used to this kind of alone. Other people considered him a recluse but, even in his insular world, there was more…interaction.

He traveled constantly, moving from one of his

family's hotels to the next. And on those trips he dealt with room service personnel, hotel managers, maids, waiters, the occasional guest. No matter how he tried to avoid contact with people, there were always some who he was forced to speak to.

Until now.

The plain truth was he hated being completely alone even more than he hated being in a crowd.

His fists tightened on the varnished wood railing until he wouldn't have been surprised to see the imprint of his fingers digging into the wood. He was used to people jumping when he spoke. To his employees practically doing backflips to accommodate his wishes. He liked dropping in on his favorite casino in Monte Carlo and spending the night with whatever blonde, brunette or redhead was the most convenient. He liked the sounds of champagne bottles popping and crystal clinking, and the muted sound of sophisticated laughter. He was accustomed to picking up a phone and ordering a meal. To calling his pilot to get his jet ready to leave at a moment's notice.

Yet now he knew he couldn't go anywhere.

And that was the real irritant chewing at him. Nathan hadn't stayed in any one place for more than three or four days since he was a kid. Which was exactly how he wanted it. Knowing that he was *trapped* on top of this damned mountain for a damned *month* was enough to make him want to call his pilot now.

Why he didn't was a mystery to him.

"Hunter, you really owe me big time," he said and didn't know whether to look toward heaven or hell as he uttered the words.

Hunter Palmer had been a good guy, but reaching out from beyond the grave to put Nathan through this should have earned him a seat in hell.

"Why did I come here in the first place?" he whispered, asking himself the question and knowing he didn't have an answer.

Old loyalties was not a good enough reason.

It has been ten years since Hunter had died. Ten years since Nathan had even thought of those days, of the friend he'd lost too young. Of the five others who had been such a huge part of his life. He'd moved on. Built his world just the way he wanted it and didn't give a damn what anyone else had to say about it. That pledge the Samurai had made to one another? It seemed to come from another lifetime.

He thought briefly of the framed photos of the Seven Samurai, as they'd called themselves back then, hanging here in the upstairs hall. Every time he passed them, he deliberately looked away. Studying the past was for archaeologists. Not barristers. He didn't owe Hunter or any of the others anything. College friendships were routinely left behind as life continued on. So why in hell was he here?

A bird skimmed the water's surface, its wings stretched wide, its shadow moving on the lake as if it had a life of its own. "And even the damn bird is freer than I am."

Pushing away from the rail, he turned his back on the expansive view of nature's beauty and walked back into what he was already considering his cell.

He glanced at the television, then rejected the idea of turning it on. There were plenty of books to read, and even a state-of-the-art office loft upstairs but he couldn't imagine sitting still long enough to truly accomplish anything, at the moment, all he could do was prowl. He could take a walk, but he might just keep on walking, right down the mountain to the airport where his private Gulfstream waited for him.

"I'm never gonna make the whole damn month," he muttered, shoving one hand through his hair and turning toward the table where his laptop sat open.

He took a seat, hit a few keys and checked his e-mail as soon as the Internet connection came through. Two new letters were there, one each from the managers of the London and Tokyo Barrister hotels.

Once he'd dealt with their questions about his schedule, Nathan was at a loss again. There was only so much work he could do long-distance. After all, if he wasn't there in person, he couldn't scowl at his employees.

When the doorbell rang, he jumped to his feet. This is what he'd come to, then. Grateful for an interruption. For someone—anyone—to interrupt the silence that continued to claw at him. He closed the laptop and stalked across the great room to the front door.

When he opened the door, he said, "I should have guessed it would be you."

Keira grinned, slipped past him into the house and then turned to look at him. "You're going to need a coat."

Nathan closed the door and didn't admit even to himself that he was glad to see her. As annoying as she was, she was, at least, another voice in this damned quiet.

"I'm warm enough, thanks."

"No, I mean, the potluck is outside so you'll really need a coat." She turned again and walked into the great room as if she belonged there. Her voice echoed in the high-ceilinged room and her footsteps sounded like a heartbeat. "We could have held the dinner at the courthouse, but it's a little cramped and the band said it would be easier to set up outside."

"The band?"

"Uh-huh," she said, looking around as if she hadn't just seen the place the day before, "it's a local group. Super Leo. They play mostly rock but they'll take requests, too, and they're good guys. They all grew up here."

"Fascinating," Nathan said, moving to the edge of the foyer, leaning one shoulder against the wall and crossing one foot over the other as he watched her move. Damn, the woman looked good.

It was the solitude getting to him. The only explanation why he was interested in a short, mouthy redhead when ordinarily, he never would have looked at her twice. The fact that he'd only been "enjoying" this solitude for a day didn't really matter.

"The town council approved new lights for this year, so the square will be bright as day with plenty of room for dancing. When I left they were already setting the food out on the tables and the band was tuning up, so we really should get going if you don't want to miss anything."

"Miss anything?" Nathan shook his head. "I told you yesterday that I had no interest in going to your town party or whatever."

"Well, I didn't think you *meant* it."

"Why not?"

"Who wouldn't want to go to a party?"

"Me." Now, if the party were in St. Tropez, or Gstaad, he'd be right there. But a small-town party in the middle of Nowhere, U.S.A.? No, thanks.

She stared at him as if he'd just grown another

head. Then she shrugged and went on as if he hadn't said a word.

"The town council was incredibly grateful for your donation."

"You told them?" An uncomfortable itch settled between his shoulder blades. He didn't mind donating money. It was simply a part of who he was. But he preferred anonymity. He didn't want gratitude. He just wanted to be left alone.

But even as he thought this, he realized that he'd been complaining about the solitude just a minute before.

"Of course I told them," she said, picking up a throw pillow from the couch and fluffing it before she dropped it back into place. "Who am I, Santa? Dropping money into the town coffers without an explanation? I don't think so. They all want to meet you, to thank you for your generosity."

"Not necessary."

"Oh, but it really is," she said and reached down to straighten a stack of magazines strewn across the coffee table. "If you don't come to the potluck so everyone can meet you…"

"Yeah?"

She shrugged. "Then I guess everyone will just have to come to *you*."

Nathan sighed. She was blackmailing him into attending her damned town function. And doing a pretty good job of it, too. If he didn't go, he had no doubt that she'd lead droves of citizens up the mountain to intrude on the lodge. He'd be hip-deep in people before he knew it.

"Extortion?"

"Let's call it judicial negotiations."

"And if I go to the party, you'll leave me alone."

She held up one hand like a Girl Scout salute and said, "I so solemnly swear."

"I don't believe you."

"Gee, attractive, crabby *and* smart."

A smile twitched at his mouth, but he fought it into submission. No point in encouraging her any.

"Fine. I'll go."

"Wow," she said, patting her hand over her heart, "I'm all excited."

Her green eyes were shining and a smile curved her tantalizing mouth. The gray sweater she wore beneath a black leather jacket outlined the swell of her breasts, and her faded jeans and battered boots made her look too tempting to a man who was going to be trapped on a damn mountaintop for a month.

So Nathan got a grip on his hormonal overdrive and turned to the hall closet. He opened it, snatched out his brown leather jacket and pulled it on over his dark green cashmere sweater.

A few minutes ago, he'd been complaining that he was too alone. Now, he was going to a block party, of all things.

Be careful what you wish for.

Keira sneaked glances at him as she drove down the mountain. His profile was enough to make her heart stutter and when he turned his head to look at her, she almost drove into a tree.

"Whoops." She over-straightened and her snow tires slipped a little on an icy patch of road.

"Was this a ploy to get me on the road long enough to kill me?"

"Everything's fine," she said, tightening her grip on the wheel. "But would you like to take a look around before we head into town?"

"No, thanks." He checked the gold watch on his left wrist. "I can only spare an hour or two."

"Why?"

"Because."

"Ah. Good reason." Keira smiled and followed the curve of the road. There was a steep drop-off beyond the white barrier and Nathan glanced down into the abyss.

"Look," he said, "I'm only coming to this party to avoid the alternative."

"Don't worry, you'll be glad you came."

"Why do you care if I attend this party or not?"

"Why?" She risked another glance at him as soon as the road straightened, then turned her gaze ahead again. "You and the others who'll stay at the lodge after you are doing something tremendous for our town. Why wouldn't we want to thank you for that?"

He shifted uncomfortably on the truck seat. "I can't speak for the others, but I'm not doing this for you or your town."

"Then why?"

His mouth flattened into a grim line. "It's not important."

"But it's important enough for you to come here. To stay for a month?"

Still scowling, he said, "I'm here. As to the month… I don't know."

A small spear of panic jolted through Keira at the thought that he might leave. If he did, then, according to the terms of the will she'd read, the town of Hunter's

Landing would get nothing and the lakeside mansion would be sold.

She couldn't let that happen.

She *had* to convince Nathan Barrister to stay for the whole month. And maybe the best way to do that was to show him the town he and his friends were going to help. To let him see firsthand what a difference a month of his time could make to all of them.

But if he really wanted to go, how could she make him stay?

"But you agreed to the month."

"I did," he said, and she sensed, more than saw, him shrug his broad shoulders. "But I don't know that it's feasible. I have businesses to watch over. Places I'm supposed to be."

Already he was making mental excuses. Giving himself an out. Looking for a way to escape the terms of the will. The panic Keira's heart felt a moment ago jumped into hyperactive life and did a quick two step in the pit of her stomach. Did he believe that by making that incredibly generous donation he didn't have to complete the terms of the will?

"You wouldn't really leave soon, would you?"

He shifted in his seat and the leather creaked as he moved. "If you're looking for guarantees, I can't give them to you."

"But you agreed to the terms."

"Yes."

"So your word's not worth much?"

He frowned at her. "Is insulting me your grand plan to get me to cooperate? If so, it's a bad idea."

"Probably." She sighed and took the final turn down

the mountain road. Just a half mile ahead was Hunter's Landing, where her friends and neighbors were celebrating and planning the changes that would be coming at the end of six months.

She wondered how happy they'd all be to meet Nathan Barrister if they knew just how close he was to ruining those plans.

Pulling the car off to the side of the road, Keira threw the gearshift into park, yanked up the emergency brake and turned in her seat to look at him head-on.

"Problem?" he asked.

"You could say so," she said. In the darkening light, his pale blue eyes shone like chips of ice—and were just as welcoming. "This might not mean much to you," she said, "but your staying here for the entire month can mean a huge difference to the people here."

"I didn't say I was leaving," he pointed out.

"You didn't say you were staying, either," she countered.

"I am for right now," he said.

"That's supposed to make me feel better? Right now?"

"It's all I can give you."

Keira wanted to grab him and shake him, but she knew that wouldn't do any good. He was so closed-off, so shut down from anything other than his own feelings, she'd need a hammer to pound home her point. Tempting, but probably not logical.

"You've been here only one day. Give it a chance. Give *us* a chance."

He looked at her in the waning light and, just for a second, Keira thought those eyes of his warmed a little.

But she was probably mistaken since an instant later, they were cool and distant again.

"If you do," she added, "who knows, you might just like it here."

One dark eyebrow rose. "I'm not expecting to like it."

"Well," she said, smiling as she turned to shift the car into gear again and head into town, "surprises happen every day."

"Whether I stay or go is really none of your business." His tone clearly stated that was the end of the discussion.

Well, Keira wasn't sure who he was used to dealing with, but she wasn't about to back down under that king-to-peasant attitude.

"That's where you're wrong, Nathan." She paused and threw him a smile designed to either put him at ease or worry him half to death. "You don't mind if I call you Nathan, right? Well, Nathan, it *is* my business to see that you stay here. As mayor, I can't let you walk away from something that will mean so much to us."

He studied her for a long minute. She felt his gaze on her and forced herself to keep her own gaze focused on the road ahead of her. As they got closer to town, she heard the still-distant sounds of the band playing and steeled herself for whatever he was going to say next.

"Just so you know, Keira, if I decide to go, there's no way you'll be able to stop me."

She took the last turn in the road and saw Hunter's Landing spilling out ahead of her. Party lights were strung across the street, tiny blazes of white in the gathering darkness. People crowded the whole area, and a few couples had already started dancing.

Her heart swelled with love for the place and the

people she'd grown up with. Determination filled her as she turned to glance at the man beside her. She smiled and said, "Nathan, never issue a challenge like that to me. You'll lose every time."

They were swept into the party the moment she parked the truck, and Keira watched with some amusement as Nathan was dragged unwillingly into the center of things. The man was so stiff, so aloof, he stood out from the crowd like an ostrich in a chicken coop.

With the band's music pouring over them in a continuous wave of sound, Keira stood to one side and watched Nathan's features tighten as a few of the older men gathered around him to give Nathan some advice on fly-fishing.

The devil inside her told Keira to leave him to it. To let him be surrounded by the townspeople she'd so wanted him to meet. But a rational voice in the back of her mind drowned out that little devil by pointing out that if he *hated* it here, he'd have little reason to stay for the month to insure the town's bequest.

So she walked up to the group of men, smiled and said, "Sorry, guys, but I'm going to steal Nathan away for a dance."

"Aw, now, Keira, we're just telling him about the best spots in the Truckee River for fishing," one of them argued.

"And it was fascinating," Nathan said, dropping one arm around Keira's shoulders and dragging her in close to his side, as if afraid she'd change her mind and leave him there for more fishing advice. "But if you'll excuse me, gentlemen, I did promise the lady a dance."

Keira hid her smile and told herself that the warmth of Nathan's arm around her had more to do with body heat than sexual pull. Although she wasn't easily convinced, since parts of her that hadn't been hot in a very long time were suddenly smoking with sizzle and warmth.

When they moved away from the crowd toward the dance floor, Nathan bent his head and muttered, "I don't know whether to thank you for rescuing me or throttle you for bringing me here in the first place."

His voice was nearly lost under the slam of sound, so Keira leaned in closer to make sure he heard her response. "But you looked like you were having so much fun."

"I don't fish," he muttered.

"Maybe not," she pointed out, "but thanks to Sam Dover and the others, you could now if you wanted to."

He stopped and, since his arm was still wrapped around her shoulder, she did a quick stop too and slammed into his side.

"You're enjoying this, aren't you?"

"Would it be wrong to say yes?"

He frowned down at her. "I don't think I've ever met anyone like you before."

"Nathan! A compliment?"

"I'm not sure that's how I meant it."

She grinned. "That's how I'm taking it."

"Big surprise."

Keira wasn't fooled. There was a twitch at the corner of his way-too-kissable mouth that told her he was fighting the urge to smile. In the last day or so, she'd noticed he fought down smiling a lot. And she wondered why.

"So," she asked, "are you really going to dance with me?"

He sighed. "If I don't, are you going to sic the fishermen on me again?"

She lifted her arms into the dance-with-me position and said, "Nothing wrong with a good threat."

Four

The music slowed down into as close as a rock band could get to a romantic ballad, and Nathan reached for Keira. The instant his arm went around her waist, he felt a charge of something that jolted him from the soles of his feet straight up through the top of his head.

She smiled at him and he knew she'd felt it, too.

Her right hand felt small in his and the featherlight weight of her left hand seemed to be branding his shoulder. The air was icy and the street was crowded with people, yet he felt as if he and Keira were alone in the tropics, heat pouring through them with enough intensity to kindle a white-hot flame.

"What're you thinking?" she asked as he steered her around the makeshift dance floor in the middle of town.

"I don't think I'll tell you," he said and deliberately

raised his gaze from the sparkling beauty of her green eyes. "I have a feeling you'd find a way to use it against me."

"Oh, you're a sharp businessman, aren't you?" she asked, and suppressed laughter colored her voice.

He risked a glance down at her and found that the power in her gaze hadn't lessened a bit. "You've already blackmailed me *once,*" he reminded her.

"For a good cause," she pointed out.

"I really don't think that's an excuse the legal system would smile on."

"Hey, I'm the mayor. Would I do anything illegal?" She smiled at him again, and damned if Nathan's body didn't do a quick lunge. His arm tightened around her waist, tucking her in even closer, and when she moved in the dance, she did things to him he didn't want to think about.

So he didn't. To distract himself, he let his gaze sweep the town, and it didn't escape him that he could see the whole thing in a matter of seconds. The buildings were old, but well cared for. Fresh paint shone in the lights and sidewalks were swept clean. Flower boxes jutted out from window fronts and he presumed that if spring should ever come to the mountains, those boxes would be full of bright flowers.

A couple hundred people crowded the blocked-off streets, and he saw everyone from old couples sitting quietly holding hands to teenaged lovers gazing at each other so intently, he half expected to see tiny cartoon hearts circling their heads.

Keira fit right in here. She was greeted by hugs, kisses, teasing laughter and shouts, and Nathan wondered briefly what it must be like to so thoroughly belong somewhere. He hadn't known that feeling since he was a kid. And he had, over the years, done everything he could to *keep* from belonging anywhere in particular. Yet he could see that Keira thrived on the very kind of life he'd avoided.

Overhead, the moon peeked through a wisp of clouds and shone down onto the town, bathing it in a silvery glow that made it look almost magical. Which was a ridiculous thought, since Hunter's Landing was clearly no more than a tiny town in between a couple of bigger ones.

If Hunter Palmer hadn't chosen this town—no doubt for the pleasure of building a mansion in a town that shared his name—Nathan would never have known of the place's existence. He wasn't a man to go wandering down unbeaten paths.

He preferred big cities. The anonymity of hotel rooms with an ever-changing sea of faces surrounding him. He had no interest in bonding with a town and people he'd never see again once he got off this mountain.

And yet…

Keira held his hand a little tighter as if she could read his thoughts and was subtly trying to hold him here, to this place.

She felt good in his arms, her curvy little body pressed up close to his, and Nathan could admit, at least to himself, that he wanted her. He hadn't had any intention of making a connection of any sort with the people of this town, but she just wouldn't go the hell away. And was it his fault if his body reacted to hers?

This reaction was chemical, pure and simple.

He'd been so long without a woman sharing his bed that he was reacting to the first female to get close.

Not that she was close.

But the thought of her in his bed was enough to set a flash fire racing through his bloodstream.

"Oh," she said, tipping her head back to stare up at him, "now I *really* have to know what you're thinking. Your face just got all stiff and your eyes went slitty."

"Slitty?"

"It's a word," she argued.

"Barely."

"You're changing the subject."

"Apparently not successfully," he said, not surprised at all that she wasn't willing to back down.

"Once you get to know me," she countered, "you'll know that I don't give up all that easily."

"Trust me," Nathan said, "that much I've already learned."

"Wow!" Her face lit up and her eyes sparkled in the overhead lights. "We're really making progress here, aren't we?"

"Progress?"

"You bet. I know that you get all stiff when you don't want to talk about something, and you know that I'm a little stubborn…"

"A little?"

"…we're practically friends already."

"Friends?"

"Nothing wrong with that, is there?" she asked and came to a stop as the song ended and a new one, one with a raw, savage beat, started up. "You have so many friends you can't use another one?"

No, he didn't have friends. Purposely. That need had been satisfied then discarded ten years ago. Now his life was streamlined. Just the way he wanted it.

Nathan let her go gratefully, though he couldn't help but notice just how empty his arms felt without her in them. A warning flag if he'd ever seen one. Keeping a few feet of space between them seemed like the smart move, here. And he'd always been smart enough to protect himself.

"We're not friends, Keira. Friends don't use extortion to get their way."

"Really?" she asked, tipping her head to one side so that her hair fell in a reddish-blond wave to the side of her head, "isn't that what your friend Hunter Palmer did?"

He felt himself stiffen again and couldn't seem to stop it. "Excuse me?"

"Well," she said, linking her arm through his and leading him farther away from the pulsing beat of the song and the jostling crowd on the dance floor, "you clearly don't want to be here, but you're going to stay the month because your old friend asked you to in his will. So, isn't that extortion?"

He supposed it was and hadn't he been thinking pretty much along the same lines earlier today? "You can be extremely annoying."

"I've heard that before."

"Again, not surprising."

"Come on, Nathan," she said, tugging at his arm, "I think it's time I fed you. Maybe your attitude will improve once you've tasted Clearwater's lasagna."

He didn't want to spend more time with her. She had a way of getting into his head that he wasn't entirely comfortable with. So he stopped dead, and Keira jolted back into him.

"Hey, a little warning before a sudden stop might be a good thing."

"Sorry. But I think I've seen enough," he said. "I came to the potluck and now, if you don't mind, I'd like to go back to the house."

"You haven't eaten yet," she said.

"Not hungry."

"Liar."

He shoved his hands into his jacket pockets and gave her a look that had been known to send hotel managers scurrying for cover. "Are you going to take me back or not?"

"You bet. As soon as we eat."

"Damn it, Keira—"

"You have to eat, Nathan. You might as well do it here."

When he didn't budge, she prodded. "You're not scared of us, are you?"

"Us?"

"The town." She spread her arms wide as if encompassing everyone there in a hug. "Hunter's Landing. You a little worried that if you stick around for a while, you just might get to like us?"

"Don't you get it?" he asked, suddenly feeling that, if he wasn't rude, she'd never listen to him. "I'm not here to make friends. I'm here because I have to be. I owe it—" He stopped himself before he gave her more information than he wanted to. "I'm not interested in liking or disliking your town. I just want to put in my time and get back to my life."

"Wow." She blinked up at him. "You did it again."

Nathan sighed and asked the question he knew he shouldn't. "What?"

"Turned on the rude," she said. "It's pretty impressive, really, just how easy it is for you to get all crabby and nasty."

"You don't listen to me otherwise."

"Oh," she said, smiling again like nothing was wrong, "I listen, I just don't pay attention. There's a difference. And whether you want to admit it or not Nathan Barrister, you're hungry. You may not want to be here, but since you *are* here, you might as well eat. Right?"

How was a man supposed to argue with that kind of twisted logic? She grabbed his arm and tugged him toward a long line of tables piled high with what looked like every kind of food imaginable.

Nathan felt like a petulant child and he didn't like it. No point in being stubborn about this, though. There was no way out. He couldn't *walk* back up the mountain. And he wasn't going to ask someone else to drive him up. So he'd wait. He'd eat. And once he got back up the mountain, he'd call his damn pilot and tell him to fire up the engines.

No way was he going to stay for the whole month. A couple of days in Keira Sanders's company was enough to convince him to leave while he still could.

For the next hour, Keira watched him with some amusement.

Nathan probably wouldn't be happy to hear it, but she found it pretty entertaining watching him try to dodge the town's gratitude. Every time someone stepped up to say thank you, Nathan turned into a stone statue. He would nod politely, close down his features and then turn away, only to be met by yet another grateful citizen.

What was it about this man that was so intriguing? She couldn't quite figure it out. But seeing him squirm uncomfortably around her friends and neighbors was just captivating enough that she wanted to know him better. To slip under the walls he'd erected around himself. To get past the arrogant stance and condescending tone to the man who lived within.

Or was she just fooling herself?

Maybe there was no inner Nathan to meet. Maybe he was just who he appeared to be. Rich, aloof, disinterested. But she didn't believe that. She'd seen the quick flash of humor in his eyes before he deliberately stamped it out, and she was willing to put in the time to see if she could reach past his barriers.

Why?

She hadn't figured that out yet.

Oh, sure. She was working double-time to make sure he didn't leave town before his month was up. But this was more personal than insuring a bequest to the town she loved. This was getting to be…interesting.

When her cell phone rang, Keira glanced at the screen, noted the number and got up to walk farther away from Nathan and the crowd to answer it. She threw him a finger-wave as she moved off and smiled to herself at the panic that zipped across his face.

Couldn't really blame him for the panic as Sallye and Margie, the town's two most talkative women, took up position on either side of him. Keira left him to his own devices as she stepped into the doorway of the flower shop and flipped her phone open.

"Hi, Kelly!"

"Hey, big sister, how's it going?" Kelly Sanders sounded like she was down the street instead of calling from her home in London.

Keira didn't even want to think about what kind of charges were going to be adding up on her cell phone. But she was so glad to talk to her younger sister, she wasn't going to worry about it.

"Everything's good," Keira shouted to be heard over the band who, even now, was cranking up the decibels to ear shattering level.

"What's going on?" Kelly demanded, then, after a heartbeat, whined, "It's a block party, isn't it? Everyone's having a good time and I'm not there."

"Yeah, but you're in Europe. Really good times, remember?"

"True," she said wistfully. "Usually I love it here, but I hate knowing life is going on at home without me."

Well, that was typical Kelly. She had always wanted to be in the center of things. Even when she was a little girl, Kelly wasn't satisfied with being in the background. Their mother used to say that Kelly had been born in a hurry and had just never stopped running.

Keira really missed her. They were each other's only family now, and this last year, when Kelly had been living in England, Keira had had a hard time of it.

"I'll tell everyone you said hi," she said and glanced down the street, making sure Nathan hadn't bolted for freedom. Nope, he was still there, sandwiched between the two very nice, very chatty older ladies. Keira grinned, leaned against the shingled wall of the flower shop and said, "So what's going on?"

"Oh, Tony's taking me to Paris for the weekend and I wanted to let you know I wouldn't be home for our Saturday night phone call."

Tony—also known as Stewart Anthony Brookhurst, was CEO of some huge conglomerate based in England and, for the last six months, the main topic of all of Kelly's conversations.

"Paris, very nice," Keira said and tried to keep the sigh of envy from slipping from her soul.

She'd had plenty of plans of her own years ago. She'd wanted to finish college, travel, see the world. But in the blink of an eye, her plans—her world—had changed. Not that she regretted being there for Kelly, for putting her own life plans on hold to see to it that her little sister went to college. She didn't resent the fact that while she had stayed here, in the town she loved, Kelly had gone off on the adventures that Keira had once dreamed of.

And, if she did feel occasional spikes of envy jabbing at her, she'd managed so far to hide them from the sister she loved.

"I know," Kelly said with a laugh. "Who would have thought that I'd be saying stuff like that? *Paris for the weekend.* But you know, K, I really love it here. I mean, I miss home and everybody, you especially, but I love living in London. I even like the rain!"

"I know." She heard that love in Kelly's voice every time they spoke. This was supposed to have been a one-year stint—a year that was almost over—in London, for the international bank that had hired Kelly right out of college. But Keira had been preparing herself for months now, to be ready for the day when Kelly announced that she would be *staying* in Europe.

Kelly loved everything about England and now that she was seriously dating a man who had been born and raised there, the chances of her ever moving back to Hunter's Landing were slimmer than ever.

"So what's going on at home, besides the party I'm not at," she asked.

Keira shook off the gloomy thoughts that had settled over her like some sort of shroud and forced a smile into her voice. "We've got our first guest in the lake lodge."

"Oh my God! You're kidding! What's he like? Did you see the inside of the place? Is it fabulous?"

Keira laughed. God, she missed her little sister. "Not kidding, he seems nice, saw the house, it's amazing."

"C'mon," Kelly whined. "There's gotta be more than that. You've been telling me about that house for a year now. So what's it like?"

"It's so gorgeous, you wouldn't believe it. Awesome views of the lake—built of glass and wood and stone, and there's a fireplace big enough to stand up in."

"Oh, wow."

"I'll say."

"And the guy?"

"What about him?"

"'He seems nice?'" Kelly laughed. "Please. Give me more than that."

More? What could she say? That he was arrogant and irritating and altogether too attractive? That she was spending too much time thinking about *him* when she should have been worrying about keeping him in the lodge long enough to fulfill the requirements of the will?

"What's his name, at least," Kelly demanded.

"Nathan." There. That was safe information. "Nathan Barrister."

"*Whoa.* Barrister? Like in the Barrister Hotel Barristers?"

"I don't know," Keira said with a shrug her sister couldn't see. "I…maybe."

"Nathan Barrister was in London a couple of months ago. Had a meeting at my bank. Tell me what yours looks like and I'll tell you if it's him."

"Tall. Dark. Pale blue eyes."

"Snotty twist to his mouth?" Kelly asked.

"Not exactly snotty," Keira argued.

"Woo hoo," Kelly crowed. "It *is* him. And you *like* him."

"Dial it down, Kel," Keira said, knowing it was way too late to put the lid back down on that particular box. Kelly was already enjoying herself.

"I don't believe this. Nathan Barrister in Hunter's Landing? That's too funny."

"Why's it funny?" She stiffened at the amusement in her sister's voice and felt like she should be defending the man for some reason.

"Well, he's just such a *stick*. The man has no sense of humor and one look out of those eyes and you practically freeze over. And I saw my boss's face after his meeting with Barrister. You remember I told you that my boss is mean enough to give the boogeyman nightmares?"

"Yeah…"

"When Barrister left his office, my boss was *pale* and shaking."

"Oh."

"Seriously, K," Kelly said, her voice dropping. It was

a strain to hear her over the crash of the band and the swell of laughter and conversation rising up over Main Street. "If you're thinking about falling for this guy, don't do it."

"Oh, please." Keira sighed, shook her hair back from her face and said, "He's here as part of that will I told you about. If he stays for the month, if the rest of them each stay for a month, the town is going to get a heck of a lot of money that we really need. And that's all there is to it. I just said he was attractive, I didn't say I was going after him."

"You didn't say he was attractive!" Kelly's voice shrieked so high that Keira jerked the phone away from her ear.

"I didn't?"

"No. K, don't do this. Don't let yourself care about this guy. Remember what happened with—"

"Don't go there, okay?" Keira interrupted her quickly, not willing to take a forced march down memory lane. "And let's remember here just which one of us is the *older* sister."

"I know," Kelly said, "it's just that you're so—"

"So *what* exactly?"

"I don't know. Never mind. Just be careful, okay?"

"I'm always careful, Kelly. Trust me. Nothing's going to happen." Even if she wanted something to happen, Nathan had already made it perfectly clear that *he* didn't, so what could happen?

Keira peeked around the edge of the flower shop wall to stare down the street at Nathan again—big mistake. He was watching for her. Even from a distance, his gaze slammed into hers with a punch that was nearly physical. Keira sucked in a gulp of air and reached out blindly with her right hand to slap it against the wall in an effort to balance herself. It didn't help much.

A flicker of heat kicked into life in the pit of her stomach and rolled through her like a storm-pitched wave crashing onto shore. She felt her world rock and had to fight to right it again.

"K?" Kelly's voice was in her ear. "Are you okay?"

"Yeah," she lied, swallowing hard past the knot of need that was lodged firmly in her throat. She couldn't look away from Nathan's eyes. "I'm fine. Don't worry about anything."

"But—"

"Look. Send me a postcard from Paris, okay?"

"Sure, but—"

"Bye, honey, be safe." Keira flipped the phone closed and straightened up just as Nathan headed toward her.

Five

Nathan had had enough.

His ears were ringing and the good manners his grandmother had drummed into him were strained now to the snapping point. He'd excused himself from the two older women who had seemed determined to trap him on Main Street forever, and now he was going to get Keira to take him back to the lodge.

He should have driven himself.

Then he wouldn't be waiting around for anyone. He wasn't a man who liked being dependent on someone else for anything. His insides tightened as people milled past him, laughing, talking, dancing. He wasn't a part of them and never would be. Didn't *want* to be. And the more time he spent with all of them, the more clear that feeling became.

He didn't know why the hell he hadn't left the mountains already. He didn't *have* to honor a promise made in college to a man long-dead. Hell, he could donate the twenty million himself and get out of this mess now.

And with that thought firmly in his mind, his steps quickened toward Keira. Her gaze locked with his and he told himself to pay no attention to the brilliant green of her eyes or the worried twist of her mouth. He refused to notice how the light dazzled the ends of her reddish-blond hair, making it almost glow in a soft halo around her head. And damned if he would remember just how good she felt when her body was pressed against his during their dance.

As he came closer, she shoved her cell phone into the front pocket of her jeans and inhaled deeply enough that her breasts rose and then fell with the rush of her sigh.

If his body tightened suddenly, desperately, he ignored it.

"Hi," she said and, somehow, her voice carried over the other sounds on the street. "Enjoying yourself?"

He frowned at her. "Yeah, it's been great. I've eaten, I've danced and I've listened to enough thank-yous to last me a lifetime, so if you don't mind, I'd like a ride back to the lodge."

"Sure."

"That easy?" He felt one eyebrow quirk. He hadn't expected her to give in without trying to talk him into staying longer.

"Why not?" she asked and looked away from him, shifting her gaze to sweep across the town square. She sighed again and this time her voice was so soft, he almost missed it. "I just wanted you to see Hunter's

Landing. To meet some of the people, so you'd know who you and your friends are helping."

"Thank you." He heard the sarcasm in his own voice but didn't bother to try to take the sting out of it.

"I can take you by the clinic for a quick look on the way back. Then you can see exactly what we're planning."

"Not necessary."

Nathan blew out a frustrated breath. Everything in him was clamoring to be gone from this place. To pick up the threads of his life and get back to living the way he knew best. He didn't do well with other people. Didn't care to. And yet now…

Screw it.

"How about that ride?"

Frowning, she said, "You're just determined not to enjoy yourself, aren't you?"

"Was that a requirement?"

She muttered, "Kelly was right. You really are scary, aren't you?"

"What?"

"Nothing." Reluctantly, she shrugged and said, "Let's go."

He followed her to her truck and when she stumbled over a crack in the road, Nathan lunged forward to grab her before she could fall. Spinning her around, he pulled her in close and she laughed up at him. The woman was so changeable, he could hardly keep up.

"Thanks, didn't see that."

"Weren't looking, you mean."

Her hands were on his upper arms and even through the thick leather of his coat, he felt the heat in her touch and wanted more. Wanted to feel her hands on his bare skin, run his own hands over every curve of her body. Hear her sigh as he buried himself inside her.

The images in his mind were suddenly so clear, so overpowering, he could hardly draw a breath past the hot fist tightening around his lungs.

He willed himself to speak. “It’s a wonder you’re not covered in bruises the way you stumble around.”

“What makes you think I’m not?” she asked, still smiling.

He pulled in another deep breath of cold, mountain air and hoped it would help chill the fire in his blood. “What the hell are you doing to me?” he demanded.

“Depends, Nathan,” she said, her smile fading as her brilliant green eyes darkened with a need he recognized. “What do you *want* me to do to you?”

“I’m not interested in a short affair,” he said tightly, despite the fact that his body clamored for just that.

“Well, who asked you?” She pulled free of his grasp, straightened up and shook her hair back from her face. “Jeez, save a girl from a fall and then accuse *her* of trying to seduce *you.* Nice. Very nice.”

He pushed one hand through his hair and wondered why in the hell he tried talking to her anyway. “Can we just get in the damn truck?”

She dug her keys out of her pocket and bounced them on her palm. “You know, you were the one looking at me like you wanted to gobble me up.”

He blew out another breath and glared at her. “Call it temporary insanity.”

“Wow, one compliment after another,” she said and turned for the truck. “You’re really on a roll here, Barrister.”

He stood just where he was and watched her open the driver's side door and step up into the cab. "You're an infuriating woman, did you know that?"

She glanced back at him over her shoulder. "Believe it or not, that's been said before."

"My sympathies to the poor bastard, whoever he was."

Her face froze up and her eyes shuttered as effectively as if she'd slapped on a pair of dark glasses. "He doesn't need your sympathy, Nathan. And neither do I. So, you getting in the truck or are you going to walk back up the mountain?"

Over the next week or so, every time Keira drove up the mountain, she was half afraid she'd find Nathan gone. After a *really* quiet ride back from the block party, she had dropped him off at the lodge and had hardly waited for his feet to hit the dirt before she gunned the engine and went home. It still embarrassed her to think about driving off in a huff like that.

She never should have let him get to her—couldn't understand why she had. But that little dig about giving his sympathies to whichever man had last been in her life had come a little too quickly after Kelly had brought up the same damn thing.

It wasn't that Keira was sensitive about her past; she just didn't like being reminded of what an idiot she'd been once upon a time.

But that was the past and this was now. And all that mattered *now* was making sure Nathan didn't leave before his month was up. She was pretty sure he was tired of having her show up on his doorstep every day, but she kept visiting him anyway, because she could practically *see* his need to leave vibrating in the air all around him.

And she wouldn't let that happen.

Parking the truck in the drive, she hopped out, slammed the door and headed for the front door. Dark clouds hung heavy over the mountains and the air felt thick with the promise of more snow. As much as she loved winter in the mountains, she was really ready for spring. Unfortunately, it looked as if nature didn't feel the same way.

She shivered, dug her hands into her jacket pockets and quickened her step, only to stop when she heard Nathan's voice shout, "Back here."

Surprised to find him outside and away from the laptop that he clung to like his last link with civilization, Keira headed down the drive. She saw him at the lake's edge and she wasn't ashamed to admit, at least to herself, that the man was really sigh-worthy.

He wore that dark green cashmere sweater again over jeans that looked worn and comfortable. His brown leather jacket gave him a piratical air, and the wind tossed his hair across his forehead, making him look more free than she could remember seeing him before. Her heart jumped a little and her mouth went dry.

She could be in some serious trouble here. Especially if he started looking at her the way he had the night of the party.

"What're you doing?" she called as her boots crunched on the gravel drive.

He gave her a quick look, then shifted his gaze back to the steel gray surface of the lake. "Just looking. Needed some air."

"Really?" she teased as she walked up to stop beside him. "I thought you were very happy breathing canned air and looking at nature through the beauty of clean glass windows."

He snorted. "Let's just say I'm feeling a little cabin fever."

There it was again. She could see how ready he was to chuck the whole month and escape from what he no doubt considered captivity. So what she had to do was take his mind off it.

"I can cure that."

"How?"

"Take a walk with me." She threaded her arm through the crook of his and smiled up at him.

"It's freezing out here," he reminded her.

"If we keep moving, we won't feel it." She tugged at his arm. "Come on. When's the last time you took a walk along a lake as beautiful as this one?"

His gaze swept out over the wide expanse of water and the pine-tree-studded shoreline before turning back to her. "Never."

"Way too long," she assured him and started walking. His long legs outdistanced hers, and Keira caught herself half running to keep up before she pulled back on his arm and said, "It's not a race, you know. You don't actually get a prize for reaching the other side."

He stopped, smirked a little, then shrugged. "Point taken. But I'm not used to just strolling."

"It's okay," Keira said, enjoying the flash of warmth in his too-cool blue eyes. "You can learn."

They walked in companionable silence for a few

minutes before she said, "The bears will be waking up soon."

"Bears?"

"Oh, yeah. Black ones and brown ones. Mamas and babies. They'll be trolling through backyards and tipping over trash cans looking for food or trouble."

"Bears." He shook his head. "Can't imagine living somewhere I could expect to bump into a bear."

"Funny, huh?" she asked, tipping her face up to the darkening clouds, "I can't imagine living anywhere else."

"You were raised here?"

"Yep. Born in Lake Tahoe, raised here. We didn't have a clinic back then. Now our new moms don't have to take that trek over the mountain for medical help." She grinned and patted his arm with her free hand. "And thanks to you, our clinic's going to be even better than it already is."

"You've thanked me enough."

"Not really," she said, "but I'll let it go."

"Thank you."

"For now."

He snorted.

"What about you?" she asked in the silence, "Where are you from?"

"Everywhere," he said, turning his gaze on the wind-whipped water of the lake again.

"That's not an answer, just so you know."

"I was born in Massachusetts. Grew up on the east coast."

Amazing how the man could give information and still make it seem like so little. But Keira wasn't a woman to be dissuaded easily. She dug a little deeper.

"Your family still there?"

"No family," he said shortly, and his gorgeous blue eyes squinted into the wind racing past them.

"I'm sorry."

"No reason to be. You couldn't know."

"Well, I am, anyway," she said and squeezed his arm companionably. "My folks died when I was in college," she said, thinking that maybe if she gave a little, he'd be willing to give a little, too. "They went skiing. Got caught in an avalanche."

His gaze shifted to hers. "Now I'm sorry."

She looked up at him and smiled. "Thank you. It was really hard. I still miss them so much."

"I was ten," he said. "Car accident."

A few words, but said so tightly, Keira could feel the old pain still welling inside him. At least she'd been grown when she lost her parents. She couldn't even imagine how lonely and terrifying it would have been to be a child and lose the safety of your own little world.

"God, Nathan, that's terrible."

"A long time ago," he reminded her. "Had my grandmother. Dad's mom. She took me in."

"That couldn't have been easy for her," Keira said, then stumbled on a piece of wood jutting up into the rocky trail.

Nathan caught her by tightening his grip on her arm and keeping her steady. "It wasn't much of a hardship. She sent me to boarding school, and I was only home for a month every summer."

"She *what?*"

He blinked at her, clearly surprised by her reaction. What kind of people farmed out ten-year-old kids to boarding schools? What kind of grandparent couldn't see that the child left in her care was in pain and needed more than the impersonal attention of someone *paid* to watch over him?

"It was a very good school," he said.

"Oh, I'm sure." A spurt of anger shot through Keira on behalf of a child who no longer existed. "No brothers or sisters?"

"Nope. You?"

God, he had been all alone with a grandmother too busy to give him what he must have craved. A sense of belonging. A sense of safety. Keira couldn't even imagine what that must have been like for him, and a part of her warmed up to his frosty nature a little more. After all, if he'd been so cut off as a child, how could she possibly expect the man to be open to possibilities?

He was watching her, waiting for her to answer his question, and so she gave him a smile that didn't let him in on the fact that she was really feeling sorry for the boy he'd once been.

"I have a sister. Kelly. She's younger than me and was still in high school when our folks were killed. So, I came home from school, watched over her and started running the family diner."

He frowned. "The coffee shop in town?"

"You noticed it? Yep. The Lakeside was my dad's baby. It's small, but it's been good to us. Made it possible for me to get Kelly into college—well, the diner and a few good loans."

"What about you?" he asked. "You didn't go back to school?"

"No," she said, still irritated with his grandmother for some bizarre reason. "I meant to, I really did. But then

Kelly was in college, and no way could we afford for both of us to go. And when she graduated, I'd already hired a manager for the diner and was running for mayor, so…" She shrugged.

"Your sister should have taken her turn in town to give you a chance to go to school."

Keira shook her head. "No, she got a tremendous job offer right out of school and there was no way she could not take it."

He was silent, but the quiet held a lot of disapproval.

"You could go back to college now," he pointed out.

"Oh, yeah," Keira said, laughing shortly. "Just what I want to do. Go to school with a bunch of kids. Sounds like a great time."

"What's your sister doing now?"

"She's living in London," Keira said, defensive of a little sister who didn't need defending. "She loves England," she added with a wistful sigh. "She sends me pictures that make me want to pack my bags and go there for myself."

"Why don't you?"

"I can't just leave because I *want* to. I have responsibilities to this town."

He sighed, frowned and turned slitted eyes on her. "Is that a not so subtle hint?"

"I wasn't going for subtle," she admitted, smiling up at him despite the glower in his eyes. "Just for a reminder about the responsibilities *you* and the others have to Hunter's Landing."

"I'd never heard of your town until a month ago," he reminded her, "and a month from now, I will have forgotten it."

"Well, don't we feel special," she mused.

"It's nothing personal," he said. "It's just…"

"None of that really matters, does it? You agreed to the terms of the will and—" The toe of her boot caught under a root and she would have gone sprawling if Nathan hadn't steadied her again.

"You're dangerous," he snapped. "Why don't you pay more attention to where you're walking?"

"Hey, I have you here to catch me."

"Don't count on that."

"I am, though," Keira said, blocking his way by stepping in front of him before she stopped dead. "We're all counting on you. You and your friends."

The wind sliced in off the lake and cut at them like a knife straight out of a freezer. Keira's hair swept across her eyes and she plucked it free so she could look at Nathan.

He didn't look happy, but what was new about that? His gaze was locked with hers and his mouth was tightened into a grim slash that told her exactly what he was thinking.

"I know you don't want to hear it," Keira said and reached out to put both hands on his forearms. And even through the icy brown leather jacket, she felt the strength of him, tightly leashed. "But it's true. I can't even tell you how important it is to all of us that you stay for the month."

"Keira—"

"I know, I know," she said, lifting both hands in a mock surrender. "You don't want to hear about this anymore."

"The night of the town party," he admitted quietly, "I had every intention of calling my pilot and flying out of here."

"But you didn't," she said lightly, despite the quick tightening around her insides.

"That doesn't mean I won't," he pointed out. "I don't want you—or anyone—counting on me. For anything."

"That's a hard way to live," she said.

"It's my way."

"It doesn't have to be," Keira said, her voice a whisper that was nearly lost in the swirl of the wind. Why was she doing this? Why did she care how Nathan Barrister lived his life?

He laughed shortly, and the sound was so surprising that Keira blinked at him.

"I *like* my life just the way it is," he said. "I'm not interested in changing it."

"Just like you're not interested in a one-month affair."

His jaw clenched.

Oops.

She didn't know why she'd said that. But now that it was back out in the open between them, she wasn't sure how to *un*-say it, either.

"Keira…"

A puff of white danced on the wind and flew between them as if trying to end their conversation.

"Was that…?" he asked.

"Snow," she said.

And in that split second, several more flakes of snow whipped around them, carried on the wind that snapped and rattled at the pine trees. The temperature dropped what felt like twenty degrees and the lowering clouds looked black and threatening.

"Of course it's snow. For God's sake, does spring *ever* get here?" He inhaled sharply, deeply, and looked at her as if there was something more he wanted to say.

The look in his eyes was nearly electric. Despite the

snowflakes just beginning to flurry around them, she felt heat arcing between them.

Her heartbeat was jittering in her chest, her blood was pumping hot and thick in her veins, and she had the most overpowering urge to reach up and smooth his hair back from his forehead.

Instead, she curled her fingers into her palms and took a deep breath. “It’s coming down harder. We should start back.”

Six

By the time they reached the lodge, snow had dusted their hair and shoulders and was thick enough in the air that every breath tasted like ice.

When Keira would have turned down the driveway to head for her truck, Nathan caught her elbow and tugged her up the back steps to the house by the lake.

"Nathan…"

He stopped on the top step, looked down into her soft green eyes and said, "You might as well wait out the storm here."

She hunched deeper into her jacket, swung her snow-dusted hair out of her eyes and said, "It might not stop for a few hours."

Glad to hear it, he almost said and was glad he'd managed to clamp his jaw shut. But the truth was, he didn't want to go back into that too-damned-quiet lodge. It was bad enough to be trapped there in the silence when the sun was shining. He had a feeling that being alone with the falling snow and lowering clouds would make him feel as though he were buried alive in a dark cave. Not something he really wanted to experience.

"And it might stop in a few minutes," he pointed out, but, as if to prove that prediction false, the wind kicked up and the snow flew in frenzied flurries.

"If I was home right now," Keira said, "I'd make myself some hot chocolate."

"I can probably handle that," he said. "Or, there's some excellent brandy."

She climbed up a step, coming that much closer to him, and the depths in her green eyes called to him, reached for him. "Brandy would be good, too. Got anything to eat?"

He held out one hand and waited for her to take it. When she did, his fingers folded tightly around hers. "There's plenty of stuff in the fridge."

She took the last step that brought her beside him and gave him a smile that warmed him through, despite the icy wind and the snow sneaking beneath the collar of his jacket. "Then why are we still standing in the storm?"

They walked across the covered deck, stepped into the mudroom and pulled off their jackets and boots. Then, together, they went into the kitchen. The room was cavernous, with built in niches for the stainless steel appliances and a mile of granite counter. The walls were painted to give them an antiqued finish, and the colors were warm cream and brown, making the kitchen seem cozy even in the midst of a storm.

"Let's get that brandy first, worry about food later," Nathan said, and led the way from the kitchen to the great room.

"Good plan," she said and shivered a little as she followed him down the hall.

A fire was blazing in the hearth and Keira moved straight toward it as Nathan walked to the wet bar. He poured them each a drink, then walked to join her by the fire. Handing her one of the crystal snifters, he watched the amber liquid swirl in the bottom of his glass for a long moment before he took a sip.

He swallowed and felt the alcohol fueled fire rush through him as he shifted his gaze to Keira. Firelight played on her skin and danced in her eyes. The ends of her hair shone with a nearly incandescent light and when she lifted her glass to her lips, everything inside him tightened.

After taking a sip, she blew out a breath, smiled and looked up at him. "Wow. Well, that warms you up fast, doesn't it?"

Nathan ground his teeth together and then took a sip of his own brandy. The heat it produced was nothing like the *other* kind of heat swamping him. Just looking at Keira made him burn.

For more than a week now, he had tried not to think about her, to put this insane attraction out of his mind. But he hadn't been able to manage it. When he closed his eyes, he saw her. When he dreamed, he touched her. When he thought he would go out of his mind from the silence in this place, she arrived and he nearly went out of his mind for different reasons entirely.

She sat down on the stone hearth, the fire at her back,

and looked up at him as she cradled the brandy snifter between her palms. “So, Nathan, are you the Barrister Hotel guy?”

One eyebrow rose and he took another sip of his brandy, welcoming the steady fire. “Hotel guy? Yeah. I suppose I am. How’d you know?”

She smiled. “Just a guess. Hunter’s Landing isn’t exactly on the moon. We get newspapers and magazines here, too. Which one of your hotels is your favorite?”

He shrugged carelessly. “I don’t really have a favorite, they’re all top-of-the-line establishments, each of them with their own unique pluses and minuses.”

“Boy, feel the enthusiasm.”

“I’m sorry?”

“Well, come on, Nathan, you own four-star hotels—”

“Five-star,” he amended automatically.

“Right. In beautiful, exotic places all over the world. You talk about them as if they’re nothing special. As if they’re no different from any other exclusive hotels. Is that really what you think?”

Nathan frowned, sat down beside her and instantly appreciated the heat of the fire warming his back. “It’s the family business, Keira. They’re valuable properties with impeccable reputations that I work hard to maintain.”

“Uh-huh,” she said and nudged his upper arm with her shoulder. “And do you ever drop in on one in say…Paris, or Dublin…just for fun?”

“No,” he said and wondered why he cared that she looked disappointed at his statement. “I have a rigorous schedule I adhere to. The managers of the hotels know when I’m coming, know to have everything ready for my inspection and—”

She sighed.

"What?"

"Do they salute? Click their heels together when you walk into a room?"

He scowled at her. "I'm not a general or something."

"Could have fooled me," she muttered, and took another sip of brandy. "Seriously, do you scare all the people who work for you? I bet you do."

"Certainly not," Nathan said and wondered why he suddenly sounded so damn pompous, even to himself.

"You know," she said, lifting her brandy glass to peer at the room through the amber liquid, "if you changed up your *schedule* once in a while, you might actually catch people unaware. Find out what life in your hotels is really like."

He stared at her, but she wasn't looking at him. Her words, though, were running through his brain as if they'd been etched in neon. Funny, but he'd never thought to do something like that. He was a man who lived his life as efficiently as possible. And to do that, he required a schedule. But…

"You mean, I should show up when they're not expecting me?"

"Why not?" she mused. "They're *your* hotels, aren't they?"

"Yes, but a schedule is necessary to maintain some kind of order."

"And if the kids know that daddy's coming home, they're on their best behavior."

Frowning, Nathan kept staring at her until she finally turned and looked at him, her eyes wide.

"What?" she asked.

"I can't believe I never thought of that."

"Me, neither," she said, smiling. "For heaven's sake, Nathan, do you *ever* do something that you don't have scheduled? Do you ever take a little time out for yourself? You're wound so tight, it gives *me* a headache."

He sighed and shrugged. "In my world, there's no time for relaxing."

"You should make time." She turned on the hearth, laid one hand on his forearm and asked, "For instance, when you're at one of your fabulous, oh-so-exclusive hotels, do you ever take a swim? Get a massage? Sightsee?"

"No. I'm not there for pleasure—"

"Why not?"

"Because…"

"People all over the world want to go to your hotels to experience something amazing. I've seen some of them on TV. And in magazines. God, the one in London, I would actually kill to stay in."

He smiled, picturing the stately stone entrance of the London Barrister with its sweeping marble floors and Old World chandeliers in the lobby.

"It is beautiful," he mused, surprised that he hadn't really appreciated the place until seeing it through Keira's enthusiasm.

"It's amazing," she said with a sigh. "Some rock star held an interview in the penthouse suite and the news covered it—there was an incredible view of London."

"The view from the owner's suite is even more impressive," he told her, picturing it vividly now in his mind. "You can see Big Ben in the distance and the Millennium Wheel."

"The huge Ferris wheel!" she cried and grabbed his

arm hard. "Have you ridden it?" She paused, and said, "Of course you haven't. Honestly, Nathan, don't you ever have any *fun?*"

A little insulted, he said, "Sure I do."

"Prove it. Name one thing you've done just for fun in the last month," she challenged.

"I sat on a stone hearth letting a beautiful woman insult me."

She tipped her head to one side, gave him a smile that made his heart jitter in his chest and repeated, *"Beautiful?"*

"Figures that's the part you heard."

Her smile brightened into a grin. "Well, *duh.*"

He really enjoyed the flash of humor in her eyes. And for the first time in way too long, he realized there wasn't a steel band wrapped around his middle. There was no pressure pounding through him. No hurry to get work done. To check his e-mail. To leave the lodge.

Because suddenly and completely, there was simply nowhere else on earth he'd rather be.

The quiet between them stretched on for another minute or two, the only sound in the room, the snap and hiss of the fire behind them. Shadows stretched across the room and, outside, dots of white swirled in ever changing patterns driven by the wind.

"I envy you," she said quietly. "All the places you've seen."

"You like traveling?"

"Never really traveled much, but yeah, I think I would." She folded her legs up beneath her on the stone, her white socks standing out brilliantly against her dark denim jeans. "I had big plans," she admitted. "When I was a teenager, I went to bookstores and bought street maps of foreign cities. If you had dropped me into the middle of Paris, I could have found my way around blindfolded, I studied those maps so often. London, Dublin, Barcelona, Rome, oh... *Venice.*" Her voice took on a dreamy quality that tugged at something deep inside him. "I wanted to drink wine while riding in a gondola. And see the windmills in Holland, and the Swiss Alps..."

"But..."

"But," she said, giving him a dazzling smile and lifting her glass for another sip of brandy, "life happened. I had to take care of Kelly, and then I got busy with the town and..."

"You stopped reading your maps?"

"Oh, no," she said, "I've still got them all and I still pore over them and plan trips and, one of these days, I'll get away." She looked down into her glass and asked, "What about you? When the month is up, where do you go next?"

"Barbados for a couple of weeks, then Madrid."

She sighed. "It sounds wonderful."

"Barbados or Madrid?"

"Both. But Barbados first. A tropical island." She sighed again.

"A beautiful one," he agreed.

She leaned her head against his shoulder and said, "Show me."

"Can't. Don't have any pictures of it."

"No," she said softly, "Draw me a picture with words. Show it to me through your memories of the place."

Nathan frowned down at the top of her head and tried to give her what she wanted. He thought about the

Barbados Barrister for a long moment, bringing it up in his mind, then slowly said, "It's our newest hotel. Only been open a few months. It sits right on the beach, stretches out almost a block. It has five stories for guest rooms and the sixth floor is the owner's suite." His voice warmed as his memories thickened and the ease of sharing them became more comfortable. "The views stretch on forever. The ocean is so blue you're not sure if you're looking at the sea or the sky."

"Keep going," she said.

He smiled. "There are palm trees and sand so white it hurts to look at it. Green-and-white striped umbrellas surround an infinity pool, and waiters dressed in green shirts and white pants carry trays of drinks to the people lounging poolside."

"More," she said, nestling in closer.

The feel of her leaning into him, the heat of the fire behind them and the quiet of the house all made for a feeling of intimacy that Nathan hadn't allowed himself to feel in years.

"Inside the hotel," he continued, "the wood is pale, almost gold. The windows are always open, and the sea wind sweeps through the lobby where pots of flowers and trailing vines make it seem almost like a jungle." He rested his head on top of hers. "There are deck chairs on a wide, white porch that stretches the length of the first floor, and people sit out there, sometimes all day, just to watch the ocean. And the restaurant has an outside deck where you can dine and watch the sunset."

"Sounds wonderful."

"Actually," he said, not a little surprised himself, "it really is."

She raised her head and smiled up at him. "I'm going to buy a map of Barbados," she said, "and I'm putting that hotel on my list."

He smoothed her hair back from her face, his fingertips lingering on the softness of her skin. She closed her eyes at his touch and shivered a little as his fingers slid down to her jaw.

"I'll put your name on the VIP list," he whispered, threading his fingers through her silky hair again just to enjoy the sensation.

"Nathan?"

"Keira…"

"The storm's still blowing," she said softly, her gaze locked with his. "What will we do while we wait it out?"

"We could eat," he offered.

"True," she said. "Or you could tell me about another of your hotels."

"Or play chess."

"Watch a movie."

"Read."

She nodded and reached up to catch his hand with hers and hold it against her cheek. "All good ideas. But, I have a better idea."

Nathan bit back a groan as she leaned in close to him. His body was hard and tight and every breath now was a victory. If he didn't have her in the next few minutes, he was going to explode. "Yeah?" he asked. "What's that?"

"I think you know," she said and took one more sip of brandy before setting her glass down on the hearth.

Nathan tipped his head back and tossed the last of his brandy down his throat before setting his glass down beside hers.

"Possibly," he said, though a voice in his brain was telling him to stop now before it was too late. But damn it, he wanted her. Keira's image had been haunting him for days—she'd gotten to him more than any other woman he'd ever known. He wasn't used to waiting for something he wanted. Usually, he simply *took* what most women were more than willing to offer. Keira was different. "Why don't you tell me, and I'll let you know if we're on the same page."

"Why don't I show you?" she whispered, and then pressed her mouth to his.

Air.

He probably needed air, because the edges of his vision were blurring and his brain felt as if it had been short-circuited. But breathing didn't seem as important as kissing her—harder, deeper—did.

Nathan groaned, pulled her in tightly to him and opened her mouth with a sweep of his tongue. She sighed into him as he tasted her, tangling their tongues together in a wild, frantic dance of need and promise.

He felt her hands tighten on his shoulders, her fingers digging into the soft fabric of his sweater to brand his skin with match-head dots of flame. Electricity hummed between them and Nathan surrendered to the sensations coursing through him.

He needed her.

Now.

He pulled her into his arms and settled her on his lap. His hands swept up and down her back, defining her curves through the soft knit of her sweater. She sighed heavily, pressed herself more firmly to him and rubbed her body against his.

Nathan's mouth moved over hers like a dying man seeking the only sustenance left in the world. He shared his breath with her and she gave it back to him. Their tongues and lips melded, savored, enjoyed. Nathan slipped both hands beneath the hem of her sweater and his palms slid across her back, his fingertips smoothing over her satiny skin.

She tore her mouth free, let her head fall back and sighed at his touch. "Nathan…"

He lowered his head, kissing her jaw, her neck, following the line of her throat with his lips and teeth and tongue. She shivered in his grasp and fed the need pulsing inside him.

Lifting his head, Nathan looked down at her as his hands, sliding beneath her sweater, swept around her body to find the front clasp on her bra. Deftly, he undid the tiny plastic clip, then pushed her bra free and cupped her breasts in his palms. His thumbs caressed her hardened nipples as his fingers kneaded her soft flesh.

Her hands clutched at his shoulders as he held her tightly to his lap, letting her feel the hard length of him.

Need roared and crashed through Nathan until he could hardly draw breath. He couldn't remember *ever* wanting like this before. He couldn't remember another woman in his life who had pushed him to the razor's edge of rationality. All he could think of was Keira.

All he wanted was Keira.

He didn't care what it might mean.

What it might cost him.

Didn't want to examine every feeling, every ache.

He only wanted to lose himself in her. For this one moment in time, he wanted nothing more than the feel of her beneath his hands and the sensation of burying his body within the hot, tight channel of hers.

"I've got to have you," he whispered, hearing the raw throb in his own voice.

"Me, too," she said, opening her eyes and pulling herself upright, leaning into him. "Oh, Nathan, me, too. Now, okay?"

"Right now." He pulled his hands free of her body, not even thinking about how empty he felt without the warmth of her pouring into him. Then he stood up, set her on her feet and led her across the great room toward the foyer and the majestic staircase that led to the second floor and the master bedroom. With their boots off, their sock feet made almost no noise at all in their rush for the stairs.

She stumbled behind him, kicked an end table and letting go of his hand, hopped ungainly for a minute, whimpering. "Ow, ow…"

Nathan turned, swept her up into his arms and said thickly, "Okay, I'm carrying you from here. I'm not taking any chances with a tumble down the stairs."

"Right, right," she said and leaned in to nibble at his throat as his long legs took the steep stairs two at a time.

He hissed in a breath, took a sharp turn at the head of the stairs and headed for the only bedroom in the place that had been furnished.

Keira looked around quickly as Nathan carried her into the master bedroom. The log walls were pale and the honey-colored floorboards gleamed from a thick coat of polish. A stone hearth, much like the one in the great room, boasted a fire that warmed the room and made it feel, for all its size, cozy. A bank of windows overlooked the lake and the forest and showcased the snow falling steadily.

But Keira didn't really care about the storm or the decor. All she was interested in now was the feel of Nathan's arms around her as he walked toward the huge, dark sleigh bed tucked against the far wall. Her heartbeat thundered in her chest as Nathan set her on her feet, grabbed a corner of the old-fashioned quilt and tossed it to the foot of the bed.

Then he grabbed her again and Keira stopped thinking in favor of *feeling*.

His mouth claimed hers again and her brain sizzled. Every nerve ending she possessed hummed with an awareness she'd never experienced before. His lips and tongue tasted her, tormented her, and she gave as good as she got.

Holding on to his shoulders, she pushed her body against his and rubbed her aching nipples across his chest. She needed him. And that thought was enough to make her splintered brain try to work for a second or two. She knew she should stop. Think about what she was doing.

But a heartbeat later, when Nathan pulled her sweater up and over her head, and bent to take one hardened nipple into his mouth, Keira silently told the cautionary voice in her mind to shut up.

Seven

Keira groaned gently as his mouth closed over first one nipple, then the next. His lips, tongue and teeth teased her already aching flesh until her whole body felt as though it were on full alert. She felt his touch in every cell. Her blood pumped thick and hot through her veins and when she closed her eyes and tipped her head back, she could have sworn she actually saw fireworks bursting in electric flashes of heat and color.

She held his head to her, half afraid that he might stop what he was doing. Her fingers speared through his thick, soft, black hair and when he sighed against her flesh, she felt the heat of his breath brush her skin in an ethereal caress.

He dropped his hands to the waistband of her jeans and, in just moments, he had the button and zipper undone and was sliding them, along with her pale ivory panties, down the length of her legs. She helped as much as she could, stepping out of her jeans and lifting first one foot, then the other, so he could pull her socks off.

The air in the room felt cool against her skin, despite the fire in the hearth. She listened to the snap and hiss of the flames on logs and let the sound fill her mind until all that remained was the music of the fire and Nathan's breath against her body.

She smiled up at him and tugged at the hem of his sweater, fingers curling into the soft fabric. "Someone here is overdressed."

"Not for long," he promised and quickly got rid of his own clothing before laying her back on the cool, soft sheets.

He looked down at her for a long minute, and Keira arched her back from the bed and stretched both hands back and over her head, enjoying the power of his gaze on her. She saw the passion in his eyes and responded, moving sinuously over the bed, sweeping her own hands down her body, pausing at her breasts, stroking her own nipples as she watched his eyes darken and his jaw clench. Finally, when she lifted both hands toward him in open invitation, Nathan groaned and leaned over her.

"No bruises," he said quietly as he studied her.

She smiled and stroked his cheek with her fingertips. "It's been a good week for me. You were always around to rescue me from a fall."

"You're making me nuts. You know that, right?"

She reached up and cupped his face between her palms. Drawing his head down to hers, she kissed him once, twice and again. "Of course I know. The question is, what're you going to do about it?"

"Return the favor," he assured her.

He kissed her, hard and long and deep, until her body was quivering and her breath was hissing from her lungs. And when she tried to hold onto him, to pull him closer, Nathan slipped from her grasp and Keira could only watch as he moved along her body, sliding his flesh across hers, kissing every inch of her skin as he moved down the length of her.

She trembled, her breath caught and she bit into her bottom lip as she moved, twisting into him, arching into his movements, trying to keep their bodies connected, their flesh burning into each other's.

But Nathan had other ideas; he continued his slow, torturous assault on her nerve endings by stroking his tongue across her abdomen and nibbling at her skin until she was whispering his name in a broken hush. He smiled against her body, and kept moving, lower and lower still until finally he had backed off the mattress.

And kneeling beside the bed, he grabbed her legs and pulled her close, until her legs hung free and she was balanced precariously on the edge of the bed. He lifted her legs, laying them across his shoulders and Keira watched him as he smiled knowingly.

"Your turn," he whispered and scooped his hands under her behind before lifting her to meet his questing mouth.

Keira sucked in a gulp of air and held it, afraid to let it out because if she did, she might not be able to draw another, and she was pretty sure she was going to need to breathe.

His mouth claimed her, and Keira pushed herself up

onto her elbows to watch him take her more intimately than anyone ever had before. Her eyes widened and locked on him, as aroused by the sight of him taking her as she was by the incredible sensations coursing through her.

Keira had never known anything like it. His tongue swept a caress across her inner folds and dipped within her body to tempt her with even more.

She was really grateful for that lungful of air, because now she had forgotten how to breathe. Her world centered on this one man and what he was doing to her body.

Again and again, he stroked and nibbled and caressed. His tongue touched a tiny bud of sensitized flesh and—" Nathan!"

She felt him smiling, and then lost herself in the wonder of what he was able to do to her. He suckled and teased and stroked until the ball of need in the pit of her stomach bubbled into a fiery cauldron that tipped and spilled an unbelievable heat throughout her body. Keira rocked her hips, reached down to cup the back of his head to hold him to her and couldn't seem to look away.

Her heels dug into his back as he slipped one finger, then two inside her body and quickened the intensity of her experience in a heartbeat. There was so much, too much. Her mind couldn't capture it all, so she quit trying and surrendered to the incredible wash of anticipation building within.

"Nathan, if you stop," she whispered through dry lips, "I'll have to kill you."

He chuckled and then closed his mouth over that one most sensitive spot. Keira cried out his name as her body shuddered with the force of the climax ripping through her. She held onto him as the only stable point in the universe and as the tremors rocking her slowly faded, like far-reaching ripples in a pond, Nathan moved, easing her legs from his shoulders, shifting her further back onto the bed and then covering her body with his own.

"I can't…I mean…" She blew out a breath and laughed shortly. "I think I may be paralyzed."

"Not yet you're not," he murmured, dipping his head to taste one of her pale-pink nipples.

Instantly, need rebuilt at the feel of his body pressing her down into the so-soft mattress. She stroked his skin, running her hands up and down his back, kissing the underside of his jaw, his neck.

"That was…" she said.

"Only the beginning," he said and kissed her, his tongue plunging into her mouth, tangling with hers, stealing what breath she had left, then giving her his own to replace it.

Keira's body lit up again with fresh need and she lifted both legs to wrap them around his waist. "I want you inside me, Nathan."

"Just where I want to be, Keira," he whispered and lifted his head so he could watch her face as he entered her.

She tipped her head back on the bed, but kept her gaze locked with his. He pushed himself home with one long, deep stroke, and Keira gasped as she rocked her hips, taking even more of him within.

Outside, the storm raged, and inside, a different kind of storm swept the two of them into a world of mindless passion. Where all that mattered was the next touch, the next kiss, the next stroke of heat to heat. Their bodies moved in an ancient dance with a rhythm that seemed as old as time and as new as her next breath.

His body moved with hers, invaded hers, claimed hers, and Keira gave him all she had to give. Her hands smoothed over his back and around to stroke down his chest, her thumbnails flicking at his flat, brown nipples until he was gritting his teeth to hold back a shout.

She liked knowing that he was as lost to sensation as she was. That his body was screaming for release as loudly as her own. That she could shatter Nathan's rigid sense of control.

Arching into him again and again, she urged him deeper, faster, harder. Her fingers clawed at his back while the pressure within tightened ferociously, demanding release.

"Now, Nathan," she groaned, moving with him at a fever pitch that couldn't be sustained without the two of them bursting into flames, "please *now.*"

He pushed himself up on his hands, stared down at her face and whispered, "You first, Keira. You first and I'll follow."

He slid one hand down the length of her body, across her flat abdomen, down to where their bodies were joined. His fingers dipped into the joining and stroked her damp heat as he continued to move inside her.

"Nathan!" Keira shrieked his name, clutched at his shoulders and bucked beneath him as an overwhelming wave of pleasure swept through her on what felt like an endless tide of mind-shattering explosions rattling just beneath her skin.

"Now," he groaned and plunged deep inside her, his

body shaking as he fell into the same tidal wave that had captured Keira and let it carry them both away.

An hour…or, for all Keira knew, a *week* later, she forced her eyelids open and stared up at the ceiling. Fire-cast shadows leaped and danced across the beams in hypnotic pulses.

"You okay?" Nathan murmured from close to her ear.

"Not sure yet," she admitted, turning her head on the pillow to smile at him. Reaching out, she smoothed his hair back from his forehead with her fingertips. "Hey, I can move my hand, so…good sign!"

Pushing himself up on one elbow, he stared down at her for a long minute or two, his eyes unreadable. A curl of unease opened inside Keira as she studied him, searching for a shadow of the passionate man he'd been so short a time ago. But the Nathan watching her now was more like the closed-off man she'd met his first day at the lodge.

"What?" she finally asked, unable to stand the silence any longer.

"I was just thinking."

"About?" she coaxed.

He looked as if he were about to say something, then thought better of it. Shaking his head, he said only, "Nothing. Never mind."

He rolled off the bed and walked naked across the room to a door that he opened to reveal a gigantic closet. It was practically empty from what Keira could see, since he'd brought only enough clothes for a month. But he stepped inside and when he came back out, he was wearing a thick black robe and carrying a dark green one that he tossed onto the foot of the bed. "I brought my own robe, but this green one was hanging in the closet when I got here."

"Thanks," she said, reaching for it and shoving both arms into the sleeves before slipping off the bed and tying the belt of the robe at her waist.

His features were tight, closed off as if he were carefully preventing whatever he was thinking from showing on his face. Which only served to really irritate Keira. A few minutes ago, they'd shared something truly amazing. They'd been as close as two people could get. Yet now…he was looking at her as if she were a stranger.

A really unwelcome stranger.

"Nathan, what's going on?"

"Not a thing," he said and started for the bedroom door and the stairs beyond. "But I promised you food, didn't I? I'll check out the kitchen. See what I can find."

Very nice, Keira thought. He'd shut her out so politely, so neatly, she had to wonder if maybe his hideous grandmother, who'd shipped him off to boarding school with hardly a wave goodbye, had taught him how to do that? How to push people away without even breaking a sweat.

Well, she wasn't going anywhere. Not until the storm stopped. And to be honest, even if the storm stopped right this minute, she wouldn't have been going anywhere. Not until she found out what the hell had happened to send Nathan from orgasmic to crabby in no time at all.

She followed him down the stairs, keeping one hand on the banister to make sure she didn't fall down the damn stairs and break her neck before she got some answers. She made a sharp right at the bottom of the stairs just in time to see his black robe disappear into the distant kitchen.

Well, if he thought she was that easy to get rid of, he really didn't know her well at all. Walking quickly, her bare feet hardly making a sound on the area rugs tossed across the gleaming wood floors, Keira got to the swinging door to the kitchen, slapped her palm against it and sent it crashing open.

He was at the fridge and raised his head to look at her when she stepped into the room. Then he dismissed her coolly, reached into the freezer and pulled out a long, flat aluminum tray.

"The housekeeper fills the freezer for me once a week. I think this is…" He read the label. "Fettuccine Alfredo with grilled garlic chicken. It's from the Clearwater, the restaurant you seem so fond of."

"Their fettuccine is great," Keira said, walking toward the granite counter and one of the stools pulled up beneath it. She sat down and tucked her bare feet up to get them off the cold floor.

"Glad you approve," he said, and turned to quickly take off the lid, turn on the oven and pop the tray inside. "Shouldn't take too long," he said, and walked to the wine cooler along the wall. "Would you like a glass of wine?"

"Sure," Keira said, trying to figure out a way to get past the wall he'd erected around himself so quickly and so completely. "Nathan, is everything all right?"

"Why wouldn't it be?"

"You're just acting a little…weird."

One black eyebrow rose as he set a bottle of white wine on the countertop. He opened a drawer, took out a corkscrew and then tore off the foil top from the bottle. Keira shivered a little and he said, "Cold?"

"A bit."

There was another fireplace in the kitchen, but this one was cold and dark. Beyond the windows leading to the covered deck, the world was a whirl of white. Light faded from the sky, the heavy clouds dropped even lower, and the flurries of snow were thick enough that it looked as though someone had hung a sheet from the edge of the patio cover.

"There's extra firewood on the deck. I'll get some."

"Okay, fine," Keira said as Nathan walked to the back door, "but first, tell me what you were going to say upstairs. When you were looking at me so funny. When you said, 'oh, it's nothing, never mind.'"

"Keira," he said with a sigh, "just let it go."

"Oh no," she assured him, shaking her head at the sheer folly of the man. "That's never gonna happen. So it'll be quicker and easier on both of us if you'll just spit it out."

"It's nothing."

"Then *say* it," she insisted.

One hand on the doorknob, he stared at her for a long moment, as if trying to decide whether to speak or not. At last, though, he nodded and said, "Fine. I was thinking about the sex. And I wondered just how far you were willing to go to get me to stay here for the whole month."

Keira felt the slap of his words like a physical blow. Stung, humiliated and furious, she glared at him with enough heat that, if there were any justice at all, he would have been a pillar of fire. "Are you serious?"

"You asked what I was going to say," he said and watched her through narrowed eyes.

"I didn't know you were going to say *that!*"

"Don't sound so offended." Nathan looked at her for a long minute. "It's not like I'm surprised."

"Is that right?"

"For God's sake, Keira, you think this is the first time a woman's used her body to get me to do something for her? We're both adults. You wanted something from me and you used sex to get it."

Fury whipped through Keira. "You…you…"

He shrugged and headed for the back door. "It was good for both of us. We each got what we wanted. No point now in trying to make it something it wasn't."

He opened the back door to a gust of icy wind and said, "Look, let's just forget it, all right?"

"Sure," she whispered as she watched him hurry barefoot across the icy deck toward the neatly stacked pile of firewood. As he gathered up a few logs and some kindling, the wind whipping the edges of his robe around his calves, Keira jumped off her stool, crossed the floor and quietly closed and locked the back door.

Instantly he straightened up, whirled around and shocked, stared at her through the glass. He crossed to the door and gave the knob a turn and a shake. "Keira, open the damn door."

"I don't think so," she said, folding her arms over her chest and tapping one bare foot against the cold wood floor.

She'd never been so mad in her whole life. *Or* so humiliated. For God's sake, she'd let him do things to her no one had ever done before, only because she'd felt a connection to him somehow. Some minuscule, apparently clearly one-sided, *feeling*. How could he ever think that she would have slept with him just to make him stay?

Did she really give off such a slutty vibe?

And what the hell kind of people was he so used to dealing with that would make him assume she was so coldblooded?

He shivered, clutched the firewood tighter to his chest and gave her a glare she was sure sent his employees scuttling for cover.

Keira, however, remained unmoved.

"Damn it, Keira, it's snowing out here!"

"You're under the porch roof."

"It's freezing."

"Start a fire."

"On the *deck?*"

"Frankly, I don't care if you freeze solid to the spot. I'll put up a small but tasteful plaque, something like Here Stands An American Moron."

"This is *not* funny!" he shouted, and hunched deeper into his way-too-thin-for-snow robe.

"No kidding!" Keira walked closer to the glass so she could burn her stare into his eyes. "I cannot believe you. You actually think I'd *prostitute* myself to get you to stay here?"

"I didn't say *that,*" he reasoned.

"Oh, yes you did, you pompous, self important, miserable son of a bitch."

"Look, I was *wrong,* okay?"

"You're just saying that so I'll open the door," she snapped.

"Damn straight."

"Well, forget it! You deserve to freeze, but you

probably won't. You're so damn cold already, I don't see how you could possibly get any colder!"

"Can you let me the hell in the house and *then* yell at me?"

"Why should I let you in?" she demanded, so furious she was seeing red at the edges of her vision. Amazing. You really *did* see red if you were angry enough.

"Because…because…"

"See? Even *you* can't think of a reason!" Keira shouted.

"Hah!" Nathan raised one hand in the air, dropped some kindling on his foot and hopped in place. "Because if I die out here, I won't be able to stay the damn month and your town won't get the money you want so badly."

"Funny," she said, thoughtfully tapping one finger against her chin, "but I don't remember it saying anywhere in the will that you had to be *alive* and here for a month. It'd probably be okay if we just prop you up out there on the deck."

"You are the most infuriating woman I have ever met."

"You've got a heck of a lot of nerve, Nathan Barrister. You call me a *ho,* and I'm the one who's infuriating?"

He flicked a glance behind him when the wind shifted and a flurry of snow rushed at him from the lake. Turning his gaze back to hers, he said tightly, "Keira, open this damn door and let me inside."

"And if I don't?"

"Then I'll break the glass with one of these logs and we'll *both* be freezing our asses off."

Hmm. Good point. Well, she hadn't really planned on letting him become an ice sculpture on the deck. Though the idea was all too tempting at the moment.

"Fine." She reached out, unlocked the door and then stomped across the room so she was as far from Nathan as she could get and still be able to give him dirty looks.

He rushed into the room, dropped the firewood into the hearth, then pounded his bare feet against the floor and slapped his hands at his arms, trying to get his blood moving.

"Cold?" she asked sweetly.

"Funny," he snapped, snarling at her.

"As cold as that tiny little marble in your chest? You know, the one you call your *heart?*"

Still shivering, he turned his back on her, started a fire in the hearth and huddled next to the flames as they sputtered, caught and licked at the dry wood. Finally, he turned a look on her. "My heart's got nothing to do with any of this."

"Since it probably gets very little use, I'm willing to bet you're right," Keira hissed.

"You tried to freeze me to death!" His voice ricocheted off the high beamed ceiling and Keira didn't even flinch.

"Don't be such a baby."

"A *baby?*" Astonishment flashed across his features and she waved one hand at him dismissively.

"You're lucky I let you back in."

There was a long moment of silence before he finally said, "Yeah. You're just crazy enough to have left me out there, so I guess I am lucky. And frostbitten."

"That was a nasty thing to think about me," she said, ignoring his complaint, "and even nastier to say."

"You wouldn't leave it alone. You had to know what I was thinking," he pointed out, raising his hands high in amazement. "What is it about women, anyway? They poke and prod at a man to tell them what he's thinking and when he does, they lock him outside in a damn snowstorm!"

"Is it our fault that what you're really thinking is so ridiculously insulting that we aren't prepared?" Keira slapped the granite counter. "We want to know what you're thinking, because, silly us, we actually think your minds *aren't* twisted little black holes."

"No, you expect us to be like you," Nathan said tightly, still scowling, still stamping his feet on the floor trying to get his circulation moving again. "All warm and fuzzy, wanting kids and a dog and a white picket fence and—"

"Are you *delusional?*" Keira interrupted his rant. "Who said anything about a picket fence?"

"You don't have to say it," he challenged, stabbing one finger in the air, pointed at her. "It's who you are. You're Ms. Roots herself. Well, I don't have roots. Don't want any and if I found some I'd rip 'em out of the ground."

Keira stomped across the room until she was right in front of him. His blue eyes were wild and hot, and the set of his jaw told her he was every bit as furious as she was. Well, good. No point in being mad all by yourself. And besides, he'd probably *never* lost his temper. Not the ever-polite, always distant Nathan Barrister. So, she'd let him rant and rave. Maybe it'd do him some good. God knows it was doing wonders for *her.*

"Your perfect little town has nothing I want or need. As soon as possible, I'll be on my jet, heading for the opposite end of the world."

"Good. Nobody's asking you to settle down in

Hunter's Landing, *Mr. Wonderful.*" Keira stabbed her finger at him, poking him several times dead center of the chest until he grabbed her finger in self defense. She shook him off a second later. "*I'm* certainly not laying out traps for you—"

"Oh, no?" Nathan countered quickly, apparently enjoying interrupting her for a change. "No traps, huh? Did it happen to escape your notice that we didn't use any protection?"

Keira blanched for a second. Damn it, it *had* escaped her attention. Then his words hit home. *A trap?* "First I'm a slut and now I'm trying to trap you and your golden sperm? Aren't I the busy little bee?"

"You're deliberately avoiding the point," he said. "We didn't use anything and—"

"Well, jeez," she said, interrupting him neatly for the umpteenth time, "color me *human.* You know, I don't actually travel with condoms in my jeans on the off chance that some spoiled, snotty rich guy will want to have sex with me and then insult me!"

He grabbed two fists full of his own hair and yanked. Hard. Then, his voice rumbled through the kitchen at a level just below howling. "For God's sake, I just told you I could have made you pregnant and you take *that* as an insult, too?"

"I'm not pregnant," she snapped. "Just so you know, I'm on the Pill, so no worries there, Mr. Barrister. Your personal fortune is safe from this particular gold digger."

"I never said you were a—"

"But as long as we're on the subject," she continued, her voice rolling right over his, "how about you?"

He grimaced. "I'm not on the Pill."

"Not the best time to develop a sense of humor, just so you know."

He raised his hands in mock surrender. "Fine. Fine. I'm healthy. No worries there. You?"

"Contrary to certain people's opinion, I am *not* a slut and, therefore, I, too, am very healthy." She crossed her fingers over her heart. "Of course, I'll be happy to get you a letter from my doctor to alleviate any further concern…"

"Damn it, Keira, I'm not calling you a slut for doing whatever you have to do to get what you want. That's how the world works. The real world, that is, not your own personal little Xanadu here."

"Believe it or not," she shouted, "I did *not* have sex with you to keep you here for the month!"

"You keep telling yourself that," he said tightly.

"Jeez," Keira muttered, shaking her head. "Are you really so far out of touch with humanity? Does *everything* in your world carry a price tag?"

"There are price tags everywhere in the world. Wake up and maybe you'll notice them."

"You lead an ugly life," she whispered.

"At least I live with my eyes open," he countered. "I know that people are mostly out for themselves and willing to do just about anything to take care of number one."

"So I slept with you to get what I want?"

"Wouldn't be the first time it's happened."

Keira flinched at the coldness in his eyes. He really did believe that anyone getting close to him was out for his money. His lifestyle. How sad. How unbearably empty his world must be. And the saddest part was, he didn't even realize it.

"And so, because you've surrounded yourself with

sycophants and users, you naturally assumed that I was one, too."

He gritted his teeth and a muscle in his jaw twitched. "And you're telling me you're not."

"Yeah," she said, "I am. And what's more, you know it. Somewhere in that cavernous emptiness you call a heart, you know it. And you insulted me on purpose."

He glared at her. "You are the most—" He caught himself, dragged in a gulp of air and then fired his gaze into hers. "Okay, yeah. I did."

"Finally!" Keira shouted and scooted a little closer to the kitchen fire, nudging Nathan out of her way. "The question is *why?*"

"Why?"

"Why did you want to insult me, Nathan?" She tipped her head to one side, stared up at him and asked, "If you wanted me to leave, all you had to do was say so."

"I didn't want you to leave," he admitted, though it was clear he wasn't happy about the confession.

"Then why?"

"I honestly don't know," he said and pulled her up close against him. When she tried to push herself free, he simply tightened his hold on her middle, pinning her body to his until Keira could feel his need building again.

Was he so unused to people wanting to be with him just to be with him? Was his world so insulated that the only people he ever saw were the ones who worked for him or wanted something from him?

Slightly mollified, Keira stared up into his eyes and saw questions still lingering in those pale blue depths. The man did things to her she had never expected. He had a way of touching her heart at the oddest moments and she was more than a little confused about that.

She could continue the fight, which, let's face it, she was enjoying. She could give him answers to his questions. She could even make him wonder about lots of other things.

Or, she could do what she most wanted to do.

Tugging the lapels of his thick, cashmere robe aside, Keira stroked his bare chest with the flat of her palms and watched his eyes narrow into slits and his jaw clench as he hissed in a long, slow breath.

Deliberately, she teased him, spreading his robe open, baring his body to her touch. She slid her hands over his still cold skin and felt heat bubble beneath the surface at her touch. Then she tugged the belt of the robe free and swept one hand down to capture his hard length in a soft, firm grip.

"You know, Nathan," she said, smoothing her fingers up and down his erection with slow caresses, "the simple truth is, I've wanted you almost from the moment I first saw you. That's why I stayed. That's why I want you again now."

He groaned as she slipped her free hand down to cup him. "Works for me."

Eight

The rich scent of Alfredo sauce was beginning to fill the kitchen, but Keira was hungry for something other than food. Strange, but even fighting with Nathan was stimulating.

Her body was quickening as his hands moved to tug her robe open and pull it down off her shoulders to let it pool on the floor at her feet. The air in the kitchen was still icy from the wind that had whooshed inside when the door was opened. Yet she didn't really mind it. Instead, that sensation added to the others already coursing through her body, mingling together, causing a ripple effect of near turmoil in her system.

His hands swept up and down her body, his long, talented fingers exploring every curve as she ran her own hands over him. His broad, muscular chest was clearly defined, sculpted and tanned, making him look as though he were carved from the same kind of honey-toned wood that graced the lodge.

But he was warm and ready, and his body was already pressing into hers, letting her know that he felt the same blood pounding need she did.

"Why do I want you so much?" he whispered, his fingers stroking, sliding down her body to caress the heat between her thighs.

Keira sighed and swayed unsteadily on her feet as a rush of something delicious began to build within. "Why do you ask so many questions?" she answered.

He smiled, and her heart flipped in her chest. A weird sensation, but a shockingly good one.

"You're the one with all the questions," he murmured, dipping his head to kiss the curve of her neck, to nibble at the base of her throat.

Her hands moved to his shoulders and she clung to him desperately as he continued to smooth his fingers over her damp heat. Instinctively, he found that one most-sensitive bud and concentrated his attentions on it, thumb and forefinger gliding, stroking until Keira's blood felt as if it were boiling just beneath her skin.

"No questions," she said, licking dry lips and trying to catch her breath. "Not now, anyway."

He slid one hand up to hold the back of her neck while his other hand continued to gently torture her with anticipation. His blue eyes caught hers and Keira wished she knew what he was thinking now. Now, when passion simmered in pale eyes gone dark with desire.

She wanted to give him what he was giving her, so she slid one hand down his body until she could encircle his length with her fingers again. He swallowed a great gulp of air before lowering his head to take her mouth with his. His tongue plunged into her mouth, claiming her fiercely, desperately, as if he couldn't wait another moment to taste her.

And Keira matched his need with her own. She shifted position, sliding her hands around his waist to splay them against his back. She felt his heart pounding and knew her own was in sync that wild rhythm.

His fingers dipped into her center, first one, then two, diving in and out of her heat, touching her deeply, but not deep enough. Not as deeply as she wanted him. Needed him.

When he tore his mouth from hers, he stared down at her and whispered, "We'll never make it back up to the bedroom."

"Not a chance," she agreed, already so hungry for him, her arms and legs were trembling.

"Here then," he said and, moving quickly, he picked her up, carried her to the counter and plopped her down onto it.

"Yikes!" The cold granite bit into her heated skin and sent a chill slicing right through her.

He grinned wickedly. "Cold?"

She narrowed her eyes on him. "You enjoyed that. Payback for locking you outside?"

"Just a little," he admitted, then leaned in and bit her bottom lip gently, swiping his tongue along the crease in her mouth. "But I'm willing to warm you up again, too."

She reached for him, sliding her arms around his neck, pulling him in closer. "A generous man," she said with a sigh as his mouth came down on hers.

As he kissed her, he parted her thighs, moved in close and entered her body on a rush of sensation that poured through the two of them, linking them in a way that neither had experienced or expected.

Keira arched into him, moving her hips on the hard granite in a desperate attempt to get closer, to take him more fully within. She closed her eyes and saw swirls of vibrant color as her body leaped into life. Her being soared, and something deep within her unexpectedly awoke. Her eyes opened again as that thought sang through her mind. She watched him and felt new feelings stir within. New emotions. New and incredibly fragile threads of connection.

Nathan's hands dropped to her hips and he held her still, trapped within his steely grip as he plunged in and out of her depths in a ferocious rhythm designed to drive them both quickly over the edge.

The world dropped away and it was just the two of them. Nothing beyond existed anymore. Passion swelled and trapped them in a silky web of desire. Keira held on to him, and lost herself in his strength, surrendering to the twist of anticipation curling inside her.

Her body tightened, her mouth mated with his and she hooked her legs around Nathan's waist, pulling him in harder, deeper. She felt his body's invasion of hers all the way to her soul and knew she would never get enough of him. Knew that this man was touching more than her body. He'd already laid claim to a piece of her heart.

Whether she wanted it or not, she cared for him. More than she wanted to think about. More than she dared to admit.

She pulled free of his kiss so she could watch his

eyes as he claimed her. His beautiful blue gaze locked with hers, as though he understood her silent plea and felt the same way.

Her body quickened, anticipation exploded and a climax stronger than anything she'd ever known before shattered inside her, splintering itself into brilliant colors that tore through her heart and spilled into her bones.

Nathan kept his gaze fixed on hers and when she cried out his name, he gave himself up to the release clamoring inside him and followed her over the ragged edge of control, into oblivion.

By morning, Nathan was rethinking the whole situation.

The night before, he'd thought it a great idea having Keira stay with him. They'd come together often during the night and each time had been more incredible than the first. He felt as though each time he touched her, he felt something more, something different. And he'd reveled in their time together, knowing that in the morning, she would be going home.

At least, that's what he had thought.

He gritted his teeth and stared out the bank of windows in the kitchen. Outside the lodge, the world was a wash of white. Snow piled on the sides of the deck and blew in under the overhang to coat the wood planks with a layer of snow at least a foot deep. And that was under the porch roof. It was much deeper everywhere else, and it was still falling.

He'd never seen anything like it.

"It's mid-March and it looks like Siberia in December out there," he muttered.

Keira came up behind him, threaded her arms around his waist and rested her cheek against his back. "Welcome to the high Sierras."

"I tried the phone," he said. "No dial tone."

"Uh-oh."

"What's that mean?" He turned his head to look at her.

"It means," she said, "that with the phone lines down this early in the storm, it's a big one."

Nathan glowered at her. "Which translates into…?"

She shrugged. "If the roads aren't completely blocked already, they soon will be."

"Surely you have crews to take care of that."

"Of course we do," Keira said, smiling up at him. "But they can't roll till the heavy snows are over, and even when they do…"

He didn't like the look on her face. The look that said *he's not going to like this.*

"What?"

"They take care of the town first and then the main stretches of highway. Those are priorities for obvious reasons."

"And…?"

"And," she said with another shrug, "the roads up here probably won't be cleared for a few days."

"A few *days?*"

"Maybe sooner," she said, he suspected simply to placate him. "But the private roads and the roads leading to them are pretty much a lower priority. Unless there's an emergency or something. If the road crews get a call like that, they'll come right away."

"The phones are out." He paused, then said, "Wait. I've got my satellite phone."

"But no one else around here has one."

"Right." Nathan shook his head.

She pulled her arms from around his waist, shoved her hands into the pockets of her robe and said, "Look, we do the best we can. And people generally privately contract to get their roads cleared, so that takes care of a lot of problems."

"And does the lodge have a private contract?"

"I don't know."

"Perfect." Nathan blew out a breath. This month was turning into a real trial. "How long is this going to keep up?" He shook his head as he shifted his gaze across the lake, watching snow slide in sideways, riding a wind that was rattling the windows.

"Well," she said, giving him a brilliant smile, "if it keeps up, at least it won't be coming down anymore."

He glanced at her. "Oh, very humorous."

She moved to stand in front of him, leaning both palms against an icy window to get as good a view as she could of the blustering storm outside. "I always laughed when my dad said it." She glanced at him over her shoulder. "Of course, I was ten."

Nathan wasn't amused. Nor was he charmed. He'd wanted her here last night—and he'd enjoyed every minute of his time with her. But that didn't mean he wanted her at the lodge for freaking *ever*. Scowling, he saw the wind spit snow at the windows and knew that she wouldn't be going anywhere. At least not today.

As if she was reading his mind, Keira turned around, leaned back against the floor-to-ceiling windows and tipped her head to one side, staring up at him. "So, what'll we do while we're stuck inside?"

He knew that gleam in her eye. Hell, he'd seen it most of the night. He was willing to bet they hadn't had more than a couple of hours' sleep. Yet even thinking about being inside her, touching her, holding her, tasting her, made him hard and eager again.

Which was clearly unacceptable.

He wasn't a kid to be led around by his groin. And damned if he'd let himself get any more tangled up with Keira than he already was. Just because she was here, with him, didn't mean she had to be *with* him.

"Uh-oh," she said, tugging the edges of her robe more firmly together over her chest. "It suddenly got very cold in here."

He nodded. "I'll turn up the thermostat."

"That's not what I meant."

"What're you talking about?" he asked as he walked to the coffee pot on the kitchen counter.

God.

The counter.

How was he ever supposed to walk through this kitchen again without remembering her sitting naked on that counter? Without thinking about how she'd taken him so deep inside her he'd thought he might never find his way out again?

Crap.

Now he had a headache.

Rubbing his temple, he asked, "Coffee?"

"Sure. I'll have a cup of coffee, black, with answers."

"Huh?" He half turned to look at her as she walked slowly across the kitchen. Did her hips always sway like that, he wondered, or was she doing it purposely now?

"I said I'd like some answers."

"To what?" He was stalling. He knew it. He poured two cups of coffee, handed her one, then stalled again by taking a long sip of his own.

"To why your eyes suddenly looked even colder than this stormy day outside."

"Keira," he said tightly, "you're making too much of nothing."

"So you're *happy* I'm here," she coaxed, taking a drink of her coffee and moving in closer to him.

"Delirious," he assured her.

"Liar."

"Why do you do that? Accuse me of lying at every opportunity?"

"A better question is why am I always right?"

He set his coffee cup down, tugged at the belt of his robe and said, "You're not right. Women always say that to win an argument, but it's never true."

"Of course it is," Keira said, sipping her coffee. "Women are right because we *see* everything and we *remember* everything."

"Sure."

"Just like I can see that you're trying to start a fight so you won't have to answer my question."

He sighed. This woman got to him like no one else ever had. And he was forced to admit that part of the reason why was because she never took any of his crap. She always called him on everything.

"Fine," he said tightly and met her gaze with a hard look designed to put some distance between them. "I was thinking that it would be more comfortable if you could have gone home this morning. Happy?"

"Delirious," she said, throwing his own word back at

him. Then she turned around and pulled a chair out from under the kitchen table. Curling one leg under herself, she plopped down, propped her elbow on the table and took another sip of coffee before saying, "Was that so hard?"

Nathan just blinked at her. Any other woman would have been insulted, giving him all kinds of frosty attitude right now. Figured Keira would react differently. She had to everything else.

"You're not mad."

"Nope, sorry to disappoint." She took long drink of her coffee, then set the cup onto the table. "Nathan, I know you don't really want me here, and that's okay. I mean, I hadn't planned on staying forever, you know."

"Yeah, I know."

"But it's really storming out there, so I'm stuck here and you're stuck with me. We might as well make the best of it, don't you think?"

A constant surprise. Keira Sanders never failed to bewilder him with her reactions to things. He couldn't depend on what she'd do next, because she never responded to *anything* the way he expected her to. How was a man supposed to find his emotional footing if a woman kept changing on him?

"I suppose that's logical."

"Excellent," she said. "I've got a few ideas on what we could do today." She hopped off her chair, stumbled over her own foot and slammed into his chest. She grabbed him in self-preservation and spilled his coffee down the front of his robe. Grinning up at him, she said, "Maybe we should do some laundry first."

* * *

Cold fettuccine Alfredo for breakfast, a load of wash done and in the dryer, and the snow was still blowing outside.

Keira wandered through the lodge, peeking into closets and exploring rooms that were still standing empty waiting for the decorator. From every room, the view was outstanding and displayed the growing storm to its advantage.

She chewed at her bottom lip and wondered how the town was doing, then reminded herself that the people of Hunter's Landing dealt with snowstorms every year. The only difference with this storm was that she wasn't there. She couldn't see for herself that everyone was fine, hunkered down to wait out the snow.

She couldn't even *call* anyone to check on them. The phone lines were still down. Remembering the look on Nathan's face when he'd tried the phone again an hour ago made her smile.

Leaving one of the bedrooms, she wandered back into the upper hall, passed the master bedroom and paused for a moment, remembering everything she and Nathan had done together the night before. Her heart filled, her body ached with tired satisfaction and the small smile on her face faded slowly. She knew that today, he was regretting their time together.

He probably wasn't used to facing his nighttime bed partner the next day. Well, this was pretty new for Keira, too. But at least she was trying to make the best of it. Unlike Nathan, who'd buried himself in busywork on his laptop. The man had avoided talking to her for hours now and the quiet—except for his fingers hitting the keyboard—was starting to really bother her.

The wind howled around the corners of the house, sounding as though it was looking for a way in. Shivering, Keira headed for the stairs. She held onto the banister, and started down, her bare feet making no sound at all on the dark carpet runner that covered the wood planks.

Walking into the great room, she headed for the fire crackling in the hearth, turned her back to it and stared at Nathan, just a few feet away. He hadn't even looked up when she entered the room.

"Ignoring me doesn't make me invisible," she said abruptly.

"Huh? What?" He raised his head, turned to look at her and asked, "What did you say?"

"I said, are you going to be sitting in front of that computer all day?"

"I have work to do."

"That you can't send anywhere because the phone lines are down."

"It's not e-mail, it's work," he said.

"Fine." She blew out a breath, walked toward him, then squatted beside him until they were eye to eye. "My point is, does *everything* have to be done *today?*"

"Keira…"

She hopped up, plopped onto the couch beside him and leaned in, staring at the computer screen. "Okay, okay. So you have to work. Tell me about it. Talk to me."

He sighed in resignation, and Keira hid a smile. "I'm working up a new schedule for impromptu visits to my hotels."

She looked at him, stupefied for a second, then burst out laughing.

"What's so funny?"

She waved one hand, shook her head and fought for breath. Laughter spilled from her throat, bubbled into the room and crashed down around them as she wrapped her arms around his shoulders and gave him a fast hug. "Nathan, you're really something," she said when she finally got control of her giggles.

"I'm so happy I can entertain you."

"Don't you get it?" she asked, grinning. "You're making a *schedule* for *impromptu* visits. The whole point of impromptu is *no* schedule."

Nathan scowled at her, then at the computer screen. He felt like an idiot. But in his own defense, he'd only been making busy work anyway. Anything to keep his mind off the fact that Keira was here and way too accessible.

He had no intention of getting in any deeper with her. And the best way to keep from doing that was to keep his hands to himself. Yet…everytime he heard her breathe, or caught a whiff of her scent, all he wanted to do was carry her back upstairs and bury himself inside her.

He wanted to experience again that incredible warmth that he'd only found with her. But it wouldn't be right. He wanted to enjoy her, enjoy their time together and still be able to walk away. Because he *would* be leaving. Nothing would stop him.

She reached out and closed the computer, then clambered onto his lap. Threading her arms around his neck, she looked into his eyes and asked, "What do you do when you're not working?"

He didn't have an answer. Strange, but he'd never really thought about it. "I'm always working."

"Well, let's see what we can do about that."

Nine

An hour later, Nathan rolled out of bed, his body replete, his mind racing. He glanced at Keira languidly stretching on the mattress and had to fight down an urge to lay back down and gather her up close. And because that thought was uppermost in his brain, he took a step or two away from the bed just for good measure.

"Now," she said, sweeping her hair up to lay across the pillow like a red-gold banner, "wasn't that more fun than planning schedules?"

He grabbed his robe from the end of the bed, slipped it on, then stood up to look down at her. "If we spend the next few days like this," he said with a smile he couldn't quite prevent curving his mouth, "by the time the storm ends, we'll be dead."

"I can think of worse ways to go."

So could he. That was one of his problems. Always before, Nathan's relationships with women had been uncomplicated and straightforward. Before he took a woman to bed, he made sure she felt as he did about affairs—that they should be undemanding, easily slipped in and out of, with no hard feelings, no promises made, so no promises broken.

Ordinarily, he never would have become involved with a woman like Keira. She had "complications" written all over her. And yet, at this moment, he couldn't really bring himself to regret what he'd found with her.

Regrets would come later. Once he was gone and safely wrapped up in his normal world. Once he was far enough away from her eyes that they didn't haunt him every damn minute.

"You're an unusual woman."

She sat up, completely comfortable with her own nudity, and swung her hair back from her face. "Thanks."

"You're welcome," he said, his gaze dipping to the swell of her breasts, then back to her fathomless green eyes. She was tempting. More tempting than anyone he'd ever known before. He was walking through unfamiliar territory here and he felt as though he were trying to negotiate his way through quicksand.

What he needed was a little space. A little time to himself to gather his defenses and shore up the inner walls she seemed so determine to shatter.

Decision made, he said, "I'm going downstairs to get some work done."

She looked at him for a long second or two, shook her head, then flopped back onto the bed, dragged the quilt up to cover herself and muttered, "Of course you are."

* * *

A few hours later, Nathan was hunched determinedly over his computer, doing an excellent job of pretending Keira wasn't in the room.

Tossing the book she'd been trying to read for the last half hour onto the sofa cushion beside her, she frowned at the back of his head and said pointedly, "What're you doing?"

"Working."

"*Again,* you mean. Well, I can see that, Mr. Chatty. Working on what? Still trying to find a way to schedule spontaneity?"

"No." He shook his head, turned back to the computer and typed something else.

"Then what?"

"You're not going to give me any peace at all, are you?"

"Probably not," she said.

"Fine." He leaned back into the couch, winced and retrieved the book she'd dropped out from behind his back and set it on the coffee table. When he was settled again, he glanced at her and said, "I'm making some notes on how to confront the manager of the Gstaad Barrister."

"Switzerland," she said with a sigh. Then she asked, "Confront? About what?"

"I gave him specific instructions last time on how I wanted him to deal with the housekeeping staff, and they haven't been implemented."

"Why not?"

He looked at her. "How the hell do I know?"

She curled her legs up under her, propped her elbow on the back of the sofa and leaned in. "What's wrong with the way *he's* handling things, then?"

Nathan sighed. "He's very…relaxed in his position. He allows the employees too much leeway in their work."

"Does it all get done?"

"Yes, but—"

"So maybe," Keira said, "he knows his people better than you do?"

"Maybe, but—"

She smiled. "So if you weren't stomping around bellowing orders like a bully, maybe you'd get more cooperation out of him?"

"I do *not* bellow," Nathan said and sat up straight.

"But you *do* bully."

He blew out a disgusted breath. "You don't understand. There's a right way and a wrong way to run a business, Keira."

"Oh, I understand," she said, reaching out to pat his shoulder, then letting her fingertips linger there just a moment or two. "Believe me, as mayor, I have to deal with people all the time. And it's just not logical to assume you can use the same strategy when dealing with different types of people."

"It's always worked before," he pointed out, scowling at her.

Keira scooted closer, leaned down and looked him dead in the eye. This she knew about. He might own all of the gorgeous hotels in the world, but Nathan Barrister was *not* a people person.

"But the thing is, Nathan, you don't know if it might work better doing things differently."

"The company's policy has been in effect since my grandfather started the first hotel."

"Jeez," she said softly. "No wonder it's out-of-date."

"I didn't say it was out-of-date."

"Nope. I did." Turning around, she sat back beside Nathan, tucked her hand through the crook of his arm and cuddled in. "Like, for instance, when Donna—she owns the pottery shop on the outskirts of town—wanted to increase her number of parking spaces in front of her shop, I went to bat for her with the town council. After all, her shop is out of the way, it wouldn't infringe on anyone else's parking. Why not?"

"Okay…"

"But, when the Clearwater wanted the same deal, I had to tell them no. Because they're in the middle of town, lakeside, and we just couldn't afford to lose tourist parking slots to make more room for their customers. Different situations, different rules."

"Ah," he said, smiling at her, "but the situations in my hotels are all the same. Each one is a Barrister. So the rules should apply evenly."

She nudged his shoulder and laughed shortly. "The hotels are all in different places. Different traditions, different employees."

"But—"

"Would you decorate your Barbados hotel the same way you decorated the one in say, D.C.?"

"No…"

"So, same thing applies." Leaning her head against his shoulder, she added, "Cut your managers a little slack, Nathan. Trust them to know their people and their hotels. Lighten up a little and you might be surprised by the results you get."

He frowned thoughtfully and shifted his gaze to the screen of his laptop, where his carefully written-up notes were marked with bullet points. "You couldn't have made your point an hour ago? Before I started working on this stupid list?"

Keira laughed and Nathan took a heartbeat of time to simply enjoy the sound as it swirled around him. She was cuddled in close and he liked the feel of her pressed against him. He liked knowing she was sitting beside him reading quietly—or that she was in the kitchen making grilled cheese sandwiches—or tripping over a rug on her way down the hall.

He just liked knowing she was here. Outside, the storm was still blowing and Nathan was willing to admit, at least to himself, that if he had been here, trapped by himself, he would have been half crazy by now.

But having her here made for a different sort of crazy. Keira was becoming too much a part of his world. He hated knowing that he was beginning to count on hearing her move through the house. That he was looking forward to their next argument. That he wanted her even more now than he had the first time they were together.

Somehow, she was worming her way right into the heart of him. And Nathan wasn't sure how to keep her at a distance anymore. Or even if he wanted to. Which worried him more than a little.

He hadn't thought about anything but business for years. Now, his life was on hold and he was in a situation where the rules had all changed on him. He was in a place where there was too little work to do and too few distractions to keep him from having too much time to think. To wonder. To ask himself a few fundamental questions. Like what his life might have been like if he'd taken a different path.

He supposed most men wondered those things from time to time, but he never had. He'd never had any doubts about his life or how he lived it.

Until now.

Until Keira.

"What're you thinking?" she asked.

"No way," he said. "I'm not playing that game again. I'm in no mood to get frostbite, thanks."

Keira laughed, gave him a punch on the arm and said, "Fine, coward. Can I use your satellite phone?"

He turned and looked at her, curiosity taking small, annoying bites of him. "Who're you going to call? The lines are all down, remember?"

"My sister," Keira said. "I know, it's really long distance, you know, to London and all. But I won't stay on long and I'll pay for the call."

Something inside him eased back and he really didn't want to explore what that might mean. Instead, he rummaged through the briefcase beside him on the floor, came up with the phone and handed it over. "Talk as long as you want. My treat."

"Wow. You'll do *anything* to get me to leave you alone, huh?"

The answer to that question should have been yes. Since he wasn't sure anymore if it was or not, he said nothing, just turned back to his computer and began to delete his well-thought-out letter.

Keira punched in her sister's number as she walked into the kitchen and poured herself a cup of coffee.

While she waited for Kelly to pick up, she took a sip and leaned back against the kitchen counter.

"Hello?"

"Hey, Kel," Keira said, pushing away from the counter and walking toward the bank of windows. Her gaze fixed on the storm still blowing like crazy out there, she listened to Kelly's excited yelp and settled in for a good talk.

"Where have you *been?*" Kelly demanded. "I've been trying to get you forever but the phone at home's out of order and, by the way, how are you calling me and whose phone is it? I didn't recognize the number."

Keira laughed, took another sip of hot coffee and said, "Big storm blew in yesterday. Phone lines are down."

"Then how—"

"It's a satellite phone," Keira said quickly. "Nathan let me borrow it."

"*Nathan,* is it?" Kelly whistled a little, then asked, "what's he doing at the house?"

"He's not at the house, *Mom*—I'm at his place."

"You mean the lodge?"

"That's the one." Keira grinned and watched her reflection smile back at her.

"So this storm. How bad is it?"

"Phone lines down, remember?"

"Which means the roads are blocked, which means you're stranded in that big lodge with Nathan Barrister?"

Keira laughed. "All that college wasn't a waste after all. You're really quick."

"Very funny. How did this happen? Oh, K. You slept with him, didn't you?"

"Kelly…" Keira glanced back over her shoulder, as if Nathan could hear her sister's voice.

"You did. I can *so* hear it in your tone. It's that, *this is none of your business, butt out, Kelly,* tone. I know it well."

"And yet," Keira said through gritted teeth, "you always seem to ignore it."

"I'm sorry. No, wait. I'm not. Honest to God, Keira, are you nuts? This is Nathan Barrister, for God's sake. He is sooooooo not your type."

A quick jolt of anger shot through Keira but she managed to squelch it before she could shout. "What exactly *is* my type then, Kel? You tell me."

"Someone remotely normal? As in, not some damn recluse? Someone who isn't one of the richest men on the planet? Someone who isn't *renowned* for strings of one night stands?"

Well, Keira thought bitterly, she'd had to ask. "You're really making me sorry I called," she muttered and took another drink of coffee, appreciating the scalding heat as it sang down her throat.

"It's not like I don't want you to find somebody," Kelly said, her voice a lot softer now, as if carrying an apology she wouldn't actually say, "it's just. Keira, you've been down this road before, remember? Remember how hurt you were?"

"Trust me," Keira said tightly. "I remember."

How in the hell could she forget? Three years ago, she'd fallen madly, wildly in love with an Olympic skier who was in town training over the winter. Max had been exciting and funny and sexy and he had seemed to care for her as much as she had for him.

In a few short months, they had gotten so close that Keira was mentally making plans for a life together.

They spent every night locked in each other's arms. And Keira had never been so happy.

She'd never seen him for what he really was. Never suspected that he didn't feel the same way she did.

Until the day his fiancée rolled into town.

And Max, smooth, gorgeous Max, had turned and introduced Keira to the woman he was going to marry—as a *"good friend."*

The pain of that humiliation was going to be with her forever. Seeing the sympathetic understanding in the other woman's eyes when they met had told Keira that she wasn't the first woman he'd cheated with. Wasn't the first woman he'd lied to.

But that information had done little to heal a broken heart.

So, when the aching misery had finally faded along with her memories, Keira had made herself a promise. To protect herself, she wasn't going to fall for anyone again. Wouldn't believe more pretty lies. Wouldn't let a man get so deep inside her that she couldn't shake him loose any time she wanted to.

And her plan had worked pretty well. Until Nathan Barrister had walked into her life. Now she knew that her sister was right to worry. Because Keira was falling for him.

Despite knowing better, despite knowing that there was no future for them, her heart hadn't learned its lesson.

"I know you remember," Kelly said softly. "And I don't want to hurt you. It's just…I don't want to see you get all torn up again."

"Kelly…"

"Keira, why don't you come to London? Right now.

Well, okay, when the storm stops. Hop on a plane and come see me. It'll give you some distance. Some time to think. And you've been promising for a year you'd come anyway."

"I can't," Keira said, leaning her forehead against the window, allowing the icy cold to sweep through her. "I can't just pack up and go. You know that."

"I know that the town would be just fine without you for a month. Or two."

Chuckling in spite of the heaviness in her heart, Keira said, "Two months? Oh, I'm sure Tony would love to have your big sister around for that long. Great idea, Kel."

"Omigod!"

"What?" Keira's heart jolted. "What is it?"

"Tony. I can't believe I forgot."

"Is he okay?" Keira asked, though she couldn't imagine that her little sister would have had time to lecture her about her love life if her own man were in danger.

"Oh, he's way better than okay," Kelly said, then without even taking a breath, continued in a rush. "Remember I told you he was taking me to Paris for the weekend?"

"Yes."

"Well, we stayed a little longer than we planned, or I would have called you sooner and then, when I did try to call, the lines were down, so just keep in mind that I *did* try to get hold of you and—"

"Will you just say it?" Keira demanded.

"He asked me to marry him," Kelly said, with a sigh that told Keira her little sister was no doubt staring at her engagement ring and getting all misty-eyed.

"He did?"

"Yes. I'm engaged."

"That's—" Keira didn't know what to say, so she said nothing at all. Her heart took a small ping of something she really didn't want to call envy, but there didn't seem to be any other name for it. Oh, God, Kelly was getting married. She was living in Europe and marrying a man who was crazy about her.

And Keira was standing still.

Not that she didn't like her life—she did.

But…she'd had so many plans once upon a time and none of them had come true. And now, despite being happy for her little sister, there was a small, whimpering voice in the back of her mind, wishing that things were different for her, too.

"I have the most beautiful ring you've ever seen, it's so amazing. We're getting married this summer. At his parents' estate in Sussex. Oh, Keira, it's going to be so gorgeous. So perfect. And Tony's so great. I really love him so much and everything is so wonderful."

No one but Kelly could cram that many *so's* into a single paragraph. Her palpable excitement hummed through the phone like a live electrical wire.

"That's great, honey," Keira said and she really meant it. She was glad for Kelly. Glad she'd found someone to love and to love her back. Glad that she was building a life she was happy with.

Really.

"So will you come?"

"To the wedding?" Keira asked, dumbfounded. "Of course I'll come to the wedding! I'm completely expecting to be in the wedding."

"You're my maid of honor, Keira," Kelly said, clearly

exasperated now. "But I'm not talking about you coming to the wedding. I want you to come see me now. Please, Keira. Come and see me. Get away for a while."

"This is about Nathan, isn't it?" Keira whispered, not wanting him to overhear her.

"Well, yeah," Kelly said. "I don't want you getting attached to somebody like him. I know you, Keira. And I'm afraid you're gonna set yourself up for another fall."

"Hey. Who's the big sister here? You or me?"

"What? Because I'm younger I can't be right?"

Keira glanced over her shoulder again to make sure Nathan was still in the great room where she'd left him, then she closed her eyes, took a deep breath and said, "Even if you're right, Kel, getting away wouldn't change anything."

"Oh, God," Kelly said with a sigh. "It really is too late, isn't it? I can hear it in your voice. You already love him."

Did she? Instantly, images of Nathan flashed through her mind. The day they met, that night at the town party, dancing with him under the stars, the panicked look in his eyes everytime someone in town tried to thank him for his donation.

Memories raced through her mind now, one after another, almost too fast to separate one from the other. She remembered his rarely seen smile and the stunned look on his features whenever she made him think beyond what he'd always done. The gleam in his eyes as his body moved within hers. The stillness of the coming storm as they took their walk around the lake.

Making love in front of the fire, shouting at him as he stood on the snow-covered deck, furious with her for locking him out. His carrying her up the stairs and catching her whenever she stumbled because she wasn't paying attention.

He was arrogant and abrasive and annoying.

And God help her, she was crazy about him.

Leaning her head against the icy glass again, she whispered, "Oh, Kelly. You're right. I *am* in love with him."

Ten

"No way this is happening," Keira whispered frantically. "I've known him only a couple of weeks."

"Uh-huh," Kelly muttered. "And just what is the time frame for falling in love? A month? Six?"

"This can't be happening." Keira thunked her head against the windowpane and welcomed the hard jolt. What an idiot she was. She'd been so busy spending time with Nathan so he wouldn't split, she hadn't noticed that she was falling in love with the man.

"Run," Kelly said. "Run fast, run far."

"I can't," Keira snapped. "Snowed in. Remember? Besides, it's too late for that."

Kelly sighed. "I know. What're you gonna do?"

"Well, I'm not telling him, that's for damn sure," she said. She might be an idiot, but she knew enough to know Nathan wouldn't want to hear her declaration of love any more than Max had.

No, thank you. She wasn't going to set herself up for another kick in the teeth. She'd made the mistake of falling in love with the wrong man. Again. But that didn't mean she had to let anyone else know.

"Probably a good plan," Kelly said, then added, "but if you want my advice…"

"I really don't."

"Well, that's nice."

"Kel, I'm sorry. But this one I'm going to have to take care of on my own."

"Fine. Just—watch yourself, okay?"

"Yeah." Keira inhaled sharply, blew the air out in a rush and said, "I've gotta go. I've got some thinking to do."

"Okay, but call me this weekend."

When she hung up, Keira didn't move. She just stood there, rooted in the kitchen, staring out at the storm and, for the first time in her life, she hated the snow. Hated the storm that was trapping her there with a man who didn't want her. Hated that she couldn't get away. Hated that she'd set herself up for more pain.

And mostly, she hated herself for being jealous of her little sister.

"Why is it that when Kelly falls in love, everything works out great?"

"Who you talking to?"

She spun around to see Nathan standing in the doorway, watching her. A flush of heat swept over her and she hoped to hell he hadn't overheard any of her conversation with Kelly. "No one. How long have you been there?"

"About ten seconds. Did you get hold of your sister?"

"Yes," Keira said, plastering a brilliant smile on her face. "She's terrific. Better than terrific, really. She's engaged."

"That's nice."

"Yeah," she said, shifting her gaze to the phone she still held in her hand, "it is."

"And you sound really excited for her."

"Oh, I am."

"Well, now I'm convinced," he said, walking over to the counter to pour himself another cup of coffee. "What's wrong, don't you like the guy?"

"Never met him, actually. Talked to him a couple of times, but they live in England, so…"

"Why don't you go visit?"

Keira looked up at him as he leaned casually against the kitchen counter, taking a sip of his coffee. "I believe we already covered that. I have responsibilities here."

One dark eyebrow rose. "So mayors don't get vacations?"

"Why do you care if I visit my sister or not?" she snapped.

"Whoa. Don't care. Just asked."

Keira held up one hand, crossed the room and gave him back his phone. "Sorry, sorry. That wasn't about you. That was about me."

He looked at her for a long minute or two and Keira stared up into those pale blue eyes of his. How could she not have realized that she was falling in love with him? And when had it happened?

When he told her about his awful grandmother? When he actually listened to her advice? When they took a walk beside the lake? When he touched her and made her body sing?

Oh, God.

Why couldn't she have fallen for the right guy this time?

"What's wrong?" he asked and his voice was so quiet, she nearly missed the words.

"I don't know," she said, because she couldn't tell him the truth. Turning her back on him, she walked to the windows and stared out at the storm that had become an enemy.

She heard his footsteps behind her, but didn't turn to watch him approach. Instead, she watched his reflection in the dark glass and, when his hands came down on her shoulders, she managed to suppress a sigh of satisfaction at his touch.

"Tell me," he said softly.

Keira shook her head and said, "I'm evil."

He laughed shortly. "Yeah? Evil how?"

"My sister tells me she's engaged and I'm envious. How evil is that?"

He dropped his hands from her shoulders and Keira thought he couldn't have made it any clearer just how he felt. He didn't move away, though. Just stood there behind her, his body sending waves of heat her way.

"You want to get married?"

Now *she* laughed a little. At the situation. At herself. At the raw panic in the reflection of his eyes.

"I always planned to," she said. "Just like I planned to travel. But things don't seem to work out the way you think they will."

"Maybe that's for the best."

She turned around to look up at him. "For the best?"

He shrugged. "Who cares what your old plans were? Thought you liked your life the way it is."

"I do," she admitted, "It's just…different from what I expected it to be. My mom used to say that life is what happens while you're making plans. And I guess that's true."

As she talked, Keira knew she was trying to convince not only Nathan, but herself, that her life was just the way she wanted it. That she would be fine when he left. That it didn't matter to her that he didn't love her. That he would be leaving without a backward glance.

She would be all right because she still had her home. Her place in the world. If it wasn't the place she'd always planned on, did that make it any less important?

No.

"I mean," she said, pulling a chair out from under the kitchen table and plopping into it, "I love Hunter's Landing. I love belonging and being a part of the town's life. So, plan or no plan, I like my life. Don't get me wrong, I'd still like to travel, but this will always be home. I'll always come back here."

He looked down at her and shook his head, taking another sip of his coffee. "I don't understand tying yourself to a place."

Keira's heart felt another twinge, but she managed to avoid showing it. "The word *home* isn't synonymous with *prison*."

"Might as well be," he said. "The best way to live is to just keep moving."

Which is just what he'd be doing in a couple of weeks. He'd be moving on so fast that he probably wouldn't even bother to say goodbye. It hurt her to know that she'd remember him long after he'd forgotten her *and* Hunter's Landing. "Because if you keep moving, you make sure you never have time to care about anyone or anything, huh?"

His gaze narrowed on her. "You like sitting still. I like moving. Who's to say which way is best?"

"Me."

"Ah," he said, setting his coffee cup down onto the kitchen table. Shoving both hands into his pockets, he said irritably, "Ms. Roots speaks. Hearth and home and everything that goes with it, right? Well, not all of us are looking to get stuck in a rut so deep you can't see over the top of it."

"Who said anything about a rut?" she demanded, standing up so she was more on an even keel with him. It hadn't taken long for the two of them to start an argument. And maybe it was better this way, she thought. Maybe if they kept fighting, then it wouldn't hurt so much when he left.

But, even as she thought it, Keira knew it for a lie. She *liked* fighting with Nathan. So this would be just one more thing to miss.

"Please. Your rut is so comfortable, you've hung curtains and had it carpeted."

"Excuse me?"

"Come on, Keira. Admit it. You're stuck here in this little town, and the only reason you keep talking about how wonderful it is, is to keep yourself from feeling cheated out of the life you wanted."

"Is that right?" Incensed, she poked him in the chest with her index finger and seriously thought about kicking him. But she wasn't wearing shoes so she'd probably break her toe. "Just so you know, Mr. Fabulous World Traveler, I do *not* feel cheated. If I wanted my life to change, I'd change it. I'm not the one who's too afraid to try something new."

"Afraid?" He snorted a laugh. "Is that supposed to mean that *I'm* afraid of something?"

She blinked at him. "Duh."

"This should be good." He folded his arms over his chest, tipped his head to one side and waited, a smirking half smile on his face. "Fine. Tell me. What am I so afraid of?"

"I don't know," Keira admitted, wishing she did. Because then, maybe she'd have half a chance to fight through the walls he'd built around himself so many years ago.

"Hah!"

"But *you* know," she added quickly. "You might not admit it to me, but deep down inside, you know damn well there's a reason you're constantly moving on."

"Yeah," he said. "I like it."

"Liar."

He blew out a disgusted breath.

"You spend your whole life running so fast that nobody can catch up," Keira said, more thoughtful now as the temper that had spiked within her slowly drained away. "The question is what're you running from, Nathan?"

"I'm not running from anything."

"Well," she mused. "I guess you've said that often enough that even you believe it now."

She walked around him, careful not to brush against

him as she headed for the doorway leading back to the great room. When she reached it, she paused and looked back at him, standing alone in an elegant kitchen. This is how she'd remember him best, she thought. Stubbornly aloof. Alone.

Her heart ached, almost in preparation for the coming pain, but she held it inside as she said, "Someday, I hope you figure it out, Nathan. Before it's too late to stop and let somebody catch up to you."

She avoided him for the rest of the day and Nathan told himself he didn't care. He appreciated having some quiet time to work uninterrupted. God knew, since he'd met Keira, he'd had little enough peace and quiet.

And after an afternoon of it, he was going quietly insane.

He kept looking for her, expecting her to run into the room and trip over a table or something. He kept listening for the sound of her voice. But there was nothing. The big lodge fairly echoed with a stillness that was starting to really grate on him. Disgusted with himself, he finally realized that his satellite phone could connect him with more people than the citizens of Hunter's Landing.

Grabbing it, he hit the speed dial and called the one person on earth he knew would understand exactly what he was going through.

"Barton."

Nathan smiled at the sound of his old friend's voice. They hadn't really seen each other since college, but Luke Barton was one of the Seven Samurai he'd managed to keep in touch with, however loosely.

"Barrister here," he said and stalked to the wide

windows overlooking the white stillness covering the front yard of the lodge.

"Hell, Nathan." Luke laughed. "Good to hear your voice. How's life in the wild?"

"Not as wild as we might like," he grumbled and turned his back on the view of Mother Nature. "Glad to say my month is almost up and yours is coming."

"That bad?" Luke asked, dread clear in his voice.

"Small-town America at its coziest."

"Jeez. Sounds horrifying."

Nathan laughed and felt better. Good to know he wasn't the only person in the world who preferred big cities to quiet reflection. "Exactly. I got your e-mail last week," he said. "How the hell did Matthias convince you to switch months at the cabin with him? Are you two speaking again?"

"Not likely," Luke admitted.

The Barton twins had been at war for years, ever since their father had cooked up a competition between the two of them for the right to run the family business. Matthias won, but Luke was always sure his twin had somehow cheated him. Not that Luke was starving or anything. He'd built his own fortune—one to rival the legacy that Matthias had inherited—by starting up Eagle Wireless, a tech company that had pretty much taken over the world.

Still, old rivalries would never die.

"So, how'd Matt get you to switch?"

"Bastard couldn't do his month—some business emergency or other. Not sure, really. His assistant talked to my assistant." Luke blew out a disgusted breath. "The only reason I agreed to the damn switch was so Hunter's last request wouldn't be ruined."

Nathan wandered the great room while he listened. The house was crouched in quiet, and he was as cut off from the outside world as neatly as he would have been if he'd been on Mars. Talking to Luke took the edge off, and he wondered why the hell they didn't talk to each other more often.

"How bad is it?" Luke asked. "Have you at least been to Tahoe? Stateline?"

"No," Nathan answered. "I can see the lights from the casinos in the distance though—when it isn't snowing."

"Snowing?" Luke echoed. "It's March, for God's sake."

"And I'm talking to you from the middle of a blizzard."

"God, if Hunter wasn't gone, I'd kill him myself."

Nathan laughed again and dropped onto the couch. "Just what I was thinking when I first got here."

"But not now?"

"Don't get me wrong," Nathan said, "I can't wait to shake this place. Get the jet fired up and leave Hunter's Landing in the dust."

"But..."

"No but."

"I heard an implied but."

Frowning, Nathan said, "But there's a woman."

"Isn't there always? Who was that last one? Some Hollywood babe who wanted you to produce her next movie?"

He smiled, then frowned again. Maybe he was too used to people using him. "This one's different."

"This must be a sign of the Apocalypse," Luke said. "Nathan Barrister in love?"

"Who the hell said anything about love?" Nathan countered and jumped off the couch like he'd been set on fire.

"Okay then, I stand reassured," Luke said, then covered the receiver with one hand and muttered something Nathan couldn't catch. "Nathan," he said a moment later, "I've got to run. I have a meeting with some new Japanese clients and want to get this deal sewn up before I have to take my place in the cottage at the end of the world."

"Right. Well, hurry the hell up and get me out of this place, all right?"

"Not a chance, pal. You finish out your damn month. I've got my own to worry about."

After he'd hung up, Nathan stood in the middle of the great room and listened to the quiet. He should be glad Keira was giving him some space. It wasn't like he needed to be around her, for God's sake. But the quiet nagged at him and, when he finally couldn't stand it anymore, he went looking for her, sure that he'd find her sitting in a corner somewhere, pissed off and thinking of ways to make him suffer.

But she wasn't anywhere in the house.

Scowling, he grabbed his jacket from the hook in the mudroom, walked outside into the slap of an icy wind and squinted into the lamp-lit darkness. Even the night seemed deeper here. More black. More all-encompassing.

The moon was hidden behind clouds that showed no sign of leaving and snow was *still* falling, though in lighter flurries than before. He walked across the deck, grabbed the railing and leaned out, scanning the area for her.

"Surely she wouldn't have gone on one of her *walks* in the snow," he muttered. And as he considered that, he imagined her lying on the ground, unconscious from hitting her head when she fell because *he* hadn't been there to catch her. She could freeze to death out there and no one would find her until the spring thaw—if spring ever really came to the high Sierras.

Ridiculous. He tried to dismiss the worry. She'd managed to survive without his help for thirty years; he was sure she'd be fine tonight, too. "But she could have told me where she was going," he said softly.

An explosion of icy wet hit the side of his head and Nathan jerked upright like he'd been shot. Almost before he realized that he'd been hit with a snowball, he heard her laugh and turned toward the sound.

Keira stood beneath the deck, her breath puffing out in white clouds in front of her. Her smile stretched across her face and her laughter rose up in the air like music.

"Got ya!"

"Are you out of your mind?" he shouted to be heard over her wild whoop of renewed amusement.

"What's the matter, Nathan?" she taunted. "Afraid of a little snow?" Then she bent down, scooped up more of the icy stuff, patted it into a ball and let it go.

This time he saw it coming and ducked. And while he was bent down low, he scooped up some snow of his own, packed a mean snowball and let it fly while she was bent over gathering new ammunition. He hit her on the back of the head and she went down on one knee.

Instantly, he worried that he'd actually hurt her. A second later though, she raised her gaze to his and said, "You realize this means war."

He'd never get used to her, he thought. While he had been expecting to find her sulking and nursing a temper—as most other women he'd ever known would have been doing—she had been outside waiting for the opportunity to execute a surprise attack.

She wasn't angry. She was laughing. And the joy in that sound touched something inside Nathan that had been locked away for more years than he could count. He didn't examine it too closely. Instead, he gave himself up to the moment. He forgot about work. Forgot about keeping a safe distance from a woman who too easily found her way around his defenses. He forgot everything in the moment that was *now.*

"You're gonna pay for this," he shouted.

"Talk is cheap," she taunted.

Setting one hand on the railing, he vaulted over the edge and landed five feet down in the snow, bending his knees to absorb the jolt.

Her eyes went wide, and stunned surprise kept her frozen just long enough to give Nathan time to form another snowball and let her have it. She shrieked when the snow hit her face and did a funny little dance as some of the cold wet stuff slinked beneath the collar of her jacket.

But she didn't let it slow her down. In seconds the war was raging and the two of them were running around the snowy yard like a couple of ten-year-olds. Nathan hadn't had so much fun in years. He couldn't remember the last time he'd done anything like this and he was loving it. Their shouts echoed off the mountain and snow flew from half-frozen hands like white bullets.

Lamplight gleamed golden and shone in her hair as Nathan circled her, waiting for an opening. When he got it, he charged her, grabbing her around the waist and carrying them both to the snowy cushion atop the cold ground. He hit the ground first, taking the brunt of the fall, keeping her on top of him until he rolled over her, pinning her in place.

"I win," he said, grinning at her.

"No fair," she countered. "I didn't know we were playing tackle snow war."

"All's fair," he said—then caught himself before he could utter the rest of the old cliché.

She smiled up at him and the warmth in her gaze started a fire inside him that burned away every icy edge he had ever carried. He felt...different somehow and, later, when he thought about this moment, he might do some worrying. But right now, all he wanted to think about was her. What she did to him with a smile. How she could constantly surprise him and jolt him out of the ordinary.

And just how much he wanted her.

Bending his head to hers, he kissed her and the cold of her lips met his, eagerly, hungrily. When he finally broke free, he said, "How about we finish this inside?"

Eleven

Two days later, the lodge phone rang and Keira nearly jumped out of her skin. Nathan grabbed it and, after a second or two, handed it over to her. A brief conversation later, she hung up, looked at Nathan and said, "Phone lines are working again."

His mouth quirked and she felt a tug in the pit of her stomach. Something like the beginnings of loneliness. Their time together was over and it was time to go back to the real world. The world where Nathan wasn't a part of her life.

"I got that. How about the roads?" he asked.

Keira raised her chin and gave him a bright smile. "Your prayers are answered. That was Bill Hambleton, the deputy mayor. He was calling to let me know the crews were out and the road to the lodge should be clear by late afternoon."

"Bill, huh?" Nathan nodded, picked up the remote and turned the TV off in the middle of the movie they had been watching. "How'd he know you were here?"

"His wife, Patti, knew I was coming here the day the storm hit." She shrugged. "Guess she just figured when she didn't see me in town that I had gotten stuck here."

"His wife," he mused.

"Yeah." Keira cocked her head and smiled at his expression. Was it possible he had been—even momentarily—jealous?

"So you'll be leaving."

"Time to go home."

"For some of us."

"You're the one who said you didn't have a home," she reminded him.

"Touché," he acknowledged with a nod. "I guess I meant that one of us will be leaving."

"So, you'll definitely stay for the rest of the month?"

Nodding, he leaned back into the couch. "Yeah. I'll stay."

"Thanks," she whispered and resisted the urge to reach out and smooth his hair back from his forehead.

"It's okay." He propped his feet up on the coffee table and said, "It's only two weeks. And, hell," he added quietly, more to himself than to her, "guess I owe it to Hunter."

Keira leaned into the couch too, curling her legs up under her. "Tell me about him."

"What?"

"Hunter Palmer," she urged. "Tell me about him. I mean, all I know is that, for some reason, he chose our town to build his lodge in—and he's arranged for some amazingly generous donations to charity."

Nathan looked at her briefly, then shifted his gaze so that he was staring at the fire burning in the hearth. As if mesmerized by the flames, he began talking slowly, as if unsure just where to start. "My guess is Hunter chose your town because its name was the same as his. Probably thought it was a good joke. Anyway, we went to college together. Hunter, me, and the other guys who'll be coming here."

"Where?"

"Harvard," he said easily, and she wondered if he knew he was smiling. "After our first year, we rented a house off campus together."

"Just you and Hunter?"

"No, all seven of us. Back then we called ourselves the Seven Samurai." He shot her an amused look. "Not real clever, but…" He shrugged and let it go. "We were all as close as brothers back then."

"I was looking at the framed photos of all of you in the upstairs hall yesterday," Keira said. "Your hair was a lot longer then."

He chuckled at that, and she thought he looked a little surprised. "Don't remind me."

"Oh, I don't know. I sort of like a man in a ponytail."

His smile slowly faded as he shook his head. Firelight shimmered in the room, and Keira watched as memories swarmed in the depths of his eyes. "We were different then. All of us," he said, his voice soft and far away. "We were so certain how life would turn out for us. That night we promised to build this lodge together, it never crossed our minds that we wouldn't all be there to see it." He paused. "Hunter got sick our senior year. Skin cancer. By the time they found it, it was way too late. He died by inches."

"Oh, Nathan."

He let his head fall to the back of the sofa and stared up at the ceiling. "I watched him sliding away and finally one night I couldn't take it anymore. I went to a bar near the campus, got blind drunk and picked a fight." A quirk of his mouth appeared and disappeared again a moment later. "Naturally, I picked the wrong guy to mess with and got my ass kicked. I ended up in the hospital."

Keira's heart ached listening to him, but she knew she had to let him finish. She had the distinct impression that he'd never said any of this before.

He turned his head to look at her. "I woke up three days later and found out Hunter had died and was already buried."

"I'm sorry."

A closed door snapped into place over his eyes and his voice lost the memory-tinged softness. "It was a long time ago."

"It was yesterday."

He turned and speared her with a look. "What's that supposed to mean?"

"Nathan, I can see it in your face," she said gently. "The pain of it is still with you."

"You're wrong," he said and pushed himself to his feet. Shoving his hands into his pockets, he walked around the room like a caged tiger looking for a way through the bars. "It was ten years ago, Keira. I'm over it."

"I wish that was true," she said softly. "But it's not." Shaking her head, she got up from the couch, crossed the room and stopped right in front of him. Reaching up, she cupped his face between her palms. "Whether you can admit it or not, you're punishing yourself for a single mistake you made when you were in pain. Don't you see that Hunter wouldn't want you to be so alone? Still suffering over something you never meant to do?"

"Oh, for God's sake," he said, pulling away from her touch, "I'm not a wounded animal, Keira. Or a child. I don't want or need your sympathy."

"Well, you have it anyway," she said.

Shaking his head, he choked out a strangled laugh. "God. I don't know how you got me talking about this, but don't think I'm looking to be *cured.* I'm not carrying around a burden of guilt for being a stupid kid. I'm not hiding myself away from people so that I never have to worry about letting someone down when they need me again."

"I didn't say that's why you're alone so much," she pointed out quietly, "but it's interesting that it's the first thing that came to you."

"This is great," he snapped, pushing one hand through his hair and looking like he'd rather be anywhere but where he was at the moment. "A mayor who's a part-time psychiatrist. Lucky for me you were here."

"Nathan…"

"Forget it, Keira. I'm not interested in being analyzed."

"I wasn't—"

"Yes, you were. Well, don't bother. I'm not 'punishing' myself," he said, his voice as grim as the bleak shine in his eyes. "I'm just living."

"Are you?" she asked. "Really?"

He laughed sourly and shook his head. "You're seeing things that aren't there, Keira. Quit fooling yourself. I'm not the man you think I am," he said. "I'm not looking to be saved. I'm not looking for roots. My life is just the way I want it. I'm happy going from Monte Carlo to Venice to London. I have friends, I go to parties, I come and go as I please and I live exactly the way I want to live. Not all of us want to be buried alive in a small town on top of a mountain."

Her heart twisted in her chest as she looked up at him and watched him emotionally pull further away from her than he'd ever been. "Nathan…"

He took a long step backward. "Just leave it alone, okay? Today you go back to your life. I go back to mine. And it's probably best if we just don't see each other again while I'm here."

There it was—the pain she'd been waiting for since the moment she realized she was in love with him. God. She hadn't expected it to be so sharp. So devastating. When Max had betrayed her, she'd thought herself wounded. But now, knowing that she was losing Nathan, Keira finally understood what real misery was. What real heartbreak was.

Instantly, her imagination played out in her mind, showing her the coming years. The long, lonely years when she would be wondering if he ever thought of her. If he missed her. If he ever wished he had stayed in Hunter's Landing.

And in the next moment, Keira had to ask herself if she would come to regret never telling him that she loved him. If she didn't, she'd never know if there might have been a chance for them. Besides, if she kept quiet about her feelings, hiding behind her fear, wouldn't that make her as big a coward as Nathan—hiding from possible pain?

That thought was enough to spur her into action. She

would take a chance because that's who she was. Who she had always been. And if he didn't want her, then she would know. If he didn't love her, she'd never have to wonder. She would only have to mourn what might have been.

"Maybe you're right," she said after taking a moment to steady herself. "Maybe we shouldn't see each other anymore. But before I leave, I want you to know something."

His jaw clenched and his pale blue eyes shone with wariness. "I really think we've said enough already."

"I don't," she countered quickly, before she could talk herself out of this. "You may not want to hear this, but I'm going to say it because if I don't, I know I'll regret it and, damn it, there are enough regrets in the world already."

"Keira…"

"I love you," she said, the words dropping into a sudden silence like stones into a well. When he didn't say anything, Keira pushed on, knowing that if she didn't get it all said now, she might never have another chance. "I didn't expect to, but I do. I really love you, Nathan."

Suspicion glittered in his eyes now, and she knew she was fighting in a battle already lost. He'd closed himself off so tightly, she could barely see a shadow of the man she'd spent the last four days with. But still, she'd come this far; she would say the rest, too.

"I'm not expecting you to say anything, and hey," she forced a short laugh she didn't feel "good thing. And I don't want anything from you, either. I just…wanted you to know that somebody loves you. That *I* love you."

She couldn't reach him. She could see it as plain as anything. He had withdrawn so far from her, it was as if she was alone in the room.

The silence screamed at her. The snap and hiss of the fire sounded as loud as gunshots. While she watched him, Keira remembered everything they'd shared here during the storm. The wild, passionate lovemaking, the snowball fight, the arguments and the laughter.

She recalled turning to him in the middle of the night and feeling his arms slide around her middle, pinning her to him as they slept, and she wondered how she would ever sleep through the night again without him. How was she going to face every day, knowing she wouldn't see him? Would never talk to him again?

A soul-deep ache washed over her and Keira wanted to moan at the swell of looming emptiness inside. But she didn't. If this was the last time she was going to see him, then she wanted him to remember her smiling. And maybe someday, when it was much too late for either of them, he would think back to this moment and wish he'd had the courage to accept the love she had offered him.

"Well," she said briskly, giving him her brightest smile and hoping it was enough to ease the shadows she knew were in her eyes, "I guess that's it. The road should be clear in a couple of hours, so I'll just stay out of your hair until then."

He nodded so stiffly, it was a wonder his neck didn't snap.

Keira walked up to him, went up on her toes and planted a quick, fierce kiss on his unyielding mouth. Then she stepped back, looked into his eyes and whispered, "Goodbye, Nathan Barrister."

Then she left him, and the only sounds in the room were the fire and her quick steps as she ran up the staircase to get her things.

* * *

Several hours later, Keira was gone and the big house on the lake echoed with emptiness. Nathan wandered from room to room, too restless to sit still, too wired to work. Instead, his mind continued to taunt him by replaying those last few moments with Keira.

She loved him.

He should have said something, but damned if he knew what. She'd caught him completely off balance and that wasn't something that happened to Nathan Barrister. He was a man who always knew where he stood. What to do. What to expect. He'd made a habit of being prepared for any eventuality.

She loved him.

He took the stairs two steps at a time, listening to the sound of his own footsteps thump like a jittering heartbeat in the big house. When he hit the upper landing, he headed for the bedroom. But, instead of averting his gaze from the old photos on the wall, he stopped to look at them all for the first time.

Echoes of the past reached out for him as his gaze moved from one familiar face to the next. There was Hunter, of course, laughing into the camera without a care in the world. And Nathan smiled at the photo of Luke and Matt Barton, back in the days when they were still speaking, holding Ryan Sperling in a friendly headlock, while Devlin Campbell and Jack Howington poured bottles of beer over them all.

His friends. More than friends, they'd been brothers—the only real family Nathan had known after his parents' death. And he'd let them all slip mostly away from him.

When Hunter died, the rest of the group had splintered, as if its heart had been removed and there was no way to keep the rest of the whole together. Nathan reached out and touched the glass covering a photo of the Seven Samurai and he realized just how much he missed them all. How he missed what they had been back then!

And he wondered what kind of man he might have been if things had been different.

Would he have known how to accept Keira's love? Would he have believed her when she said she wanted nothing from him? Shaking his head, he stepped back from the images of his past and walked on, into the master bedroom.

No. How could he believe her? *Everyone* wanted something from him, he thought as he laid down, fully clothed across the bed. Why should she be any different?

One day bled into the next and that one into another until a week had crawled past.

And Nathan hadn't gotten a damn thing done.

No lists. No memos. No e-mails to hotel managers setting up meetings. Instead, he was restless. Couldn't think. Couldn't sleep. Couldn't keep his mind from turning to thoughts of Keira, damn it.

She was everywhere in the lodge. He couldn't take a step without remembering something she had said. He couldn't lay in bed without recalling the feel of her body pressed to his. He couldn't walk into the kitchen without seeing her naked on the counter. He stepped outside and was whisked back to the night of their snowball fight. He went for firewood and remembered her locking him outside and shouting at him through the glass.

He walked down the stairs and remembered catching her as she fell—and, damn it, he was worried about who was going to catch her when he wasn't around.

"Not my problem," he grumbled into the silence. "If the damn woman is too busy to watch where she's going, she'll just have to fall. Probably break her damn neck one of these days."

The quiet mocked him as his own voice faded into the stillness crouched in the big, empty lodge. One week to go and then he could leave. He had to stick it out now; he'd promised Keira, and a Barrister never went back on his word. No matter the temptation.

Scowling, he told himself that Keira was probably worried that he was going to leave anyway. Probably hadn't believed him when he'd promised. Well, he could just go into town and assure her that he would be right where he said he would be. That he was staying until the end of the month and then he was going to leave this town and *her* behind him as fast as he was able.

But, even as he thought that, something else occurred to him. Something he hadn't considered before and, frankly, at the moment, he couldn't figure out why not. It made sense. It fit the situation and would give both he and Keira what they wanted.

Damned if he wasn't a genius.

A week with no word from Nathan, and Keira was forced to admit that he just wasn't interested in what she felt for him. Of course, she hadn't really expected him to do an about-face, shout *I love you, too!* and carry her off to his castle—er, favorite hotel.

"But damn it, he doesn't have to completely ignore

me, either." She kicked her living room couch and limped into the kitchen for yet another cup of coffee. "It's my own fault," she muttered before taking a sip. "I knew who he was and how he felt, and I went ahead and fell in love with him anyway."

If she could have figured out exactly how to do it, she would have kicked her own ass.

"Idiot." She cupped both hands around her coffee mug and hoped that the heat would wipe away the chill sweeping through her. But it didn't help. Nothing would and she knew it. She was going to carry this icy loneliness around with her for the rest of her life. All because of one stubborn, miserable, selfish son of a bitch who didn't have the decency to accept an offer of love freely given.

"There. That's better," she whispered. "Be mad, not sad."

But the sad went too deep and the mad wasn't nearly enough to bury it.

When the doorbell rang, she set her coffee down and went to answer it. With any luck, there was some town crisis she could lose herself in. She threw the door open and stared up at Nathan, way too shocked to think of anything to say.

He smiled, and Keira swallowed hard. "What're you doing here?"

Stepping past her, he walked into her house, looked around, then turned to look at her, a wide smile brightening his features. "I have a surprise for you."

Intrigued and, damn it all, a little hopeful, Keira closed the door, shoved her hands into her jeans pockets and said, "A surprise?"

"Yes." He looked so pleased with himself, Keira

didn't know what to think. "I took care of everything this morning. You don't have to do a thing."

Worry began to nibble at her. He was taking care of everything? Taking care of what, exactly? "What is this great surprise then?"

He walked toward her, took hold of her shoulders and held on as he looked down into her eyes. "You know I'm leaving for Barbados at the end of the month."

"Yeah…" That sinking sensation in the pit of her stomach simply refused to go away.

"You're going with me."

Keira staggered and probably would have fallen down if his grip on her shoulders hadn't tightened perceptibly. "I'm what?"

He grinned, apparently taking her shock for pleasure. "I talked to your deputy mayor—Hambleton?"

"Bill, yes." She was struggling for air. Her chest felt tight and her whole body was tingling with nerves that were pushing her to do *something*.

"Right," he said. He released her, then walked into the living room and spun around, folding his arms across his chest, looking like a king who had finally figured out how to please the peasants. "I told Bill you'd be leaving with me and we didn't know how long we'd be gone. He's fine with it. He can handle whatever happens here—" He shrugged. "Town this size, running it can't be too difficult anyway."

"Is that right?" Cold. She felt cold all the way through. How weird. For the last week, she'd alternated between fury and grief, and now all she could feel was this body-numbing iciness.

"I called the hotel in Barbados," he was saying. "Told

them I would have a companion accompanying me and arranged for a personal shopper for you the moment we land. You don't even have to pack for the trip. While I'm working, you'll have the run of the shops—unlimited expense account, of course—and we'll have every night to ourselves."

"I see." She really did and she was hurt in more ways than she could count.

"From Barbados," he said, hurrying on to fill the silence growing between them, "we'll head to London. Maybe visit your sister. Or even better, we'll go to Venice—I'll send for your sister, make all the arrangements. You can have her with you as long as you want."

"How nice for me—you can arrange Kelly's life, too."

He frowned briefly, shoved one hand through his hair and said, "If you don't want to go to Venice, we'll go somewhere else."

"Oh," Keira said, walking past him now, into the kitchen where she picked up her coffee cup. "I get a vote?"

"What?"

She took a breath, hoping to steady the swell of fury rising up to choke her. "And if I tell you I can't afford to take off work? To go and travel around the world with you?"

"I didn't ask you to pay for anything," he said, frowning. "I've taken care of it. I told you that."

"Right. Silly me. So *you* decide what I do and where I go. *You* pay for me and I'm supposed to just be grateful to be taken care of."

"Is there something wrong with that?"

He was looking at her like she was speaking Greek. Could he really be this clueless?

"You really don't see it, do you?" Keira felt like her head was exploding. How could she ever make him see who she really was if he was convinced his bank account would fix any problem?

"I'm offering you the travel and excitement you always dreamed of and that makes me a bad guy?"

"You didn't even *ask* me, Nathan. You just order me here or there, and I'm supposed to come trotting along behind you fluttering with gratitude?"

"I'm confused," he admitted and stopped in the doorway between the kitchen and the living room. "You said you wanted to travel."

"Yeah, I did."

"You want to visit your sister. See Venice."

"All correct," she admitted, and took a sip of coffee that she didn't even taste. Heck, she was half amazed that she could force the liquid down past the knot in her throat.

"Then what's the problem? Why the hell aren't you happy?" He was shouting now, and that at least made her feel a little better. She'd finally cracked through his wall of blasé.

"Because you *told* me what I was going to do," she countered, slapping her cup down onto the counter with enough force to slosh coffee over the edge. "You didn't ask. You just arranged everything the way you wanted it to be. God, you went to Bill and told him we'd be traveling together. That's just fabulous."

"You said you loved me," he said tightly. "I naturally assumed you would want to be with me."

Keira choked out a laugh. "And because I love you I would want to be your 'companion'? How many times have your hotel employees been told to prepare for your current 'guest'? What number am I in line? Is there a salary that goes with the position? How much does your own private whore make? Am I paid by the hour? Or is my new wardrobe my payment?"

"For God's sake, that's not how I meant—"

"You're unbelievable," Keira said, striding across the kitchen to slap both hands against his chest. "You go behind my back to *arrange* my life. Oh, and you don't even stop there. You think you can arrange my *sister's* life—she has a job, you know? And a fiancé. She can't just entertain me when it's convenient for you."

"This is not the way I expected this conversation to go," he said.

"Well, maybe you should have written out a script for me."

"Damn it, that's not what I meant. I thought you'd be happy. I thought you wanted to travel. To see the world. That's what you said."

"I said a lot of things. Some of them you obviously ignored. I *love* my home. I don't want to leave it forever, and I can't just walk away from my responsibilities here because you say so."

He inhaled sharply, deeply, and blew the air out in a long rush of exasperation. Well, now she knew just how he felt. She loved the man and now she knew all too well that he would never love her back.

"I didn't tell you I loved you so that you would *do* something for me, Nathan," she said, and all of her anger drained away in the wash of despair swamping her. "My love doesn't come with a price tag. You don't have to throw presents at me to try to even the playing field. I didn't ask for anything from you. I offered you my love, free and clear. No strings attached."

"Keira—"

"You know what? I think you should go, Nathan," she said, moving past him to the front door, locking her knees so that she wouldn't slump to the floor until long after he left. "You just don't understand me and you never will."

He stopped beside her and looked down into her eyes for one brief moment. "You're right," he said. "I don't understand you. I offered you everything you ever wanted and you turned it all down."

"Not everything, Nathan," she said, and quietly closed the door behind him.

Twelve

Keira smiled and tried to focus on her friend standing in front of her. It wasn't easy. For a week now she'd been moving in a fog. She couldn't get Nathan out of her mind and she wondered if she'd spend the rest of her life like this—only half aware of the world going on around her.

She'd had to tell several people that she wasn't actually leaving with Nathan at the end of the month. And she'd had to put up with their knowing smiles and nods of sympathy for a love affair gone bad. Damn Nathan anyway. By trying to run her life, he'd made it that much more complicated.

"The contractor says he's ready to start on the clinic next week," Mike McDonald was saying, and Keira made an effort to concentrate.

"He wants to start before the thaw?"

Mike, an older man with long gray hair that he kept in a neat ponytail, shrugged and said, "He says he wants to start on the inside and then, by the time the snows are gone, his crew will be ready to begin the structural changes."

"Okay," she said, nodding as she shifted her gaze to the clinic that was going to become so much more, thanks to Nathan's contribution and the promise of Hunter Palmer's legacy. "I'll tell the town council and you can give the contractor the go ahead."

"Great," Mike said, adding, "and you're gonna be here, right?"

She sighed. "Yes, Mike. I'll be here. I live here. Where else would I be?"

He clucked his tongue and patted her shoulder before heading off down the sidewalk.

Alone, Keira turned and took in all of Hunter's Landing in a single glance. A sad smile curved her mouth as she realized what an idiot she had been to think that a man like Nathan would want to give up his travels to exotic cities and countries in favor of settling down in a tiny town like this one.

Kelly had been right. Nathan was *so* not the right man for Keira. He'd proven that himself only two days ago when he'd tried to hijack her life. "Unfortunately," she whispered, her heart as heavy as it had been the last time she'd seen him, "he's the only one I want."

"Talking to yourself, Mayor?" Francine Hogan called from the doorway of the post office.

Jolted, Keira forced a smile. "Nobody understands me better than me," she joked.

Just as Keira had hoped, Francine laughed and went

about her business. Stuffing her hands into her pockets, Keira walked down the street, nodding and smiling at the people she'd known her whole life.

The sun was shining and the temperature was finally starting to climb. Maybe spring was actually going to arrive at last. Just in time for Nathan to shake off the dust of Hunter's Landing and move on to Barbados. Without her. She felt a twinge around her heart and knew that it was something she was just going to have to get used to.

Then she stopped and blinked. Okay, she was worse off than she'd thought. If she didn't know better, she would swear that Nathan Barrister was standing outside the grocery store, chatting with Sallye Carberry. Oh, Keira thought, she was really losing it.

Putting one hand up to shield her eyes, she took a better look and could hardly believe what she was seeing. It *was* Nathan. Smiling and talking as if he and the older woman were the best of friends. As she stood, rooted to the spot, she watched him say goodbye to Sallye, then move along the walk on the opposite side of the street, stopping now and then to greet someone else he'd met at the block party three weeks before. For a man so determined to be alone, he had already made connections with some of these people, whether he realized it or not.

"What is he doing?" she murmured, then followed that up with, "and why do I care?"

It was no business of hers what Nathan did. He had promised to stay in town through the end of the month and that was all that mattered now. And, since their last fight two days ago, she knew that any chance they might have had together was gone. Still, her heartbeat quickened and her mouth went dry just watching him walk. Oh, she really didn't want him to see her.

So, to minimize the risk of that happening, Keira hurried her steps, heading to the diner. She needed coffee and some comfort food, and the diner was the best place to find both.

Several days later, Nathan sat, having a solitary drink on the Clearwater restaurant's deck. He'd been in town every day now for nearly a week and he hadn't seen Keira once. Everywhere he went, people told him he'd just missed her. How was that possible in a town this size? Was she deliberately avoiding him? All because he'd wanted her with him? What in the hell did the woman want, anyway?

He stared out over the lake and watched the first deep, rich colors of sunset stain the sky. Around him, families laughed and talked together; waiters moved through the crowd with expert agility and, directly across from Nathan, a young couple sat so lost in each other they might as well have been alone on a deserted island.

A ping of envy rattled Nathan enough that he took a long drink of his Scotch and shifted his gaze back to the lake. Rose and gold streaks lay across the surface of the water and the cool evening breeze was so different from the icy wind that had held the mountain in a tight grip just the week before, it amazed him.

"Your usual, Mr. Barrister?" The waiter was standing beside his table, smiling.

"Yes, Jake. Thanks." As the young man moved off to get his dinner, Nathan surprised himself by smiling. He had, over the last few days, become a regular at the

Clearwater. The waiters knew his name and his favorite meal—the chicken Alfredo, no surprise there—and always greeted him like family.

But then, he'd been experiencing the same feelings all over town. The shop owners smiled, people stopped to talk with him and he had begun to feel as if he actually *belonged* in Hunter's Landing. A strange feeling for a man who had spent most of his life on the move. Even stranger…he liked it.

In a couple of days, his month would be over and he would be leaving. And the truth of it was, he'd never been less interested in moving on—alone. But Keira wouldn't come with him and he didn't know *how* to stay. Didn't know how to become a part of something greater than himself.

Didn't know how to love someone like Keira—and the thought of somehow screwing up what they had so briefly had together…making her sorry she'd ever said she loved him, was enough to make him see that leaving was really his only option.

He finished his drink and ordered another.

An hour later, Keira took her sandwich into the living room, dropped onto the couch and flipped on the television. She used to love sitting in the quiet, letting her mind rest after listening to people chatter all day long. But these days, she needed the noise. The distraction.

Because, in the quiet, her brain was too free to wander—and inevitably, it went straight to thoughts of Nathan. She took a bite of her grilled cheese sandwich, blindly stared at the game show playing out on the screen and thought about how Nathan had looked that afternoon.

She'd hidden inside the diner and watched him laughing with Bill Hambleton. The man who had fought so hard against staying in Hunter's Landing now seemed perfectly at home here. She'd been ducking him for days, not wanting to get close enough to be hurt again, but somehow needing to see him while she could.

"Pitiful. A thirty-year-old sixth grader," she muttered, setting her sandwich down on the coffee table. "That's what you are now, Keira. Aren't you proud?"

She flopped back into the couch cushions and pulled a pillow onto her chest. Wrapping her arms around it tightly, she hugged it to her, stared at the blasted TV and tried to concentrate on the inane game show host who was trying to be funny.

But how could she focus on anything but the fact that Nathan would be leaving in a few days? She thought about calling him now, telling him she'd changed her mind and would go with him, but she couldn't. She couldn't let him think that what she felt for him was temporary. Or that she was just another woman in a long line of impermanent lovers. But how could she let him go without talking to him again? And how could she face him without wanting to kiss him? Or kick him?

"God. I'm an idiot."

A knock on the door sounded out and she rolled to her feet, reluctantly pulling herself up and out of her own misery. As much as she wanted a distraction from her own thoughts, she was in no mood for company. She walked across the room, pulled the door open and said, "Nathan?"

He looked so good, it made her heart hurt. Why was he here?

"Keira," he said, shoving one hand through his hair, as his heated gaze raked her up and down. "I had to see you."

Hope leaped up into her chest and nearly strangled her. Was he here to admit that he cared? To tell her he wanted her as much as she wanted him? Her mouth went dry and her stomach did a weird pitch-and-roll that made her reach out and slap one hand to the doorjamb to keep herself upright. "What is it?"

He stepped past her into the house, not waiting for an invitation. When she closed the door and turned around to look at him, he was looking around her house. "I didn't say anything the other day, but this is a nice place."

"Thanks," she said, glancing at him over her shoulder as she moved past him into the living room. "Smaller than the lodge, but I like it."

Her knee caught the edge of a chair and Nathan reached out to steady her. His hand on her elbow sent bolts of heat rocketing through her body like frenzied lightning strikes in the middle of a summer storm. God, she'd missed that sensation.

"Still tripping, I see," he whispered, then let her go.

In a few days, there'd be no one around to catch her when she stumbled. She'd have dozens of small aches and bruises competing with the giant ache in her heart. She rubbed her elbow as if she could ease away the hum he'd created, and looked up at him. "Why are you here, Nathan?"

"I'm sorry we ended things the way we did," he said tightly.

"But not sorry we ended," she whispered, feeling a quick stab of fresh pain. So he wasn't here to grovel and beg her to take him back. When would she stop being an idiot?

He scrubbed one hand over his face, then reached into his jacket pocket. "I wanted to see you in person again. To give you this."

He handed her a folded slip of paper. Keira knew what it was before she opened it. Hadn't he given her one before? A personal check. Made out to Hunter's Landing. Only this check was for *one million dollars.*

"I want the town to have that," he was saying, and she could barely hear him over the roaring in her ears. "The clinic can become a first-class hospital and I want—"

"What?" Keira ground the word out as she tore her eyes from the check to meet his gaze. "You want what exactly? To be a hero? To be remembered? Well, the money isn't necessary, Nathan. I'll remember you just fine without it."

"Keira…"

"No," she snapped, fury rising up to swamp her pain, "you already made a huge donation, and I don't need you to throw more money at me because you're feeling guilty."

"Guilty?" he repeated.

"You're unbelievable," Keira said, riding that anger gratefully, because rage was so much easier to handle than pain. "I offered you *love* and you offer to make me your mistress. And when I turn that lovely offer down, you offer me cash."

"Damn it, Keira, this is all I *can* do. All I know how to do."

"Bull," she said and angrily swiped at the one stray tear that coursed down her cheek as she faced him down. "I can see in your eyes that you want to stay. I've watched you with everyone these last few days. I've seen you in town and you *like* it here, Nathan. I know that you want to be more, have more in your life. But you're too scared to try. Too caught up in your own careful world to take a risk—even if it means cheating yourself out of a real life."

He stalked away from her, whirled around to face her again and said, "I offered to take you with me."

"As your 'companion.'"

"I wanted you with me, I don't care what you call it," he said. "I never promised you anything, Keira. I made it clear right from the first that I wasn't the kind of man you needed."

"How the hell do you know what kind of man I need?" she argued. "Nathan, look at you. You've completely forgotten how to give *yourself* because giving money is so much easier. You hand out checks so you don't have to get involved. It lets you stay in the shadows, safe at a distance."

He didn't say anything though she waited a moment or two, desperately hoping he'd argue with her, tell her she was wrong and he *did* want a life. With her. When the words didn't come, Keira shook her head, crumpled his check in one tight fist and then shoved it into his jacket pocket.

"You already donated money for the clinic," she said, pride coloring her tone now as much as fury. "And the town will get its share of Hunter Palmer's bequest when the six months is up. We don't need more from you."

"Keira—"

"Go away, Nathan," she said, sorrow filling her voice and staining the words until she was sure she could see the pain she was feeling actually coloring the air. "Just leave. Go back to your travels. Go to Barbados. Find some woman who'll want your money so you'll know what to do with her. Move from hotel to hotel, making sure to never speak to anyone. Keep your insulated life because I don't want you *or* your money."

Nathan couldn't breathe. He looked into her stormy green eyes, heard her order him out of her house and knew that if he left, he was a dead man. He'd come here telling himself he only wanted to give her money for the town she loved. Telling himself he only wanted to see her one last time.

When she'd turned down his offer to travel with him, he'd been lost. He had been so sure she'd accept. He'd never had anyone turn him down before. Never had anyone tell him that what he could buy for them wasn't enough. He'd been so damned sure that she'd throw her own life away to follow him. And he hadn't even admitted to himself how important it had been that she come with him. He hadn't wanted to see just how much she meant to him.

When she told him to leave, he'd felt more alone than he ever had before. He couldn't see the coming years without Keira in them. He couldn't see himself without her in his life.

She was right. He was a damn liar.

Panic clawing at him, he reached out, grabbed hold of her and yanked her up against him. Wrapping his arms tight around her waist, he bent his head to the curve of her neck and inhaled her scent, drawing his first easy breath since the day she'd walked out of the lodge and out of his life.

"Keira, don't," he whispered, his words muffled against her skin. "Don't ask me to leave again. I'll do anything in the world for you but that."

She pulled her head back to look up at him, and it tore at him to see tears swimming in those brilliant green depths. This is what he'd brought her to. He'd reduced an incredibly strong woman to tears. He felt like the biggest jackass in the world.

"Nathan, I can't do this anymore," she said, shaking her head and squirming in his arms, trying to get free.

"Keira," he said quickly, holding her as if his life depended on it—because it did. "Don't cry," he said, bending his head to kiss away her tears before saying, "I'm so sorry. I tried to tell myself I could go back to my old life. Tried to believe it. Tried to convince myself that nothing had changed and that my life could continue along as usual. Hell, I tried to drag you into my old life, thinking that having you temporarily would ease the need I feel for you."

"Nathan—"

He moved his hands to cup her face, to stroke the pads of his thumbs across her cheeks. "But the truth is, nothing is the same for me anymore, Keira. You changed everything. I *love* you."

She sucked in a gulp of air and hope lit her eyes. Nathan smiled, finally feeling hope himself. Maybe it wasn't too late for them. Maybe he hadn't already completely screwed it all up.

"I need you, Keira. Can't imagine my life without you in it." He kissed her hard, quick. "We'll live here on the mountain if you want. Build our own place however you want it. I'll still have to travel, but I want you to go with me—only when you want to," he added. "It's up to you. I won't try to make plans without talking to you again. Won't tell you what to do—"

She laughed at his pained expression.

"Fine, I'll probably *still* tell you what to do. It's who I am. But you'll fight me on it because that's who you are. And it'll be good. Damn it, Keira, it'll be *great.* We'll be great. I need you so much. I want to show you the world. I want to give you everything you've ever wanted."

He paused for breath, gave her a half smile, swallowed what was left of his pride and admitted at last, "I'm just not sure how to do it without messing it all up. I've never loved anyone before, Keira. And I don't want to hurt you."

"I don't know what to say," she whispered, her voice breaking.

"Say you'll forgive me. Say you still love me," he urged before kissing her again, this time long and hard and deep. "Say you'll marry me, Keira."

"Nathan…" She laughed, reached up and grabbed hold of his hands, still on her face. "I can't believe you're here. Can't believe you're saying all of this. And I *do* love you. So much. Of course I'll marry you."

"Thank God," he said with a rush of breath. Grinning now, Nathan pulled her in close for a hug that nearly cracked her ribs. "It's your own fault, you know," he said, kissing her hair, resting his head atop hers. "You're the one who wouldn't let me stay on the outside. Now, you're just going to have to find a way to deal with having me on the *inside.*"

She hugged him back, nestling in close, tucking her head beneath his chin. "I think I can handle that."

When he pulled back and held her at arm's length, he said, "I don't have a ring to give you, yet. We can go now—wait. Damn it, the lodge thing. I can't leave for a few more days."

She laughed. It sounded wonderful to him, the sweetest music Nathan could ever remember hearing.

"I don't need a ring right this minute," she said.

"I *need* you to have one," he told her, grinning as he suddenly saw the rest of his life stretch out in front of him, bright and beautiful. "The biggest damn diamond we can find. No, wait. Not one. Two diamonds. Or three or four. We'll look."

She laughed even harder and leaned into him to wrap her arms tightly around him, and Nathan sighed, completely content to stand here with her pressed against him forever. Just feeling her heart beat in tandem with his made him feel that his life was finally the way it should be.

Whispering now, he said, "I promise you, Keira, I will spend the rest of my life loving you and I will do everything I can to make you happy."

"I'm happier now than I've ever been, Nathan," she said, cuddling closer, holding him. "I will love you forever, and we'll make each other happy. I know we will. And I swear, you'll never be on the outside again. Neither of us will be."

He kissed her, feeling the magic, the rightness of it, and knew that for the first time in his life, Nathan Barrister had finally found home.

At the end of the month, Keira was practically dancing in place, impatient to board Nathan's private jet for their trip to Barbados—after a quick stop in London to visit Kelly. Before hoisting their bags, Nathan taped a note to the wall in the foyer of the lodge where his life had changed forever.

> Luke,
>
> It's been a hell of a month. Turns out, the middle of nowhere isn't exactly the black hole I thought it was. I hope you get as much out of your time here as I have.
>
> Nathan

Then he left his past behind and hurried out to keep his future from breaking her leg in a fall.

* * * * *

THE PRINCE'S MISTRESS

by
Day Leclaire

Dear Reader,

Welcome again to the imaginary country of Verdonia and the princes and princesses who people it and offer such rich material for their various love affairs. I want to thank the Mills & Boon® Romance readers who have followed me to Desire™. And a special thanks to Desire readers for giving THE ROYALS trilogy a try.

This book was a special one for me because I love dealing with issues of trust – or the lack of it. I've always felt that learning to trust completely and utterly is what love is all about. This book also gave me the opportunity to introduce the hero for my fourth Desire book, *The Billionaire's Baby Negotiation*, available in June, and I hope you fall in love with him as much as I did. He's a special one.

Please come and visit me at my website: www.dayleclaire.com.

I love hearing from readers

Best,

Day Leclaire

PS Don't miss next month's conclusion of THE ROYALS, *The Royal Wedding Night*.

DAY LECLAIRE

Day Leclaire is the multi-award-winning author of nearly forty novels. Her passionate books offer a unique combination of humour, emotion and unforgettable characters, which have won Day tremendous worldwide popularity, as well as numerous publishing honours. She is a three-time winner of both The Colorado Award of Excellence and The Golden Quill Award. She's won *Romantic Times BOOKreviews* Career Achievement and Love and Laughter awards, the Holt Medallion, the Booksellers Best Award, and has received an impressive ten nominations for the prestigious Romance Writers of America RITA® Award.

Day's romances touch the heart and make you care about her characters as much as she does. In Day's own words, "I adore writing romances and can't think of a better way to spend each day."

To Jada Andre, who can't be thanked often enough. You've been an unbelievable help.

One

Mt. Roche, Principality of Verdon, Verdonia

Prince Lander Montgomery gripped the phone and spoke in a low, forceful voice. "You owe me, Arnaud. You've been in my debt for years. It's time for you to pay up, and I have the perfect way you can do it."

"I don't owe you a damn thing," Joc snapped. Even from half a world away his voice was as clear as though he stood in the same room. "You and your cronies made my life hell at Harvard. You're lucky I haven't tried to even the score. But now that you've taken the time and trouble to remind me of those good ol' days, I may reconsider."

Lander glared in disbelief. "Payback? After all this time?"

"Why not? When you have as much money as I do,

payback can be a real bitch. A fact you'll soon discover firsthand, Your Highness."

"You have a convenient memory. I'd almost think you'd forgotten about graduation night." Lander paused. "Not to mention the promise you made."

Joc snarled a curse. "I was out of my mind when I made that promise."

"No doubt. But still, you made it. Or doesn't the infamous Joc Arnaud honor his promises? Given your background, I thought honor was everything."

There was a moment of dead silence and Lander wondered if he'd pushed too hard. Then, "What do you want, Montgomery?"

Lander fought to disguise his relief. Years of practice maintaining an impassive facade came to his rescue and was reflected in the calmness of his voice. "I want to discuss a business proposition. I'm throwing a charity ball this Saturday. I understand you'll be in the vicinity."

"If you consider Paris in the vicinity."

"It's a hell of a lot closer than Dallas. Where should I send the invitation?"

"Corporate headquarters. And make it two. There's someone I'd like to invite to your little shindig."

"I'll courier them to you today."

"You never did say…" A hint of curiosity climbed into Joc's voice. "What do you want from me?"

Lander smiled in satisfaction. When it came to Arnaud, curiosity was a good thing. A very good thing. "Not much. I just want you to save Verdonia."

She was late. Unforgivably late.

Juliana Rose mentally willed the cab to hurry, to cut through the heavy traffic overflowing the streets of

Verdonia's capital city of Mt. Roche and reach her destination while she could still enjoy what remained of the evening's festivities. Even if she made it to the palace within the next five minutes—highly unlikely—she didn't doubt for a single moment that she'd be the last guest to arrive.

Peering through the window, she struggled to see how much farther they had to go. In the distance the palace of Mt. Roche topped a nearby hill. It gleamed silvery gold beneath an early June moon, its graceful turrets and glittering stonework reinforcing its fairy-tale appearance. A hunger built deep inside, a hunger to believe in fairy tales and happily-ever-after endings, even though she'd learned long ago that such things were impossible—at least for her.

This was her very first ball, a reward for all her charitable work for Arnaud's Angels. The fact that the fates were busily conspiring to prevent her from enjoying the fruits of her labor simply underscored her suspicion that some things were never meant to be. Besides, wasn't it considered a major no-no to arrive after the royal family? Would they even let her in? Or would she be turned from the door before she had the chance to peek inside? Well, she'd find out whether they'd let her in soon enough. And if they didn't… She shrugged philosophically. She had a briefcase full of work back at her apartment and a dozen potential candidates who would benefit from Angels' benevolence.

As the cab turned onto the winding approach to the palace, Juliana struggled not to fuss with her hair or tug at the scrap of beaded silk that bared more of her breasts than she found comfortable. Instead she folded her hands in her lap and cleared her mind by silently working her way through a complex mathematical equation. She'd stumbled across the trick as a child, starting with simple multiplication tables to calm herself whenever she'd been upset. Since then, she'd refined the technique, increasing the level of difficulty until it took all her focus and concentration to work her way through the problems. To her relief, the exercise worked, easing her tension and allowing her to regain her poise.

At long last the cab pulled through the palace gates and cruised slowly around the sweeping circle to an entryway as elegant as it was imposing. "Lion's Den," the driver announced in near perfect English. But then, most Verdonians were fluent, since it was their second language. Even the children she worked with spoke English as well as she spoke Verdonian.

"Why do you call it the Lion's Den?" Curiosity compelled her to ask.

He shrugged. "Prince Lander is the Lion of Mt. Roche."

"So you call the palace the Lion's Den?"

He acknowledged her amusement with an answering grin. "Well…perhaps not to His Highness's face."

"No, I imagine not."

With a quick word of thanks, she added a generous tip to the fare and exited the cab. She could practically hear the clock ticking a frantic warning that time was passing, but she refused to rush, choosing instead to soak in the beauty of her surroundings. Normally she wouldn't have dared attend an affair like this. But she was in Verdonia, a small European country that rarely gained media attention, and far—she hoped—from the intrusive focus of the paparazzi. No one knew her real name here, that she was an Arnaud. Instead, she'd been using her first and middle name. She was just Juliana

Rose, charity worker, invited to the ball as a generous afterthought.

Tonight she had an opportunity she'd never experienced before. Tonight, she'd be able to cut loose from her conservative image and allow a tiny piece of her natural personality to take over. To shine as hot and brightly as she dared without worrying about who was watching or taking note of every word she spoke, or dress she wore, or man who danced with her.

Tonight she could be herself and damn the consequences.

Footmen lined the great hall, unobtrusively directing her along the corridor. As she suspected, she was the only guest not yet in the ballroom. The spiked heels of her sandals fired off a rapid tattoo against the endless expanse of marble flooring. With every step she felt more and more like Cinderella, though if she were fortunate her Elie Saab gown wouldn't dissolve into rags on the stroke of midnight any more than the cab she arrived in would revert to a pumpkin with a mouse for a driver.

Passing between huge Doric columns she found herself on a large curved landing overlooking the gathering. A majordomo guarded the wide staircase that led downward into the mass of glittering partygoers. She paused to absorb it all, to savor every single aspect of this moment out of time. Flowers of endless variety and hue overflowed urns and vases, filling the room with a lush, heady scent. Elegant French doors were thrown wide, allowing a soft warm breeze laden with the advent of summer to filter through the throng, and causing the candles that lit the room to flicker and dance. Eventually her attention drifted to the staircase leading downward. And that's when she saw him, positioned at the foot of the steps as though he'd been waiting for her.

He was tall. Even standing a full story above him she could tell his height was impressive. He wore his black tux with casual ease, his chest and shoulders a virtual wall of immovable masculinity. Thick, wavy hair swept back from his face, streaks of sun-bleached blond competing for supremacy over the rich nut brown.

She could see his chiseled features were striking, with high arcing cheekbones and a strong, square jaw that warned of a stubborn nature. But it was his mouth that fascinated her the most. It sat at odds with the hard, forbidding lines of his face and jaw. That mouth betrayed him, the lips full and sensuous and perfectly designed to give a woman pleasure. There was a volcano of passion brewing beneath that mountain of calm control, passion requiring only a single spark to ignite an explosion. The knowledge stirred a secret smile, one that faded the instant she realized he was watching her.

While she'd been studying him, curious and unguarded and exposed, he'd been busy returning the favor. Their gazes locked and held for an endless moment. Heat pooled low in her belly, lapping outward in ever-increasing demand. Never in all her twenty-five years had she experienced anything quite like it. She'd heard of women who'd been struck by that sort of sexual lightning bolt, had even scoffed at the possibility, but she'd never believed it possible.

Until now.

Now, she was faced with an urgent demand she could no more restrain than deny. She knew this man. Oh, they'd never met. But somehow she recognized him. Connected with him on some primal, instinctive level.

For instance, she knew with every fiber of her being that he was a strong man. Powerful. A leader. And she knew that he'd taken one look at her and decided he would have her. He wanted her, wanted to sweep her into his arms and carry her off to his own private lair. To lock her away and possess her body, heart and soul until he'd had his fill of her.

The knowledge almost had her stumbling backward. Pride kept her locked in place. He wasn't the first of his kind she'd had to sort out. She'd spent her entire life dealing with strong, powerful men. They were nothing but trouble. They demanded full control and considered everyone and everything within their world a challenge to either conquer, absorb or destroy.

She also knew that if she were smart she'd turn around and flee the palace. The safest recourse open to her was to hail a cab and return to her apartment where she could hide herself in precious anonymity. There was only one problem.

She wanted him, too.

Flight or confrontation? Rationality or insanity? She hesitated for a telling second before lifting her chin. To hell with it. She'd never before thrown discretion to the winds. Tonight would be her one chance and she intended to seize it with both hands. Gathering up her silk chiffon skirting, Juliana started down the steps and toward whatever fate the gods decreed.

Prince Lander Montgomery stood at the bottom of the staircase leading to the ballroom and stared at the vision standing, still as a statue, in the shadows on the landing above. She was absolutely magnificent—statuesque, with the sort of figure capable of making grown men weep. Her skin rivaled the color and beauty of the white lilies that dotted the floral displays, and set off hair that at first appeared brunette. But then she stepped into the light, and flames erupted from the darkness, smoldering like hot ruby coals. It reminded him of the fire that hid in the richest of Verdonia's world-renowned amethysts, the spark of hidden red that would heat the blue and purple to a blistering inferno and had made the unusual gems some of the most coveted in Europe.

She wore an elegant silver gown, the low-cut corsetted bodice and capped sleeves forming a triangle that framed her neck, shoulders and breasts. Her gaze drifted across the ballroom and a smile broke free, chasing the aloof expression from her face and completely altering her appearance. In the space of a heartbeat she went from cool and regal to warm and vibrant. And then she glanced in his direction.

Heaven help him, it was one of the most intimate looks he'd ever received—open and direct, and as arousing as a lover's caress. A matching hunger consumed him, a ravenous need. One look and he knew he had to have her. It didn't matter why. It didn't matter how. He'd never felt such urgency before, had never felt on the bitter edge of control. Not over a woman. He'd always been the one in charge, the one to set the terms. It was his right and one he'd taken full advantage of.

Until now.

She handed her invitation to the majordomo and then swept down the staircase toward him, crystal beads glittering with every movement. Lander found himself blessing whichever designer god had created her gown, mesmerized by the way the silver material clung to her shapely hips before flaring outward. Layer after layer of tissue-thin skirting lifted and fluttered to show off a spectacular pair of legs.

It was like a scene straight out of *Cinderella.* Except this prince had no intention of falling madly in love. In lust, perhaps. Hell, definitely. But love belonged right where Cinderella found it—in a fairy tale.

Reaching the final step, she hesitated. She continued to stare straight at him, her eyes the color of gold-flecked honey. He read barely suppressed excitement there combined with an inner fire that burned so fiercely he could feel the scorching heat from where he stood. It drew him, stirring an uncontrollable desire. It also roused the predator in him. He wanted to have her focus that iridescent gaze on him and only him, to discover the cause of her suppressed excitement. Free it. Just as he wanted to free her inner fire and bask in its searing intensity.

A ripple lapped outward among the nearby guests, warning of gathering interest. Verdonia was a small country, the people attending tonight's charity gala familiar with one another. This was the first ball since his father's death, a traditional affair Lander had known his father would have wanted them to hold, despite being in mourning. And into the darkness this exotic stranger had appeared, cutting through their grief with fiery brilliance. It wouldn't be long before one of the unattached males—or even a few of the attached ones—approached her.

Before that could happen, Lander closed the distance between them. She was tall. In her four-inch heels she easily hit six feet. "Welcome," he said simply. "I've been waiting for you."

Wariness clouded her eyes and she retreated a pace. "Do you know me?"

Odd question. Did she think they could have met in the past and not remember each other? Not a chance. "No, I don't know you. But I hope to change that."

Her relief was palpable, a fact he found intriguing. "My mistake," she murmured. Her husky accent held the unmistakable sultriness of the American south and tugged at something visceral deep inside him. "I thought perhaps we'd met and I'd somehow forgotten."

"No. It was my rusty attempt at a pickup line." Lander's mouth twisted. "It would appear I'm seriously out of practice."

For some reason his admission succeeded where the line hadn't. "In that case, you can practice on me. I promise I'll go easy on you." She leaned forward and lowered her voice. "I wasn't certain they'd let me in if the royals had already arrived. I don't suppose you know the proper protocol? Is there someone I should speak to? Apologize to?"

As a pickup line it worked far better than his had. "Prince Lander, for instance?" he suggested with a teasing smile.

To his surprise, alarm flared. "Definitely not him. I'm just here for the party, not to hobnob with any luminaries. In fact, the first one I see will be the last, because I'll be out the door in two seconds flat."

He fought to keep his face expressionless. How interesting. Unless she were the best liar he'd ever met, she didn't recognize him. That had to be a first. Nor did she want to know him, which meant keeping her far from anyone who might give his identity away.

"As it happens, I do know the proper protocol," he

responded in a grave voice. "You've missed the receiving line. Fortunate, since it's damn boring. But it's a serious lapse in etiquette to arrive so late. You'd be smart to get onto the dance floor as quickly as possible before someone notices and has you removed."

Alarm flitted across her face before she caught the wicked gleam in his eyes. Her smile flashed, filling her expression with a sweetness as unexpected as it was appealing. "I don't suppose there's anyone here who knows how to dance?"

He made a show of looking around before shaking his head. "I've seen these men in action. It's not worth the risk. Considering how late you are, it's either me or the dungeon."

Her eyes widened and she managed to appear suitably shocked. "The dungeon, huh?"

"I'm afraid so." He shrugged. "Blame it on Prince Lander. He takes this whole I-am-lion-hear-me-roar stuff pretty seriously."

"So it's either dance with you or be dragged off to the dungeon. Tough choice." She pretended to consider. "I suppose I'd be safer in the dungeon."

"True." He held out his hand. "But safe isn't always as much fun."

"And rarely does it give us our heart's desire." She came to a swift decision. "I'll dance with you."

With that, she accepted the hand he offered. The instant they touched it was as if time slowed to a crawl. Outside of their tiny world, sound grew muffled. Light dimmed. Movement paused. Her fingers were long and supple within his, revealing both strength and softness. He found he didn't want to release her, didn't want to sever the connection between them. Rather he wanted to draw her closer, to taste her, inhale her, touch far more than just her hand.

Her breath quickened as he continued to stare, the pulse leaping at the base of her throat. Her lips parted in anticipation and in that twilight of stillness he could feel the heady rush of scented air as she swayed toward him. It was all the agreement he needed, the most subtle of feminine signals giving him permission to take what he wanted. He tugged her into his arms, and just like that, time clicked back into its normal rhythm. He had enough self-possession—barely enough—to turn his actions into the first steps of the waltz the orchestra was performing.

Sweeping her onto the dance floor, he circled the room. She fit beautifully within his hold, her height making her a perfect match. He kept the dance simple and basic. She followed him without hesitation and he increased the intricacy of his movements, delighted when she matched him step for step.

Her scent tantalized him, and he drew it deep into his lungs. "What's the perfume you're wearing? I don't recognize it."

"You wouldn't. It was a gift from—" She broke off self-consciously. "It's a special blend, number 1794A."

He couldn't help but wonder who had given it to her. A former husband? A current lover? Aw, hell. The fact that he cared was a bad sign. A very bad sign. He gritted his teeth, searching for something to say that would distract him from the futile path his thoughts were taking. "What have you named it?"

She tilted her head to stare at him blankly. "Named it?"

"You're kidding, right?" Okay, now he was distracted. "You have a perfume blended just for you and you haven't named it?"

She shrugged, disconcerted. "Was I supposed to? I didn't realize."

"Most women would have." Hell, most women would have named the perfume after themselves.

"I'm not most women."

"So I'm discovering." And he found that fact fascinating. "I just realized we never introduced ourselves. Tell me your name."

"Juliana Rose." The mischievous expression in her eyes accentuated the burnished gold flecks. "And shall I call you Prince Charming?"

He shot her a swift, suspicious look, but couldn't detect so much as a hint of guile. "There are those who'd disagree," he replied, sidestepping the question.

"That's because you threaten your partner with the dungeon if she refuses to dance with you. I don't suppose there's any chance of a tour of the palace?"

"I could show you the gardens. But the rest will have to wait for another night."

Her smile flashed. "In other words, we're allowed in the gardens but the main part of the palace is off-limits."

"Something like that."

"And here I thought you were an influential man with unlimited power."

He stiffened. "What makes you say that?"

"Instinct."

"Do you know me?" he demanded, throwing her earlier words back at her.

In response, she eased away from him, distancing herself. A wash of cold air cut between them, while wariness stole the open warmth from her expression. "Should I?"

"Verdonia is a small country."

"I'm not Verdonian."

"No. American, if I'm not mistaken. And you still haven't answered my question."

"Okay, fine. Yes, I'm American." It wasn't what he'd asked, and she damn well knew it. The contest of wills was brief. It took a strong person to stand up to him. And though he believed Juliana possessed unusual strength, it was no match for his. With an exclamation of annoyance, she conceded, "No, I don't know you. As far as I'm concerned we're two strangers who have the opportunity to enjoy a single evening together before going our separate ways."

"Instead of happily-ever-after we indulge in happy-for-one-night? Is that why you came here?" he demanded. "So you could meet a stranger and spend an evening with him? Is that the current American euphemism for a one-night stand?"

Instead of reacting in anger she grew more remote, more regal. "I came because I received an invitation to the ball," she said with devastating simplicity. "And I have to settle for a single evening because that's all I've been given. After tonight I return to real life. You see, I discovered long ago there's no such thing as a happily-ever-after ending. One night at a royal ball won't change that."

"Then I suggest we make the most of the one night we have together. Have you ever been to a ball before?"

"No." Her voice dropped, the wistful quality underscoring her words hitting him low and hard. "At least, not to anything like this."

"I'm surprised."

"Really? Why?"

"Because you look like you belong. You act like it."

"I don't," she replied shortly.

"I'm not so certain. You're wearing a couture gown. Your shoes are handmade and would have cost the average citizen a month's pay." He could sense her dismay and wondered at it. "Shall I continue?"

"If you must."

"You walked into the palace as though you were a Verdonian princess. Proud. Confident. At ease with your surroundings. It tells me that even if you've never been to a royal ball, you're accustomed to elegant affairs."

"I may have been to one or two," she conceded.

She'd aroused his curiosity. "Why is it so difficult for you to acknowledge that fact?"

"Because it's in my past. This gown?" She swept her hand over the silk chiffon skirt. "The shoes? Even my invitation are all gifts. If they hadn't been I wouldn't be here. It's not a lifestyle I enjoy. Not any longer."

Lander didn't have a single doubt there was a man involved in that decision. Had she been some wealthy man's mistress? A plaything for the rich and powerful? Any man would have been delighted to have such a woman gracing his arm, not to mention his bed. The thought infuriated him, rousing a primitive possessiveness he'd never before experienced and one he fought to restrain. What did it matter who or how many men she'd been with? Right now she was in his arms. And if he were extremely fortunate, later tonight would find her in his bed.

"So you've chosen to leave this sort of lifestyle behind," he managed with impressive lightness. "Or you have until now."

"Well..." He caught a hint of self-mockery. "It *is* a royal ball. What woman could resist indulging in that sort of fantasy for one night?"

The dance ended and she stepped free of his embrace before he could prevent it. "Then allow me to make your night as special as possible."

His offer gave him the excuse to touch her again, to take her hand and gather her close. To put an unspoken stamp on her that read *mine.* He'd learned over the years how to throw up a protective wall on the rare instance he needed privacy, a subtle signal for others to keep their distance. Most recognized and obeyed, and this occasion proved no different.

Of course it helped that his staff ran interference whenever he gave them that certain look. Footmen shifted their positions. Matrons were intercepted and their hopeful daughters distracted by accommodating friends. It all occurred with the beauty and timing of an intricate dance with no one, he hoped, the wiser—especially not the woman on his arm.

A clear path opened to the buffet set up in an anteroom adjacent to the ballroom, and Lander headed in that direction. Helping himself to one of the fragile china plates embossed with the Montgomery family crest, he filled it with a selection of tidbits. He dipped a strawberry in the molten chocolate fountain and offered it to her. To his amusement, she bit into the strawberry, her eyes half closing as she savored the rich dark chocolate.

"Come on. I know someplace private we can go to cat this."

Bypassing the scattering of linen-covered tables, Lander led Juliana through the open French doors to the gardens beyond. Subtle lighting glowed along the gravel walkways and in the trees and shrubbery. He hooked a sharp right onto a path that most overlooked.

"You know your way around," she observed.

"I've been here once or twice before."

The path dead-ended at a small lattice-covered gazebo. Vines twined up the posts and across the top, dripping fat white rose blossoms. Their fragrant scent hung heavily in the air, ripe and eager to lend assistance to a scene set for seduction.

Lander plucked one of the plumpest roses, and after thumbing off the thorns, threaded it behind her ear. He allowed the back of his hand to trail along her cheek and down the endless length of her neck. He was amazed at the softness of her skin, the color and texture putting the rose to shame. Even the scent of her rivaled the most potent flower.

"How did you come to be here?" he demanded.

"Does it matter?"

"No. Right now it doesn't matter in the least. Only one thing does."

He tossed aside the plate he carried. Neither of them were hungry, at least not for food. Sliding his hands up along the bare length of her arms, he dipped his fingers into the heavy mass of auburn curls and tugged her close. She came willingly, lifting her face to his.

Night shadows turned her eyes black, the moonlight picking out the occasional glitter of gold that slipped past the darkness. Her heart thudded against his, tripping light and eager. A soft smile tilted her mouth and he wondered if her lips were as soft as her skin.

His younger brother, Merrick, had been labeled the impulsive one in the family practically from the moment of his birth, with his stepsister, Miri, close but not quite as bad. Lander had always chosen a more disciplined route. Steady. In charge. He allowed little to sway or influence him.

But he had only to look at Juliana to want with a ferocity beyond his control. He didn't care that the Verdonian election to choose whether or not he'd be the next king was only months away. He didn't care that the press had him beneath a microscope. He didn't even care that in all likelihood the woman he held within his arms wouldn't make an appropriate wife, let alone an appropriate queen. All that mattered was finding a way to carry her off to his bed and lose himself in the fiery heat of her.

Taking his time, he lowered his head and captured her mouth. Lightly. Just a gentle sample. Just enough to test flavor and texture. But that was all it took. One taste and he was lost. His mouth returned to hers and her hands curled into his shirt, anchoring him in place. Not that he planned on going anywhere.

The kiss seemed to change with each and every breath. First fast and impatient, two people discovering a new, irresistible sweet—and desperate to sate their craving of it. Then curious, each eager to explore every detail about the other. Next came slow and languid as they savored what they'd discovered, relishing the ability to please, before the want grew too strong, the urgency too powerful to deny. The kiss turned stormy again. Demanding. Pulsing. Hard and reckless. Robbing them of all thought. He heard her moan and inhaled the sound, reveling in the helpless sign of desire.

With each passing minute, with every hungry, biting kiss, his need for her coalesced into one inescapable certainty. Once she found out who he really was, there would be hell to pay. But he didn't care. It would be worth it. Because no matter what obstacles he had to overcome, no matter who stood in his way, this woman was his and he intended to have her.

Two

She was lost. Totally lost.

Juliana opened her mouth to his and drank greedily, aware that if there had been a bed here in the middle of their private glade, she'd have been on her back, opening herself to this man, giving herself to someone she'd known less than an hour. The knowledge had her shuddering in a combination of disbelief and desire.

His hands drifted from her hair to her shoulders before skating down the naked length of her spine. He cupped her hips, tugging her against him until she was locked tight against his pelvis. She struggled to think, to speak, to plead. But even that was beyond her. All she could do was moan her encouragement. His hands were large and hard and she wanted them on her, wanted them to touch her in the most intimate ways possible, just as she wanted to touch him.

Impatient, she snagged his bow tie and ripped it from its mooring. The pearl studs holding his shirt closed scattered beneath her urgent fingers. And then finally, *finally,* she hit hot, masculine flesh. She ran her hands across his chest and downward over hard, rippled abs.

He returned the favor, finding the crystal button at the nape of her neck and slipping it through its hole. The cap sleeves of her gown slid down her arms and he eased back, tracing the swell of her breasts above the corsetted bodice. Gently he slid the silk downward, baring her. They both stood motionless for a long moment. The only sound was the desperate harshness of their breathing. Moonlight silvered them, giving ripe flesh an unearthly glow. The scent of roses mingled with that of desire.

"God, you're beautiful," he murmured.

"I want you. As crazy as that sounds, I do." She laughed unevenly. "Maybe it's something in the air."

"Or maybe we were meant to be here, like this."

"Fate?"

He shrugged. "It's as good a reason as any."

As though unable to resist, he reached for her, tracing his fingertip down the swell of her breast to her nipple. His face remained taut and hungry, filled with a determination she found impossible to resist.

It took two attempts before she could speak. "I don't even know your name." That simple fact both bewildered and excited.

"We know this." His hand cupped her breast and he leaned down to feather a kiss across the tip, eliciting another helpless moan. "This is all that matters."

She hovered between common sense and lust. She craved this man, craved his touch, his kisses, his body.

It didn't matter that she'd only met him a scant hour ago. It had only taken one look, one single touch, for her to be willing to compromise the values and mores she held most dear.

She'd never done anything like this before nor wanted a man quite so desperately. Even with Stewart, with the man who'd ultimately betrayed her, she'd never come close to experiencing such a total rending of control. If she'd learned nothing else from her past, it had been to live with the utmost caution. To keep rampant emotions in tight check. As a result, she'd turned logic and rationale into her own personal religion. And yet, here she stood, ready to dive headfirst into a fast-moving river leading straight over a waterfall. Not that she cared. This one man, along with this one moment in time, governed every thought and deed.

"We can't do anything here," she felt compelled to protest. "Someone might find us."

"In that case we have two options. We can stop. Or we can take this somewhere else." He made the suggestion without inflection. And though he continued to hold her, he didn't use those clever hands to try and influence her decision. "It's up to you."

He was offering her a clear-cut choice, an opportunity to back out while there was still time. But she'd already made that choice. There was only one option available to her. She lifted her arms and wrapped them around his neck. Finding his mouth with hers, she sank into the kiss, offering herself without saying a word. It was glorious. Delicious. A fantasy beyond compare. If this were a dream, she hoped never to awake. His arms offered a world she'd never known, but one that she wanted more than anything. A world of passion and seduction, and oddly enough, protection. If she were very lucky, this night would never end.

She snatched a final kiss before pulling back. "I'd like to go somewhere else," she said answering his question. The ease and simplicity of her response amazed her. How right it felt and how deliriously free she felt saying it. "I'd like to go with you very much."

With an exclamation of triumph, he swept her into his arms. She grinned up at him about to demand that he carry her off to his fairy-tale castle and have his wicked way with her, when the sound of someone clearing his throat came from the edge of the copse. Instantly her "prince" spun them around into shadow, putting his back to whomever had joined them. He lowered her to the ground, refastening her gown to conceal her nudity.

"Bad timing, Lander?" a laughing voice asked.

"Damn it, Joc. Two minutes more and we'd have been gone."

Juliana stiffened. No. Oh, please no. It couldn't be. A single, swift glance confirmed her worst fears. She gave herself a few precious seconds to catch her breath while mustering what little poise she still retained. Circling the man Joc had referred to as Lander—and why did that name send a warning bell screaming though her fogged brain?—she stepped into a patch of moonlight.

"Hello, Joc," she greeted her brother.

"Juliana?" He uttered her name in sharp disbelief.

Lander's gaze switched from one to the other, his eyes narrowing. "You two know each other?"

"I work for Arnaud's Angels," she responded calmly, shooting her brother a look, warning that she didn't want him to reveal their relationship. To her relief, he gave a subtle nod of understanding. "I didn't realize Mr. Arnaud would be here tonight."

"No," Joc murmured dryly. "Obviously, you didn't."

"If you'll excuse me…Lander, is it?" She knew that name. How did she know that name? If only she could think straight. "I'll leave you two gentlemen to your business."

Joc lifted an eyebrow. "Don't be rude, my dear. As a representative of Arnaud's Angels you owe His Highness more respect than that. After all, he is your host."

Lander started to speak, but after making a sound of disgust, fell silent.

Juliana stilled. "What are you talking about?" But deep down, she knew. His name had sounded familiar, and perhaps if she hadn't been so drunk on kisses she'd have recognized it sooner.

Joc released a bark of disbelieving laughter. "Didn't you realize? The man you've been kissing is Prince Lander. Or to be more precise, Prince Lander Montgomery, Duke of Verdon. The Lion of Mt. Roche."

Oh, no. It couldn't be. What wicked-humored fate had put her in the path of the one man she wanted most to avoid? And why hadn't she figured it out sooner? How was it possible that the very first time she'd chosen to cut loose, she'd selected to do it with him? When it came to ignorant fools, she took top prize in both categories. Lifting her chin, she faced Prince Lander with what little remained of her tattered dignity.

"How very amusing," she said, her tone making it clear she was anything but amused. She swept him a deep, formal curtsey. "I'm delighted I could provide Your Highness with tonight's entertainment."

"It wasn't like that and you damn well know it."

She could hear the frustration underscoring his words, but didn't care. He'd kept his identity from her for reasons of his own, even after she'd made it clear that she had no interest in meeting Prince Lander. Maybe he'd remained silent because she'd warned him that she'd run if she came across anyone of consequence. Otherwise, he'd have revealed his name if only in the hope that it would have her tumbling into his bed all that more quickly.

More quickly? She almost groaned aloud. How much faster could she have tumbled? It had only taken him a brief hour to sweep her off her feet, and that was without pulling rank, as it were. Murmuring an excuse, she skirted her brother and returned to the palace. She hesitated in the shadows just beyond the spill of lights from the ballroom, struggling to regain her self-control.

How could she have been so idiotic? How could she have let a man—even a prince—rob her of every ounce of intelligent thought? But from the moment she'd first seen him, she'd been utterly lost, willing to go anywhere he demanded, give anything he requested, do whatever he required. The knowledge ate at her. With one painful exception, she'd never allowed a man so much control over her. And yet in the space of a single hour, Prince Lander had not only demanded that control, but had been given it without a single word of protest. Had she learned nothing from her past? Clearly not.

Taking a deep breath, she stepped into the light and headed across the ballroom, walking casually, if determinedly, toward the nearest exit. Before she'd taken more than a half-dozen steps, a hand landed on her shoulder, spinning her around.

"I'm sure you don't intend to leave without dancing with me," Joc stated. Not giving her a chance to protest, he swung her onto the dance floor. "So, tell me... What's a nice girl like you doing in a palace like this?"

"Oh, ha-ha. The more interesting question is, what are you doing here?" Juliana retorted in a furious undertone.

"Visiting you, of course."

Blithe and casual. Typical of him. But she wasn't buying it for a minute. She knew that beneath that good-ol'-boy routine hid the soul of a brilliant, hard-as-nails businessman. Whatever reason Joc had for being here, it was neither blithe nor casual. "You came all the way to Verdonia just to visit me? Try again, big brother."

"Maybe I should ask what you're doing with Prince Lander."

As usual, he'd turned the tables on her with annoying ease. She focused on the dance for a full minute before replying. "I didn't know he was a prince."

"Or you'd never have been with him?"

She hated the gentle concern in Joc's voice almost as much as she hated the question. "Not a chance."

His breath escaped in a sigh. "Just as well. I wouldn't want any sister of mine mixed up with a Montgomery."

Her head jerked up at that. "Why not?"

"We have a...history."

"What sort of history?" she pressed.

"That's not important."

Impatience lined Joc's face, warning her to drop the subject. It was a striking face, lean and golden, with the blood of their Comanche ancestors contributing to the impressive bone structure. Black eyes, black hair and what some would call a black heart completed the package, though she knew better. Joc was the kindest, most generous man alive. Unless crossed.

"Explain something to me, Ana—"

"Juliana," she corrected. "I don't use my nickname, anymore."

"And why is that?" he demanded. "Why don't you want him to know who you are? What does it matter if I tell him you're Juliana Rose Arnaud, my sister, rather than Juliana Rose, charity worker? You won't be seeing him again." He waited a beat before pushing. "Will you?"

"No." But how she wanted to.

Deep grooves formed on either side of his mouth. "It's because you're my sister, isn't it? That's why you only use your first and middle names these days. Because you're afraid of the attention you'll receive if anyone finds out you're Ana Arnaud, sister to the infamous Joc Arnaud."

Tears filled her eyes and she blinked them back before lifting her gaze to his, praying that he wouldn't be able to tell how close to the edge he'd pushed her. She lifted a hand to his cheek. "It's not that. You know I love you. I'm proud to be your sister."

"Then what stopped you from telling Montgomery the truth?"

She shivered at the coldness of the question…and the underlying hurt. "I haven't told anyone. I want the focus to be on the charity, not on me. Now that I know Lander is a prince, it's even more imperative that I remain silent. He's in the public eye. If the media gets a whiff of our involvement, they'll be all over us. I can't handle that. Not again." Not ever again. "Don't you see? It's not just what will happen to me. It's not fair to throw Prince Lander to the wolves without any warning."

"Is that the only reason? Because if it is, I can take care of the media."

The hard look in Joc's eyes worried her. There was

another reason she couldn't be with Prince Lander, but she didn't dare mention it. It would only anger her brother. "I came to Verdonia to escape scandal, not stir up more. Besides, it isn't like I'm seriously interested in Prince Lander."

"Liar." He hesitated, no doubt torn between whatever history stood between the two men and his love for her. "I may not care much for your choice, but if you're serious about him, I can fix things," he offered grudgingly. "Though to be honest, I'd rather you kept your distance. I don't trust the man. Not with you."

"What you saw in the garden, it was just a bit of harmless fun. Nothing consequential. And it's not like I'll be in Verdonia for very much longer. A few more weeks at most." Could Joc hear the desperation in her voice? Probably. Her brother was as skilled at reading people as he was at making money. In fact, she doubted he'd have amassed his current fortune if he hadn't possessed both abilities. "Tomorrow I'll be back at work and tonight will have been nothing more than a sweet dream. Just a meaningless interlude."

"And Montgomery?"

She took a deep breath. "Since you don't want me to see him again, I won't be seeing him." For some reason the realization caused a stab of pain.

"Montgomery's a powerful man. If he wants you, he'll find you."

She shook her head. "He won't waste time trying. After all, it was only one dance."

"And one kiss," Joc added. "No big deal."

She flinched. "Exactly." She deliberately changed the subject. "I guess I have you to thank for the ticket to the ball, as well as the dress."

"Considering how hard you've been working, you deserve it," he answered, accepting the new topic with good grace. "It only seemed appropriate to send a suitable dress and shoes. I'm willing to bet you didn't bring anything with you."

"Good guess. Maybe that's because I'm here to work, not play."

"Speaking of which, the reports I've received have been glowing."

"Thank you." His acknowledgment of her accomplishments delighted her. Although Joc wasn't stingy with his praise, he also didn't offer it gratuitously. "And thank you for tonight. It's been—" Amazing. Incredible. A dream come true. "Very nice."

He leaned forward and kissed her brow. "You're welcome. I don't suppose you're ready to come home now?"

"Home?" It took her a minute to catch his drift. "Oh, you mean to the States?"

"Of course I mean to the States." Amusement competed with impatience. "Honey, as wonderful a job as you're doing here, I need you back in Dallas. You're my best executive accountant."

"Was," she stressed. "I *was* your best executive accountant. Now I head up your European branch of Arnaud's Angels."

He waved that aside. "A total waste of your talent."

Her mouth tightened. "I don't happen to agree. The children need me."

"You mean…you need the children."

Sometimes it didn't pay to be subtle with her brother. "I'm not returning to Dallas."

"It doesn't have to be Dallas, if you'd rather not."

His instant willingness to compromise warned of his seriousness. "You can work out of whichever city suits you."

"What suits me is the job I'm currently doing. Considering how much work there is for me in Europe, I may never return home." Her hand tightened on his shoulder. "I need you to back off, Joc, and let me live my life my way. Either I continue with Angels or I offer my services to some other charitable organization. I guarantee they'll snatch me up in a heartbeat."

To her surprise, he let it go. "Fine, fine. If that's what you want, stay in Verdonia. Hell, stay wherever in Europe you want." A frown touched his brow. "So long as it's away from Montgomery, I can live with it."

Lander stood on the sidelines, watching Joc and Juliana dance with an ease that spoke of long intimacy. Damn it all! It might have been a replay of their years at Harvard. For some reason, they'd constantly found themselves in competition. On the playing field. In the classroom. And in their most contentious battles, over women. After the first few years where they'd taken loutish delight in poaching, their attitudes had changed. Lander hadn't wanted any of the women Arnaud had been with, anymore than Joc had wanted Lander's.

But that changed the moment Lander had met Juliana. Now only one question remained…was Juliana fair game? And what did he do if she wasn't?

The dance ended. But Joc didn't release his hold on his partner. Rather, they spoke quietly for a moment before he bent forward and gave her a second kiss, this one on the cheek. It took every ounce of self-control for

Lander to keep his shoulder glued to the wall instead of striding across the room and planting his fist in Arnaud's nose. If that kiss had landed any closer to Juliana's mouth he might have, regardless of the consequences.

The couple reluctantly parted—at least, it appeared reluctant to Lander—and the crowd chose that inopportune moment to surge forward, blocking his view. When next he could see, only Joc remained, who offered a nod of acknowledgment and headed toward Lander, joining him on the sidelines.

"I think it's time we spoke, don't you?" Joc asked.

Screw that. "Where is she?"

"Gone."

"Is she yours?" Lander demanded with single-minded intensity.

Anger flared in Joc's gaze. "That's a hell of a thing to ask. Juliana doesn't belong to any man. Not me. And for damn sure not you. Not now. Not ever."

Not ever? He'd see about that. "If she's not yours, I want to know where I can reach her."

"Did you hear what I said?"

"I heard. Are you telling me she's off-limits?"

A silent battle of wills ensued with Joc blinking first. "Is she that important to you?"

"Yes."

Joc shrugged his concession, but Lander could see the wheels turning. Ever the businessman, he was no doubt trying to figure out how to turn the situation to his financial advantage. "Fine. But don't you have more important issues to deal with than some woman you only met tonight? Isn't that why you called me?"

It shouldn't have taken Lander a full minute to switch his focus from Juliana to affairs of state. But it did. Aw, hell. He scrubbed a hand across his face. He had it bad. Without another word, Lander led the way to his private office. It was a large room with floor-to-ceiling windows that offered an unparalleled view of each day's sunrise. The room also overlooked the front of the palace, and Lander made a point of crossing to the window just in time to see a distinctive flash of silver silk disappear into the back of a cab.

Deliberately forcing himself to redirect his focus to the current problems plaguing his country, he turned to face Joc Arnaud. His nemesis stood in front of a map of Verdonia, his hands clasped behind his back.

"So when will you be crowned king?"

"Either in two months—" Lander shrugged "—or never."

"Never?" Joc swiveled, his brows climbing. "I don't understand. Wasn't your father king? I assumed when he died that the crown would fall to you. Isn't that how those things work?"

Lander inclined his head. "In a true monarchy that would be correct. But in Verdonia it's a little different. We have a popular vote among the eligible royals."

Joc frowned. "You and your brother have to compete for the throne?"

"As a second son Merrick's not in the running. No, the eldest royals from each principality are the only ones eligible."

"Well, hell. Who are you up against?" Joc leaned in and tapped the southernmost principality. "I gather you represent Verdon."

Lander joined Arnaud in front of the map and indicated the principality farthest north. "Prince Brandt von Folke is the eligible royal from Avernos."

Joc traced the principality snuggled between north and south. "And this one in the middle? Celestia, is it?"

"There aren't any eligible royals. You have to be twenty-five to rule Verdonia and Princess Alyssa won't turn twenty-five until after the election. She's my brother, Merrick's, wife. They married just a few days ago."

"A political affair?"

Lander nodded. "It started out that way. She was going to marry Brandt until Merrick intervened."

"Why would Merrick inter—" Joc broke off, his brow furrowed. "Oh, I get it. If Alyssa and this Brandt fellow had married, it would have united the royal families of Avernos and Celestia. Wouldn't that have ensured Prince Brandt the popular vote?"

"Astute as always," Lander commented. Joc's talent at grasping the salient points and analyzing how they affected the big picture had always—reluctantly—impressed the hell out of him. "Yes, Brandt would have won the election if Merrick hadn't interfered. He abducted Alyssa and married her himself."

Joc barked out an incredulous laugh. "Gutsy."

"Would have been if he hadn't fallen in love with her."

"I don't know." Joc's expression turned dubious. "You certain he wasn't ensuring you the win by uniting the Montgomerys with her people? Sounds damn convenient if you ask me."

Lander fought back a stab of anger. "I think he'd have claimed it was quite inconvenient. But if you saw them together—" he shrugged "—they appear disgustingly happy."

Joc glanced across the room and brightened. Crossing to Lander's desk, he helped himself to a Havana Corona from the humidor. "Okay, so now that you've caught me up on the political situation, why don't you explain what I'm doing here." Making himself at home, he clipped the cigar and passed it to Lander before repeating the process for himself. "I gather there's a serious reason or you wouldn't have imposed on our…friendship."

Lander didn't bother couching his words. "I need your help." He took his time lighting his cigar, before lifting his gaze to stare at Arnaud through the haze of pungent smoke. "Verdonia's in trouble."

"I assume you mean financial difficulties. I suppose you expect me to bail you out just because I owe you over a half-forgotten college debt?"

"If it were half-forgotten, you wouldn't be here." He allowed his comment to hang, before adding, "And I'll only accept your help if you can do it aboveboard."

Joc bit down on his cigar, fury burning in his gaze. "You have a hell of a nerve." A hint of rawness ripped through his voice. "My father may have walked the wrong side of the line. At least, that's what the feds claimed. And he may have fathered a pair of bastard children on my mother and then refused to give them his name. But I'm not, and never have been, my father. I only deal aboveboard and if you've had me investigated, as I'm sure you have, you damn well know that."

Lander inclined his head. "That's the only reason we're talking. Tell me something, Arnaud. How many failing businesses have you turned around?"

"Too many to count."

"Right now Verdonia is a failing business. I need your skill—and maybe a few Arnaud business interests relocating here—to get my country turned around."

Joc worked on his cigar before slowly nodding. "If

there's money to be made helping, I'll help. But I'll want an airtight contract before I let go of one thin dime."

"Perfect. First we'll talk money." Lander opened a decanter and splashed a couple fingers of single malt into a crystal tumbler. He held it out. "And then we'll talk women."

Three

Juliana cuddled Harver in her arms as she spoke quietly to the baby's mother. Born with a cleft palate, the little boy would be another of Arnaud's Angels. At least, he would if Juliana had her way. She had doctors standing by once she received approval from Harver's parents for the operation.

The mother was understandably fearful, while the father appeared suspicious of the offer of such an expensive procedure for free, despite her having explained everything with meticulous care. It helped that the surgeon was Verdonian, his calm voice of reason allaying most concerns. At long last the parents signed the consent forms and Harver was carried off for the necessary testing in preparation for his surgery.

After wishing the parents well, and receiving a fierce hug from Harver's mother, Juliana gathered up her paperwork and filed the various forms and folders in her briefcase. As always, an irrepressible excitement bubbled through her now that her task was completed, now that she knew another baby would receive the life-altering procedure. How could Joc think an accounting job, no matter how lofty the position, could compare to this?

She exited the hospital, her high spirits giving a swing to her step as she headed toward a nearby cab stand. A light breeze tugged at her hair, loosening a few of the curls that she'd secured at the nape of her neck with a clip. She hadn't gone more than a dozen paces when a black stretch limo pulled up beside her. She sensed who it was even before the door swung open to reveal Prince Lander.

Dismay filled her. So he'd found her. She shouldn't be surprised. It was bound to happen. Her grip tightened on her briefcase as she inclined her head. "Your Highness."

"Please, get in, Ms. Rose," he said. "We need to talk."

Just because he was a prince didn't mean she had to go with him. She'd made enough of a fool of herself the previous evening without making it worse in the harsh light of day. "No, thank you. I think we said everything we needed to last night."

"Perhaps." He paused a telling moment. "But we didn't do everything we planned, did we?"

She fought to control the flush that heated her cheeks. "Fortunately. Now if you'll excuse me—"

"I'm not going anywhere. And neither are you." Determination settled into the hard lines of his face. She recognized that expression. She should. Joc wore it often enough and it always signaled an unwillingness to budge from his position. "Now are you going to get in, or do I continue to draw attention to us by following you?"

He couldn't have found a more effective way of convincing her to join him. Caving to the inevitable, she slid in beside him, placing her briefcase between them. Let him read whatever he wished into that small, pointless gesture.

"Okay, speak." She closed her eyes, drawing on every ounce of self-control. "Please excuse me, Your Highness. I apologize if that sounded rude. How can Arnaud's Angels be of assistance to you?"

"I'm not interested in your charitable work," he bit out. "I'm interested in you, as you damn well know."

"Yes, sir. I believe you explained that last night. Perhaps we didn't have an opportunity to finish that conversation, after all. So allow me to finish it now."

She forced herself to turn and offer her coldest stare. It was a major mistake. She'd mapped out precisely what she'd intended to say, worked it almost like a mathematical equation—the words, the intonation, the expression she'd use. But in the space of the two heartbeats it took for her to fall into his intense gaze, every last thought vanished from her head. She could only stare at him in complete and utter bewilderment.

"Fine," he prompted. "Finish it."

"Finish it." She moistened her lips. "Right. I'll do that right now."

Held by those brilliant hazel eyes, she racked her brain, struggling to remember what she was supposed to finish. Something. Something about…finishing. Her confusion must have shown because his mouth twitched. And then a chuckle rumbled deep in his chest. "Hell, woman. We do have a bizarre effect on each other, don't we?"

She couldn't help it; his laughter proved too contagious. Shaking her head, she gave in to her amusement. "What am I going to do about you, Your Highness?"

"Whatever you want. And make it Lander."

"Thank you." She regarded him with sudden suspicion. "How did you find me? Joc?"

"No. He refused to help."

She could be grateful for that much, at least. For some reason their shared amusement had her relaxing enough for her brain to function again. "I remember what I was going to say."

"Something about finishing?" he offered with a slight smile.

She nodded gravely. "Finishing things between us."

"Excellent. I'll instruct my driver to drop us off at the palace so we can finish what we started last night."

She fought to keep from laughing again. She didn't want to be charmed by him. Yet she was. Utterly charmed. Enthralled. Entertained. Filled with an impossible yearning. It had to stop, and stop now. "I meant finishing, as in ending things between us," she clarified.

"Why?"

The simple question caught her off guard. "Last night… It wasn't meant to happen."

"But it did. You wanted me. You can't deny that."

Honesty came hard, but she refused to shy from it. "I don't deny it. I wish I could blame it on the moonlight. Or on too much to drink."

"It wasn't even close to a full moon. And you didn't have anything alcoholic."

"No, I didn't." If only she had, it would be some balm to her pride. "I take full responsibility for what happened."

"Noble, but unnecessary." Irony laced his words. "I seem to recall you weren't alone in that garden."

"But I let you—" She'd let him kiss her. Incredible, amazing kisses. And he'd touched her. Just remembering had her aching to have his hands on her again.

He studied her, pinning her with a look that had her brain misfiring again. "Are you feeling guilty because of Joc?"

She blinked in bewilderment. "Joc? What does he have to do with this?"

"He asked for two invitations when I invited him to the ball. I assume he sent the second to you. And I'm also guessing he might have had something to do with your designer gown, as well. Didn't you tell me it was a gift?"

He didn't know. Relief swept through her. He'd assumed she and Joc were lovers. Her brother had promised he wouldn't tell Lander of their connection, but she'd been concerned that the prince might have guessed the truth. She nodded. "Joc arranged for both the clothes and the invitation."

"Is that why you want to end things between us? Are the two of you involved?"

"Not the way you mean."

His eyes narrowed in thought. "In that case, there can only be one other reason. It's because of who I am, isn't it?"

She couldn't hold his gaze. "Yes."

"Hell." She could hear the ripe frustration vented in that single expletive. "You're probably the first woman I've ever met who didn't want to have anything to do with me once she knew who I was."

"Takes all kinds," she joked.

"Explain it to me."

She forced herself to look at him, to be as honest as possible. He deserved no less. "I don't like living in the spotlight. Being with you, even for a short time, would mean precisely that."

"Been there, done that?"

"Yes."

"With Joc."

He didn't phrase it as a question or ask for a confirmation, so she didn't offer one. Instead, she reached for the door. "May I go now, Your Highness?"

He gave an impatient shake of his head. "I'll take you home." Before she could protest, he signaled his driver. "Samson Apartments," he instructed.

"How do you know where I live?" When he simply smiled, she released her breath in a sigh. "Why do I bother asking? You're Prince Lander, Duke of Verdon. I suppose all you have to do is wave your royal scepter and your every command is granted."

"If that were true, we wouldn't be having this conversation. We'd both be in my suite at the palace and you'd be gracing my bed."

There was nothing she could say to that, so she closed her mouth and turned her head to stare out the window. The drive through the city was accomplished at a record pace, and in short order they pulled up outside her apartment complex.

"I guess this is goodbye," she said, reaching for the door handle.

"It is." He paused a beat. "If that's what you really want."

"We settled this already."

"You can leave." He shifted closer and covered her hand with his, preventing her escape. His breath stirred the curls at her temple while his voice murmured seductively in her ear. "You can get out and we'll never see each other again. Or you can stay. Think about it. We can have one evening together before we go our separate ways. No one has to know. I can arrange that. No media attention. No spotlight. Just a man and a woman doing what men and women have done throughout the ages. One night, Juliana."

One night. The insidious words were all too tempting. She could see it, as clearly as though it had already happened. A night she'd never forget, held within the arms of a man who filled her with a desire beyond anything she'd ever before experienced. Limbs intertwined. Heated flesh sliding against heated flesh. An intimate exploration as soft and gentle as it was hard and fierce. She'd never allowed herself to give in to such basic, primitive demands. For the first time, she wanted to.

"Don't," she whispered.

"Because you're not interested in what I'm offering?"

She shook her head. "Because I am."

He tucked a lock of hair behind her ear, his mouth following the same path as his fingers. "Then why resist?"

She fought back a moan. It was an excellent question. Why did she resist? She was far from home. No one knew her true identity. Nor did anyone know about the various scandals in her past. Hadn't she been cautious her entire life, watching every step she took? And even that hadn't prevented her from tripping. Now she had an opportunity that would never come her way again. A chance to seize what she wanted. Have the sort of fling she'd never dared indulge in before—never been tempted to indulge in.

"If I come with you," she began hesitantly, "what would you expect from me? Where would we go?"

"I expect nothing more than what you're willing to give. And we can go anyplace you'd like."

He interlaced her fingers with his and lifted them from the door handle. She allowed it, realizing as she did so that she'd just committed herself to insanity. She didn't know whether to laugh at her daring or call herself every sort of fool. Perhaps both.

"Can we go somewhere other than the palace?" she asked.

He inclined his head in agreement. "Someplace private."

"You're actually allowed privacy?"

"Allowed? No. But every once in a while I take what I need." His smile came slow and deliberate. "And right now what I need is you. Give me a moment to arrange everything."

The entire time he was gone she sat in utter disbelief. What had she done? How could she have agreed to see him again when she knew the potential consequences? Last night she could blame on moonlight and roses, on wanting so desperately to believe in fairy tales that she'd behaved in ways she never would have believed herself capable. Now, with a clear, bright June sun shining down on her, she couldn't delude herself any longer. The facts were as black-and-white as a column of numbers. It didn't matter how many times she totaled the figures, the bottom line didn't change. And the bottom line right now was she'd just agreed to spend the night with Lander.

Her mouth firmed. So what if she had? Why shouldn't she indulge in a single night of bliss before returning to real life? It wasn't that she deserved it, or had earned it. She simply wanted it. Wanted the fantasy. Wanted the intense pleasure she'd shared with Lander to continue a short time longer. She slid her hand over the plush leather seat. For once she'd be greedy. She'd put aside all her fears and worries and grab with both hands what fate had so generously provided. As for tomorrow?

She lifted her chin in defiance. Tomorrow could take care of itself.

A few minutes later Lander returned to the limo. "Everything all right?" he asked.

"Perfect."

"I was hesitant to leave you alone in case you had second thoughts."

"Oh, I had second thoughts. And third and fourth and fifth."

"You're still here."

She offered a blinding smile. "Yes, I am."

He cupped her chin in response. Lifting her face, he took her mouth in a slow, deliberate kiss. She was curious to see what would happen, whether she'd react to him the same way as before. To her dismay she found it far different.

Last night she'd been lost. Totally and utterly lost. It had been like discovering a glorious private world, filled with beauty of sound and taste, scent and sensation. She'd been intrigued by what she'd discovered, but able to explore only the smallest part. Last night she'd barely stepped into that world.

Today it exploded around her, everything twice as intense, twice as spectacular, twice as overwhelming. And it left her utterly bewildered. A kiss was supposed to be just a kiss. A sweet joining of lips. A mild physical pleasure. Not this blistering desire that melted all intelligent thought. That had never happened to her before.

Lander reluctantly released her. "We're in serious trouble. You realize that, don't you?"

"We can handle it," she insisted. Did he catch the hint of desperation in her voice? "One night. That's all we can have. After that, we go our separate ways."

"Hell, woman. We can barely handle a simple kiss. You think after I make love to you, we'll be able to walk away from each other?"

"You promised!"

A hint of anger glinted in his eyes. "I've never broken my word, and I don't intend to start now, no matter how much I'd like to."

She'd have to be satisfied with that. "Where are we going?" she asked, intent on changing the subject.

"I have access to an apartment on the outskirts of the city. It's a secure location. With luck, no one will discover we're there."

To her relief, he was right. The limo pulled into a deserted underground garage and dropped them off by a private elevator before departing again. In less than two minutes the elevator whisked them upward, opening onto a penthouse suite. Lander locked the elevator in place to ensure they didn't receive any surprise visitors, before joining her in the middle of the foyer.

"It's lovely," Juliana murmured, struggling to conceal the distressing awkwardness sweeping through her.

"Feel free to look around."

Taking him at his word, she wandered from the foyer into a great room walled on two sides with windows overlooking the city of Mt. Roche. Adjacent to that she found a formal dining room with a compact kitchen beyond. Lander didn't follow her. Instead, he took up a stance between the foyer and great room, his gaze on her the entire time. Returning to her starting point she glanced toward the one section of the apartment she hadn't yet explored.

"Don't," Lander said.

She looked at him, startled. "Don't what?"

"It's the bedroom. You're welcome to check it out." He tilted his head to one side. "But somehow I don't think you're ready for that."

She wrapped her arms about her waist. "Is it so obvious?"

"What's obvious is that you're not ready for any of this." He straightened from his stance and approached. "If I were less selfish, I'd take you home. But I can't. I want you too much. And I think you want me, too."

As nervous as she was, she couldn't deny the truth. "You know I do."

"If you were willing to give me more than one night, we could avoid tonight's dilemma. We'd have the time to take our relationship slow and easy. What do you say? Wouldn't a gradual progression suit you far more than fast and reckless?" Wordless, she shook her head and he accepted her refusal with a shrug. "In that case, will you stay, or should we end this now?"

She hesitated. How could she have thought herself capable of a one-night stand with him? To go into it so cold-bloodedly when she'd never indulged in one before. She glanced uneasily across the foyer. If Lander hadn't locked the elevator, she'd be over there right now, stabbing at the button, determined to escape. She needed an out, even just the promise of one, so she wouldn't feel quite so much like a mouse caught beneath a cat's paw.

She cleared her voice. "If this doesn't work—"

"I'll take you home." Amusement rippled through his

words and she realized he'd been able to read her thoughts as though she'd shouted them aloud. "In the meantime, no pressure. I'll open a bottle of wine and we can talk."

"Sounds perfect."

And it was. They decided to watch the sunset from the balcony off the great room. Lander chose a French Beaujolais that went down as smooth and light as the conversation. He asked about her work with Arnaud's Angels, a subject dear to her heart. As they talked and drank, Juliana could feel her tension ease. They finished their wine just as the sun vanished behind the Mt. Roche skyline. The city lights sparkled in the growing darkness, winking up at the stars dotting the velvet canopy overhead.

Lander rose, offering his hand. "Are you hungry? I arranged for dinner to be delivered. It won't take long to heat."

She gazed up at him, wishing with all her heart that Lander were an ordinary man, or that she didn't have a past that curtailed any possibility of a relationship. That she were the sort of woman he could be seen with in public. Or he was in a position not to care about propriety or scandal.

Taking his hand, she stood. "Thank you, I'm starved. I worked through lunch today."

He maintained his stance, his face cast into shadow, while hers was bared by the light seeping onto the balcony from the great room. "What were you thinking about a minute ago?" he asked unexpectedly.

She regarded him warily. "Nothing important."

"Did you know that your eyes darken when you're not being honest?" He cupped her face, sweeping his thumbs along her cheekbones. "The brown swallows up the gold. Tell me the truth. What were you thinking?"

"That I was sorry we don't have longer than tonight," she confessed.

"That's your choice, not mine."

"Trust me when I say I have a valid reason."

"Tell me what it is."

"Maybe after dinner." He shook his head, rejecting the possibility, and she sighed. "My eyes, again?"

"Dead giveaway."

"Joc could always tell when I was lying, too. Now I know why."

She'd made a mistake mentioning her brother, she realized. Lander's hazel eyes didn't darken as hers had. Instead they flamed with odd green sparks. He shifted closer, joining her inside the circle of light. It sliced across his face, revealing the fierceness of his expression.

"I think it might be wise to leave your boss out of our conversation tonight." His voice scored the balmy dark with a wintry coldness. "Unless you want this night to end far differently than planned."

She considered backing down. But it had never been her style. She might be unwilling to reveal her true relationship with Joc or confess to the various scandals in her background. That didn't mean she'd allow him to believe she was one of her brother's women. "Are you jealous? Is that why you don't want me to mention Joc?"

"Yes."

He'd surprised her with his honesty. "Then allow me to reassure you. He and I aren't lovers. Not now. Not ever."

"Your relationship is strictly professional?" Lander asked dubiously.

"No," she admitted. "It's more than that, and always will be. We've known each other most our lives."

"Let me guess. He's like a brother to you."

She couldn't help but smile. "Exactly."

"I find it impossible to believe there's a man alive who could be around you for any length of time and not want you in his bed. Especially a man like Joc."

"Look at my eyes and tell me what you see. Truth… or lie?"

He took his time, his hands continuing to skim across her face as if he could absorb the information through his fingertips. After an endless minute his mouth curved to one side. "Truth."

"Is there anything else you want to ask me about Joc? Now's your chance."

"Not a thing."

"Good." She grinned. "In that case, let's eat. I really am starving."

She helped him heat their dinner and carry the meals to the table. "My stepmother was quite disgusted that we weren't expected to learn any domestic chores," he told her as he thanked her for her help. "But my father explained that it would have shocked the staff if we showed up in the kitchens expecting to cook our own meals or the laundry room to clean our clothes. My brother, Merrick, and I got off easy. Our stepsister, Miri, wasn't so lucky. When she joined our family, she learned the consequences of being stepdaughter to a king. Poor thing."

Juliana cupped her chin in her hand and gazed at him across the candlelit table. "Why poor thing?"

He shrugged. "She found it difficult to deal with the restrictions and all the protocol." His brows drew together. "Wasn't there a movie a while back along those lines? Something about an American girl who discovers she's a princess and has to learn how to act the part?"

"I remember it. Cute movie."

"Well, Miri lived it. Merrick and I had been trained for our roles since birth. Miri was seven when she came to live with us. It took a while before she fit in. And Merrick and I didn't make it easy for her, either. At least, not at first."

Something in his tone roused her curiosity. "What happened to change that?"

Lander's mouth compressed. "Merrick and I overheard someone telling her that she wasn't a 'real' princess. It was true, of course. She wasn't a princess. But I don't think she understood that until then. I'll never forget the expression on her face. It devastated her. From that moment on, Merrick and I closed ranks. She was our sister, if not by birth then by choice, and we weren't about to let anyone hurt her like that again. When my father discovered what happened, he adopted her and had her crowned Princess Miri."

"What a wonderful thing to do," Juliana marveled.

"My father was an amazing man." Lander's declaration held equal parts love and sorrow. "Not a day goes by that I don't miss him. I can only hope that if I'm elected I'll make half the king he did."

"I'm sure you will."

"Thanks for the vote of confidence, but everything considered, it won't be easy. Verdonia is facing some challenging times."

It didn't take much to read between the lines. "I've heard rumors about the amethysts. There's growing concern that the mines are played out. What will happen if it's true? Aren't the gems Verdonia's economic mainstay?"

"We'll find alternatives to help bolster the economy.

I'm considering a number of possibilities." Determination filled his expression. "It might take a while, but we're a strong people. We'll adapt."

Juliana lowered her gaze, a puzzle piece clicking into place. She'd wondered why Joc had come to Verdonia. He'd claimed it was to see her, to pressure her back into her old job. But she'd had trouble buying that. Now she suspected she had the answer. If Verdonia faced financial difficulties, who better to call in than financial wizard Joc Arnaud?

She didn't have long to dwell on the matter. Lander leaned forward and took her hand in his. "So, tell me, Juliana. Have you made a decision?"

His question caught her by surprise. "About what?"

"About tonight. Do you want an out?"

Didn't he know? Hadn't he sensed her decision? "I don't need an out." She fixed him with an unwavering look. "I'm staying."

"In that case, let's try a little experiment." Releasing her hand, he rose and crossed to her side. When she would have stood to join him, he pressed her back into her chair. "No, no. You don't need to move. Just sit for a minute."

"What are you going to do?" she asked, torn between apprehension and amusement.

"Just this." He released the clip anchoring her hair at the nape of her neck and filled his hands with the curls that tumbled free. "Soft. And much prettier loose."

"It's too curly." Her voice had grown thick and heavy. "It gets in the way."

"It won't get in my way."

His hands drifted downward to her neck, circling her throat. Sliding his palms along the lapels of her suit coat, he reached the first button and flicked it through the hole. One by one, he released them until the jacket parted. Still standing behind her, he turned his attention to her blouse. Again he took his time, unfastening button after button.

Her breath quickened with each one he loosened, and she fisted her hands around the arms of her chair. It seemed to take forever before he finished. Was he waiting for her to protest? To change her mind? It wouldn't happen. It was as though her inhibitions were released with each practiced flick, freeing her to express every sensation crashing through her. At long last he finished, sliding both jacket and blouse from her body.

"Nice," he commented, tracing the scalloped lace edging her bra. "Very nice. Who'd have guessed you were hiding something this sexy under such a prim business suit? Which is the truth, do you suppose? The suit or the lingerie?"

"What makes you think they're not both the truth?"

His index finger dipped beneath the lace and stroked. "Are they? Or is one truer than the other? Siren or businesswoman? Which is the better fit?"

"This morning, trying to change a baby's life, it was the businesswoman. Although I'm not sure that's even an accurate description. Perhaps *advocate* suits best. As for tonight…"

She stood, praying her legs would hold her. The instant she turned to face him, he kicked the chair out of the way. "What about tonight?" he asked.

"I'm not a siren. But I am a woman, a woman who wants you." She stepped closer. "You're wasting time. Are you going to take me or just talk about it?"

Four

Lander didn't need any further prompting. He swept Juliana into his arms and carried her to the bedroom. He didn't bother turning on the lights. A half-moon shone through the windows offering the perfect amount of illumination. He released her legs and allowed her to slide down his body, inch by luscious inch. The moon turned her into a palette of charcoal and silver—skin kissed with silver moonbeams, eyes as inky as the coal-black sky. Even her hair picked up the shades of the night, dousing the flames, if not the heat the color imitated.

He lowered his head, burying a kiss in the silken juncture of shoulder and throat. "One night," he whispered against her heated skin. "I swear I'll make it unforgettable."

He could feel her hands on his head, her fingers trembling as she threaded them into his hair. "I want unforgettable," she told him, holding him close. "Even more, I want to give it to you, as well."

"You already have."

He feathered kisses across her face, determined to taste every part of her. He was so intent on his exploration that he barely felt her unbutton his shirt or loosen his belt buckle. He fought against the urge to take, quickly and thoroughly. Juliana deserved more. If they only had one night, he would make certain they took their time and enjoyed every single second.

He found the zip at the side of her skirt and lowered it. To his amusement she rested her hands on his shoulders, and gave a rolling shimmy that sent the skirt drifting to the floor before nudging it aside. It left her standing in a pool of moonlight, clad in stockings and heels and a bra and thong. She paused then, and he caught a hint of vulnerability in her upturned face.

He traced her cheekbones with his thumbs. "What's wrong?"

"Nothing. I mean—" She made a small, fluttering gesture. "Nothing's wrong, exactly. It's just that I've known you barely a day."

"And yet you're standing in my bedroom, practically nude, about to make love to me."

He could feel a flush gather along her cheeks. "Yes."

"And it feels wrong."

"No." She shivered from the sudden chill that seemed to have invaded the room. Instead of wrapping her arms around herself or reaching for her clothes, as he half expected her to do, she shifted deeper into his arms, drawing warmth from him. "It feels right. It scares me how right it feels. How could that be in just a few short hours?"

She'd stunned him with her confession. Even more

unnerving was how her observation mirrored his own subconscious thoughts. Holding her, loving her, having her in his bed, his apartment, his life, did feel right. It wasn't a possibility he was willing to deal with, not when they only had this one night available to them.

This rightness, it had to result from the novelty of the situation. No more than that. Just lust. Once sated it would diminish, easing from this clawing necessity to something more manageable. Something that didn't tear him apart inside. Years from now when this time with Juliana came to mind, he'd smile reminiscently, savoring the faded memory the same way he savored a fine port or a Cuban cigar.

He glanced down at the woman he held, certain their reaction to each other was simple sexual attraction. How could it be anything more? Resolution filled him. He'd make the most of what they shared in the next few hours. Give her a memory she'd never forget, something she could savor, as well. And then it would end.

"It feels right because it is right," he reassured. For now. Knowing he had to be fair, he added, "We can stop. If it's only sex, it'll pass. We'll come to our senses, eventually." Maybe.

She laughed at that. "I don't think this will pass, not until we've done something about it."

Nor did he. "Then let's see how right we can make it."

There wasn't any talking after that. Focus narrowed, tightened. He could sense the slow build within her, the gradual drift from sweet want to desperate need. He curbed his impatience, the instinct to take her fast and thoroughly. To mark her as his. Instead, he continued on a slow, languid path, savoring each progressive step.

He unhooked her bra while she made short work of

his unbuttoned shirt. His slacks came next, along with her heels. He knelt to roll her stockings down the endless length of her legs, pausing periodically to kiss the path the drift of silk bared.

She clung to him for balance, shuddering beneath his caresses. "Hurry," she urged.

"Not a chance." He gave his undivided attention to the inner curve of her thigh, catching her as she sagged in his arms. "This is too important to rush."

Clothes ringed them in a tangled circle. Snatching a final kiss, he lifted her into his arms. He stepped from the circle of clothes and moonlight toward the shadowed bed, following her down onto the plush comforter. Her dark curls flowed out around her, captivating him. She was one of the most beautiful women he'd ever seen. Satin soft. Warm and generous. Filled with a hunger that matched his own. She returned his look, seducing him with a laugh as she melted against him.

"What would make you happy, love?" He filled his palms with her breasts and gently nipped at the rigid tips before laving them with his tongue. "This? Or how about…"

He trailed kisses downward, over the valley of her belly to the edge of her thong. Hooking his thumbs in the elastic riding her hips, he tugged, baring her. The perfume of her sex threatened to drive him insane. He found her with his mouth. Loved her. He heard her choked cry, her pleading words escaping in swift, desperate pants. Her muscles bunched, buttocks and thighs rippling beneath the strain, while she gathered up fistfuls of the comforter. Within minutes a high keening sob broke from her and she shattered in his arms.

"No, no." Her head moved restlessly back and forth. "It can't be over."

He soothed her with a gentle touch. "It's not over, love. It's just beginning."

He covered her body with his, stroking initially to calm, then to arouse. He'd promised himself when they'd met that he'd explore every inch of her body, and tonight he intended to do just that. They exchanged kisses, tentative at first, then with growing ardor. He'd anticipated a slow burn, building bit by bit, log heaped on burning log. But it was nothing like that. Wildfire exploded, sweeping fierce and reckless in one direction then another, overrunning sense and sensibility until they were both caught up in a maelstrom beyond their control.

His hands played over her until he heard the hitch in her breath that warned of her approaching climax. He sought out the heart of her, cupping the source of the fire. He'd done this to her. His touch had brought her to the brink once again. The knowledge roused something indescribable in him, awakening an emotion he couldn't put name to or fully understand. It was primal and viscerally male. A word echoed in the deepest recesses of his mind. A single word, chanted over and over again, like a mantra, offering both promise and intent.

Mine.

Juliana's voice joined the chorus. "Please. Please, Lander. Take me now. Make me yours."

He levered above her and dipped himself in her liquid heat. She wrapped her legs around him, locking him tightly against her. He surged, deep and hard, stroking into her. He'd never in his life felt anything like it. So snug and sleek. Almost virginal. She gasped out his name and when he moved even that one word was lost to her.

Still, he heard her singing, a soft musical cry of urgency and delight. Of wonder. Of rapture. And somehow he knew—knew without doubt or question—that it was a song she'd never sung before. That the woman in his arms wasn't almost virginal. Until just seconds ago, she'd been a virgin. She'd given herself to him without condition or hesitation, despite there being no future in it for either of them.

He mated their bodies, filling her again and again, whispering words, endless words, he couldn't afterward recall. They poured from the very heart of him as he poured his heart and soul into her. She arched beneath him, and the building came, faster and more powerful than before. It pounded unrelentingly until they reached the dizzying crest, teetering there for an endless second. The climax came, so hard and merciless, that all they could do was surrender to its taking, clinging to each other in its aftermath.

Breathless, they collapsed in a tangle of slick arms and legs, utterly spent. He had no idea how long they lay there while their bodies cooled, then chilled. Flinging out a hand, Lander snagged a section of comforter and pulled it over them, cocooning them in a silken nest.

Forever passed before passion eased and his brain began to function again. "Why, Juliana?" He rolled onto his side, levering himself upward onto an elbow. "Why didn't you tell me?"

To his frustration the bed remained in shadow, concealing her expression. Even so, he could hear the wariness in her voice. "Tell you what?"

"Don't pretend. You've never done anything like this before. Why now? Why me?"

She shrugged. "Because it felt right."

"That's not good enough."

She sat up, and this time the moon did find her, cutting across her face and lapping over her bared shoulders. "Do you think I wanted it to be you? That I wasn't hoping for more than you have to offer? More than I can give you? But when you touch me..." She turned her face away. "Is it just me? Or do you feel it, too? Isn't that why I'm here?"

"Hell. I'm sorry." He snagged a rope of curls and tugged until she looked at him again. "It just caught me by surprise. I find it hard to believe that there hasn't been a man in your life before this."

"There was a man."

A possessive stab caught Lander by surprise. "Obviously things didn't work out, because there's no question in my mind that he never had you in his bed."

"No." The intense pain in that single word had him wanting to gather her up and protect her from everyone and everything that might hurt her again. "He wanted to seduce me for reasons of his own. I found out before I made the ultimate mistake."

Possessiveness turned to cold anger. "A Verdonian?"

"No, Your Highness." A hint of gold flickered in her eyes, highlighting her amusement. "Not a Verdonian. The dungeons and torture rooms won't be needed."

"I'd have done it," he growled.

"Let's forget about Stewart." She rolled on top of him and captured his mouth with hers. "Isn't there something else you'd rather be doing?"

It was an offer he couldn't resist. The remaining hours of the night flowed from one unforgettable moment into another until exhaustion overtook them and they finally slept. When next Lander awoke, sunlight enveloped the room, filling it with a sparkling brilliance. But the warmth had fled.

Juliana was gone.

Juliana lifted her face to the first rays of the morning sun. Rather than hail a cab, she decided to walk for a while, needing the exercise to help center herself. Initially, her steps were light and joyous, the blood singing through her veins. Last night was the most incredible of her life. She'd never imagined lovemaking could be so earth-shattering. The fact that one man could make her feel so loved and cherished, amazed her every bit as much as it confused her. But Lander had done that and more.

A secret smile swept across her mouth and a passing pedestrian returned the smile with a wink and a grin. She shook her head, marveling. Imagine a lifetime filled with nights like the one she'd just experienced. Greeting each day locked in Lander's arms, having the right to stay there as long as she wanted. And imagine waking each morning filled with a jubilance and contentment that surpassed anything she'd dared believe possible. She hugged the emotions close, reveling in them.

Until she remembered.

Lander could never be a part of her life. She'd never know what it felt like to awaken in his arms, because it would never happen. She'd agreed to give him a single night, no more. And he'd accepted the offer and promised not to ask for another. Even if he wanted to see her again, to continue their relationship, it was impossible.

Maybe he'd have succeeded in tempting her if he could have guaranteed that their affair would remain secret. But she'd had enough experience with the paparazzi to know better. Eventually they'd discover Lander was seeing her. And once they did, they'd ferret out her identity. Her real identity. When that happened, it would cost Lander big-time. He might very well lose the election because of her and she couldn't bear it if that happened. Besides it wasn't like she'd be staying in Verdonia much longer. Soon she'd move on to another European country.

Her energy drained away, her earlier euphoria fizzling like a spent firecracker. Hailing a cab, she sat in the back, fighting tears. She tried to run through a series of mathematical equations to calm herself, but even that was beyond her. Ten minutes later she arrived outside of her apartment building. Paying the driver, she entered the complex and took the elevator to the tenth floor, grateful that she had no work pending and could take the day off to lick her wounds. To her dismay, even that was denied her. Stepping into her apartment, she found Joc waiting. She took one look at her brother and burst into tears.

"Aw, hell," he muttered, gathering her into his arms. "What did that bastard do to you?"

"Nothing. Everything." She fought to regain control with only limited success. "I'm sorry, Joc. I don't know what's the matter with me."

"I told you to stay away from him. Naturally you didn't listen and now he's made you cry." Beneath the brotherly concern she heard a ferocity that alarmed her. "No one's made you cry since Stewart."

His comment stopped her cold. She remembered all too well what he'd done to Stewart for that single affront. The only jobs still available to him involved mops and buckets of soapy water.

"No!" She pulled back, fisting her hands in her brother's shirt. "Now you listen up, big brother. You stay out of this. Lander didn't make me cry. I'm serious. He didn't."

He greeted her reassurance with skepticism. "Then why are you so upset?"

"Because he wanted to continue the relationship and I refused to even consider it."

It wasn't precisely accurate, but she didn't doubt for a minute that if she'd made the offer, Lander would have accepted without hesitation. He'd wanted her to stay with him. The desire had been buried in every whispered word, in each hungry kiss, in his first tender caress, straight through to his last. He'd overwhelmed her with want, seduced her with a need she'd never realized she possessed. If she'd been able to find the least little excuse for remaining with him, she'd have seized it without hesitation. But there hadn't been any reasonable excuses. The risk was too great, protecting Lander's reputation paramount. That far outweighed her petty wishes.

Joc shook his head. "You're not making a bit of sense. That alone is peculiar, considering you're one of the most rational, analytical women I know. If Lander still wants you, then what's the problem?"

"You know what the problem is."

A muscle jerked in his jaw. "You're afraid people will find out who you are and dig up old history about you. And you don't want to be in that sort of media frenzy again."

"Yes." She let go of his shirt, trying to smooth the wrinkles as assiduously as she tried to smooth the pain from her face. "You were right to warn me away from him. He's a prince. I'm no one. I'm worse than no one.

If his people find out who I am or about my background, he'll lose the election."

"You don't know that, not for sure," he protested.

"Yes, I do." She took a step back and offered her most implacable expression, the one she used when dealing with recalcitrant clients. "It's over, Joc. I had my one night with him. That's all I asked for or wanted, and it's exactly what I received." It would be foolish to hope for more.

"Are you certain? I can fix this, if you want."

"I'm positive. And no, I don't want you to fix a thing." She managed a quick, bright smile. "Seriously. Stay out of it."

Joc met her smile with one of his own, his a hard flash of white against his sun-darkened skin. "Okay, Ana." He tucked a tumble of curls behind her ear. "After all, haven't I always given you everything you wanted?"

"Yes, you have." But he couldn't help her this time, she realized. What she wanted wasn't his to give.

The instant the door closed behind her brother, the dam broke and with it came the realization that by allowing herself to become emotionally involved with the one man she couldn't have, she'd totally and completely ruined her life.

Lander stared at Arnaud in stunned disbelief. "What did you say?"

"You heard me." Determination was carved into every line of Joc's face. "I want you to marry my sister. In fact, our negotiations hinge on that very point."

Lander sliced his hand through the air, cutting him off. "Forget it. Maybe if you'd approached me a week ago. *Maybe* I'd have considered it. I'm that desperate. But not now."

"Because of Juliana."

He hadn't felt this possessive toward a woman ever. "Yes, because of Juliana."

"I thought it was a one-night stand."

"You bastard! Did she tell you that?"

"I have no intention of betraying her confidence." A hint of mockery crept into Joc's voice. "As far as I'm concerned you have two choices. I can either beat you to a bloody pulp for messing with Juliana, or I can make you pay for what you did to her by forcing you to give up your precious freedom. Personally, whaling on you for a bit holds far more appeal."

In two strides Lander was across the room and had Joc by the throat and up against the nearest wall. "What's your relationship with her?" he demanded. "She swore you weren't lovers, something I can verify as fact. So, why are you throwing up roadblocks between us? Why put your sister in the middle of all this? You want Juliana for yourself, don't you?"

To Lander's surprise Joc didn't try and break his hold. "I want Juliana to be happy."

"And marrying your sister will make her happy?" That didn't make sense.

"I believe so." Joc actually had the nerve to laugh. "Why don't I show you a picture of my sister."

"What the hell good will that do?" He released Joc with an exclamation of disgust. "You think I'm going to take one look at her and fall madly in love?"

Joc shrugged. "It could happen." He removed a snapshot from his wallet and spun it in Lander's direction. "Why don't we try it and see."

Lander caught the photo midair. Flipping it over, he stared at the picture in sheer disbelief.

"My sister. Juliana Rose Arnaud. I always called her Ana." Joc shrugged. "I guess the nickname carries bad memories, so she doesn't use it anymore."

It took Lander two tries before he could speak. "This has been a setup from the beginning, hasn't it?" He shot Joc a furious glare. "I call you for help and who shows up at the ball while I'm waiting for you, but your sister—a sister who's conveniently forgotten her last name's Arnaud. She falls into my arms like a ripe peach and after we spend one unforgettable night together all of a sudden I find out the two of you are related. And coincidence of all coincidences, the very next day you're holding our contract for ransom."

Joc shook his head. "Clever plan. I wish I could actually take credit for it. But I can't, because it didn't go down that way."

"I don't care how it went down. I suggest you get the hell out of Verdonia while you still have your head attached to your shoulders."

Joc held up a hand in an appeasing gesture. "Look, I swear there was no setup. I tried to warn her about you, Montgomery. I can't tell you how many times I advised her to give you a wide berth. But Juliana has a soft spot for jackals like you and once your relationship took a turn for the worse, this seemed an obvious solution."

"Not to me."

A hint of anger glittered in Joc's black gaze. "Maybe you should have thought of that before your North Pole got overruled by the southern half of your equator. Now let's talk turkey because this is how it's going down. I'm making a one-time offer. You refuse, I walk. And your precious country can go bankrupt for all I care."

Son of a— "What do you want?"

"Your end of our business arrangement is simple. Get my sister to fall in love with you. Should be easy since she's halfway there already. Marry her. Treat her like the queen she deserves to be. Live happily ever after. Hell, have babies if you're so inclined." He paused, shooting Lander a keen look. "Think you can do that?"

Babies? An image of redheaded toddlers racing through the palace came all too easily to mind. He took a step back, mentally and literally. "I think you're interfering where you don't belong."

The two locked gazes for an endless minute. "But you'll do it, won't you?" Joc demanded. "You'd do anything to save your country, including marry my sister."

Lander ground his teeth in silent fury. "Yes," he finally bit out.

"Even if it means being related to me?" Joc pressed harder. "And even if our connection causes you to lose the election?"

It very well might. Lander turned away and allowed the possibility to settle into his heart and mind. Not that it took much thought. He'd seen Arnaud's plan for Verdonia. It was a good one, one that had an excellent shot at ensuring full financial recovery. Setup or not, if the price he had to pay for that was marriage, he'd do it. If it meant saving Verdonia from economic disaster, he'd have married a two-headed goat, and Juliana was far from that.

Still, he didn't like Joc's tactics anymore than he liked suspecting someone as open and candid as Juliana of deceit. Granted, she'd concealed her full name from him, but he had a feeling that was a one-time aberration. What he liked least of all was being forced to marry on command. He'd always been the one in charge of his own destiny. He'd always been the one to command. It rankled more than a little to play puppet to Joc's puppeteer.

Turning, he asked, "I gather she's not to know about the addendum to our contract?"

"That would be a definite deal breaker."

It confirmed Lander's suspicion that if this was a setup, Juliana had played the part of unwitting pawn. "Just one question." He approached. "Why? You can't honestly believe this is in your sister's best interest?"

He didn't think Arnaud would answer. Emotions swept across the Texan's face. Anger. Stubborn determination. And—hell, could it be?—an odd vulnerability. "You're wrong, Montgomery," he said at last. "This is in her best interest. I couldn't protect her growing up. I'm not even much good at protecting her now." His expression hardened. "But you can do what I can't. You can give her everything she needs, everything I've never been able to."

Lander wanted to argue the point. This was a huge mistake, one he didn't doubt he'd live long to regret. But he didn't see any other choice. He wanted to explain what a disservice it was to Juliana to be married for financial gain rather than love. That she wouldn't appreciate this sort of manipulation any more than he did. But he knew from long experience that once Arnaud set his mind to something, he was impossible to budge. There might be room for negotiation later on, a better opportunity to apply calm reason to reckless obsession. Until then, Lander had no choice.

"Do we have a deal?" Joc asked impatiently.

"Yes, it's a deal."

He took Arnaud's hand in a tight grip, grinding bone against bone as he fixed the man with a fierce stare.

"Someday you'll find yourself boxed into a corner like this. Remember me when that happens, Arnaud. Remember, and know that you brought it on yourself when you forced this agreement on the woman you should have protected, and the one man who will do whatever it takes to see that you pay for your arrogance."

Five

Juliana finished the last of her paperwork, signing her name with a swift practiced stroke, before shoving the folder to one side of her desk. Swiveling to face the window, she leaned back in her chair and closed her eyes. Exhaustion threatened to overwhelm her. The past three days had been hideous, perhaps because she'd chosen to work nonstop rather than pacing herself. But at least it had kept her from obsessing over Lander and that one unforgettable night.

A knock sounded at her door, and she stifled a groan. The clock on the wall warned it was well past seven. The office staff should have long since cleared out, with the possible exception of her assistant. She heard him push open the door but didn't bother to open her eyes. "Colin, I thought I told you to go home an hour ago," she complained. Her assistant didn't answer, but she could hear him approach, no doubt to get the last of the papers she'd signed. "Didn't you have a date tonight?"

To her shock, he put his hands on her, his fingers digging into the knots of tension ridging her shoulders. Her eyes blinked open and she shot straight up in her chair. "Good Lord. Colin?"

"Gone."

"Lander!" She swiveled around, staring up at him in disbelief. "What are you doing here?"

"I came to see you, of course."

He plucked her out of the chair and into his arms. For an instant she allowed herself to relax against him before common sense prevailed and she fought her way free of his hold. "Please don't take this the wrong way, but…why?"

"Because of this."

Lowering his head, he teased her mouth with his. She had every intention of stopping him, of pulling back from those coaxing lips. Of telling him firmly and unequivocally that she had no interest in seeing him ever again. Her good intentions lasted all of two seconds.

With a groan she gave up and fell into the embrace. She twined her arms around his neck and practically inhaled him. He walked her backward the two paces to her desk and lifted her onto the wooden surface. Her skirt hitched upward and he planted his hands on her knees and parted them. Stepping between, he tugged her tight against him.

"What are we doing?" she demanded, torn between laughter and tears.

"What we were meant to do."

"We agreed to a single night."

"Your choice, not mine. And like a fool, I didn't push

hard enough." He broke off to kiss her again, deep, drugging kisses. "But I've decided I want to renegotiate the terms of that agreement."

She started shaking her head before he'd finished speaking. "No. No, I can't. You have to trust that I have an excellent reason. Several of them, actually."

"Give me one."

She struggled to balance truth with caution. "You have an election coming up. You need to focus on that."

"My personal life has never interfered with my duty to my country. You should know, that takes primary importance over everything. Always," he emphasized. Sweeping the clip from her hair, he forked his fingers through the mass of curls. "But that doesn't mean I don't have time for you, as well. What's your next excuse for ending our relationship?"

"A point of clarity, if you don't mind. We don't have a relationship."

He merely smiled. His hands dropped to her legs, sliding upward, gathering her skirt as he went. "Tell me what you call it."

She shuddered beneath his touch, struggling to maintain an ounce of reason in the midst of this insanity. "A one-night stand."

His grip tightened on her thighs. "Don't." The single word sounded harsh, almost guttural. "Don't denigrate what happened between us."

"I'm just being honest." She struggled to tidy a messy situation, regardless of the pain it caused. To fit it neatly into its appropriately labeled box, a sealed box etched with "one-night stand" on the lid in indelible marker. "And though I can't explain all the problems it will cause if we continue to see each other, it's important you believe me. That you believe that it's best for Verdonia."

He dismissed her assertion with a shrug. "Why don't you let me decide that. There's only one question you need to answer. Was our one night together enough?"

She closed her eyes, dropping her head to his shoulder. "Please don't ask me that."

"Too late." She could feel his smile against the side of her neck. "Be honest, Juliana. You want more, just as I do."

The temptation to admit the truth was overwhelming. "Yes," she whispered. "I want more. But I'm begging you to walk away. There's so much you don't know about me."

His mouth traced a path along her neck to a sweet spot just beneath her ear. "In time, when you learn to trust me, you can tell me all your secrets."

Didn't he understand? With an effort, she lifted her head to look at him. "You're better off not knowing."

"At some point you'll tell me." He repeated the assertion with casual certainty. "You won't have any choice."

"You're probably right." She released her breath in a sigh. "If I agree, there are conditions."

"Name them."

"No one can know about us. And I mean no one."

"Agreed. Next."

"No falling in love."

To her surprise, that gave him pause. "You think you can order love? Where have I heard that before?"

"I don't know." Where had he? "But we can try."

"Sex and nothing but sex?"

It sounded so crude. So harsh. Not that she had any other option. She couldn't afford to fall in love with Lander. "Would that be so wrong?"

"Yes." He lifted her chin, forcing her to meet his

green-flecked eyes. She caught a hint of amusement, softened by tenderness. "Yes, it's wrong. But you'll need to discover that for yourself. What other conditions do you have?"

She hadn't a clue what else. Maybe if she'd anticipated this conversation, she'd have had a list prepared. Neatly numbered and bulleted, of course. But she'd ended things between them. She distinctly remembered doing it, even though it had ripped her apart. She'd cried over him and everything. And yet here he was, standing between her thighs with her skirt hiked to her hips and eighty-six combined inches of leg locked around his waist.

She shook her head. "I don't know. I'll give you the rest when I can think straight."

"In that case, I'm not sure I want you thinking straight." To her surprise, his grip firmed on her hips, pulling her so tightly against him that his belt buckle bit into her abdomen. "If that's everything, I suggest we get on with it."

"Excuse me?" She wriggled in discomfort. "You can't mean—"

"I do mean," he confirmed. "Right here and right now."

Had he gone crazy? She eyed him uncertainly. "Some women might want to make love on top of a desk, but I'm not one of them."

"Really?" A slight smile curved his lips and his gaze ran over her, lingering. "What happened to sex and nothing but sex?"

She became vividly aware of how she must look, her hair rioting around her shoulders, her skirt flipped back to expose everything from her waist down, her legs clasped about him. Heat scored her cheekbones and she had trouble meeting his gaze. "Not here," she whispered. "Not like this."

"I don't understand. I thought you said it's just sex, no emotion involved." He ran the tip of his finger over the swell of her breast. He'd touched her in a similar manner on a number of occasions, but this time it felt different. Careless. Distant. Carnal. "It's not like we need a bed. We can do it right here." He glanced around. "Or up against the wall over there. Or on the floor. Rug burns, but what the hell. I'm hungry, I eat. Isn't that how it works?"

She unwound her legs from his waist and shoved at his shoulders. Not that it did any good. He remained as unyielding as granite. "Please, move. I want to get off the desk."

"I'm serious, Juliana. Explain it to me. What does it matter where?" His hands dropped to her thighs. "Or how?"

She covered his hands with hers, attempting to stop those clever fingers from exploring any further. To her horror, tears pricked her eyes and her throat closed over, making it a struggle to respond. "It just does, okay?"

His hold eased. Gentled. Cupping her face, he leaned forward and kissed her. "And that, my beautiful Juliana, proves my point. Sex alone will never be enough for either of us because it's innately wrong." Stepping back, he helped her off the desk. With a few swift tugs, he straightened her clothing. "I'm sorry if I upset you."

She wobbled on her heels, struggling to regain her composure. "If that's how you feel—that it can't just be about sex, then why did you agree when I suggested it?"

He shot her a wicked look. "Oh, I'd have been willing to give it a try, if you insisted."

"Magnanimous of you," she muttered.

"I thought so." His smile faded. "But in the end, we'd have failed."

"And one of us would have gotten hurt." She rested her head against his shoulder. "So why are we doing this?"

His arms slid around her. "Because we don't have any other choice."

He made it sound as though fate had set something in motion, something they could neither change nor escape, assuming they wanted to. She felt a sudden urge to run. To return with Joc to Dallas. She was good at running. She'd done it often enough. Her breath trembled in a sigh. She'd done it often enough to know it never worked. If people wanted to find you, they could. If they wanted to expose you, they did.

Chances were, running and hiding wouldn't work this time, either. But until the truth came out—and it always came out—she'd enjoy however much time she had with Lander and hope it was enough. It would have to be.

"So what now?" she asked.

"Now we play."

She glanced up at him, intrigued. "Play?"

"You look confused. Haven't you ever played before?"

She thought about it before slowly shaking her head. "Not really."

"Then it's past time you started."

The nights following flew by as though part of a dream. During the daylight, Juliana worked harder than she thought possible so she could enjoy those few precious nighttime hours with Lander. It became like a game. Late each afternoon she'd receive a phone call giving her a different location to meet, each in a section of the city free from curious eyes. And every evening she'd escape work and race to wherever she'd been directed.

She always found a different vehicle waiting for her, the only thing they had in common a unifying anonymity in appearance that guaranteed they'd fade in with every other car on the busy streets of Mt. Roche.

The first night she was driven to an underground garage, and had expected to find herself back at the apartment complex where she'd made love to Lander. But that hadn't happened. Instead, she ended up in one of the downtown malls. Even though all the shops were lit, to her astonishment not a soul stirred. She and Lander spent the entire night wandering through the mall, laughing at the insanity of having the entire place to themselves. Every once in a while she'd catch a glimpse of the security guards who shadowed their every move. She hadn't noticed them the night she'd spent at his apartment, but she had an uneasy feeling they'd been there, regardless.

Most of the time she could ignore their presence and dart from store to store, trying on clothes or jewelry or shoes, or wandering through the bookstores or among the craft stalls. Just as exhaustion set in, dinner miraculously appeared at a small table inside a trendy café. They dined by candlelight, soft music playing in the background. When they'd finished, Lander escorted her back to the car she'd arrived in, which, to her astonishment, delivered her home again.

The next night Lander arranged for a private showing at a movie theater. Another evening found them wandering through a wild animal park on the outskirts of the city. He took her ice skating. Swimming. He even arranged for a night at a spa. But not once did he take her back to the apartment and make love to her as she longed for him to do.

He must have been aware of her confusion, just as he must have been aware of how much she wanted to be in his arms again. She didn't understand it. As impossible as it seemed, it was almost as though he were… wooing her. But that didn't make a bit of sense.

On the tenth night, her car pulled into another underground garage. Once again she thought perhaps it was the apartment complex, and hope flared. But when she stepped from the vehicle, one of Lander's private bodyguards whisked her along a set of unfamiliar corridors dotted with security. He paused before a heavy steel door, guarded by his hulking counterpart.

Opening the door, he gestured for her to enter. "Please go on through, Ms. Rose," he said. "Tell His Highness that I'm here if he needs anything."

Before she could ask the guard where she was, the door clanged shut behind her. Subdued lighting suffused the room, and it took a minute for her eyes to adjust. Once they had, she was astonished to discover she stood in a museum.

"It's one of my favorite places to come." Lander spoke from the shadows across the room. He flicked on a light switch, flooding the room with a brighter glow. "Do you like museums?"

"Yes," she confessed. "Very much."

"This one has it all. Art. History. Science."

The hours flowed one into the next as he led her through each wing. As they explored the section detailing Verdonia's rich history, Lander brought it to life with stories that gave added depth and color to each exhibit. Later, they ate picnic-style on the floor in front of a

Monet and a Renoir with a Rodin sculpture guarding them from the corner. And they talked, endlessly.

The evening concluded in a small secure room housing the crown jewels of Verdonia. "The ones not in use," Lander teased.

To her astonishment, he opened the cases and lifted out various pieces for her to try on. "I'm afraid to touch them," she told him. "I half expect your guards to burst in here and arrest me."

"I have to admit, you're the first woman outside the royals who's ever had the opportunity to do this." He fastened a necklace dripping with diamonds and amethysts around her neck. "What do you think?"

Mirrors lined the back of each display case and she stood in front of one to look, watching the gems dance and glitter with her every breath. "It's stunning."

"It was a wedding gift from my father to my mother, along with these." He lifted out a tiara and settled it in her curls. Then he slipped a ring on her finger, the central stone a huge amethyst, the purplish-blue depths flashing with red fire. "This ring's called Soul Mate, which is actually what the Verdonia Royal symbolizes."

"Verdonia Royal? Is that what the amethyst is called?"

"That particular color. There's not another shade quite like it anywhere else in the world. We also have pink stones which are far more common, but popular, nonetheless."

"A Rose de France? I've heard of them."

He glared at her in mock anger. "Please. Celestia Blush."

She swept him a deep, graceful courtesy. "I beg your pardon, Your Highness. I misspoke. I swear it won't happen again."

"See that it doesn't."

Rising, she studied the circle of Blushes that surrounded the Royal. "Does the Blush have a special meaning, too?"

Lander nodded. "It signifies the sealing of a contract. When it's set in a circle like this it denotes a binding agreement, in this case a marriage."

"It's beautiful." She glanced at him hesitantly. "You must miss your mother very much."

"She died when I was very young, Merrick little more than a baby. My memories are more…impressions. Feelings of warmth and comfort."

His expression remained open, so she risked another question. "You said it took a while to adjust to your stepsister's advent in your life. What about your stepmother's?"

"She's an impressive lady." An odd smile curved his mouth. "Did you know she designed her own engagement ring?"

"Really? What does it look like?"

"There's a replica of it over here."

She joined him in front of a display case and stared at the ring. It was quite different from the one belonging to Lander's mother. Three gem stones—a diamond, an emerald and a ruby—made up the central portion of the ring, the trio surrounded by a circle of alternating Verdonia Royals and sapphires.

"It means something, doesn't it?"

"Yes." A poignant quality had crept into his voice. "And once Merrick and I figured it out, we became a family."

"Birthstones?"

"Clever, Juliana. Yes, they're birthstones. The three in the center represent Merrick, Miri and me. All of them are of exact equal weight, cut and clarity."

"And the circle of amethysts and sapphires? Your father and stepmother?"

"The amethyst, ironically enough, is my stepmother's birthstone. The sapphire, my father's. And if you look carefully at the gold filigree that makes up the rest of the ring, it spells out two words in Verdonian."

It took Juliana a moment to find the words hidden in the pattern. "Love and…unity?"

"A circle of love and unity around the three most precious people in their lives. She's a special woman, my stepmother." He paused a beat. "You'd enjoy meeting her, as she would you."

His comment brought her down to earth with painful swiftness. Her reflection bounced back from a dozen different mirrors, mocking her. She stood in fantasy, arrayed in jewels she had no right to wear. A tiara worn by a queen. A necklace given as a royal wedding gift. A ring that connected two soul mates.

It hurt. It hurt to know that she would never be the recipient of such gifts. Oh, not the gems. She didn't care about those. It was the love and commitment and promise they stood for. Perhaps the women in her family were never meant to know those things. Certainly, her mother had never received as much from her father, though she'd kept hoping against hope, right up until her death.

Without a word Juliana turned her back on Lander, at the same time turning her back on a reflection that was just that—a reflection of reality. "I don't think I can work the clasp," she said, relieved that she sounded so calm. With luck she'd concealed her inner turmoil. "Would you mind?"

"Are you certain? I thought we could—"

She rounded on him, not so calm anymore, the

turmoil slipping from her control and spilling loose. "Could what? Indulge in a little make-believe? Were you going to put on a crown and play Prince Charming to my Cinderella again?"

He twined a length of her hair around his fingers. The curls clung to him like the roses had clung to a midnight arbor in a dream they'd shared on a night not long ago. "I've hurt you. I'm sorry. That wasn't my intention."

Pain threatened to overwhelm her, and it took a full minute to recover her equilibrium. "Thank you for a lovely evening, but it's time for me to return home now."

Home. Not that she actually had one. Her Verdonian apartment wasn't a true home. An image of a Texas hacienda flashed through her mind, filling her with a vague yearning. Nor was Dallas. Not any longer. She'd lost all that at the tender age of eight. Her mouth twisted. Or rather, she'd lost the illusion then. The pretense of hearth and home.

Without a word he reached behind her and unclasped the necklace. The tiara proved more problematic, tangling in curls that seemed reluctant to part with it. When she would have yanked it free, Lander stopped her, gently coaxing it loose.

"There," he said at last, dropping a kiss on top of her head. "Not a single hair lost."

His comment knocked her off-kilter. He hadn't been careful out of concern for the tiara, but so he wouldn't hurt her. Her breath escaped in a gusty sigh. "What are we doing? What are *you* doing?"

"Don't you know?"

She shook her head. "To be perfectly honest, I haven't a clue."

"You're a smart woman. You'll figure it out eventually."

"I don't want to figure it out eventually." She studied him, attempting to analyze the situation. She should be able to logic it out. To add it up or puzzle it through, or apply reason to the problem and come up with a simple solution. One plus one always equaled two. But no matter how hard she tried, nothing made sense. "You're playing some sort of game. I wish I knew what it was."

He paused in the process of returning the pieces of jewelry to the display cases. "This is no game."

"Are you trying to seduce me?" She shook her head as soon as she'd posed the question. "That doesn't make sense. I vaguely recall you did that already."

He lifted an eyebrow. "If it's such a vague memory, I must have done something wrong." He locked the case. "Perhaps there's another explanation. A very simple, very obvious one."

"Wait. You forgot the ring." She slipped it from her finger and held it out to him. "The only explanation that makes any sense is that you're still trying to prove that what we feel isn't lust. Like you did in my office."

He took the ring from her. But instead of returning it to the display case, he pocketed it. "Close, but not quite there."

"I give up. Tell me what's going on."

"What about love?"

He shocked her so that she couldn't think of a single thing to say. Taking her arm, he escorted her through the door protected by his bodyguards and to the car that had delivered her to the museum. The engine started with a soft purr and they exited from the garage onto a rain-slicked street. Lightning speared the sky while thunder cleared its throat. Heavy droplets pounded the front windshield, their descent as fast and dizzying as her thoughts.

In no time they pulled into a garage, and this time she recognized it as the one to his apartment. He parked the car and glanced at her. There wasn't an ounce of question in that silent look, just heated demand. She gave him her response by exiting the car and slamming the door. Then she stalked to the elevator, thunder rumbling approval with every step she took.

"It's not possible," she announced the minute they stepped from the elevator into the apartment.

A crash of thunder shook the building and Lander waited until it had died before asking, "What isn't possible?"

"True love. Fairy-tale romances. Happily ever after."

He glanced her way, the soft glow from a nearby lamp providing enough illumination to reveal his curiosity. "You don't believe in love? Or you don't believe in love at first sight?"

"I'm not sure I believe in either one," she confessed.

"Interesting, considering what happened when we met."

Her throat tightened. "What did happen, exactly?"

"Why don't I show you instead."

He lowered his head and sampled her mouth. Her lips parted beneath the onslaught. It was such a sweet joining, thorough and tender. When he would have pulled back, she thrust her fingers deep into his hair to prevent him and deepened the kiss. She couldn't deal with tender right now, couldn't handle all that it suggested about their relationship. But she'd accept thorough—accept it, as well as give it. She drank with greedy abandonment, consumed with a driving need to seize what he'd been promising for the past ten days.

The storm broke overhead, and the air quickened,

filled with an energy and electricity that fueled their taking, one of the other. It was fast. Edged with violence. A battle for supremacy between male and female. He drove her toward the bedroom just as lightning flared, turning the room a stark blue white and revealing a man pushed past reason. Exhilarated, she pushed harder.

"Show me more," she demanded, ripping at his clothing.

"Until there's no more to show." He stripped her with swift economy before dealing with the few remaining pieces of his own clothing. And then there was no more talking. The first moment of intense rapture caught them both by surprise, a swift, needy explosion of sheer ecstasy that mirrored the storm raging overhead.

"Tell me now that you don't believe in love," he demanded as he drove into her, sending her soaring again. "Deny it if you can."

Her breath caught on a sob. "I can't. You know I can't."

And as the heavens opened, flooding the earth, Juliana opened herself, heart and soul, no longer able to hide from the truth. She loved this man. Loved him more than she believed possible. It was as though her revelation gentled the storm. The thunder lost its voice, fading to a distant grumble, while the lightning flashed a soft farewell.

In that perfect moment they came together again. Slowly. Easily. With piercing sensitivity. Moving together in exquisite harmony.

Juliana closed her eyes, forced to accept the truth. They moved together in the ultimate expression of love.

Six

Lander woke, delighted to discover he still held Juliana in his arms. Rain-washed sunlight spilled across the bed and into her eyes, causing her to stir. With a gasp she sat up, one elbow just missing his jaw, the other nailing his gut with pinpoint accuracy. Whereas the night before she'd been all grace and poetry in motion, the morning turned her awkward and uncertain. He found it unbelievably endearing.

"Good morning," he said, once he could draw breath.

She gazed up at him, blinking the remnants of sweet dreams from her eyes. "I overslept, didn't I?"

"A bit." Unable to resist, he buried his hands in her hair, realizing as he did so how much he enjoyed the soft, springy texture, as well as the way the curls clung to his fingers. He gave her a slow, lingering kiss. "But if that means waking with you in my arms, rather than finding you've slipped out the door, so much the better."

"It's definitely better," she confessed with an abashed smile. "If not conducive to good work habits."

In that moment she looked as far removed from the self-confident businesswoman as he'd ever seen—not to mention the seductive siren who'd first captured his interest. He wasn't certain which aspect of her personality appealed the most. Right now he found the rumpled urchin a fascination he'd love to spend the rest of the morning exploring.

Before he could suggest it, a tiny frown crinkled her forehead. "What time is it, do you know?"

"Ten."

She nearly hyperventilated. "Work. Office. Late. Very, very late."

He shrugged, unconcerned. "Tell them you're with me."

That gave her pause, if only for an instant. At least it gave her enough time to calm down. "Wait a minute. Are you telling me that sleeping with the Prince of Verdon gives me a free pass at work?"

A smile slashed across his face. "Duke of Verdon," he corrected. "Prince of Verdonia. And I've been thinking of making it a royal decree. Any woman who sleeps with me is excused from work the next day. How does that sound?"

She inched toward the edge of the mattress. "You'll have them lining up at the palace doors."

He scooped her close before she could escape. "There's only one woman I want at my door, and that's you."

He saw the delight blossom in her face and felt the eager give of her body. She laughed up at him and that momentary indulgence completely altered her appearance. A mischievous pixie peeked through the regal facade of the Fairy Queen, and Lander found he couldn't take his eyes off her.

She was so beautiful, her eyes tilted at the corners, just enough to give them an exotic slant, while specks of gold glistened hungrily in the honey brown. The sunlight danced across the spill of auburn curls turning them to flame against the elegant angles of her face. And her body. Lord help him. Plump and rounded where it needed to be and long and lean everywhere else, with skin so milky it looked as though it had been painted on by a master artist.

His arms tightened. "Stay," he whispered. "Just this once."

"Just once? I tried just once. It didn't work, as I'm sure you recall." With a regretful sigh, she rolled away from him, and as much as it pained him, he let her go. "I'm sorry, Lander. I have to get to work."

"The children are depending on you, aren't they?"

"Yes." She gathered up her clothing and hugged the pieces to her so that all he could see was acres of leg vanishing into crumpled green silk.

He swept back the covers. "Give me a minute to dress and I'll drive you."

"No, don't bother. I'll just catch a cab back to my apartment."

"Why bother with a cab if I'm willing to do it?" It didn't surprise him when she avoided his gaze, not that he needed to see her eyes to guess what she was thinking. "It's because you're afraid someone will catch us together, isn't it?"

"Too many people already know. It's going to leak sooner or later." She did look at him then, and the pain he read there struck like a physical blow. "We don't have much longer."

He erupted from the bed and dragged on a pair of jeans, not bothering to fasten them. "We have as long as we want," he insisted, stalking toward her.

"My work in Verdonia is almost finished. I've already been up north in Avernos for six weeks. And I spent more than two months in Celestia. I may need to go back there for an additional week or so after I'm finished here, but..." She trailed off with a sigh of regret. "There are other countries. Other children. Europe's a big place."

He couldn't resist touching her. Needed to, for some reason. "How much longer here, in Mt. Roche?"

"A few days," she whispered. "Maybe a week."

"It's not enough."

"It'll have to be."

She ended the discussion by vanishing into the bathroom, emerging a short time later wearing her clothes from the night before. She'd somehow managed to tame her hair, ruthlessly knotting it at the nape of her neck. In her business suit, all neatly tucked and buttoned, she looked every inch the self-possessed professional. Lander took one look at her and all he could think about was freeing that glorious mane and rumpling her tidy suit until he'd released the heart of passion that beat within the woman of calm reason standing before him.

"I'll send a car for you tonight," he said.

She caught her lower lip between her teeth. "Maybe we should take a night off. I'm getting behind on my work and—"

"Your work isn't going anywhere."

"No, it isn't," she conceded. "But the children are hurt by any delay."

Hell. She'd gotten him with that one. "I wouldn't want that. Are you certain I can't give you a ride?"

"Thank you, no."

He could hear the unspoken "Your Highness" in her tone, the polite curtsy buried within her words. His hands folded into fists. "I'll call you. If we can't see each other, you can at least take five minutes to talk."

She attempted a smile, but he caught the faint wobble and realized she wasn't anywhere near as in control as she'd like to pretend. He took a step in her direction intent on breaking through the vestiges of that control, but she flung up a hand, stopping him at the last second.

"Don't." Her voice broke on the word. She shot a swift, hunted glance toward the door. "Please let me go."

It wasn't what either of them wanted. He could change her mind with a single touch, but he didn't have the heart to stop her, to hurt her any more than she was already hurting. "I'll call you later," he repeated, more forcefully this time, and stepped aside.

She broke for the door, snatching up her purse as she went. He didn't waste any time. Dressing as swiftly as she, he made a beeline for the elevator. Juliana was already gone, but had sent the elevator back up for him. He shook his head as he stepped inside and stabbed the button for the garage.

He found her fascinating. Passionate. Kind. Wary. Like a wild creature in need of help, but fearful of becoming trapped. He could sympathize. Soon she'd discover they were both trapped in a situation not of their making, one with only a single solution. He fingered the ring he'd taken from the museum. It weighed heavily in his pocket. It was time to end this nonsense once and for all, he decided. Time to spring the trap.

He commandeered the car from the previous night and started it with a roar. Pulling out of the garage, he turned onto the street fronting the apartment complex. To his surprise, a crowd had gathered there. He glanced over as he passed, and what he saw had him slamming on his brakes and screeching to a halt.

Damn it to hell! Someone had sprung the trap ahead of him.

The elevator ride to the lobby seemed endless, stopping at every other floor. She'd been a fool to get involved with Lander. She'd known it from the start. At least with Stewart she could claim a certain level of naiveté. She'd been woefully inexperienced. Unfortunately, with Lander she could make no such claim. She'd committed the ultimate folly. She'd allowed herself to fall in love. To believe—if only for a moment—in fairy tales and happily-ever-after endings. It had been a mistake, one she'd never make again. She had no right to involve herself with a man who would be king. None.

The doors opened on to the lobby, and after returning the car to the penthouse, she walked briskly toward the exit, the rapid-fire chatter of her heels marking the speed of her passage. She never even looked up as she pushed through the doors leading outside, never saw them until she'd burst right into their midst.

"What's your name, miss?" The question was asked in Verdonian.

Flashbulbs exploded in her face and she flung up a hand to protect herself. "What…?"

Dozens of men and women hemmed her in on all sides, pressing, pressing, pressing. Microphones were shoved toward her, along with tape recorders and camera lenses. Everything took on a surreal quality. Noises grew too loud—the shrill, demanding voices, the desperate thrum of her heartbeat, the labored sound of her breathing. Odd, unwanted sensations heightened—the harsh feel of the sunlight scouring her face, leaving it naked and vulnerable to prying eyes. The stab of heat her panic induced, countered by the dank chill of fear. The stench of too many perfumed bodies, pulling, pulling, pulling.

"How long have you been seeing Prince Lander?" Verdonian again.

"What's he like in bed?" American. Female. City-slick and cynically amused. Followed by, "Who are you? You look familiar. You're not from Verdonia, are you, sweetie?"

Oh, God. Had she been recognized? "Please—"

"American," another crowed. "Definitely American."

She tried to push her way clear, but they weren't about to allow that. They reminded her of a pack of hyenas cornering a foolish gazelle who'd strayed too far from the herd. She was struck with a hideous sense of déjà vu. Another time, another place, but with the same rabid mob mentality, pushing, pushing, pushing.

"Did you know your father was already married?" the voices had shouted at the helpless eight-year-old she'd been back then. "How does it feel to be a bastard?"

The flashback to that hideous, long-ago moment only lasted an instant, but it was enough to cause her chest to tighten. "Please, move." She could feel the panic gnawing at the edges of her self-control and she fell back a pace only to be shoved stumbling into the center ring once again. "I don't know what you're talking about. I need to get to work."

"Where do you work?"

"Do you work for Prince Lander?"

"I wouldn't mind that sort of work." Laughter erupted at the American reporter's comment. "Hell, I'd be willing to pay for the pleasure, if it meant spending the better part of my day in bed with Prince Lander."

The laughter had cut off in the middle of the woman's comment, so the final words rang crude and unpleasant in the morning air. An uncomfortable silence descended, though Juliana remained too shocked and confused to judge the cause.

And then she heard him. He uttered just a single word, one that sang of salvation, even if it sounded more like a growl than a song. "Move."

As one, the reporters and paparazzi parted and Lander stood there looking as much like the Lion of Mt. Roche as she'd ever seen him. His hair swept back from his face like a mane, the sunlight picking out the streaks of blond among the tawny brown. Fierce green lights burned in his gaze, and every line of his face held an implicit promise of violence. He sliced through them with a jungle cat saunter, and took what belonged to him—her.

He caught her by the hand and she felt something slide onto her finger before he turned with her, facing the press. He eyed them one by one, his gaze lingering for a fraction of an instant on the American reporter.

"Remove her." Security closed in, security Juliana hadn't even noticed encircling the mob until then. "Escort her to the airport and see her on the first plane out of Verdonia." He cut off the woman's furious protests with a single glare. "No one treats my fiancée with such disrespect and continues working in this country." He lifted Juliana's hand to his mouth with old-fashioned gallantry and kissed it. "No one."

Every last person drew a collective breath, including Juliana. Before anyone could fire a single question, Lander draped an arm about her shoulders and whisked her through the crowd to his car. It sat in the middle of the street, the engine idling, the driver side door hanging ajar. He bundled her into the passenger seat before climbing behind the wheel. In the next instant they shot down the road, security cars clearing a path in front and behind.

"Are you okay?" Lander spared her a swift glance. "Damn it. You look like you're going to faint. Even your lips are white." He took his hand off the wheel long enough to stroke her cheek. "And your skin is like ice."

"It was… It was—" She drew in a deep, shuddering breath, striving to speak through chattering teeth. "I don't handle crowds like that very well."

"No one does. I'm sorry. I swore I'd protect you from that sort of media circus and I failed." A muscle jerked along his jawline. "I promise it won't happen again."

"Of course it will." It always did. Numb acceptance vied with a visceral fear. She twisted her hands together in silent agitation and suddenly realized she was wearing a ring. Glancing down, she gaped. It was Soul Mate, though she didn't have a clue how it had come to be on her finger. She thrust her hand beneath his nose, her fingers trembling so badly that red sparks exploded outward from the center of the amethyst. "What? How…?"

"I slipped it on your finger right before I announced our engagement."

For some reason, she couldn't get her brain to wrap around his explanation. "But we're not engaged."

He shot her a swift, humorous glance. "We are now."

Disjointed bits and pieces from her rescue coalesced into a less-than-cohesive whole. The *snap, snap, snap* of the reporters' jaws as they bit off pieces of her for public consumption. Her helplessness and fear. And then Lander had arrived, her knight in shining armor. And he'd said…he'd said, *No one treats my fiancée with such disrespect….*

She closed her eyes. That's right, she remembered that part. He'd called her his fiancée. He'd made that one reporter leave for being disrespectful. Then he'd lifted her hand and— She sucked air into her lungs and her eyes flashed open in shock. Her *left* hand. He'd lifted her left hand and kissed it, so that everyone would notice the ring he'd surreptitiously slipped onto her finger. She'd seen the astonished delight on the faces of the reporters. Had cringed from the speculation in their eyes as they'd scribbled their notes and recorded the moment for posterity with their cameras and video. She'd just been too far gone to comprehend the significance of what had happened.

"No!" She looked around with a rising sense of desperation. "Pull over. Pull the car over, right now. You don't realize what you've done. We have to go back and fix this before you're ruined. You have to tell the press we're not engaged. Please, Lander!"

He shot her another look, one of deepening concern. "Two more minutes and we'll be there. Hang on until then."

He was as good as his word. He spun into the winding drive that led to the palace and zipped up the road and through the gates at a rate of speed that spoke of long practice, and yet had her closing her eyes out of sheer panic. When they slowed, she peeked through her lashes in time to see him turn onto a small access road that circled toward the back of the palace.

"This way," he said as soon as they'd exited the car.

He led her through a warren of walkways and it was everything she could do to keep from battering him with a barrage of questions and demands—questions as to why he'd claimed they were engaged, and demands that they return to the apartment complex and tell the press the truth. A few minutes later they found themselves once again in a small, familiar glade at the path's end. In the center of the clearing stood the trellis gazebo she remembered so well, the structure barely visible beneath its canopy of white roses. Their heady perfume scented the air, stirring bittersweet memories of the last time she'd been here.

"Back to where it all began," she felt compelled to say.

"It didn't start here." He closed the distance between them. "It started in the ballroom when I looked up and saw you standing above me. I'd never seen anyone more beautiful than you."

"Love at first sight?" If only that were possible. "I already told you I don't believe in that. It's the stuff of fairy tales and fantasies and—" Her voice broke before she managed to harden it. "And make-believe."

"Don't." He gathered her close. "It'll all work out. I promise."

"How can it?" She pushed away from him. "You just don't get it. You think I'm Cinderella. But I'm not. I'm the ugly stepsister. You have to go back to the apartment. You have to tell all those reporters that you made a mistake. That you were just joking about our engagement."

"But I wasn't joking. And it's not a mistake." Even though she'd pulled free of his embrace, he didn't let her move beyond his reach. If she'd been the imaginative sort, she'd have suspected he was stalking her. "Besides, mistake or not, it's too late to take it back."

She stilled. "What do you mean?"

"By now the information is everywhere," he explained matter-of-factly. "Newspapers. Television. The Internet. All of the media outlets will be trumpeting the news. And every last one will be in the midst of a pitched battle to be the first to identify you."

She fought to draw air in her lungs. "Oh, God. You have no idea what you've done."

"What's wrong?" The sensation of being stalked intensified as he caged her against the gazebo. "Why are you in such a panic?"

Soft white roses kissed her face and shoulders while the vines snared her hair, delicately coaxing the curls loose from their confinement at the nape of her neck. "I warned you there were things you didn't know about me."

"Like what?"

Tears blinded her. *Say it! Just say the words.* "I'm illegitimate, Lander." There. It was in the open now. She'd claimed the awful truth. Even after all these years it still had the power to wound, stirring some of the most traumatic memories of her life. "I was eight when I found out, in a manner not that different from what happened outside the apartment complex. It was…it was a big scandal at the time. My mother, my brother. We were crucified by the press."

"Easy, sweetheart. It's all right."

"No, it's not all right!"

She covered her face with her hands, struggling to contain the flood of emotions, with only limited success. It was time to get this over with, to tell him the truth and be done with it. Past time, if she were honest. She'd known this moment was coming but had been too much of a coward to face it any sooner because her desire for Lander had outweighed basic common sense. Now she had no other choice but to deal with the situation and put an end to their involvement, once and for all. Slowly she dropped her arms to her sides and stood before him like a prisoner facing a firing squad.

"No one in Verdonia knows my name yet. But that American reporter recognized me. Once she's had time to think about it, she'll remember where she's seen me." Pain underscored each word, despite her best attempts to keep her voice emotionless. "And she'll be angry because you made her leave the country. She'll want to get even. She'll put things in the paper. Or online. Or go on some hideous talk show and air all the sordid details."

"What sordid details?"

She forced herself to speak unemotionally, though it was one of the toughest things she'd ever done. "My name is Juliana Rose…Arnaud. I'm Joc's sister. Most people in the States know me as Ana Arnaud, rather than Juliana. When it gets out that I'm the illegitimate daughter of a crook, the sister of a man who amassed his fortune through—what the press regards as—questionable means, you'll be crucified."

Lander's hands tightened on her shoulders. "It doesn't matter who your father is, or your brother. I'll protect you."

"It's not me who needs protecting!" She drew a ragged breath, staring at him in disbelief. "You say none of this matters, but you're wrong. It does matter. Don't you understand what I've done? I've ruined your reputation. At the very least, I've cost you the election. No one in Verdonia will want their king married to a bast—"

He stopped her with his mouth, cutting off the word before it could be fully uttered. It was as though he refused to have the air they breathed sullied with such an ugly declaration. Every last thought in her head evaporated beneath the heat of his embrace. He took her to new heights with that kiss, reassuring her without words. Adored her. Gentled her. Loved her.

"I don't care," he said between kisses. "The circumstances of your birth aren't what matter to me."

"My illegitimacy should matter. Don't you understand—"

"Trust me, Juliana. I understand more than you know." He snatched another kiss while she puzzled over that. Reaching behind her, he removed the clip at the nape of her neck, and with a swift flick of his wrist, sent it spinning over the nearest hedge. "God, I've wanted to do that since the first time you wore your hair in that annoying knot."

Before she could utter a single protest, he sank his fingers deep into the loosened strands and tumbled it into a fiery halo around her face. In between swift, teasing kisses he stripped off her suit jacket and released the top three buttons of her blouse. The entire time he edged her closer to the gazebo until they scaled the half dozen stairs and stepped inside.

Shadows draped the interior, and the scent of roses hung more heavily in the confined space. Intent on putting some distance between them, Juliana retreated to the padded wrought-iron bench in the middle of the gazebo and attempted to do up her blouse. Before she could get more than a single button through its hole, Lander sat next to her and swung her legs across his lap. Removing her heels, he tossed them through the archway onto the verdant grass beyond.

"What are you doing?" she demanded.

"Making love to my fiancée."

She stared at him, wide-eyed. "Stop calling me that. It's not a real engagement and I'm not making love in the palace gardens where anyone could stumble across us."

He shrugged. "Okay, then we'll talk some more. Have you told me everything you need to?" He smiled at her with such tenderness that it nearly broke her heart. "Any more confessions, my scandalous wife-to-be?"

"Aren't you listening? I'm not your wife-to-be. You haven't asked and I haven't accepted. This is nothing to make light of, Your Highness. It's serious."

He sobered, the laughter dying from his eyes. "I promise I'm not making light of it. The circumstances of your birth don't make any difference to me, or to how I feel about you. Nor does your relationship to Joc. But it infuriates me that you've been made to feel ashamed of something beyond your control."

Dear God, she'd have to tell him all of it. It was the only way to get him to understand. "It isn't just the circumstance of my birth," she insisted. "There's something else. Something worse."

If she were going to get through this next part she needed every ounce of control she possessed. She fixed her gaze on where Lander had tossed her shoes, one sitting as neatly as if she'd placed it on the grass, the other facedown, its stiletto heel stabbing skyward like a finger of doom. She retreated into a math equation to help clear her mind, working it through step by step. She'd nearly finished when Lander spoke.

"Would you mind telling me what the *hell* you're doing?"

She blinked. "I'm sorry. What did you say?"

"I asked what you were doing. It's like...you went away. One minute you were here and—" he snapped his fingers just shy of her nose "—the next you were gone. This isn't the first time it's happened, either."

"Oh. That."

"Yes. That."

"I was solving a second-order-linear-difference equation."

"Second order linear—"

"Difference equation. With constant coefficients." A reluctant smile broke through. "It's a mathematical equation. It helps reduce stress."

"And you do that in your head?"

Her brow crinkled in a frown. "I'm not sure I always get the answer right, but that's not the purpose."

"Of course not," he muttered. "Damn, woman, you never cease to amaze me." He gestured for her to continue, bringing them back on point. "Okay, let's hear it. What's the other scandal in your background? I don't suppose it has anything to do with a certain man named Stewart?"

"I'm afraid so."

She started to lace her fingers together, but finding she still wore Soul Mate threw her off stride and she hesitated, not quite certain what to do with her hands. Lander settled the matter for her. He pulled her closer and twined her arms around his neck. It seemed easiest to submit rather than to protest. He'd release her soon enough—once he heard all she had to say.

Juliana rested her head on his shoulder. "I used to be an accountant," she began.

"Too bad you didn't tell me when we first met. I might have offered you a job working for me. Our chief executive accountant, Lauren DeVida, left when my father died." His voice rumbled deep and soothing against her ear. "I assume you worked for your brother as an accountant?"

"Before heading Arnaud's Angels, I was his CEA."

"See? I was right. You'd have been perfect as Lauren's replacement. I'd bet you'd find keeping track of our amethyst exchange far more interesting than Joc's wheeling and dealing." He twined a rope of curls around his finger and gave it a playful tug. "And I'm sure you'd be as devoted to me as Lauren was to my father."

"No, I wouldn't," she retorted. "Because I no longer mix business and pleasure."

"Ah. Cue Stewart's entrance into your life," Lander guessed.

Juliana nodded, her cheek rubbing against downy-soft Egyptian cotton. "And then came Stewart. It's not a pretty story."

"Let me guess. Stewart worked in Arnaud's corporate headquarters, and the instant he discovered you were Joc's little sister, he moved in." When she stared at him in astonishment, he shrugged. "It's an old story, sweetheart."

She grimaced. "Then I guess this next part won't surprise you, either. He decided to steal from Joc and use me to do it. I was so madly in love with him—" She offered Lander an apologetic look. "Or thought I was, that I didn't catch on to what he was doing until too late."

"I assume when it all came out, you were vilified right along beside him, despite being the innocent in the story?"

It took her a long moment before she could bring herself to speak. "Thank you for believing in me. Not many people did, because of who my father was."

"And your brother."

There was a harsh undercurrent to his voice that disturbed her. "Joc may have gotten his start skating a slippery line. But as soon as he found his footing, he made sure all his dealings were dead honest. It's become a point of honor with him. Unfortunately, the press has a long memory and a suspicious nature. They've never forgotten those early days."

"You're a loyal sister."

"I have reason to be. He's always done everything in his power to protect me." She returned to the issue at hand with painful deliberation. "As for my part in Stewart's scam… Though I didn't help him, at least not directly, I wasn't innocent, either. I made it easy for him to pull it off. I was careless with passwords which allowed him access to computer documents he shouldn't have seen. I also let slip information that I should have kept confidential."

"Did he embezzle money?"

"No, he was too slick to remove it directly from any of Joc's accounts. Instead, he used insider knowledge to line his own pockets. You see, Joc has hundreds of businesses under dozens of corporate umbrellas. Stewart was able to gain access to records on outstanding bids, and on proposed buyouts and sell-offs. He acquired client lists, employee records, profit-and-loss statements." She splayed her hands across Lander's shoulders. "Basically, he used his position for insider trading. In addition, he influenced clients, revealed bids to competitors. You name it. If he could profit from it, he did it."

"I assume you discovered what he was up to."

"Eventually. But not until it was too late to fix. The scandal broke within weeks of my figuring out what was going on. By then it couldn't be covered up."

"Your own brother fired you?"

"No, I quit. I couldn't let Joc take the fall for my error in judgment." She removed Lander's ring and held it out to him. "You do understand why you have to call off the engagement? Why you have to tell the media it was all a huge misunderstanding? Even though Joc corroborated my side of things, there's always been a suspicion that I was more involved than anyone could prove. Especially since my last name is Arnaud, a fact that only added to the taint of suspicion."

"What I see is a young and naive woman taken advantage of by an experienced scam artist. You aren't the first person to have that happen, and you sure as hell won't be the last." He took the ring as she'd expected he would, then stunned her by saying, "The engagement stands. And just so you know, in my world a marriage always follows an engagement. Always."

Her eyes widened. He couldn't be serious. A fake engagement was one thing. But marriage? "You can't—"

"Think about it, sweetheart. How would it look if five minutes after I announce our engagement, I claim it was all a mistake? They have photos of you wearing my mother's ring." He took her left hand in his and slid Soul Mate back into place. "I wouldn't have given this ring to someone without due consideration, and the people of Verdonia know that."

Her fingers trembled in his grasp. "If you don't put a stop to this, you'll lose the election."

"Then I'll lose the election," he retorted implacably. "Better that than my honor."

His tone warned that their discussion was at an end, something she recognized from a lifetime's experience dealing with Joc. She inclined her head in apparent agreement, but she couldn't bring herself to give voice to the lie. When he pulled her back into his embrace, she went willingly enough. But inside she wept for the loss to come.

She told Lander about her relationship to Joc, expecting him to release her from their impromptu engagement. To distance himself from her. It was one thing to maintain an arm's-length business dealing with someone, even a man suspected of amassing his fortune through dubious means; it was another to marry into the family. Once the people of Verdonia discovered she was Ana Arnaud, the stain on Lander's reputation would be irreparable. Which left her with only one choice.

If Lander's honor prevented him from breaking their engagement, she'd have to see to it personally.

Seven

"You can't do this, Ana."

"Yes, Joc, I can and I will." Juliana put the finishing touches on her makeup, then slipped a pair of plain pearl studs through the holes in her ears. "If Lander refuses to stop this insanity, I'll do it for him. The press conference stands."

"Maybe Montgomery doesn't want to end your relationship. Maybe he's in love with you. Maybe he used the situation to force you into an engagement you'd never have considered otherwise. Have you thought of that?" Joc paced from one end of the bedroom to the other, before pausing behind her. "Well? Have you?"

It took her an instant to control the wild surge of longing, the reckless hope that flared to life before she could tamp it down. "Doubtful. It's a question of honor, not love."

Joc seized her by the shoulders and spun her around. "Why do you say that? Do you consider yourself unlovable?"

"Stop it, Joc." She wriggled free of his hold. "This isn't about love, and you know it. Lander feels responsible. He pursued me after I tried to end things between us, pushed us into an affair—not that I required much pushing. It's only natural that when the press found out about us, he felt honor bound to act. He practically told me as much."

"Bull."

She drew herself up. "Excuse me?"

"You heard me. Do you think I'd be so easily trapped into a marriage I didn't want? Hell, no. Nor would Lander. He could have found some other solution if he'd wanted. A less extreme one than announcing your engagement." Joc planted his fists on his hips and lowered his head in thought. "Didn't you tell me Lander had his mother's ring on him."

"Right. It was in his pocket. So?"

"So…" Joc lifted his head and pinned her with a keen gaze. "So, what was it doing in his pocket?"

She stared blankly. "I…I don't know." How *had* it ended up there? She struggled to recall. "I handed it to him when we were at the museum. And I think he stuck it into his pocket instead of returning it to the display case."

"Wait a minute. Take me through this step-by-step. His mother's engagement ring was at a museum, the national one here in Mt. Roche?"

"Yes. He was showing me the crown jewels after hours last night."

Joc cocked an inquiring eyebrow. "Just showing? If

it was all just showing, how did the ring end up outside the case? There had to be a bit of touching going on for that to happen."

"Okay, fine," she responded defensively. "Maybe I was also trying on some of the pieces."

He grinned. "Montgomery let you wear the crown jewels of Verdonia?"

"He might have." Her cheeks warmed. "No big deal."

"Yes, it is a big deal. Have you any idea how much expense and effort that would take to secure the premises so you two could play?" Joc glanced at her finger, then frowned. "Speaking of your engagement ring. Where is it?"

"I sent it back."

"Damn it, Juliana!"

"That's enough, Joc. The subject isn't open for debate. In case you've forgotten, there's a pack of reporters gathering outside my apartment. It would look odd if I wore Lander's engagement ring to a press conference announcing the end of our engagement."

She turned her back on her brother and started to pull her hair into a sleek knot at the nape of her neck until a memory of Lander tossing her clip into the shrubbery intruded. She hesitated, combing her fingers through the strands and watching the curls riot around her face and shoulders. Maybe she'd leave her hair loose. Just this once.

Joc came to stand behind her. "Okay, I won't debate the matter with you or try and explain why you're the biggest idiot I ever met. But I'd think, at the very least, you'd be curious to know why Lander stuck that ring in his pocket instead of returning it to the display case. Admit it. Aren't you curious?"

"No, I'm not." She glared at her reflection. She was being ridiculous. The only reason she wanted to leave her hair loose was because Lander liked it that way. With ruthless intent, she scraped back every last curl, anchoring the weighty mass with a spare clip. "He could have been stealing the ring, I suppose."

"Very funny." Joc leaned in, whispering close to her ear, "Maybe he took it because he'd been planning to propose all along."

Hope flamed anew. Was it possible? It did explain his keeping the ring. The next instant pain subdued every last spark of hope. No, no, no. She didn't dare allow herself to think along those lines. She'd drive herself crazy wondering about the what-might-have-beens. What might have been if she didn't bear the Arnaud name. If she hadn't been illegitimate. If she hadn't fallen for a scam artist and ruined her reputation beyond repair. She shook her head, forcing herself to focus on her one and only goal—protecting Lander.

"I have to go." She turned to confront her brother. Stubborn determination had settled into the crevices of his face, warning he wouldn't easily give up the argument. She didn't understand it. Why was he pushing this? She released her breath in a sigh. "What do you want, Joc? I mean, really."

"I want you to stay away from the press for a few days. Allow the situation time to settle down."

"You mean, do nothing?" She couldn't believe he was suggesting such a thing. "You always taught me that whenever a problem arose, you had to deal with it right away, before it had a chance to escalate. That's what I'm doing. Besides, if I don't act now, Lander will be the one paying the consequences. There's not much more the press can do to me."

"You don't give your fiancé enough credit."

"My fiancé," she repeated. Her eyes narrowed. "What are you up to? I would have thought you'd do everything possible to help me straighten out this mess, instead of throwing up roadblocks to maintain the status quo."

"I just want you happy. And I think Lander will make you happy."

Her expression softened. "That's sweet, especially considering your earlier opinion." She raised on tiptoe and planted a kiss on his cheek. "Thank you for caring."

"You aren't going to listen to me though, are you?"

"I can't. There's too much at stake. An entire country at risk."

She checked the mirror a final time. She'd chosen to wear her most conservative dress, the unrelenting black of the raw silk relieved by a simple strand of pearls and matching earrings. She'd also kept her makeup to a minimum, just a hint of blush, a swipe of mascara and a touch of lip gloss. Satisfied, she collected her purse and turned to leave.

"Are you coming?" she asked her brother. "Or am I on my own?"

"I wouldn't miss this for the world. If you need me, I'll be right behind you."

Her mouth twisted wryly. "Lurking in the shadows?"

He lifted a shoulder. "I do my best work from there."

Juliana took the elevator to the lobby, struggling with nerves. It didn't help that each blinking number mocked her descent, as though marking her fall from grace. She dreaded the next fifteen minutes with a passion that left her shaking. She couldn't think of anything worse than facing a horde of frenzied reporters. But she'd do it. She didn't have any other choice.

The doors parted, opening like the gates to hell. "Here goes nothing," she murmured bleakly.

She walked steadily across the lobby. The media circus milled just beyond the double glass doors with two uniformed apartment security guards all that kept them from storming the building. Sparing her brother a hunted look, she forced herself to push open the doors. Just as she stepped outside, she felt something tug at the back of her head, and the next instant her hair sprang free. Damn it! Somehow she'd lost her clip, not that she could do anything about it now.

A stray breeze kicked up as she stepped onto the landing outside the doorway, and fiery curls rioted about her face and shoulders. She shoved at the windswept barrage, then gave it up as a lost cause. Forcing herself to move forward, she paused at the head of the steps that led down into the sea of journalists. More than just journalists, she realized with a start. People from all walks of life swelled the press corps ranks. How had they known she'd be here, giving a press conference? Someone must have tipped them off.

A late-afternoon sun spotlighted her, shining into her eyes, which proved a blessing in disguise since it made it impossible to pick out individual faces. Questions pelted her from the moment she appeared, so many she couldn't single out one from another. She lifted a hand, and the clamor died to an unnerving silence, giving her an opportunity to speak.

"Thank you all for coming." She hesitated at the top of the steps, relieved to have at least that much space between her and the seething mob. Since her voice carried well from her position, she elected to remain where she was. "I'd like to make a statement, after which I will not be taking any questions."

Steady. She could do this. She had to; there was no other choice. "I'm here to announce that I'm formally breaking my engagement to Prince Lander. I'd like to assure all of you that I am both honored and flattered by His Highness's proposal and I wish—" To her horror her voice broke and it took her a heartbeat to gather up her control once again. She felt Joc edge closer and signaled him that she was okay and to stay back. "And I wish circumstances could have been different. Unfortunately, I wasn't forthcoming about my background with Prince Lander. He had no idea of my true identity when he proposed, since I was using my first and middle name in an attempt to protect my anonymity."

She bowed her head. "I was a fool. I should have told him the truth the moment we met, explained why any sort of serious relationship between us was out of the question." Looking up she offered a wistful smile, one that trembled around the edges. "Maybe some of you can understand how I felt. I wanted—just for a few hours—to believe in the fairy tale. To believe that I could find true love and live happily ever after. It was selfish and rash of me, not to mention unfair to Prince Lander. And for that I apologize to him, to you and to the people of Verdonia. I should have refused Prince Lander's proposal right from the start. Because I didn't, because I was self-indulgent, he's in this mess and it's all my fault."

"You still haven't told us your name," someone called from the middle of the pack of reporters.

No she hadn't. She drew a deep, calming breath and

stared over the heads of the crowd, into the setting sun. "It's Juliana Rose…Arnaud." She twisted her hands together and the absence of Soul Mate made her feel as though part of her had been cut away. "Most of you know me as Ana Arnaud."

All hell broke loose. The questions came fast and furious, one over top of another. She held up her hands. "Please. There's nothing left to be said. Be assured that Prince Lander had no idea who I was when he announced our engagement. This was all my fault, one I've now corrected. Thank you for coming."

She turned from the deafening shouts and escaped inside her apartment building, followed close behind by Joc. She'd done the right thing, even though it hurt more than she could have believed possible. The people of Verdonia needed Lander, a need far more urgent and vital than her own.

It was her fault they'd become engaged. Her fault that he felt honor bound to offer such an extreme solution to their predicament. And her fault that he stood to lose the election by insisting they marry. The only way he'd be the next king of Verdonia was if she released him from their engagement and ended their relationship. It struck her as the ultimate irony that his honor insisted he marry her, while hers insisted they part.

"It's better this way," she told her brother as they waited for the elevator.

"If this is better, then why are you crying?"

She lifted a hand to her cheek, surprised when her hand came away damp. How odd. She hadn't realized she'd been crying. "They're tears of joy for being out of this mess," she lied.

"It's interesting that your tears of joy look exactly the same as tears of misery. Why is that do you suppose?"

Her chin quivered. "When I figure it out, then we'll both know."

Lander faced the members of the press with calm determination. They all stood respectfully, waiting to hear what he had to say. No one shouted out comments or questions as they had with Juliana. The fact that they gave him the respect they refused to give her, annoyed the hell out of him. Not that he allowed his feelings to show.

"Thank you all for coming." He hesitated before admitting, "It would seem I'm in need of your help."

His opening statement was greeted with murmurs of surprise and a few encouraging smiles. So far, so good. "My fiancée, Juliana Arnaud, is under the mistaken impression that the people of Verdonia won't accept her as my wife. I'd like to see what we can do to change that."

"We?" one of the reporters asked.

"We Verdonians. You see, I believe she thinks her illegitimacy is an unacceptable stigma." Lander gave a what-can-you-do sort of shrug. "I've assured her on numerous occasions that this isn't true. That Verdonians judge people on their merits, not on their lineage. But she's having trouble accepting that fact. She feels that should we marry, it'll cost me the election."

Another of the reporters raised his hand and Lander pointed to him. "Your Highness, you referred to Ms. Arnaud as your fiancée. Are you saying the engagement *isn't* off?"

So, it was Ms. now, was it? That wasn't what they'd called her when they'd been shouting questions the night before. "As far as I'm concerned, it's not off. Ms.

Arnaud has a different opinion." Lander offered a smile that encouraged them to join him on his side of the dilemma—and once joined, to help. "I'd like to try and change her mind."

"I don't understand, Your Highness," a man in front spoke up. "What do you expect the Verdonian citizens to do?"

"First, I'd like to introduce all of you to the Juliana Arnaud *I* know. A woman who's kind and intelligent and compassionate, who puts honor before self-interest. If her press conference yesterday proved nothing else, it should have proved that she only wants the best for me and the people of this country." He leaned forward, speaking earnestly. "Juliana is a woman who, at the tender age of eight, discovered her father was a crook masquerading as a respected businessman. Imagine discovering not only that, but that your father had two families, one legitimate, the other not. And then imagine spending the next thirteen years branded with that illegitimacy and judged by it—hounded by some—despite the fact that you're the innocent byproduct of your parents' affair."

A woman in the middle of the pack raised her hand. "I don't see that the circumstances of your fiancée's birth have any importance. But other aspects of her background certainly do. According to my sources, she was suspected of helping her lover steal from her brother. That concerns me, as I'm sure it does most Verdonians. Any comment?"

He used silence to his advantage, waiting until it had stretched to the breaking point before responding. "First, Ms. Arnaud and the individual in question were never lovers." He paused to add impact to his statement.

"Secondly, she never helped this person, nor knew what he was up to until too late. She was thoroughly investigated and cleared by the authorities, but condemned by the jury of public opinion simply for being an Arnaud. The worst you can accuse her of was an unfortunate excess of naiveté. As soon as she discovered this man's duplicity, she reported him and resigned her position as a point of honor."

"Why is she in Verdonia?" questioned another reporter.

"I'm glad you asked." He'd hoped someone would. "She works for Arnaud's Angels, a charitable organization providing medical treatment to children in need. If you check, you'll discover that Verdonia has benefited greatly from the generosity of Angels, and that's largely thanks to Juliana."

"What do you hope to gain by this press conference, Your Highness?" came the final question.

He answered with absolute sincerity. "This is the woman I want to marry. I'm hoping the people of Verdonia can do what I've failed to do. Let Juliana know how you feel. Let her know that you'd welcome her as your princess." He held up Soul Mate, allowing the lights from the cameras to flicker off the brilliant amethyst. "I'd like all of you to help me put this ring back on her finger."

Juliana yanked the door open. The minute she saw who stood there, she started hyperventilating. "You... I..." She flapped her hand toward her living room where the television was replaying Lander's press conference for the umpteenth time that day. "What were you thinking?"

He strolled past her. "Oh, good. You're watching it."

She finally managed to wrap her tongue around the words clogging her brain. "Have you lost your mind?"

she demanded. "Have you any idea what you've done with that little performance you staged?"

He lifted an eyebrow in a regal fashion. "If you're going to speak to me like that, perhaps you should address me as Your Highness."

"You think I'm being rude? Too bad! I had it all fixed. I protected your honor. I fell on my damned sword for you." She pointed a shaking finger at the screen. "Why would you do…do *that* after all I went through to put an end to a bogus engagement?"

"Because I never considered it a bogus engagement, merely a premature one." He approached, and she realized she'd caged herself with a lion, a lion in deadly pursuit. He backed her against the edge of her couch and pinned her there. "I didn't want you to fall on your sword for me, Juliana. There was no need. I had everything under control."

He was too close, muddling her thoughts and rousing emotions she had no business feeling. Not anymore. "You consider that—" she gestured toward the television again "—under control?"

He tilted his head to one side. "What do you think is going to happen as a result of what I did?"

"I suspect everyone will erroneously believe we're engaged again."

A swift smile came and went. "Besides that."

"You'll lose the election," she stated flatly.

The fierceness of his frown had her catching her breath. She didn't know why, perhaps watching the respect and deference he'd garnered during his talk with the press had affected her in some strange way. But more than anytime since they'd first met, Lander struck her as every inch the royal. "I'm going to tell you this one final time, and then

I'll consider the topic closed. My relationship with you will not affect the outcome of this election. Are we clear?"

She nodded, wide-eyed.

"Topic finished?"

"Not quite," she dared to say. "I have one final question."

"One and only one." He folded his arms across his chest. "Ask."

"Why won't it affect the outcome?"

"Because within the next couple of weeks all of Verdonia will fall in love with you. I guarantee it. What you watched today is just the beginning."

She wanted to believe him. More than anything she hoped it was true. But she didn't dare. She'd spent too many years hardening herself against the callous stares and objectionable assumptions people made about her. That sort of thing didn't change overnight, not even by royal command. "How can you be so certain your people will accept me?" she asked.

His gaze held so much tenderness it brought tears to her eyes. "Because everything I said was true. You are kind and intelligent and compassionate. Most of all, you're honorable. As soon as the country sees that for themselves, they'll realize that not only do you belong here, but we need you."

She didn't know what to say to that, which was just as well since her throat had closed over. Taking her hand in his, he slipped Soul Mate back onto her finger. She started to stammer out a protest, one he stopped with a simple shake of his head.

"Don't refuse it. Not yet. Listen to me first."

"This is insane, Lander. We don't know each other all that well. It's happening too fast." The excuses flooded from her in a nervous rush, the one that concerned her the most, coming last. "You can't want to marry me."

"You're wrong. I do want to marry you. And I think you want to marry me, too." He gathered her up, fitting her into his embrace. They locked together as though they were missing puzzle pieces, finally made whole. His hand swept across her cheek in a light caress before his fingers forked into her curls and he tilted her face up to his. "There's no hurry, Juliana. We don't need to get married tomorrow or next week, or even next month. Wear the ring. If you decide our relationship is a mistake, you can always return it. In the meantime, we'll take it slow and easy."

She moistened her lips, afraid to believe. Afraid to trust or hope. Those qualities had been lost to her so long ago, she barely remembered possessing them. "Why don't we take it slow and easy, and then decide whether or not that ring belongs on my finger?"

He shook his head. "Everyone will be looking to see if you're wearing it. So, it's all or nothing, sweetheart. Right here and right now we either make a commitment or call it quits and go our separate ways. Your choice."

"But—"

"That's my offer. I refuse to go back and forth with the media playing 'is she or isn't she.'" He held her with a demanding gaze, his eyes an intense greenish gold. "Take a chance, Juliana. Trust me."

Oh, God. Trust. He would use that particular word. She leaned into him, closing her eyes against the urge to throw caution to the winds and give in to sweet temptation. "What happens if it doesn't work out?"

"You walk away, and I let you." She opened her eyes to discover the hard lines bracketing his mouth had softened. "I'm hoping you won't walk, because I'm not sure I can keep my side of that particular deal if you do."

His admission filled her with joy, a joy she forced herself to curb. She had another concern that might end everything before it ever began. "There's something else I need to know. Not about the election," she hastened to add.

"Why do I have the feeling I'm not going to like your next question?"

"Maybe because it has to do with Joc."

"Ah." His voice soured. "That might be it."

She caught her lip between her teeth. "You two don't like each other, do you?"

Lander shrugged. "We've had our differences."

"Then...what's he doing here in Verdonia? If you're not friends, why is he here?"

Lander's face lost all expression, filling her with apprehension. "I assume he came here to see you."

Not a chance. Joc adored her, she'd never doubted that. But he adored business more. If he'd come all this way, there was more drawing him to Verdonia than trying to talk her into resuming her old job at corporate headquarters. Her brother was a strong believer in the adage, "killing two birds with one stone." "Tell me, Lander. Do the two of you have some sort of business deal in the works?"

He shook his head. "You should ask your brother about that."

Her heart sank. "I'll take that as a yes. When he danced with me at the ball, he...he warned me about you. He warned me to stay away from you." She grimaced. "Now that I think about it, he pretty much warned me to stay away from you every time I saw him."

A smile of satisfaction eased the grimness from Lander's expression. "You didn't take his advice."

"No, I didn't." She gripped his arm, the amethyst on her ring glittering with red-blue fire. "I need you to tell me the truth. If we continue our relationship, will it hurt your business deal with him?"

He stared at her for an endless moment, his jaw tightening with growing tension. His eyes had darkened with some emotion she couldn't quite decipher, but it worried her. "Throwing yourself on your sword again?" When she stared at him in open dismay, he relented. "It hasn't and it won't."

Juliana couldn't disguise her relief. "You promise?"

"I promise."

His reply was so short and abrupt she wondered if she'd offended him again. But then he lowered his head and kissed her, putting an end to any further discussion, and she realized that he was far from offended. She tumbled back onto the couch with him and lost herself in his embrace. Somehow it would all work out. Somehow the people of Verdonia would accept her, maybe even love her. They had to.

Because she'd just realized that she was madly in love with their future king. And, though he hadn't said he loved her, too—the only dark cloud on the horizon—for the first time in years, she'd begun to trust again.

Lander flipped open his cell phone and placed a call. "It's done," he announced as soon as Joc answered.

"She's wearing your ring again?"

"That's what 'done' means, Arnaud," Lander snapped. He fought for control, fought even harder to keep his voice pitched low, though his intensity still came ripping through. "If your plan backfires, if she's hurt because of this, I will find a way to make you pay."

"You make sure she doesn't find out about our contract and she won't get hurt."

"This is wrong, Arnaud."

There was a momentary silence that Lander took for agreement. "I want her happy," Joc said gruffly. "For some reason, you make her happy. Since you're what she wants, you're what she gets. As for the contracts, they should be ready to sign by the end of the month. We don't sign until you two are married, so I suggest you keep things moving at your end."

Hell. "I promised her time."

"Take all the time you want…so long as it doesn't go past the end of the month. Juliana's not stupid. You take too long sealing the deal and she'll figure out what we're up to. Get her to the altar and fast."

Lander snapped the cell phone shut, wanting nothing more than to hurl it at the nearest wall. So much for honor. He didn't know who he was more disgusted with, Joc or himself. The only part in all this that brought him any pleasure was Juliana. He didn't know what to call what they had. Not love. He wasn't the type to allow his heart to rule his head. But he wanted her. He cared about her. And he looked forward to having her for his wife. Whatever that was, it would have to do.

He could only hope it would prove enough for Juliana.

Eight

"Your Highness, please." The dressmaker fluttered behind Lander as he entered the bedroom. "You can't be here. It's bad luck to see the bride in her wedding dress before the ceremony."

"Of course I can see her, Peri. My palace, my rules."

Across the room sheer pandemonium broke out. He grinned as Peri's assistants fell over each other to hold up lengths of fabric in an effort to hide Juliana from his view. From behind the makeshift barrier, he heard a crash, followed by a muffled oath, the sound of ripping silk and another louder curse. Then, "Damn it, Lander! What the hell are you doing here?"

He laughed, in part at the exasperation in his darling bride-to-be's voice and in part at the shocked expressions of the dressmaker and her assistants. "Why, I came to visit you, of course."

"I was with you not thirty minutes ago. You couldn't wait another thirty until I'm through here?"

"No, I can't." He settled cautiously onto a dainty davenport. When it proved sturdier than it appeared, he flung one leg over the armrest and settled back against the cushions. "The latest newspapers just arrived and I wanted to share them with you."

"I try and avoid newspapers whenever possible. I usually find them depressing, if not downright unpleasant."

He winced at the hint of vulnerability threaded through her comment. "These are neither depressing nor unpleasant. In fact, in the few days since our press conferences, they've all been rave reviews. For instance…" He selected a newspaper at random and turned to the appropriate page. "May I be the first to inform you, you are officially the cat's meow."

The assistants dropped the fabric they held, revealing a hand-painted dressing screen. Lander could see Juliana's silhouette on the far side as she was assisted in removing a billowing gown that one of the dressmakers whisked away for further alteration. Lord, she was gorgeous. All long, sweeping lines and soft, feminine curves. She poked her head around the side of the screen. In her haste to hide from him, her carefully knotted hair had become delightfully unknotted. For some reason, he found those bountiful curls fascinating.

"The cat's meow?" Her eyebrow winged upward. "Should I assume you're the cat?"

"You may so assume."

"Really?" She pretended to be disappointed. "I thought you were a lion."

"Cat. Lion." He shrugged. "If you don't like that nickname, how does Angel Ana grab you? It's the most popular of the dozen or so choices, although Angel seems a little much to me. And not terribly accurate, based on the words I just heard come out of that angelic mouth of yours."

Her eyes narrowed and he could see the warning flash of gold from clear across the room. "Would you please tell me what you're talking about?"

He held up a stack of newspapers. "I told you. I'm talking about these news articles."

She gripped the edge of the screen in alarm. "All those? They're all articles about me?" she asked in disbelief.

"Well, and me, too." His brows drew together. "At least, I think I'm in here somewhere. Probably listed in one of the footnotes as Angel Ana's bridegroom."

She started to come around the screen, only to be shoved back in place by one of Peri's assistants, who then bustled around the room, pretending not to listen as she straightened bolts of satin and tulle. "Are you trying to tell me that the press is saying nice things about me?" Disbelief underscored the question. "The press never has anything nice to say. You must have read it wrong."

"Did not." He riffled through the papers. "Here's one that's fairly illustrative. And I quote, 'Verdonia's princess-to-be, Angel Ana Arnaud, has the entire country at her feet. Standing before a crowd of reporters and local citizens, vibrant red hair tousled by the wind—'"

"Darn clip."

"'Angel Ana confirmed her engagement to Lucky Lander is back on—' Oh, there I'm mentioned. See? I'm also known as—damn, I hope Merrick and Miri don't read this, I'll never hear the end of it—Lander the Lovestruck, and Lovelorn Lander."

"They actually had the nerve to call you that?" Juliana asked faintly. "And the reporters are still breathing?"

"Breathing, just not functional. And you're interrupting. Let me read you the best part of the article. Where was I? Oh, yes. And I quote once again. 'All of Verdonia rallied in their efforts to encourage Ms. Arnaud to accept Prince Lander's offer of marriage. Now that she's once again wearing his ring, the entire country is celebrating the good news.' There, you see? Rave reviews."

"I don't understand." She sounded sincerely puzzled. "Usually all they want to print about me is scandal."

He tossed the papers aside and stood. "People are coming forward from all over Verdonia, sweetheart. All in support of you and full of reports of your many good deeds and kindnesses."

"You've helped so many of our children," one of the assistants offered.

"They even support you in Avernos," the dressmaker concurred. "As well they should."

Lander chuckled. "I'll bet that has von Folke's tail in a twist. What I wouldn't give to see that."

"Now, Your Highness," the dressmaker scolded, making shooing motions toward the door. "You need to go now so I can finish my job."

"Yes, yes. I'm leaving." Before anyone could stop him he crossed the room in a half-dozen swift strides. Yanking Juliana from behind the screen, he gave her a long, thorough kiss. "To hell with bad luck," he muttered against her mouth.

The instant he released her, Peri and her assistants ringed him, urging him toward the door. They almost succeeded in ousting him when he noticed piles of silk folded on top of her bed. "What are these?" he asked, detouring in that direction.

"Nightgowns. Please, Your Highness—"

He dug in his heels and gave the garments his full attention. "I'm not going anywhere until I see what you have here." He shook out each piece and studied it with an experienced eye. "I like this one. A definite yes for the green. This one's perfect. Great color. Please, God, yes. And—fair warning—" he swiveled toward Juliana and held up one of the selections "—if I ever see you in this, I rip it off and it goes directly into the fire."

"In that case, I'll be sure to wear it on our wedding night," she returned.

"Huh." He tilted his head to one side, considering. "Not a bad plan. Okay, fine. In another two weeks you can wear this one."

"Two weeks!" Juliana shot out from behind the screen again. "What are you talking about…two weeks?"

"Didn't I mention?" he asked with the utmost casualness. "We have an official wedding date."

"There must be some mistake," she began.

Returning the nightgowns to the bed, Lander cut her off. "Ladies? If you'll excuse us?" Without a word, the dressmaker and her assistants vanished from the room, leaving him alone with his bride-to-be. "Problem?"

Regarding him warily, Juliana snatched up her silk robe and belted it. "What happened to taking our time? To having a slow and easy engagement period?"

He approached and caught the ends of her belt. One hard tug sent her tumbling against him as the robe came undone. "We can wait, if that's what you'd prefer." He slid his arms inside her robe and around her waist. "I just felt the timing was good."

"Why? Why so soon?"

He shrugged. "It gives the country something to focus on other than my father's death. Instead of grieving, they have the opportunity to celebrate. It also pulls the focus off the amethyst crisis, giving me time to get to the bottom of the problem without worrying about media scrutiny."

"And the election?" She gave him a searching look. "Our marriage will help with that, too, won't it?"

"Now you're going to win the election for me?" He smiled in genuine amusement. "I seem to recall that just a few short days ago you were certain you would be responsible for my losing."

She shot him a teasing look, relaxing. "Hey, that was before I became the cat's meow. You marry me and the election's in the bag."

His amusement faded. "Tell me something, Juliana. Do you think I'd marry you…or not marry you, if it meant winning the election?"

She didn't hesitate. "No, of course not." She nibbled on her lower lip. "Do you really want to go through with this so quickly? You don't have any doubts at all?"

He found he could answer with absolute sincerity. "None."

She took a deep breath and then nodded, undisguised happiness giving her face a breathtaking radiance. "Then it looks like we have fourteen days in which to finish organizing a wedding. Maybe you'd better call Peri back in. We have a lot to do if we're going to be ready on time."

"Later." He took her mouth in a lingering kiss, one she returned with utter abandonment. "Much later."

When Lander finally left Juliana's room, he found

himself thinking that while his bride thought two weeks far too soon for the ceremony, he found it an endless wait. He groaned in frustration. He'd never make it. Someone would slip up before then. Somehow she'd find out about that ungodly bargain he'd made with Joc. If the truth came out before the wedding could take place, she would walk. Hell, she'd run. And Verdonia would be ruined.

He shook his head in frustration. He should be worried about putting his people first, about his country's economic future. Instead, all he could think about was Juliana. If she found out the truth, it would be worse than anything she'd experienced before. Being told in such a harsh manner that she was illegitimate had been bad. Having Stewart betray her trust and the public scandal that had resulted from that betrayal, had been worse. But this…this would destroy her. And it would be all his fault.

A rolling drum of thunder woke Juliana on her wedding day, while a white staccato blaze of lightning greeted her the instant she opened her eyes. Rain peppered the windows blown there by a gleeful wind that rattled the sashes and shutters in a vain attempt to invade her bedroom. Before she had an opportunity to do more than groan in dismay, the lights flickered on overhead and an entire platoon of determined women bustled in, Lander's stepmother, Rachel, leading the parade.

"Perfect weather for a wedding," she announced. "An excellent omen."

Juliana sat up in bed and drew her knees toward her chest, eyeing the intruders with sleepy annoyance. They were all Montgomery family members, the connections so convoluted she needed a detailed genealogy to keep them straight. But it was tradition for them to help Juliana prepare for the wedding and keep her company, so she accepted their presence with good grace.

"A downpour on my wedding day is considered lucky?" A yawn interrupted the question.

"Without question." To a woman, the others gathered in the room nodded in agreement. "Rain on your wedding day means you'll be blessed with fertility and good fortune."

Juliana glanced dubiously toward the window. "And what does thunder and lightning mean?

"It signifies a very passionate love affair." Again the nods of agreement. Rachel came and sat on the edge of her bed. "Normally your mother would be performing the task I am today," she said, taking Juliana's hand in hers. "Lander told me she died when you were only ten. I hope you don't mind that I'm substituting for her."

Juliana shook her head. "Not at all. In fact, I appreciate it very much. It makes this part so much nicer."

Rachel brightened. "That's a relief." She tugged at Juliana's hand. "Up you go. You can't believe how much there is to do if we're to get you to the chapel on time."

The first item on Rachel's checklist was for Juliana to have breakfast with her and Lander's stepsister, Miri, so they could discuss the day's schedule. The two women were unmistakably mother and daughter, both with midnight-black hair as straight as Juliana's was curly. Both had the same unusual bottle-green eyes and flawless complexions, just as both were delightfully unreserved.

To Juliana's surprise, she sensed a certain strain between them and couldn't help but wonder if they'd just had an argument, or if the thread of discord she sensed indicated that they disapproved of the wedding. Juliana could understand if that were the cause. She'd only conversed with Rachel on a handful of occasions. And she'd never met Miri before. No doubt they questioned the speed with which the wedding was taking place.

She waited until they'd been served before tackling the issue with customary directness. "Do you disapprove of Lander and me marrying so quickly?"

Both woman glanced at her, startled. "No," they said in unison. It broke the tension and they all laughed.

Rachel leaned across the breakfast table and patted Juliana's arm. "You can't govern love. Or the speed with which it happens. Lander's father and I only knew each other a week before he proposed. Merrick met his bride no more than two before they wed. And yet, I've never seen a couple more in love." Juliana couldn't mistake the sincerity in the older woman's voice. "I'm delighted for you and Lander, and wish you only the best."

"Thank you." Relieved, she turned to Miri. "Lander speaks of you all the time. I'm sorry we haven't had an opportunity to meet before this. Have you been away?"

It was as though she'd hit them with a live wire. Both women jolted in shock and after exchanging one startled look, were careful to avoid the other's gaze. Juliana frowned. Oh, dear. If she didn't miss her guess, she'd just discovered the source of the strain she'd noticed earlier.

"My daughter has been enjoying a brief vacation," Rachel explained smoothly.

Miri's chin jerked upward in clear defiance and she tossed her waist-length hair back over her shoulder. "Actually, I was hiding out on the Caribbean island of Mazoné after helping Merrick abduct his wife."

"Miri!"

"Give it up, Mom. I'll bet Lander's already told her." She shot Juliana a challenging look. "Hasn't he?"

Juliana dabbed her mouth with the linen napkin. So much for asking what she'd assumed was an innocuous question. She'd opened up a veritable can of worms with that one casual inquiry. "He told me just the other day that Merrick had abducted Alyssa and that they ended up falling in love. But he didn't mention your part in the affair."

"I took Alyssa's place at the altar in order to give Merrick time to get away."

It was everything Juliana could do to keep her jaw from dropping open. She snatched up her teacup and buried her nose in her Earl Grey until she could control her expression. "Let me get this straight." She couldn't come up with a delicate way to phrase her question. "You're married to Prince Brandt, the man Lander will face in the upcoming election?"

"It's not legal." To Juliana's amusement, both women spoke in unison again.

"At least, we don't think it is," Miri added.

"What's he like?" Juliana asked, curious to know more about Lander's rival for the throne.

"He's tall, dark and handsome, of course."

"How can you call him handsome?" Rachel demanded. "He's too austere to be considered handsome."

"I don't agree. You just think that because his features are more severe than the Montgomerys', which sometimes makes him look hard." An odd quality crept into Miri's voice. "To answer your question, Juliana, he's self-contained yet passionate. And he has this old-world charm about him. He puts honor and duty and responsibility before everything else. Everything. And once he makes up his mind about something, he's impossible to sway."

"Interesting."

Juliana had learned to make swift assessments of people. Like her brother Joc, her judgment was rarely wrong—with the one disastrous exception of Stewart. Instinct told her Miri's feelings toward Brandt ran deep. Secrets burned in those spring-green eyes, as well as pain. Not wanting to add to her pain, Juliana deliberately changed the subject, addressing Rachel.

"So, what's next on my checklist?"

"After we've finished breakfast, you'll meet with Father Lonighan. He'll give you his formal blessing for the union and offer marital advice."

"Have fun with that."

"Miri! Then you have an hour to soak in your bath before the fun part begins." Rachel ticked off on her fingers. "A massage, facial, manicure and pedicure."

"Good Lord," Juliana murmured faintly.

"Then Miri and I will return to help with your hair and makeup."

Miri grinned. "What she means is, we'll watch while the experts take care of it. Then, in accordance to Verdonian tradition, Peri will sew you into your gown."

"Yes, she told me about that part," Juliana said. "But if I'm sewn in, how do I get out again, later?"

Rachel and Miri exchanged quick, mysterious smiles which worried Juliana no end. "You'll see," was all they'd say.

The rest of the day proceeded as outlined and the hours flew by. In no time she was having her hair fashioned into a gorgeous Gibson Girl hairstyle with ringlets framing her face and teasing the nape of her neck. Then the tiara she'd tried on at the museum was added to the arrangement. She hoped Lander would appreciate that she'd chosen something his mother had worn as a bride on a day very much like this one. She had the odd notion that it connected the two of them spiritually, one generation to another. As though aware of her feelings, Rachel gave her hand an understanding squeeze.

"Lander asked me to give this to you," she whispered, and offered Juliana a square jeweler's box.

Opening it, Juliana found the most striking pair of earrings she'd ever seen nestled inside on a velvet bed. They were a teardrop confection of diamonds and amethysts, both Royals and Blushes. Her hands trembled so badly she could barely put them on.

And finally came the gown itself, with Peri sewing her into it. As soon as she'd finished, she stepped back and nodded in a combination of approval and pride. The fitted bodice glittered with tiny amethysts of every shade. Layer after layer of tulle swept out from the narrow waistline in an endless train behind Juliana that folded and hooked to form an elegant bustle to make for easier maneuvering both before and after the actual ceremony.

And then they brought out her veil. A glorious confection of lace and tulle, it, too, glittered with amethysts. The lace and gemstones had all been set in an intricate pattern of swirls that managed to obscure her features while still allowing her to see. Now she understood how Miri had managed to fool Brandt when taking Alyssa's place at the altar.

As soon as Rachel twitched the veil into place, Juliana was escorted from her bedroom suite to the front of the palace where a flower-bedecked horse-drawn carriage awaited. Joc stood beside it wearing a dove-gray tux and looking more handsome than she'd ever seen him.

At some point the storm had passed, leaving the air scrubbed clean of humidity and filled with the delicious scent of early summer. A soft mist rose around the carriage, giving everything a fairy-tale quality. They rode through streets lined with Verdonians who cheered her passage. In no time they arrived at the chapel and Joc literally lifted her from the carriage and swung her to the flagstone entranceway.

"You know I only want the best for you," he said gruffly.

"Of course I know that."

"I'd hug you, but you're all—" He gestured to indicate her veil and dress. "I don't think I can wade through all that and back out again without getting it messed up."

She smiled, though she doubted he could see it through the veil. "I appreciate your restraint."

He offered his arm. "You ready?"

She took the question seriously. Was she ready? There were certain aspects of her future life with Lander that worried her, mainly living as a public figure. She'd spent a lifetime fighting the negative labels affixed to her name. How long would it take before she went from acclaimed to infamous again? It could happen. Public favor was a fickle thing.

And then she thought of Lander and how she felt about him. How much richer her life had become now that he was a part of it, and nothing else mattered. Nothing. "I'm ready," she said, and slipped her hand into the crook of Joc's arm.

Music drifted from the dim interior, Handel's "Minuet." They paused in the foyer where attendants straightened Juliana's gown and unhooked the train, spreading it behind her. "His Highness said he cut these himself," one of the women whispered, handing her a bouquet of fragrant white roses. "He said you'd know where they came from."

The gazebo. Tears sprang to Juliana's eyes and she started to lift the heavy blossoms to her nose, but the veil prevented her. As though realizing she was on the verge of ripping through the layers of lace and tulle, Joc urged her toward the sanctuary. The rippling majesty of horns broke into Stanley's "Trumpet Voluntary" the minute she appeared.

And that's when she saw Lander. He stood at attention waiting for her, dressed in full military whites, including a chest rippling with medals and an ornate saber belted at his hip—the Lion of Mt. Roche at his most majestic. Late-afternoon sunlight struck the stained glass windows on the west side of the chapel. The colors shattered, forming a rainbow of hues leading from where she stood to where she most wanted to be.

And then she was walking toward him. No, not walking. Floating, as though in a dream. The wedding service began, vanishing into the mists of memory almost as soon as it occurred. She vaguely recalled Joc joining her hand with Lander's. Father Lonighan spoke at length, his deep voice rumbling over her. Through it all, her full attention remained on the man professing to love, honor and cherish her, to protect her from all harm.

One of the clearest moments of the ceremony, a shard so piercing in intensity that it would forever remain a part of her, was when he slipped a pair of rings on her finger. The first was a heavy band of gold studded with Verdonia Royal amethysts. The second had her catching her breath. Instead of Soul Mate, he slid a far different ring on her finger, a delicate confection of diamonds and amethysts in a trio of unusual shades that complemented the earrings he'd given her earlier.

"I had it designed just for you," he murmured so only she could hear.

"Does it mean something?"

"Of course." His hazel eyes glowed with tenderness. "We'll see how long it takes you to figure out."

There wasn't further opportunity to speak. Father Lonighan gave them a final blessing, and the ceremony concluded with their being declared husband and wife. As tradition dictated, Lander had waited until the very end to lift her veil.

"I've never seen you look more beautiful," he told her.

Cupping her face, he took her mouth in the sweetest kiss they'd ever shared. Her eyes drifted closed as she lost herself in his embrace. The only thing that would have made the moment more perfect would have been if he'd told her he loved her. Just as the kiss ended, trumpets flared to life in a triumphant recessional. Lander took her arm and escorted her down the aisle and then outside where a roar of cheers greeted their appearance. The sun dipped low on the horizon spreading a rosy glow across the city. With a laugh, Lander swept his bride into his arms. Her train caught the breeze and billowed around them as he carried her to their waiting carriage. And in that moment Juliana didn't think she'd ever been happier.

Nine

After the wedding, Lander hosted a dinner reception for close friends and relatives. Laughter flowed as easily as the sparkling wine, both bright and effervescent and full of good cheer. During those brief hours, Juliana knew what Cinderella must have experienced after she'd married her prince. A rightness. A completion. For the first time in her life, Juliana felt loved and cherished. She felt like a real princess.

Toasts followed the dinner, some funny, some poignant, others heartwarming. Just as the last glass was raised, the majordomo appeared, inviting the guests to adjourn to the balcony to watch the fireworks display celebrating the royal marriage. When Juliana would have followed, Lander caught her hand and urged her in the opposite direction.

"We'll watch them from a more private location," he told her.

She didn't need any further encouragement. Gathering up the voluminous skirts of her wedding dress, she raced with him through the deserted corridors. At least, they appeared deserted. If security was stationed between the dining hall and Lander's private wing of the palace, they remained well hidden.

The two of them arrived at his bedroom suite breathless with laughter. She couldn't say what they'd found so amusing. Perhaps it was just their happiness bubbling over like uncorked champagne. Or maybe it was being alone together at last, the joyful anticipation of the hours to come. Pushing open the door, Lander swept Juliana into his arms and carried her across the threshold.

When he set her on her feet, she glanced around, her breath catching in her throat. Candles lit the room, dozens upon dozens of them on every surface, encircling them in a soft, warm glow. White rose petals were strewn across the carpet, providing a romantic pathway from door to bed. More of the petals were scattered on the satin sheets, their fragrance filling the room. Soft music issued from hidden speakers, and she paused to listen for a moment. It sounded so familiar. And then she realized why. The songs were selections from their wedding service.

"You did this, didn't you?" she asked in a broken voice.

"I'm forced to admit, I didn't light the candles. But, the rest..." He nodded. "I wanted it to be special for you."

"Thank you."

In the distance she heard a faint boom signaling the start of the fireworks, and she crossed to a set of French doors that opened onto the balcony. Lander joined her there, coming up behind and wrapping his arms around her waist, enfolding her in the warmth of his presence.

They watched the initial fireworks in silence, a blaze of color and explosion of sound that celebrated their union.

Gently he turned her. "Come. Let's get you out of that gown."

"I'm sewn into it, you know. I'm told it's traditional." Did he hear the sudden nervousness in her chatter? But then, how could he miss it? "No one's explained the origins to me."

"I believe it's to ensure the safe passage of the bride from her family's loving arms to that of her husband. Proof that no one has touched her during the interim."

"I've got news for you. There's plenty of touching that can go on without the bride removing her dress."

"Not if it's done right."

Juliana's mouth twitched. "Good point." She lifted an eyebrow. "So how do you propose to release me?"

"Like all good Verdonian husbands, I come prepared." He picked up a jeweled dagger resting on the bedside table. "This is called a *koffru*."

"I'm almost afraid to ask."

"You should be. It's a bride cutter."

"Lovely," she said dryly. "You're going to cut me with that thing?"

He responded to her jibe with a grin. Pulling her close, he spun her around so her back was to him. "It's not you I plan to cut. It's your gown."

"Don't ruin it!"

"Trust me, wife."

After sweeping her veil to one side, he sliced through the seam holding the back of her gown together with delicate precision. Inch by inch the knife skimmed down her spine until he reached her waist. And then it dove lower still, to a point just past her hips. Finished, he slid the dress from her body as well as the layered petticoat beneath. Offering her his hand, he helped her step free of the yards of satin and tulle. She stood before him, oddly self-conscious considering that they'd already been lovers, her only covering a few flimsy scraps of lace, her stockings, heels and garter, and her amethyst-studded veil and tiara.

"So beautiful," he murmured as he unhooked the veil and set it aside. When she would have removed the tiara, he stopped her. "My job." He slid the tiara from her hair, freeing the few curls that insisted on clinging to the jeweled hairpiece. "I wondered if you'd choose to wear this." His voice deepened. "It's in honor of my mother, isn't it?"

"Yes." Tension gripped his jaw, while sorrow cut brackets on either side of his mouth. Seeing him like that nearly broke her heart. "I wanted her to be a part of the ceremony in some small way."

"Thank you for that. She would have appreciated the gesture." He placed the tiara out of harm's way before turning back to her. "And now my favorite part."

One by one Lander removed the pins restraining her hair, catching the loosened pool of curls in his palms. Behind her fireworks lit up the night sky, flinging brilliant flashes of color across the hard, masculine planes of his face. Rich, vibrant sparks of green glowed in eyes filled with unmistakable hunger.

She reached for him with trembling hands, fervent and unabashed, fumbling with buttons and zips as she helped him remove his clothing. If she lingered over the corded muscles she found beneath his dress whites, he didn't complain, though she could feel the tension gathering across his shoulders. Nor did he complain when she followed the plunging vee of crisp, masculine hair that darted from chest to abdomen and farther still. She followed that line until she found the heart of his passion. She cupped him, stroked him, playing along the full length and breadth of him. It made her keenly aware of her own femininity and of his unrelenting maleness.

He took her mouth with a groan, plying her with fierce, desperate kisses. Her few remaining garments were a barrier swiftly eliminated and then it was her turn to be filled with an unnerving urgency, one painful in its intensity. He stroked her, the sensations growing hotter, headier, more concentrated. Just when her legs were on the point of giving out, he lifted her in his arms and carried her to the bed.

She drank in the aroma of the roses surrounding her, felt their silken caresses against her bare skin. But they were overlaid by another aroma and another caress, a more elemental, pervasively masculine one. He braced himself above her, touching, barely touching. Sliding with excruciating slowness. Rousing sensations that had her fevered one moment and chilled the next.

"Please, Lander. Now," she urged. "Make love to me now."

He didn't need a second invitation. He lowered himself to her, crushing the rose petals against her skin in an explosion of scent. Palming her thighs, he parted her legs, releasing his breath in a rough sigh as she welcomed him home. He surged into the liquid warmth, sealing their wedding vows as he sheathed himself fully within her.

"My bride," he whispered. "My princess. My wife."

He moved then, taking her with the utmost tenderness and care. Stroke built upon stroke, gathering the heat, driving it toward a burning need, escalating toward a frenzied desperation that left her utterly exposed, utterly abandoned to this most intimate of embraces. Her muscles tensed in anticipation of the ultimate surrender. When it came it stormed through them, demolishing every defense in an explosive release, one echoed by a final barrage of fireworks.

And in that moment of shattered completion, they became husband and wife in body, as well as name.

"Damn it, Joc. Could we get this over with?" Lander growled. "Juliana will wake any minute now. Considering it's our first day of marriage, I'd like her to do it in my arms, rather than waking to a cold bed."

"The final contracts are right here. All we have to do is get these lawyers to agree on the remaining two points and we're done. A few months from now, new business will flow into Verdonia, and hot damn—" he rubbed his hands together "—you've got a source of revenue to fill in the gaps left from the declining amethyst trade."

Lander grimaced. "It can't be soon enough. The Royals are becoming scarcer by the day. If something's not put in place to augment that lost income—and soon—it's going to have a disastrous effect on our economic stability. Nine months, a year from now, we're going to be hurting."

"We'd have an easier time finalizing our plans if you had an executive accountant working with us. What happened to yours?"

"She left after my father's funeral."

"Any chance she'd be willing to come in and lend a hand?"

"None. Lauren made that clear before she left. She

took my father's death pretty hard. I guess she'd been with him since—" Lander shook his head "—must have been before the death of my own mother. I believe she's somewhere in Spain enjoying an early retirement."

"I'm tempted to call Ana in and have her go through everything."

"Not a chance in hell."

Joc waved him silent. "I know. I know. It was just a thought."

"A bad one. We'll cope using our current accountants, not to mention the team of lawyers we both seem to have in excess." He shot a fulminating glare in the direction of the conference table. "Will they never finish?"

A light knock sounded at the door. Before Lander even saw the tumble of auburn curls and the gold-spiced eyes, he knew who it would be. Sure enough, Juliana poked her head around the door. She was dressed in a simple off-white silk shell and billowing skirt that had him remembering how beautiful she'd looked in her wedding gown. Even though her face was bare of makeup, she'd taken the time to put on the earrings he'd given her as a wedding present. It took every ounce of his self-possession to keep him from sweeping her into his arms and carrying her back to their bedroom.

"Oh, there you are." Relief brightened her face. "I thought I'd lost you."

"Not a chance." Lander pulled her into his arms, not giving a damn who was watching, and kissed her. "Good morning, wife. I'm sorry I wasn't there when you woke up," he said, and meant it.

"What's going on?" She glanced at her brother. "Hey, Joc. What are you doing here?"

"Business," he replied easily. "Just moving some of

my interests over here. You know me. Spread the wealth around."

"Right." She smiled at her brother. "Lander wouldn't discuss it, but I had a feeling you two were in negotiations over some deal or another."

"Oh, we're long past the negotiation stage. We should be done within the hour."

"Why did you have to wait until this morning to finalize everything?" To Lander's amusement, she shifted into scold mode. "In case you didn't realize, your timing stinks, Joc. That's not like you. You usually have impeccable timing."

"Sorry, Ana." Joc worked to appear suitably chastised. "I guess your wedding threw it off. If it makes you feel any better, we're at the sign, seal and delivery stage. As soon as that's done, you two lovebirds can take off on your honeymoon."

Juliana laughed, slanting a mischievous glance up at Lander. "I've worked with Joc on countless contracts. I know all about the delivery stage. One of the first things my brother taught me was to always wait until every last precontractual condition has been met before signing any agreement. He drummed the importance of it into me during every negotiation." She lowered her voice in a mocking imitation of Joc's Texan drawl. "Don't sign based on promises, Ana. Wait until they've done what they said they'd do before putting your name on the dotted line. It's all about leverage. It's all about getting what you paid for." Her gaze flashed from husband to brother. "So, what's left to do? Anything I can help with?"

"No!" Joc and Lander replied in unison, far too emphatically.

Juliana froze, and the tiniest of clouds drifted across

her expression. The silence thinned. Sharpened. Became painfully acute.

"Your Highness?" One of Lander's team of lawyers rose. "Excuse me, sir, but we can't move to the next stage until Mr. Arnaud has signed the papers indicating that you've fulfilled all the preconditions to the contract."

Juliana stiffened and the clouds from earlier deepened, piling darkly across her face and dimming the brilliance of her eyes. She untangled herself from Lander's embrace and took a quick step in her brother's direction. "What conditions are they talking about? What did Lander have to do in order to get your business?"

"It's not important," Joc dismissed the question. "Details. Nothing for you to worry about."

One look warned Lander she wasn't buying her brother's glib reply. He signaled the lawyers, jerking his head toward the door. "Out."

They didn't wait for a second invitation. Within thirty seconds they'd cleared the room. The minute the door closed behind them, Juliana spoke again, her analytical brain focused to a pinprick. "Joc, did you ever refuse to do business with Lander because he and I were having an affair?"

Lander relaxed ever so slightly, as did Joc.

"No, Ana. I didn't."

She spared Lander a swift, wary glance that had him freezing up again. "Maybe…maybe all this time I had it backward," she murmured. "Let's try it from this direction. Did you ever refuse to do business with Lander unless he and I became involved? No, you wouldn't have done that. You wouldn't have settled for anything less than—" She broke off, wide-eyed.

"Ana—"

She stumbled backward toward the door. "Oh, no. Tell me you didn't do that. Tell me *that* isn't one of the conditions of your contract."

Lander took a step in her direction. "Honey—"

She held up a hand. "I'm so stupid. How could I still be so naive after Stewart?" She shook her head, curls frothing around her face. Her complexion had turned as pale as her ensemble, stretched fragile and translucent across her elegant bone structure. Her heart fluttered at the base of her throat like the wings of a wild bird fighting the bars of her cage. "One plus one always equals two. Always. You'd think I'd remember that."

Joc frowned in confusion, but Lander instantly understood. He wished he could deny the conclusions she'd reached, but how could he when she was all too right? He'd never before seen such a look of devastation on a woman's face. The fact that that woman was his wife nearly destroyed him.

"Am I actually written into the contract, Joc?" she asked with amazing composure. "Section C, Subparagraph Four, Line Sixteen. In exchange for my basing X, Y and Z business in Verdonia you will marry my sister. If I read those contracts on the table over there, will I find my name in them?" When neither man twitched so much as a muscle, she swept relentlessly onward. "No? Not there? Then you must have decided my future over brandy and cigars. I'm a gentleman's handshake, aren't I? Marry my sister and I'll do this contract with you."

"Sweetheart, don't—"

Her composure shattered, her breath escaping in a sob. "Oh, God. You don't have to say another word. I get it. I do. My marriage is nothing more than a business deal." Her laugh was a painful splinter of sound. "Do I have all the details right? Have I missed anything?"

"Listen to me, Juliana," Lander began.

But she had no intention of listening. Before he'd even gotten the words out, she'd turned and made a beeline for the door. Flinging it open, she darted into the corridor. She heard Lander giving chase behind her. He caught up with her just as she burst into their bedroom suite.

Slamming the door closed behind them, he snagged her arm and spun her around. "Listen to me, damn it!"

"Listen to what?" She could hear the fury in her own voice and fought to modulate it, fought for a measure of restraint. Once upon a time, she might have succeeded. But this hurt went too deep to keep inside, the pain too raw to bottle up. "Whatever you have to say to me will either be a lie or an excuse. Which one were you planning on using?"

"Neither. I was planning on giving you the truth… and an explanation."

She cut him off with a swipe of her hand. "You don't need to explain. You did that weeks ago. I just wasn't paying close enough attention."

"I have no idea what you're talking about." He forked his fingers through his hair, the lion rumpling his mane. "What did I explain to you? Where? When?"

Her breath came far too quickly, her thoughts racing too fast for coherency. "We were in my office. Don't you remember? You were trying to convince me to continue our relationship after our one-night stand. And when I told you it wouldn't be in Verdonia's best interest, you said—" Her eyes fluttered closed as she strove to calm down enough to recollect his exact words. "You said your personal life has never interfered with your duty to your country, that duty takes primary importance over everything. Always."

Oh, God, why hadn't she listened? Why hadn't she understood? She'd been so caught up in the dream, in the fairy tale, that she'd forgotten what reality was all about. Well, she remembered now. It had come crashing down on her with a vengeance, destroying her from the inside out. "But I get it now, Lander. Marrying me meant that Verdonia would be protected from economic ruin. You didn't marry me because you loved me. You married me to protect Verdonia."

"You're right. You're absolutely right." Desperation had him pacing, and he ate up the length of the room with long, swift strides. "Joc came to me with his proposition. Said he had a sister he wanted me to marry."

"Me."

He swiveled to face her. "No, not you. Ana Arnaud." He closed in on her and she drew inward, flinching away from him. "I told him to go to hell. I told him I might have considered such an outrageous suggestion the week before, but not then. I'd met someone, I told him. Juliana Rose. But the joke was on me, wasn't it? Because when he showed me a picture of his sister, damned if Juliana Rose and Ana Arnaud weren't one and the same person. An interesting coincidence, don't you think?"

Her eyes narrowed. "Coincidence? You say that like you think—" Her breath escaped in a hiss and her control snapped. "You believe I was in on it?" she demanded, livid. "You think I plotted with Joc to force you to the altar?"

"The possibility occurred to me. You show up at the first ball we'd thrown since my father's death. You're using your first and middle name, conveniently omitting your last. Your brother arrives the same evening. We spend one unforgettable night together, and all of the sudden Joc is talking contracts and marriage."

She shook her head in disbelief, too full of anguish to speak, afraid she might break if she tried. If that happened, all her most private emotions would come spilling out in a hysterical flood. Once loosened from her control, she could no more call those emotions back than she could gather up a single raindrop out of a downpour.

Lander started toward her again. "So, yes. I admit it. I considered the possibility that you and Joc were setting me up. And you know what I decided?" He pursued her until he'd backed her against the bed. "I decided, who cares if that's how it went down? I wanted you. You wanted me. And then there was Verdonia to consider. With the amethyst mines played out, the country's on the verge of economic collapse. So, hell yes, Princess. I agreed to marry you. What would you have done?"

"I'd have told you the truth," she argued bitterly. "Given you a choice."

"Really?" He cocked an eyebrow, his expression skeptical. "Would you have agreed to marry me if I'd been upfront with you?"

She hesitated. Would she have? "I don't know," she conceded.

"At least you're honest about it." He lifted a shoulder in a weary shrug. "I suspected that might be your answer, and I couldn't afford to take the chance you might refuse my proposal. When the press found out about us—Joc's doing, I assume—I took advantage of the situation and had my ring on your finger before you had an opportunity to react."

"You put your country first, just as you warned you would."

He wanted to deny it, she could tell. "Yes. And let me be clear about something else, as long as we're being so damned honest. I'd do it all over again. The situation is too critical for me to leave anything to chance."

Resolution took hold, hard and implacable. "I can't live like that. I wish I could, but I can't." She looked around the room, seeking an avenue of escape. "I have to leave."

He reached for her. Fingers and curls seemed to find each other of their own accord, snaring and tangling. Clinging. Joining. "You're my wife."

"Bought and paid for." Her voice broke on the final words. Helpless tears gathered in her eyes. "That makes me property, not a wife. At least not a real one."

He snatched a kiss, then another. She remained helpless beneath the onslaught, her body softening, responding, betraying her need. "Stay," he demanded between kisses. "We'll find a way to work this out."

The tears fell then. Hopelessness drove them, a despair so deep and pervasive that nothing he said or did could make it right again. After Stewart, she'd thrown up a protective wall and hidden behind it, afraid to allow anyone access in case they hurt her again. Lander had pulled down that wall, brick by brick. He'd set those emotions free and she'd allowed it to happen, because she'd wanted—more than anything—to find love.

A coldness slipped through her veins, stealing the warmth his arms provided. She'd believed this man fulfilled her in every way possible, aligned her, balanced her. She'd thought she'd found her soul mate. And instead it had been an illusion. What he'd offered hadn't been real. What she'd hoped to find with him hadn't existed. Now all that remained was an empty shell.

She untangled herself from his embrace. He didn't want to release her any more than she wanted to go. Fingers and curls fought her, resisting, before being forced to part. No matter what it took, no matter how difficult, she had to walk away. She had to run. She wouldn't survive the pain if she didn't.

"I'm sorry, Lander. I can't stay." Her voice wobbled, not that there was any way to prevent it. "I'm going to ask Joc to take me back to the States while I consider my options. You two can decide how best to settle any outstanding contractual issues."

She started to remove her wedding rings and earrings, and he stopped her before the rings left her finger. "Keep them," he ordered.

Her gaze lifted to lock with his, a desperate, searching look. If only he'd say the words, just three simple words that would make all the difference in the world. But either he didn't know them, or he didn't feel for her what she felt for him. Time to concede defeat. It was over, the fairy tale ended before it had even begun. Without another word, she turned and left her husband.

Juliana was already on Joc's plane when her brother arrived. After shooting her a single look of concern, he gave his full attention to the pilot and attendants, issuing instructions in a low voice. He must have asked for privacy because they were immediately left alone in the spacious cabin.

"Ana, I'm so sorry." He came to sit on the armrest of the seat across the aisle from her. "I screwed up. I know that. But I swear I was acting in your best interests."

There had never been any question in her mind about that. Her brother had spent most of his life caring for her. Protecting her. Trying to provide everything she could ever want or need. But this…! "Why did you do it, Joc?" The blistering anger from earlier had gone, leaving behind a cold, bottomless fury. "How could forcing Lander to marry me possibly be in my best interests?"

"Because you deserved to be a princess." Determination filled his voice. "To be a queen, if that's what the people of Verdonia decide."

"How dare you!" she snapped. "What made you think I wanted to be a princess, let alone a queen?"

He stilled, taken aback. It had been a long time since anyone had ever questioned the rightness of his decisions, and having his little sister do it clearly left him unsettled. "Do you think I don't know how hideous the past seventeen years have been?" he tried to explain. "How you've suffered at the hands of the media? For a while I thought you'd come to terms with it. Put it behind you. You seemed to love your job." His expression darkened. "Until Stewart."

"And because of that you forced Lander to propose to me? To marry me? Was a contractual marriage supposed to protect me somehow? To ensure I live happily ever after?" Her mouth worked. "How could you do that to either Lander or me?"

"Don't you see? It's because I love you so much that I want what's best for you."

"You can't order the world and everyone in it to your convenience."

His jaw took on a stubborn set. "Why not?"

"Joc!"

He waved that aside. "Listen to me, Ana. There's something I haven't told you about my relationship with Montgomery. *I* owe *him.* That's why I came to Verdonia. That's why I agreed to help him."

Her brows pulled together. "What are you talking about?"

"We had a rather contentious relationship at Harvard." His mouth twisted. "I guess that would be a generous description considering how much I hated the man."

"You hated Lander? But, why?"

Joc's eyes were black with emotion. "You know why. Because he represented everything we weren't. He had the name, the heritage, the perfect life. He was the golden child. So I went after him to prove who was better. Grades, women, sports. You name it, I had to beat him. And in the end, I did. I graduated just ahead of him." He grimaced. "The bastard even had the nerve to shake my hand when he congratulated me."

Juliana shook her head. "I don't understand. How does that translate into your owing him?"

"His cronies decided that the only way I could have come out ahead of Montgomery was if I cheated. They beat the snot out of me, determined to get me to confess."

Understanding struck. "Lander rescued you, didn't he?"

"Yeah. I've never seen anything like it. He mowed through every last one of them and then carted me off to the hospital. I swore to him that day that if he ever needed anything, if it was in my power, I'd give it to him." His gaze fixed on her. "So, you see, he didn't have to marry you. If he'd refused, he knew damn well I would still have lived up to my part of our agreement.

There's only one reason he went along with my condition. He loves you. You have to believe that."

"But I'll never be one hundred percent certain," she shot back. "If someday he decides he does love me, I'll never know if it's what's actually in his heart or if it's part of his contract with you. I'll suspect every word he says. Every gesture he makes. Every gift he gives me. I'll never know. Not for sure."

Her brother stared at her in stunned horror. "No. That's…that's not right."

She bowed her head. "None of this is right." She pushed herself to her feet. She'd never felt so tired before, nor so defeated. "I'm going into the back to lie down. Please ask the attendants not to disturb me."

He caught her hand and squeezed it. "I'll watch out for you."

"You always do." She couldn't bring herself to look at him. "The problem is, I'm all grown up now. It's time I watched out for myself, even if it means falling down on occasion and skinning my knee. It's time to let go, Joc. You have your own life to live. Now let me live mine."

She didn't wait for his response. It didn't matter what Joc said or did anymore. Her declaration had been as much for her own benefit as it had been for her brother's. There had been the ring of truth to her words, a message from herself to herself. It was past time she took charge of her life. Long past time.

Ten

Juliana never did recall those first bleak days back in Dallas. They passed in a blur of pain and confusion, as well as a desperate, bone-deep despair. The minute she landed in Texas, she yearned to turn around and fly right back to her husband. But she couldn't. Not the way things stood between them. By the end of the first week, she knew she had to follow the advice she'd given herself on that last hideous morning in Verdonia. It was time to take charge of her life. There were decisions to make and a resignation to tender to her brother, something she intended to do that very day.

It didn't take long to drive into the city. Joc owned a full city block worth of office building in the heart of Dallas, a soaring glass and chrome structure that stabbed skyward in a gradually narrowing column. It was simply labeled Arnaud's. Security waved her through to Joc's private elevator, and upon exiting she found his personal assistant, Maggie, sitting in her usual spot outside his office.

The older woman looked up from her typing and smiled at Juliana over the top of her reading glasses. "Hey, there, girl. Or should I say, Your Highness?"

"You should not." Juliana cast a determined glance at the door leading to Joc's inner sanctum. "Is he around?"

"Can't you tell from the growls and snarls coming from in there?"

"That bad?"

"The worst I've seen him in a long time. Maybe you can snap him out of it."

"I'll see what I can do."

"His employees would be most grateful."

Taking a deep breath, Juliana entered Joc's office. She found him standing with his back to the door, staring out of the floor-to-ceiling windows at the Dallas skyline. "Damn it, I want some answers," he snapped as she slipped into the room. Realizing he was on speaker phone, she remained silent.

"You heard me." Juliana jumped in shock at the sound of her husband's voice. "I don't want her back in the country. I don't care what you have to do, just keep her with you in Dallas. Is that clear?"

"You don't give me orders, Montgomery."

"I do about this. I won't be changing my mind. If she tries to return, I swear I'll ban her from the damn country."

She must have made some small sound because Joc spun around. The words he uttered were some of the coarsest she'd ever heard him use. "Would you care to repeat that for your wife's benefit, Your Highness? She just walked into my office. Judging by her expression, I'd say she overheard every word you said."

An endless pause followed. Then the man she loved more than life itself replied, "If she heard, there's no point in my repeating it. I'll assume my message has been delivered and we can be done with this nonsense." He made the statement in a flat, emotionless voice, one so unlike his own, if she hadn't known it was her husband, she'd have thought she was listening to a stranger.

It took her three tries to answer him. "I'll have my wedding rings messengered to you first thing tomorrow."

"Don't bother. I don't want them back." And with that, the connection went dead.

Juliana stared blindly at her brother while she fought to breathe. "I…" She tried again. "I just came by to tender my resignation. If you'll excuse me—"

"Ana, wait." He started toward her. "There's something you don't know."

But she didn't wait. Turning, she walked steady as a rock from the office. Later, much later she'd break. But not here. And not now.

As Lander hung up the phone, he knew that he'd completely and utterly lost his wife—the one woman he'd ever truly loved.

Who'd have thought him capable of that particular emotion? How had that happened? When had it happened? Before their wedding, he knew that much. Certainly before he'd implemented the design for her wedding rings. Maybe it had happened the first time he'd seen her, when he'd mistaken love for lust. Leaning back in his chair, he closed his eyes, images of Juliana flashing through his mind.

His bride floating up the aisle toward him in that spectacular wedding gown and veil, her eyes gazing at him through layers of tulle, glowing a brilliant brown seasoned with gold. His wife, her skin more silken than the sheets she lay on, opening herself to him, crying his name as he brought her to completion. His princess, breaking their engagement in order to protect him, while facing down a pack of snarling reporters. She'd done all that for him. How could he do any less for her?

Even so, it hurt. A deep, immeasurable hurt. He'd thought his love for Verdonia outweighed everything. That he was incapable of the sort of love touted by poets and romantic fools. But that wasn't true. He was more than capable. It had hidden within, asleep until Juliana had come into his life. And what had he done with it when it had been gifted to him? He'd done everything in his power to destroy it.

"Excuse me, Your Highness." His majordomo stood in the open doorway to his office. "The Temporary Governing Council has requested your presence."

"Thank you, Timothy. Will you inform them that I'm on my way?"

"Yes, sire. Immediately." He hesitated. "Is there anything I can do to help?"

"There's nothing." Lander offered an encouraging smile. "Everything will be fine. I haven't done anything wrong, any more than my father did. The truth will come out."

"Yes, sir. Of course it will. No one doubts that for a minute."

Lander only wished that were true. Unfortunately, someone somewhere had pointed the finger in his direction, blaming the Montgomerys for the amethyst crisis. And he wasn't certain he could prove them wrong. The TGC, put in place to govern Verdonia until after the election, had no choice but to act on the allegations.

Added to that, news of Juliana's return to the States on the morning following their wedding had leaked almost as soon as she'd stepped onto Joc's plane. He'd anticipated the resulting public outcry and had been prepared to deal with it. But when news of the investigation had broken later that same afternoon, her disappearance had only added fuel to the fire of suspicion. Why would she have left the day after her wedding if she hadn't believed her husband guilty of wrongdoing? The fact that she'd flown out with her brother had only made the entire affair more suspect. Even the infamous Joc Arnaud had refused to stand by Prince Lander, the gossips had whispered.

The scandal threatened to rip his country apart. Until he could get it straightened out—*if* he could get it straightened out, he wanted Juliana well away from the media bloodbath.

The minute Juliana hit the street, she hailed a cab. "Drive," she instructed the cabbie as soon as he pulled curbside.

"Where do you want me to go?"

"Anywhere. In circles for all I care."

Sliding into the back, she began to shake, her hands trembling so badly the diamonds and amethysts on her rings flashed with urgent fire. She stared blindly at them as she fought for control, and when her cell phone rang, it was all she could do to answer it. She expected to hear her brother's voice. Instead her mother-in-law responded to her abrupt greeting.

"Have you heard?" Rachel asked without preamble. "About Lander?"

"I…I spoke to him ten minutes ago." If those few terse sentences could be considered speaking. "Has something happened to him?"

Rachel groaned. "He hasn't told you about the charges, has he?"

"Joc tried to tell me something when I left his office, but—" As her mother-in-law's comment sank in, she straightened in her seat. "What's wrong, Rachel? What charges are you talking about?"

"He and his father are accused of…misappropriation, I guess is the most tactful word."

Misappropriation? Did she mean…*theft?* "Did I hear you right? Lander's been accused of embezzling money?"

"Amethysts. He's been charged with skimming a portion of the outflow and selling the gems on the black market. Apparently, there's conclusive documentation to back up the accusation."

"That's a crock, and you know it," Juliana declared irately. She thrust a hand through her hair, sending curls flying. "Lander would never do anything so dishonorable. Nor would he be party to anything that would harm Verdonia."

There was an instant of silence, then Rachel whispered, "Thank you, Juliana. I was so afraid you left because you believed he was guilty."

"I left because I found out he didn't love me," she responded without thought.

"No! Whatever gave you that idea?" There was a momentary pause and then Rachel continued. "Never mind. That's none of my business." She hastened to change the subject. "Your brother told me you were the best there is when it comes to accounting and finance. Would you be willing to examine the records and see if there's something our people have missed?"

Juliana didn't hesitate. "I'll be there as soon as I can." Of course, returning to Verdonia meant facing Lander again, something she wasn't prepared to do. Not after their phone conversation. "There's one condition."

"Name it."

"I don't want Lander to know I'm in Verdonia."

"Oh. I…I guess I can do that. At least, I can promise I won't tell him. I can't promise that he won't find out from some other source. Will that be acceptable?" When Juliana reluctantly agreed, Rachel added, "Tell me, my dear. Did you ever figure out what your wedding rings meant?" Without waiting for an answer, she hung up.

Juliana flipped her cell phone shut, and after a momentary hesitation, held out her hand. She stared at the rings curiously. They were such a beautiful set. Her mouth curved upward in a wistful smile as she remembered the moment when Lander had slid the band and engagement ring onto her finger. She recalled that he'd said the design meant something, as well. Something she was supposed to figure out. With everything that had happened in the interim, she'd forgotten until Rachel's reminder. Now she looked, really looked at the pair.

The wedding band itself was set with an unbroken circle of Verdonia Royal amethysts. Royals, for soul mates. Hah. As if. But the engagement ring, was another matter. On the outer portion of either side were a scattering of tiny Blushes set in gold filigree. Farther inward the amethysts grew progressively larger and changed in color to a shade she'd never seen before, becoming mixed with diamonds until the very middle where a huge diamond and a matching Verdonia Royal were connected in a swirl of gold.

What had Lander said about the Blushes? That they symbolized a contract. Wasn't that how their engagement had begun, as a contract? She might have been unaware of it, but that didn't make it any less true. She frowned in concentration. The Blushes were only on the outer rim. As they grew in size, they also changed to an unusual reddish-purple color that was neither Blush nor Royal. She wasn't sure what this new shade symbolized. None of the jewels Lander had shown her had contained anything similar. But at the center of the ring the stones were the deepest, richest purple-blue she'd ever seen. A diamond and a Royal mated together. She shook her head. No. It couldn't possibly mean what she thought.

The tears came then, tears of regret mixed with a surge of hope so expansive and strong that it drowned out every other emotion. It took two circuits around the block before she'd recovered sufficiently to decide on her next step. Fumbling for her cell phone, she punched in a number. Her brother answered on the first ring.

"I need three things from you and I need them an hour ago," she announced.

"Name them and they're yours."

"I need your jet. My old team of accountants. And the meanest, nastiest, sharkiest bunch of lawyers you have on staff. I want to be airborne before nightfall."

"Going somewhere?"

"Verdonia."

Joc let out a sigh of relief. "About damn time."

"Lander! Lander, where are you going?" Rachel called breathlessly.

He paused, his hand on the knob of the conference room door, and glanced over his shoulder at his stepmother. To his surprise, she approached at a near run, alarm clear in her eyes. "I'm checking in with my lawyers and accountants, of course. I've called down at least six times today for an update and haven't heard a word."

"Maybe if you left them alone so they could get some work done—"

"This will only take a minute."

He pushed open the door and stepped into the room. Everyone froze, and the animated conversation came to an abrupt stop at his entry. And that's when he heard it, a soft gasp. He knew that tiny hiccup of sound, had heard it every time he'd kissed his wife, every time he'd made love to her, every time he'd brought her to completion. Slowly he turned his head and there she was, standing off to one side of the room, staring at him.

Of course her eyes gave her away, brilliant flecks of gold burning within the honey brown. He flinched at what he read there. Apprehension, longing, wariness. Even a heartrending hint of sorrow. But worst of all was the unadulterated pain.

He didn't hesitate. He was beside her in an instant. Cupping the back of her neck, he tumbled her into his arms. His mouth took hers with an intense kiss that told her more clearly than words how much he missed her. His tongue breached her lips and she responded to him the way she always did, with a generous passion that threatened to unman him. She wore her hair up in a style similar to the one on their wedding day, and he thrust his hands into those perfectly arranged curls and set them free.

At long last he pulled back and gazed down at her. "You're here."

"Yes, I'm here," she agreed breathlessly.

"Don't take this the wrong way, but…why?"

"I thought I could help."

Help. She meant help with the embezzling charges. Damn it! If the media got wind of her presence they'd be all over her. If she thought her previous experiences had been bad, it would be nothing compared to this. And there wouldn't be anything he could do to protect her. "I left specific instructions with Joc—"

"Yes," she cut in. "I heard those instructions, remember?"

Hell. Lander thrust a hand through his hair. "We need to take this someplace private where we can talk." He started to urge her from the room, only to discover that they were already alone. He paused, tempted to carry her off to their rooms while no one was watching and allow his hands and mouth to do his speaking for him. Duty battled desire for supremacy. Duty won. "You shouldn't be in Verdonia. You need to leave before word leaks of your return."

"I'm not going anywhere. At least, not yet." She stepped away from him and folded her arms across her chest. "Why didn't you tell me about these charges you're facing?"

"You left, remember?"

Hot color scorched her cheeks. "Vividly. I also remember the reason I left."

"And still you came back?" he couldn't help but ask. He didn't understand it. After everything he'd done to drive her away, here she stood.

She waved that aside as though it weren't important. "Why did you tell Joc to keep me out of Verdonia?" she countered. "Was it to protect me?"

He shrugged. "You've had enough trouble with the media to last a lifetime. You don't need any more."

"Falling on your sword, Lander?"

He managed a brief smile. "We seem to make a habit of it, don't we?" His smile faded. "Not that it matters. You're returning to Texas right now, even if I have to put you on the plane in handcuffs."

"Just one last question before I go." She hesitated before rushing into speech. "I couldn't help noticing that all the Verdonian wedding rings you showed me at the museum had names. Does mine?"

The change of topic caught him off guard and he answered automatically. "Of course."

"What is it?"

He should have seen the question coming and diverted her before she could ask. "We can discuss this later." He attempted to dismiss the subject. "The plane—"

"Can wait." One look warned she wouldn't be budged from her stance. "If you want my cooperation, we'll discuss it now."

He made the best of a losing hand. "If I tell you the name, do you agree to leave? To get on whatever plane brought you here and return to Texas within the hour?" At her nod, he bit out, "Metamorphous. Your ring is called Metamorphous."

"Ah." A strange smile tugged at her mouth. "I'd hoped it was something like that."

He started for the door. "If we're careful, I think I can get you to the airport with no one the wiser."

"In a minute." She laced his hand in hers and tugged him toward the conference table where papers were piled high. "I want to show you something first."

"We had an agreement, Juliana." Determination filled

him. This time he wouldn't fail. If she didn't come soon, he'd take more drastic action. Whatever necessary, so long as he protected her. "You promised you'd leave."

"I'll be quick." She shoved her loosened curls back from her face. "Normally I wouldn't allow a client in here while I'm working."

She was chattering from nerves, and his eyes narrowed as he watched her. "I'm not your client."

"It wouldn't matter if you were, not anymore." She edged around the table away from him and gathered up a sheaf of papers. Tidying them, she reached for another. "I'm through with my investigation."

He took the comment with calm stoicism. "Don't let it worry you. I know you did your best. Now if you don't mind—"

"I always do my best." And she smiled at him.

He saw it then. The quiet satisfaction. The breathtaking radiance that eased the lines of strain from his wife's face. "You figured out what happened to the amethysts," he marveled.

"Yes. Lauren DeVida happened to them."

"Our chief executive accountant?" He couldn't disguise his shock. "Not a chance in hell. She was devoted to my father. Devoted to Verdonia."

"No, she was pretty much devoted to stealing amethysts. I have to admit, she was good at it," Juliana reluctantly conceded. "She was really good."

"But not as good as you." There wasn't a doubt in his mind.

She struggled to appear modest. "No one's that good."

He sat down across from her. "Are you sure it was Lauren?"

"Sure enough that the accountants are reporting to

the Temporary Governing Council as we speak." She reached out and squeezed his hand. "She was like family, wasn't she?"

"Yes. My father adored her. We all did."

"Huh." Juliana's brows pulled together in thought. "I hadn't considered that possibility."

"What possibility?"

She riffled through some of the documents. "When were your father and Rachel married?" She flicked a piece of paper across the table toward him. "Was it around about this date?"

"Not around. Exactly."

"That's when the scam began. It ended the day your father died."

Damn it to hell. What had Juliana once said? One plus one always equals two. "You think Lauren was in love with my father, don't you?"

She nodded. "And when he married Rachel, that adoration turned vindictive. From what I've been able to uncover, she set up the entire operation to make it appear that your father, you and Merrick had run it. There are even documents that implicate Rachel and Miri. I'm guessing she sent copies of some of this to certain interested parties."

"Von Folke."

"It's possible. I haven't found any proof of that."

Lander glanced around the room, taking in the controlled chaos. "What's left for you to do here?"

"Nothing. As soon as we let everyone back in, copies will be made. Reports written." She shrugged. "Details finalized."

"You're certain? There's no question that it's finished?"

"I'm positive."

"That leaves one last task for me to deal with." Without warning, he circled the conference table and swept her up into his arms.

She released a muffled cry. "What do you think you're doing?"

"I'm taking a page out of Merrick's book."

"I…I don't understand." A heartbreaking ache underscored her words. "Are you still sending me home? I know I promised to go, but—"

"I'm abducting you, not sending you home," he explained gravely. "It worked so well for Merrick that I thought I'd give it a try."

"You're going to—"

He silenced her with a kiss. When he came up for air again, he said, "Abduct you. Yes. Would you prefer to be tied up?"

"That won't be necessary." Looping her hands around his neck she released a disgruntled sigh. "It would seem I don't have a choice." She peeked up at him, her eyes shining like burnished gold. "Do I?"

"You can fight. But I recommend cooperation. That way you don't invalidate Section C, Subparagraph Four, Line Sixteen of my contract with Joc."

She stiffened within his hold. "Dare I ask?"

"I believe it has to do with love, honor and cherish until death do us part."

Something shifted in her expression, a slow undoing, a helpless breaking signaling the final release of a lifetime's worth of barriers. Without a word, she closed her eyes and lowered her head to his shoulder. He carried her from the room. In no time he had a limo arranged to transport them to the apartment building where he'd first made love to his wife.

"I should have sent Joc packing the minute he proposed that outrageous contract," he told her, once they were inside.

"Why didn't you?"

"Verdonia," he said simply. "And then later, there was no reason to terminate our agreement. Why would I? It gave me everything I wanted." He reached for her. Now that she'd returned, he couldn't seem to keep his hands off her. "It gave me you."

"Oh, Lander." She clung to him. "You should have told me you were in trouble sooner," she informed him fiercely. "I would have been on the next plane back to you. We could have had this resolved a week ago."

It was all he needed to hear. She lifted her face to his kiss at the same instant as he lowered his. Their mouths collided, setting the mating dance into motion. Clothes were shed with overwhelming haste. Limbs entwined. And then they were on the bed, with nothing between them but a desperate urgency.

They surged together, the crest building, the subtle upheaval like waves fomenting before a distant storm. Juliana undulated beneath him, arching into the ebb and flow of their mating, the depth and intensity increasing before the steady advance of the tempest. And then it was on top of them, breaking loose from all restraint. Crashing and clawing at emotions drawn bow-string taut. Howling for release. They were swept high into the storm's embrace, and in that instant, she came undone, shattering in his arms.

Lander watched her, reveling in the knowledge that he'd brought her to crisis. Humbled by the fact that his hands, his mouth, his body, his touch—and his alone—could cause such an intense climax. The storm lashed out with a final violent kick. Roaring through him. Furious. Wrenching. And he followed her into the very heart of it, clinging to the one person in the universe who completed him. Who sheltered and fulfilled him.

His bride. His princess. His wife.

Much later, Lander rolled onto his back and scooped Juliana tight against him. By then dusk had settled in, leaving the room in semidarkness. He slid his fingers into her hair, filling his hands with her curls. He experienced a loosening deep inside, the knowledge that his world would only be right when it was like this—with his wife in his arms and his hands on her.

"Why did you return?" he felt compelled to ask.

Her calm gaze remained fixed on his, filled with an absolute certainty. "I returned because I realized you loved me as much as I loved you."

His brows drew together. "Of course I love you."

"You never said the words," she replied simply.

Hell. How could he have overlooked something so obvious? "Then how did you know?"

"The wedding rings. I'd forgotten what you'd told me on our wedding day, about their having a special meaning. But then Rachel reminded me." Her voice softened, grew richer. "That's when I put it all together."

"What did you put together?"

"That you loved me." She held up her hand, her rings giving off a subdued flash of fire. "The Blushes on the outside represent how our relationship began, as part of a contract. But then the stones change and grow, just as our feelings for each other changed and grew. At the very heart, it's a metamorphous from contract to soul mate."

"I couldn't have put it better myself." He smoothed

her hair away from her face. "I love you, Juliana. I have for a long time. But I knew you wouldn't believe words alone. They're too easy."

"Even so, you put the words in the ring. I found those, too. In the gold filigree. It says 'true love' in Verdonian. There's only one thing I don't understand."

"And what's that?"

She ran her fingertip over the stones set between the Blushes and Royals. "The meaning of these other amethysts. The ones between the pink and purple. They're such a unique color. Not quite red, not quite blue, nor purple. Yet, all of them mixed together. I've never seen an amethyst quite like it."

"My father came across the stones years ago. Apparently just these few were coughed out of the mines. Nothing like them has been found since."

"They're so distinctive."

"So is their name."

"Really?" She looked up at him, innocent curiosity reflected in her face. "What are they called?"

He stroked her ring, touching each stone in turn. "The Celestia Blush. The sealing of a contract. The Verdonia Royal. To represent soul mates." His finger lingered on the final group of stones. "And these were named by royal proclamation on our wedding day. This color is now known as the Juliana Rose, and will forever after symbolize true love."

She wept then, helpless tears of disbelief and joy. He held her patiently until they'd eased. Wiping the dampness from her cheeks, she wound her arms around his neck. Her eyes shone brighter than the sun as she kissed him three times, each deeper and more passionate than the last. The first kiss sealed their marriage contract. The second was reserved for soul mates. And finally, she gave him the kiss of true love.

"You should know that you've done something for me no one else has ever been able to do," she whispered against his mouth.

"What's that, Princess?"

She laughed away the last of her tears. "You've made all my dreams come true."

He smiled contentedly. "Now that sounds like the perfect job for a prince."

* * * * *

Day Leclaire's THE ROYALS *series*
continues next month.
Don't miss The Royal Wedding Night,
available in April from Desire.

0308/06

0308/064a

3 NOVELS ONLY £4.99

On sale
21st March 2008

Bestselling novels by your favourite authors back by popular demand!

The Barones: Rita, Emily & Alex

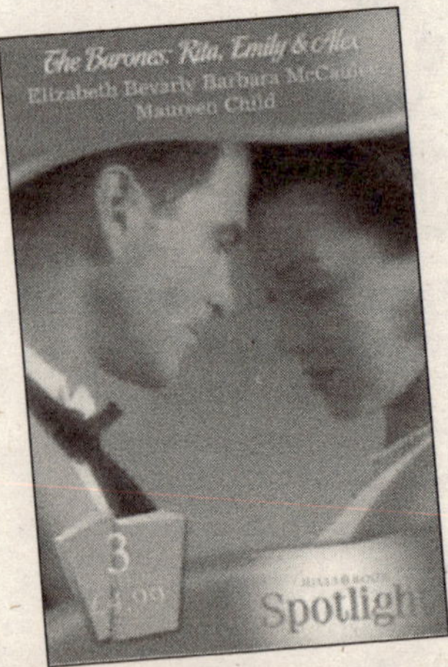

Featuring

Taming the Beastly MD
by Elizabeth Bevarly

Where There's Smoke…
by Barbara McCauley

Beauty & the Blue Angel
by Maureen Child

MILLS & BOON
Spotlight

We would like to take this opportunity to thank you for reading this Mills & Boon® book by offering you the chance to take TWO more specially selected titles from the Desire™ series absolutely FREE! We're also making this offer to introduce you to the benefits of the Mills & Boon® Reader Service™—

- ★ **FREE home delivery**
- ★ **FREE gifts and competitions**
- ★ **FREE monthly Newsletter**
- ★ **Exclusive Reader Service offers**
- ★ **Books available before they're in the shops**

Accepting these FREE books and gift places you under no obligation to buy, you may cancel at any time, even after receiving your free shipment. Simply complete your details below and return the entire page to the address below. You don't even need a stamp!

YES! Please send me 2 free Desire books and a surprise gift. I understand that unless you hear from me, I will receive 3 superb new titles every month for just £4.99 each, postage and packing free. I am under no obligation to purchase any books and may cancel my subscription at any time. The free books and gift will be mine to keep in any case.

D8ZEF

Ms/Mrs/Miss/Mr .... Initials ....

BLOCK CAPITALS PLEASE

Surname ....

Address ....

....

.... Postcode ....

Send this whole page to:
UK: FREEPOST CN81, Croydon, CR9 3WZ

Offer valid in UK only and is not available to current Mills & Boon® Reader Service™ subscribers to this series. Overseas and Eire please write for details. We reserve the right to refuse an application and applicants must be aged 18 years or over. Only one application per household. Terms and prices subject to change without notice. Offer expires 31st May 2008. As a result of this application, you may receive offers from Harlequin Mills & Boon and other carefully selected companies. If you would prefer not to share in this opportunity please write to The Data Manager, PO Box 676, Richmond, TW9 1WU.